OUT OF THE DARKNESS

First Printing: 2022
ALANNA RUSNAK PUBLISHING
an imprint of CHICKEN HOUSE PRESS

Library and Archives Canada Cataloguing in Publication
CIP data on file with the National Library and Archives

ISBN hardcover edition: 978-1-990336-30-0
ISBN trade paperback edition: 978-1-990336-29-4

Artwork by Rick deHaan and Kristine Wannamaker
Author photo by Tiffany Buchanan

Chicken House Press
282906 Normanby/Bentinck Townline
Durham, Ontario, Canada, N0G 1R0
www.chickenhousepress.ca

To those who only see the darkness in life,
May you find your light.

Empire of Remisia

VISADAS

Kli

Cisero Bay

Amarisa

Fort Karrlun

Healicine

Tondro   River

Cavar

REMEAD

R E M

Masseson

OLEND   SEA

AZUK

OUT OF THE DARKNESS

ELISABETH RODGERS

PROLOGUE

A man's right to rule does not come from the blood of his body;
It springs forth from the richness of his soul.
The silver trees of Reeza are the gods' will incarnate
Sprouting into the hand of the king who is true
And leaving its mark upon his skin.

King Emil was the first to be chosen after five brothers waged war.
Hail Marcus! Hail Balven! Hail Egnatius!
Hail Ilius! Hail Lucanus!
The descendants became five generals to serve the king.
To the North! To the South! To the East! To the West!
To the Centre!
And to ten thousand years of peace.

But when Azuk attacked the kingdom nearly fell.
A king of peace was not what they needed
and the people prayed and prayed.
Angered by humanity, the gods chose the son of a butcher,
Who relished the taste of power,
And a king of war arose.

He conquered lands and the leaves of Reeza wilted.
Many became a slave while the dwarves slept and the elves wept.
The king survived beyond the tests of time
As his armies desperately search for the elven capital
And an elf of the elvian, goddess of life.

I

THE MEADOW

General Leganous glared up at the endless sea of trees. His entire villa could fit inside one of the trunks of the ancient forest, and no matter how long he led his men through the cobblestone maze, he still felt like a tiny insect in its vastness. The daylight of the morning hardly breached the canopy of branches, and in over two decades he'd yet to catch a glimpse of their elusive enemy.

But he knew the little elf demons were watching.

The hairs on his neck rose and he reached for his blade, conscious of a mysterious figure looming in the branches. He searched but only the birds chirped from tree to tree, and they were enough to put him on edge.

It had been over five hundred years since anyone had seen an elf and forty years of scouring the godforsaken forests. When Gretafold, the elven queen died, it seemed the entire race died with her. He'd found a few villages and all of them were abandoned.

King Zoren had a few on his side, called the tamrasa, cursed to forget their way home, and rarely ever seen outside the castle walls. Bound to the king in mind, body, and soul, a sickness devoured them as their eyes raged silver. At night they took to the skies with wings of skin and bone, resembling creatures of darkness, living in caves beneath the falls of Sidabras.

Finding Amarisa had never been more dire. The king had written him a letter. One he burned. He'd not told a soul its contents and he never would. Thinking of it made him sit taller in his saddle and urge his horse to move faster.

The tattered and mended boots of his soldiers picked up the pace, shifting the packs on their shoulders and ignoring the sweat on their brows. The black armour bearing the silver tree of the king was fading across their breasts.

One of the new recruits had tears in his eyes as he peered up at the birds.

Another soldier tearing up at birdsong. Leganous rolled his eyes and wanted to kick the man upside the head. The birds may have left Remisia when the elves did and the young man was probably hearing them for the first time, but the sound wasn't worth his tears of wonder.

First Commander Grayson, his right hand, saw it as well, and his whip struck the air. "Eyes forward!" he called, daring any of the men to break rhythm.

The general knew one day his meagre battalion would savour the blood of elves on their tongues. They'd be on the front line of the greatest battle ever witnessed, and he prayed to Karas he'd live to see it as time was turning against him.

The road curved around the trunk of a massive tree, and on the other side of the bend the forest parted into a small meadow. The scouts and slaves he'd sent ahead of the army stood there waiting where the path of stone ended.

Leganous's horse reared and the beast whinnied in protest, jittery from the forces it sensed. He lifted his right hand, ordering his men to halt.

Commander Grayson rode up beside him.

Leganous didn't take his focus off the field. His eyes studied it, but only those with magic could comprehend what lay before them. He only saw the not too distant tree line on the other side, where the road ventured deeper into the forest.

Ralakai, the lead scout with the tinted green eyes of those with magic, which contrasted his dark skin, approached the general. "No way around it from what I can see. There's a cliff on the west side and a steep hill to the east. The ragatis would never make it to the top."

"Shall I call it, sir?" asked Grayson.

Leganous nodded.

Commander Grayson blew a horn made of animal bone and the soldiers parted formation as two large wagons emerged from the back.

The ragatis pulled against the iron chains, reeling their heads in protest as low grunts vibrated through their bodies. The drivers urged them forward, and the yoke cracked under the strain. Larger than horses and thicker than rhinos, containing such power was only made possible in their infancy. The trainer ripped out

3

their eyes and sewed the lids shut leaving them at the mercy of a firm hand. A set of hefty horns lay across their brows curving upwards, yet the horns had been broken to place them so close together. What was once white fur now grew in patches, stained yellow from their own excrement.

The wagons themselves were built long before, capable of both land and water travel, should the need ever arise. Moss grew between the fading boards and the rusted iron was adorned in human bone. Rib cages, pelvic bones, and skulls crisscrossed over one another, containing what lay inside.

General Leganous winced at the putrid aroma as they drew near. He'd ordered his men to toss buckets of water onto the carts, hoping to get rid of the smell, but nothing could wash it away. The odour had sealed itself shut into the very fibres of the cage and would never be removed, except by a flaming torch.

The wagons reached the front and the general's veins filled with adrenaline. He never tired of what came next. The field sat in silent wait as he fought to keep his horse in line.

"Lower spears!" commanded the general.

Commander Grayson repeated the order.

The soldiers in the front ranks lowered their silver tipped weapons.

Grayson turned to Leganous. "How many would you like to send first?"

"Let's not waste time," said the general, surveying the landscape. "Make it twenty."

II

FORSAKEN

Deformed hands and blank eyes stared through the bars of the wagon as Commander Grayson opened the door. Clamouring out of his reach, men and women deemed too disfigured, weak, or out of their minds, fought to get away.

The unsympathetic commander wrenched the first prisoner out, tossing the forsaken old woman to another soldier. "Take out ten from each. I don't care which," he stated as he returned to the general.

Soldiers invaded the wagons, pulling people by their hair, limbs, or whatever they could get their hands on. The forsaken screamed and scrapped, but their strength faltered against the king's men.

A young man sat on a wooden bench at the back of the wagon, his face downcast as though in prayer, yet his lips never moved. His once perfect dreads were in tatters, his facial hair, long and thin, as he waited for what he knew was about to happen. He, like all the men in the cart, wore neither shirt nor shoes. A pair of old frayed pants held up by a piece of string was all he possessed, yet he differed from the others. On his shoulder he bore a family crest of the citizens, not a branded Z of the slaves. Insignias were distinct for every bloodline. His was a circle with a hollow arrow, pointing south, like a compass. A woman cried out, and he lifted his head, revealing his blinded eyes, which burned in silent anger.

"What are you looking at?" The soldier scowled as he yanked the blind man to his feet and shoved him to join the rest.

Not seeing where the floor ended and the open air began, the man tumbled to the ground, wincing through his teeth as pain shot through his shoulder. Rough hands lifted him and he joined the others spread across the field in a single line. A soldier fastened heavy shackles connected by a short iron chain around his ankles.

From the other cart, a slave woman was being carried onto the field. Her body was broken when a mine collapsed, and she'd lost the ability to use her lower half. A healer patched her up to survive the journey and her two functioning arms would be sufficient enough for Leganous's purpose. The soldiers dumped her as close as they dared, eyeing what lay ahead of the forsaken and shuffling backwards to keep their distance.

They brought another man out, his slanted eyes shifting between the wagon and the field, his lower jaw grinding back and forth as he whimpered like a little boy. Since the day of his birth his body had grown, but his mind had not. An empty child they called him. Kept in the shadows, lifting heavy sacks of grain in a mill until they came for him. The skin on his chest and thighs hung on his bones like half empty wineskins. Arms once accustomed to lifting large sacks of grain were sunken. He tried to turn back, but he could not.

A soldier reached down to place shackles around his ankles, and when it clicked the man bolted into action. Kicking the soldier in the face and pushing another away, he took them by surprise. Darting for the cart, child-like tears flowed from his eyes. He was searching for his mom, who'd crossed the week before. She'd been perfectly healthy, but refused to send her son alone. She'd told him to stay in the wagon. That she'd see him soon. He slammed against the wagon, trying to figure out how to get back in. He pounded the door and cried until the guards came up behind him and he ran towards the forest.

In a couple strides he was two lengths ahead of the soldiers. The forsaken prayed he'd escape. The distance between him and his pursuers grew until an arrow pierced through the back of his skull.

He fell to the ground, his body twitching like he was having a seizure. The arrow breached the top of his head, the tip penetrating through the base of the chin, nailing his tongue to the bottom of his jaw.

Priestess Cyrene lowered her bow, riding her grey horse over to the man. Her flowing white toga trailed behind. Dressed for elegance and war, her silver breast plate glistened as she came to a halt. Dismounting, the soldiers gaped up at her before she crouched down over the man, her bow never leaving her hand. She grabbed the arrow and pushed it the rest of the way through. The blade and fetching remained undamaged. She used the dead man's clothing to wipe the arrow clean and carved a small notch into it. She yielded it to her leather quiver where other arrows surrounded it, covered in the same markings. Getting back on her steed, she returned to her position in the background, ever watching for anything amiss.

The forsaken watched the king's men throw the body into the tree line, left to be devoured by wild animals as they brought the final few out of the wagons.

General Leganous nudged his horse towards them, a false mask of tenderness upon his face.

Soldiers turned the forsaken in his direction and he began his speech.

"Forsaken. Today you have the tremendous honour of serving our merciful King Zoren with your lives. You will perish at the hands of our great enemy, the elves, but rest assured, we will avenge every single one of you. When we reach Amarisa, every life we take in the name of our monarch, will also be in your name." He peered down into the petrified faces of the forsaken and savoured it. "This may not be the end you'd choose, but it is the end for which destiny has blessed you. For those about to die on this field, remember that it is not in vain you give your life. It is for the sake of the many." Leganous nodded his head in fabricated respect. "Look to the end."

"Look to the end!" shouted the soldiers as the forsaken were turned to face their doom.

"Forsaken! Advance!" commanded Leganous.

No one moved. No one was eager to find out what came after.

General Leganous turned to Commander Grayson. "I think they may need a little more encouragement."

Grayson lifted his fist. "Infantry, forward!"

The soldiers closed in on the forsaken.

An elderly woman was the first to take a step. Her shrieks pierced the blind man's ears as vines grew out of her entire being, overwhelming her until she was barely visible and rooted to the earth, lifeless. With hopeless tears, more people walked forward, some suffering the same fate as the woman who'd crossed first. Others froze where they stood, terror their last expression.

The blind man instinctively lifted his hand to feel where he was going. His palm bore a brand from the handle of a fine sword. He gave the birds one final listen. All his life living in the dark he'd never heard such wonder. Perhaps there were birds in Valganen and their song would welcome him home. Taking a stammered breath, he stepped towards what lay ahead, but instead of pain, his hand ignited with energy. Withdrawing it, his heart raced in fear, but the footsteps in his wake edged him on.

The forsaken next to him exploded into a thousand pieces, splattering his right side in blood and flesh.

Pressing forward, the barrier moved around him like a river, its current guiding him left and right. He couldn't help but give in. Back and forth it went, always moving ahead, until there was nothing except the grass between his toes and he stood before the forest on the other side of the small meadow.

The silence was deafening. Not even the birds chirped as those who'd turned away stared at the one who'd done the impossible.

The clearing behind him smelled of burning flesh and freshly chiseled stone, for some had transformed into statues. Never again would a smile light up their eyes or a chuckle escape their lips.

The blind man's legs faltered under him. Screams of the dead ringing in his ears as the blood of the one who'd been beside him crawled down his skin. He wiped it away, trying not to think about who it was. There was no time to explain to himself why he was alive and they were not. He stumbled back to his feet.

"That's far enough," General Leganous hollered from the other side of what remained of the barrier as Priestess Cyrene drew back her bow.

Turning his head to Leganous's voice, he contemplated his choice. He'd made it through the barriers and it would be foolish to run. He'd crash into the first obstacle. The trees creaked in the nearby woods directly behind him. There had to be a road, but if he took it they'd only catch him quicker. He would have to muddle his way through the forest and hide if he stood any chance of escape.

They wouldn't put him back in the wagon and pretend this never happened. They'd want to know how he did it. Torturing him for days or weeks to get information he neither understood nor possessed. It's what his father would have done. But his father had also taught him to never surrender.

It's not in our bloodline, he remembered his father saying. To sit down and wait for the king's army to claim him would be surrender. His breath came in spurts and he took a step.

An arrow pierced through his leg.

He cried out in pain and his leg gave way. Writhing on the ground, he reached for the arrow. At the slightest contact, a fresh surge of agony shot up his leg, yet he was too stubborn to stop. Warm blood covered his palm as he shakily touched the tip of the blade and snapped the arrow in two. His leg shot out as he bit his lip to stop himself from wailing and his entire body shook with the effort. The arrowhead clutched between his fingers, he employed his other hand to pull the rest of it out of his leg. The relief was a small mercy. He rolled onto his stomach and dug his fingers into the earth, feeling for the path away from the barrier.

In the distance, the general called for another round of forsaken.

The blind man moved along the grass until his hand struck a root, and he used it to guide him into the forest. Immediately it dipped downwards into the woodland and he felt shaded by the canopy of trees above. Dead leaves cracked under the weight of his body and he shifted small twigs to the side. Every move he made filled him with nausea and he suppressed his desire to give in. There was no time to cover his tracks and a trail of blood marked his direction. The chains around his ankles clicked and clanged, preventing the full mobility of his legs. He used his good leg as much as he could to push him on. His hand seized another root, but when he pulled it, the branch gave way. It was long enough to use as a walking stick. Hera wasn't there to guide him; the tree limb would help. He gripped the arrowhead tighter and, gritting his teeth, forced himself to his feet, putting his full weight onto the limb.

He made quick work with the branch, using it to

walk and scout what lay before him, passing other obstacles, but despite his efforts, it wasn't long before he heard hooves pursuing him. Enough of the barrier had been destroyed and now they hunted him.

He moved as fast as his legs could carry him, the chain pulling taut with every step, but he was easy prey and she caught him in her sights.

Priestess Cyrene dismounted her horse while in stride, her sword thrust into the air, and the beast ran right past him.

Listening, he followed the closeness of her footsteps and thrusted the arrow in her direction. Cyrene shifted out of the way. She grabbed his wrist and hit it with her knee, knocking the weapon free. The man put all of his weight on his injured leg, pushing through the pain, and tried to strike her with the branch.

She replied with her sword, severing it in two.

Dropping the fragments of his walking stick, he punched the air, missing her completely as she stepped on the chain between his ankles and drew it towards her, knocking him onto his back.

Cyrene's steed returned, and she acquired a pair of shackles from her saddle. The man crawled along the earth in a last attempt of escape, but it was to no avail. She put the irons around his wrists and threw his feeble frame over the withers of her horse.

When they returned, the soldiers were moving the statues and hacking away at the branches rooting the fallen forsaken to the ground, clearing the way for the wagons to pass through. Other soldiers were making camp.

Priestess Cyrene brought the blind man to the

general's feet and made him kneel.

"What's your name citizen?" questioned the general.

The man kept his lips pursed.

Leganous's hand grabbed his shoulder and the man heard the general's slight intake of breath as he recognized the coveted tattoo of the House of Marcus.

Leganous punched him in the head to loosen his resolve. "What is your name?"

"Marcus, son of the fallen General Barsadias," he stated.

Commander Grayson butted in. "That's not possible." He pulled his sword out, but the general stayed his hand.

"Truth can be extracted, Commander. It's only a matter of patience and endurance," remarked General Leganous. "String him up."

Soldiers dragged Marcus away and Commander Grayson went for his whip and knives as the slaves pulled tents off the donkeys and gathered wood for the fires. Up in the trees, beyond the eye of any human, perched two birds, a falcon and a frogmouth, their eyes intent on the one who'd run the barrier.

III

WINGS OF FIRE

King Zoren ran the blade of his fillet knife across the tenderloin of a white-tailed deer. The fresh kill sunk into his palm like melted butter. With each slice of the blade, his hands steadied as he severed the white skin from the good meat, just as his brute of a father had taught him.

He was left to his own devices. Fresh kills hung from the roof. Some were skinned and others were waiting to be. The warmer the body, the easier it was to rip off the hide. Pigs snorted and cows nestled in the hay, unsuspecting of their fate.

He'd dreamed of the first time he'd met his beloved Queen Lina as he held his gashed arm like the idiot he was for falling off a spooked horse. Her mother, Queen Gretafold, had finished welcoming him to Amarisa and he swore every elf in the room heard his pulse flutter as she entered. She'd worn a blue sleeveless dress matching the colour of her eyes, and her long brown hair trailed behind her, only to be broken by her pointed ears. All over her arms, chest, and back were water droplets and he'd thought it strange because it wasn't raining outside.

She approached him like a vision of a goddess in light. He'd almost forgotten he was injured until she tenderly took his arm and let the sun flow through the vertes on her skin; she was an elvian.

Lina smiled at him and a warmth he'd never known filled him as the cut on his arm healed. Then the dream shifted and his hands were covered in her blood. Her smile turned to anguish.

Zoren closed his eyes and took a deep breath, letting the dream go before it could continue. Butchering eased his soul, but distraction could not stop the questions plaguing him. Her people would have the answers he sought, and the silent war was deafening. There was no path to recompense with the elves, for it was a desire neither side shared.

Zoren put the knife down and let his fingers graze his tattooed arm. The branches of a tree stretched from his wrist and high onto his shoulder, mirroring the trees of Reeza. The unnatural vertes brushed the tips of his fingers, varying in shades of grey to black, and it was like Lina was in the room with him.

He released his arm and picked up his knife when the air next to him churned. Wings sprouted from the centre of a hovering flame and contorted into a bird. The age old messenger of the gods. In its talons was a letter.

Zoren didn't waste time washing the blood off his hands and took it before the bird disappeared. For someone to use magic to communicate, its contents had to be dire or they would suffer. Opening the letter, he read:

My King,

I apologize for the use of magic, but the contents of this letter could not wait. A blind man has crossed the barrier unharmed. He is Marcus, son of the fallen General Barsadias. I was led to believe he'd been killed along with his entire village eighteen years ago and the line of Marcus ended. Commander Grayson digs into his flesh to discover his secrets, but your presence would be beneficial. Come as soon as possible. If the secret to crossing the barriers is discovered, we can increase our presence in Visadas and find the city of Amarisa and the power you so desperately need. Our blades may soon be shimmering with the blood of elves.

General Leganous

King Zoren removed his leather apron and left the cutting shed at all haste, his hands still covered in crimson.

A slave waited outside and fumbled to speak.

Zoren ignored him, but the slave followed. He picked up the pace and the slave fell behind. There was much to do before he could depart.

Zoren looked over the heads of the people. Slaves scurried around him and kept their heads down, moving to the side to avoid his attention. Some wagons headed for the market turned down vacant alleys when they saw him from afar.

Every soldier on their way to the temple stood to the side to honour him. The priestesses rang the gongs and he headed towards the sound. The members of the elected council would be there and before his departure he wanted Karas's blessing.

The temple rose in front of him like a sunrise. Built with the magic of elves and the skills of the dwarves it was the greatest temple in all of Remisia. Not a crack marked the age-old stone, though Zoren had made a few changes. He'd destroyed any sign of the elves and rebuilt the statues to reflect the people. The original statue of Karas at the front of the temple had pointed ears. He remembered the day the people of Remisia tore it down and elected a new statue be built. The new statue stood taller than the original and when it had been unveiled, he could not help but notice the similarities to himself. He blushed at their admiration. So many of the people had come to believe that he was the reincarnation of Karas. Many others like it rose up throughout Remisia, confirming it in the people's minds. When the trees had chosen him to be king, he had been their battle cry and led them out of the darkness and into the silver age.

Marching up the steps and through the temple door, a priestess sprinkled water on him. His senses filled with the smell of a burning sacrifice and incense.

At the front of the sanctuary stood the Iron Pyramid of Valganen, depicting the four levels of the afterlife. The multitudes of slaves and corrupt were on their hands and knees at the bottom. The warriors of the land stood on their backs lounging in paradise.

Over their heads were the gods of the four elements. Dirva, god of earth, Casiro, god of fire, Brisa, goddess of wind, and Vandus, goddess of water.

It irritated Zoren to see Dirva the god of earth next

to his siblings. If he could rebuild the pyramid he'd put him at the bottom for the way he fought.

Fire, earth, water, and wind sprung from each of the gods hands to the very top of the pyramid where Elvian the goddess of life and Karas the god of death stood under a tree of Reeza. All within the pyramid were connected by the roots of the immortal tree. There were two places the gods had allowed them to grow on earth. One tree stood in the elven capital of Amarisa and the rest grew around the walls of the king's castle.

The High Priestess, Nerva was watching him as he caught sight of her. Her silver armour reflected the fire from the altar and her white tunic accentuated her every curve. She was a vision of war and it took his breath away, though there was a fresh cut on her arm and cheek. It was deep and seemed to come from a sword.

She waited for him to come to her and when he reached her he lifted his bloodstained hand to the bleeding scar on her face, ignoring the wrinkles around her eyes.

"You should have this tended to," advised Zoren, glancing at the blackening necklace he'd given her at the height of their passion when she was a woman of thirty-one. The magic in the vertes stone was fading and time was beginning to eat away at her. Soon she would fight like a woman in her late sixties and wouldn't have the strength to counter the young priestesses who coveted her title.

"After morning prayers." Her guard raised and her eyes focused on the happenings of the room. "Tatiana chose her moment well to challenge me, but she's young and plagued by emotion. She'll bear the mark of her first attempt to take my place on her wrist and can add to her collection whenever she pleases." Nerva smirked as the young priestess she was referring to scowled at the edge of the sanctuary. "Hopefully when she does she'll be wiser and not driven by arrogance and selfish ambition, but you did not come to ask about my troubles."

Zoren handed General Leganous's letter to her.

Nerva's eyes lit as she read it. She returned it to him when she was finished. "You must leave at once."

"I am," said Zoren.

"I will bless your journey."

"The council must be informed first."

"As you wish." Nerva cleared the way for him to go.

The council of seven: Augustus, Cassius, Livius, Brennon, Kinkade, Leon, and Zabba, sat in their chairs at the front. Some of them were alarmed by their king's appearance. His black pants and simple sleeveless shirt were not his typical attire. Concerned faces eyed the blood on his hands.

Zoren smirked to himself, thinking about who they thought he'd killed this time.

Best to keep them guessing, he thought. They knew he'd never kill without reason or cause. If someone attacked him with a sword he met it. If someone betrayed him, depending on the severity of their betrayal, they died. And if someone had information he needed, he always gave them the chance to speak before they lost too much blood. To protect his people he would do it, even if part of his soul was sacrificed along the way.

He handed Augustus the letter and each one read it, passing it to the next, excited at the prospect of advancement in Visadas.

"The letter is definitely in General Leganous's hand," observed Cassius, not that his confirmation was needed.

First Commander Othos approached and King Zoren took the letter from Leon and gave it to him.

"You must send for General Zale while I'm away."

"How will you travel?" asked First Commander Othos.

Council member Leon snatched the letter back from him.

"Elian will take me," replied Zoren.

Council member Leon interrupted after he'd re-examined the letter. "Not before you've consulted a seer. In the height of the elven war, the elves sent false word in their efforts to destroy you. We must be certain this isn't a way for them to lure you away from where you are strongest."

Zoren cursed under his breath. These retired soldiers did not know what truly awaited in Amarisa. They'd become content in this silent war between elves and men and they grew fat on complacency. But each of them was elected and their word had to be heeded.

Leon continued. "If you are meant to go, it will be with her blessing."

"Of course," Zoren sneered. "Prepare the men. If a way through the barriers is found we will increase our presence in Visadas."

The King turned to Priestess Nerva and bowed his head. "I apologize I can't stay for morning prayers."

Priestess Nerva cut off a piece of the burnt offering and slipped it between Zoren lips. "That you receive a favourable word from the seer will be in our prayers."

King Zoren bowed his head and ate the piece of

meat as he walked away. He needed to consult with his mother.

IV

THE GATE

King Zoren pushed open the door to his mother's chambers and saw her chair tossed over. Remnants of her papers had fallen to the ground and heaps of them covered her desk. Zoren picked one of them up. It was a mix of childlike drawings and illegible scribbles. The fire under the hearth still smouldered. She hadn't been gone long. He cursed under his breath. He didn't have time for her foolish nonsense.

He strode back into the hallway, looking and listening for the sound of her steps and her veil of vertes stones smacking against her face. She couldn't have gotten far. His men were instructed to turn her back to her room if they saw her leaving the castle.

The animal blood made Zoren's fingers stick together as he moved them. If anything happened to the queen, they would be drenched in fresh blood.

He wouldn't wait for her to come to him. There were a few places her mind took her to ease the visions which plagued her, and he headed for the one she frequented most. Long ago his mother had given herself to the tides of time and lost herself. She neither knew the day nor the hour. Her mind was in a constant flux of time, living in the past, present, or future. Whenever he saw her, he wasn't sure which he would encounter. If in the past, she might confuse him for his father and defend herself against any advancement. If in the present, she would tell him what he needed to know. But if her mind was in the future, there was no determining how the conversation would go. He would have to play off wherever her mind was and work from there.

One of his mother's favourite spots was the castle wall overlooking the eastern waterfall. Stepping outside, the thunder of raging water grew. He raced towards the walls made of interlocking silver branches and climbed the rooted stairs to the top. Each tree was bent over to make a smooth path for his men to patrol, and from his vantage point, he could see for miles. The river parted the forest and smoke rose from chimneys of distant homes.

The silver trees of Reeza shone like a ring around the walls, but every time he saw the empty branches swaying in the wind, he could hardly look at them. Both the elves and dwarves turned their backs on him when the leaves fell. They saw it as a sign and called him cursed, though the trees remained loyal.

Zoren scanned the branches of the trees, searching for his mother. There was no sign of her. She rarely attempted to wander across the bridge on either side into the city. If she had, he hoped it wasn't the western side. The apartments and cracking structures of the slaves were nestled so close together, one had to know the way to the market or be lost. It would take his men days to find her, and that was if she wasn't murdered by the masses.

The solider on guard flocked to his king the moment he saw him.

"Are you looking for the queen?" he asked.

"Have you seen her?"

"She was headed towards the eastern gate. I sent Ronin to prevent her from leaving."

Zoren's worry abated. "How long ago was this?"

"Not long."

Zoren took the soldier at his word and headed for the eastern gate. As he passed under limbs of the tree hanging over the gate he saw a crowd gathered. A slave he recognized as his mother's handmaiden waved her hands to get his attention.

"I'm sorry, Your Majesty. I couldn't stop her," she pleaded.

Ronin, the soldier, rushed to his king's side. "I was about to send for you."

Zoren paid him no mind, and the people surrounding his mother rushed from his sight. She was lying on her back in her black tunic, holding her gut as she struggled for breath. Her veil of vertes obscured her facial features, but he could see her lips pursed in pain. Concerned, he knelt down beside her.

Over his shoulder, he commanded his soldier. "Don't let anyone leave. If my mother's been injured her attacker will be among them."

Zoren reached down and inspected his mother. He touched her hand and she slapped his away with her perfectly clean hand.

"Stop it, Zoren," she said. "Can't you see I've been stabbed? —Or did I stab myself? Why would I stab myself? I need Lina to come and heal me."

Zoren stood to his feet. "There isn't any blood."

"Yes, there is," she exclaimed, pointing at Zoren's bloody hands.

"Look at your hands, mother."

Queen Cecilia turned her wrist that bore the tattooed eye of the seer and her eyes went wide as she realized it was empty. She turned on her hands and knees, searching the bridge for something.

"Where is it?" she wept. "I can't have lost it."

Zoren could stand her episode no further. He put his hand around her waist as she hastily grabbed the closest pebble she could find. She held it close to her chest, like it was the most precious thing in the world. Zoren handed his mother to her caretaker. "Take her back to her room," he said. "I'm headed to Visadas."

"No!" she yelled, breaking her servant's grip. Queen Cecilia grabbed her son's arm, turning him back to the palace gates.

Zoren wrenched his arm back, his hand flexing open to slap her, even though he'd sworn to never be like his father.

"You cannot go to Visadas! It's not time!" The queen looked down at the ground and mumbled over and over. "Not time, not time, not time." She turned away from him and her eyes turned white as snow. "If he goes now, surely nothing seen will come to pass. He's only just crossed the barrier. So much more must transpire before the armies of Remisia take their course."

Queen Cecilia looked over the city, her eyes welling with tears as she saw a future the others could not. Her legs gave out from under her, the weight of what she was seeing too much for her to bear.

Zoren knelt next to his mother. "Tell me what you see."

Queen Cecilia opened her mouth, her head shaking in an effort to speak, but what escaped her lips was nothing but gurgles. She screamed at the top of her lungs. "It cannot yet be revealed! You must leave this matter in the hands of your generals. Another seer will reveal the next step. You will receive no blessing for this journey to Visadas from me."

King Zoren stroked his hand through his black hair, unable to conceal his frustrations. His mother surrendered herself to the care of her handmaiden and leaned heavily on her as the branches of the trees allowed them to pass through the gates and into the palace. He wondered if it might have been kinder to have let her pass when her time had come, all those years ago. Lina had insisted she live and gave her half of the vertes. All she'd said was that his mother would have a role to play in the coming days, but what that role was had yet to be seen. By her words he could not play an active role in Marcus's fate, but another one of his generals could. He would bring Marcus out of Visadas where he could keep a close eye on him and discover the secrets he might possess.

V

EMPTY PROMISES

Hanging from a branch by his wrists, Marcus reeled in pain as his own weight pulled down on his shoulder, which didn't feel right. He'd lost track of time. His only measurement was when they stopped and when they started. The sensation in his fingers was gone and all he had left in his soul was the unquenchable desire for his life to end. Marcus had no information to give. He wished he had answers to tell, but he'd tried lying and paid for it. The stripes of his deception dug deep into the soft spots of his back.

Commander Grayson was an unyielding force, knowing exactly how far to push his body without losing its focus. His seasoned brow gave him a vastness to draw from. He'd tortured many in his day, more than his general would ever know.

Grayson's fist struck him again in the gut, and the

chains jingled overhead as Marcus convulsed back and forth before the masters.

General Leganous sat at a table drinking a cup of warm calda, waiting for the armour to crack. The smell of the watered-down wine and spices reminded Marcus of home. Whenever he was sick as a child, Mizpah would give him a sip of calda to help him feel better. In his delirium he could almost feel her hand wiping his brow.

The more impatient Leganous became, the more sips he took, but he never interrupted.

The commander's one hand reached out and stopped Marcus from moving, as the other seized the back of his head.

Grayson took a step closer.

Blood dripped from Marcus's lip. Half of his face swollen beyond recognition, he tried to pull away, and winced at the movement.

"Speak," demanded the Commander, unsheathing his knife.

Marcus let his head go slack in Grayson's grasp.

Commander Grayson drew nearer and as Marcus's torturer whispered in his ear, a dagger hovered over his heart. "I can ease your pain, if you tell the general what we need to know." His voice dripping with honey.

Marcus scoffed at Grayson's empty promise. He knew the commander could hurt him, but to take his life would be to surrender his own. It was against the law to kill a citizen who'd committed no crime outside the laws of combat. Marcus had been sent to the barriers because to die within them was to be killed by the enemy. It was a less than honourable end, but any family left behind walked the streets with their heads held high.

"You might want to say that a little louder," slurred Marcus, "I don't think the general could hear you."

Grayson dragged his knife across Marcus's chest.

Marcus's head flew backwards, his hands straining to break free and defend himself, but his bounds prevented it.

Commander Grayson came at him like a battering ram against crumbling doors. Hitting him over and over again.

Marcus took a fresh grip of the shackles around his wrists and tried to fight back using his legs, kicking blindly at the Commander. But Grayson only used his momentum against him. Grayson held the knife in the path of Marcus's leg, and the blade plunged itself into his thigh.

Marcus shrieked. His limbs shaking beyond control. He tried raising his wounded leg, yearning to pull the dagger out, but it dug deeper with every move.

"Commander," interrupted Leganous. "You forget a corpse cannot speak."

"He'll live," muttered Grayson, a hint of joy passing his lips.

"Stop the bleeding."

Grayson departed and Marcus heard General Leganous's chair creek as he sat back, studying the boy who resembled a butchered pig on a hook more than a man.

"You seem to have a knack for surviving the impossible. First Naiden, then eighteen years on your own in the wilderness, and now the barriers. If you were a gladiator, people would place wagers on you based on luck alone. Thousands have died where you've tread and yet you survive."

Marcus's head hung low.

"Yet you do not speak of your past." Leganous took another sip of his calda. "In battle, if a lone man returns with no details of how the conflict was lost, it's clear only the back of his heels witnessed the destruction of his comrades. His nose, ears, and hair are severed from his body and he's left to row in the dark of a galley where he'll live out his cowardice. A disgrace to all who knew him; and his wife, she remarries because in eyes of the law the man is dead."

Marcus's hoarse voice broke silence. "I'm not a coward."

"Of course." General Leganous smirked, his eyes possessing secrets Marcus could not see. "Before the kings were chosen to rule by the trees of Reeza, Marcus, Balven, Egnatius, Ilius, and Lucanus nearly killed each other for the right to rule. Then all of their descendants killed each other in the arena for the chance to be general. Leaving you the last of any of their bloodlines. A descendant of the original five would never admit to running from a fight. Your father was the same way. I hated him."

"I'm sure the feeling was mutual," stated Marcus.

The chair creaked again as General Leganous rose. A twig snapped and Marcus wondered what the man was up to.

"It wasn't always." Something moved in the general's hands. "There was a time I would have laid on my sword for your father's sake. A friendship sealed in blood until blood and opportunity separated us. But we don't have

30

to repeat the past."

"Fall on your sword now if that will ease your conscience. I will say nothing more, for there is nothing for me to say that has not already been spoken."

"Fine," said Leganous, shoving a stick between Marcus's teeth as footsteps drew near. Whoever approached spit and something sizzled. Hands grasped his wounded leg and extracted the knife.

Marcus screamed and experienced the relief of his mind slipping beyond awakening.

VI

SIGHT

"No one has travelled up this mountain," protested Grayson, who pointed to it on the map.

Priestess Cyrene thought differently, but was unable to voice her opinions. The High Priestess Nerva had sworn her to silence so she could hear the will of the gods more clearly. *Here*. She wrote on the map; insisting they go where the forest grew thickest.

"No. General Ambrose spent years exploring there and found nothing. We need to go somewhere new. General, explain it to her."

General Leganous sat back in his chair and studied his family crest on the ceiling. It was a maze in the shape of a circle with a blooming gladiolus flower at the centre. His eyes tracked the path, symbolizing the journey a man took to find the warrior within. The road was never a straight line. There would always be moments of failure. When the warrior reached the middle, they'd be ready for any task.

The maze reminded him of Visadas. When he emerged at the root of the ancient forest he would be a warrior in full bloom and the king would be pleased.

Leganous turned a ring with a silver band and dimming jewel on his finger as he thought.

Commander Grayson and the priestess sought his answer, waiting for him to pick a side, when the flap of his tent opened.

General Leganous hoped it was Ralaki bringing word of the king's arrival, but letting in the night air was a poor foot soldier from the south named Gregor.

"Aren't you supposed to be guarding the forsaken?" inquired the disappointed general.

"Yes, sir."

Leganous glared at the intruder. "Then why have you come here?"

"One of them wants to speak with you," trembled Gregor.

Leganous laughed at the prospect.

Gregor spoke over them. "She's a seer. Says she's got something to show you."

"And you believe her?"

"I trained in the barracks of Sidabras, near the House of Seers. I know the mark. Sent here from Ironwood, I'd expect, since she's got no brand or family crest."

Commander Grayson moved to throw the soldier out and reprimand him. "Probably because she didn't pass the seer's tests."

"Send her in," Leganous ordered, much to his

commander's surprise.

"But sir, you don't know for certain she legitimate."

General Leganous ignored him. He had nothing to lose. Only the "seer" did.

Gregor went out and brought the woman into the light.

"Or she was sent to Ironwood because she looked like that and couldn't find a man to take her even in the dark," mocked Grayson.

She was a decrepit old woman, frail, with skin stretching down to her bones. Leganous could tell by the way her lips fell that she didn't have any teeth. Her hair was a mess of grey, long and brittle. If she'd been born a slave, he would've left her in the wagon to rot, but as a seer, her word may be valuable.

The soldier released the hag, offering her a certain level of respect, which Leganous wondered if she deserved.

She held out her palm in anticipation of his first question, revealing a tattoo of an eye below her thumb. She went to the water basin and dipped her calloused hand into it, rubbing at the tattoo with her thumb, ensuring the mark was genuine before she spoke.

"That proves nothing," Leganous scorned. "Many women have claimed to be seers. Stirring up dissension and conflict amongst the people. The true seers burn heretics alive in the Aurelius. Searing an image into the minds of those who come after to never try to do the same."

"I'm a descendant of the Prorok family. My mother named me Favil, after her grandmother, who was seer to the High Priestess Vesta," she said. "I am bound to the temple and my vow to the eye unbreakable. I can only show you truth."

Leganous stood to his feet and walked around his desk towards her. "Marks can be forged or covered." Leganous's eyes searched her shoulder for the faintest hint of a mark.

Grayson piped in. "Yet another reason we should send her to the wagons and mark her to be killed at the earliest convenience."

Leganous noted Cyrene, who'd moved to the corner of the tent, yet made no attempt to stop him.

The seer kept her eyes on Leganous. "It is your choice to see."

Leganous looked down at her and held her gaze. "Show me nothing and you'll be the first my men toss into the barrier."

Favil extended her hand to him, and he took it. "One hand to keep you in reality, the other to take you into the world beyond." She placed her other hand to his temple.

Both their eyes turned white as a power beyond the general's control took over his mind and he entered the realm of prophecy.

At first he saw nothing but black. Voices murmured and came into focus.

"Once the heart is broken, my men will be led directly to the city." Leganous heard himself say. *"The enchantment will find the weakest part in the defences and with a spell from Ralakai on the other side it will crumble. We'll enter where they believe there's no door."*

The voice that responded was the last he thought he would hear, *"Start preparing your men and send for reinforcements. The city won't fall on a whim,"* said Marcus.

"We'll attack on the third morning after the heart has been broken."

The sounds of war echoed somewhere far in the distance. Birds cawed and screeched as horses whinnied and voices faltered into death. The emptiness cracked before him and a light formed as the world opened up; his heart quickened in anticipation.

He saw himself. His sword and black armour, bearing the silver tree, glistening in a crimson river of blood. The magical stone on his finger restored to its former glory, clear and full of power.

Behind him was the elven queen's silver tree of legend, and all around him his soldiers battled against the elves. Overhead elven houses like he'd never seen before swayed like torches, wreathed in flame. Smoke blocked the sky, and whether it was day or night, he couldn't tell.

But he knew where he stood. He had reached the city of Amarisa.

"For the King!" He saw himself yell.

Human magicians expelled what magic they possessed against the elves. His army attacked with net, spear, and sword; slaughtering their enemy and advancing towards the tree.

Leganous watched himself lead his men deeper into the city at war, as the vision dimmed. His mind returned to his body as the old woman drew back.

The general stammered and Commander Grayson reached out to steady him. His eyes shimmered in joy at what he'd seen.

"Commander, I'm going to extract the information myself. Take her back with you." Leganous went for his armour and readied himself to go back out to Marcus who was still hanging in the tree.

Grayson reached for Favil, but she stood her ground.

"If Marcus dies by either of your hands before he's helped you reach the city, nothing I've shown you will come to pass. And the king will never get what he truly desires from the city. The pigeon's heart will guide you. Broken over the soil of Amarisa by the very one you torture. You will sell him for silver and one day silver will lead him back to you."

General Leganous threw his armour on the ground. "Until I have silver in my hands, he'll run every barrier, and if he dies by them, you will have my personal attention," he threatened.

"What are your orders, General?" asked Gregor.

"Take her back to the wagon."

The young soldier did as he was told, and she was gone.

Leganous went back to his desk and sat down, ignoring the worthless maps. "We head for the mountain. Have the men leave the seer be. Who knows what other visions she may have to reveal when the future becomes clearer. Bring Ralakai to me. I've another message for the king and I want to speak to him about our route."

General Leganous pulled out a blank piece of parchment and started to compose all he'd seen and learned about Marcus from the seer. But mid-sentence he put down his quill and opened a drawer in his desk. Inside was a small wooden box. The lid was embellished with a carving of two pigeons with their foreheads pressed together. He placed his hand upon it and felt the beat of a tiny heart that would lead him to glory and his king's salvation.

VII

PUT BACK

Marcus's body jolted against the floor of the wagon and he heard the door screech shut behind him. Hands turned him onto his back, and he couldn't refrain the sounds of his agony.

"It's okay, son. We've got you," uttered the concerned voice of Favil.

More of the forsaken rose to their feet to help, but they stopped when a man spoke.

"Don't move him yet," he said, looking at Marcus's shoulder. "There's something we need to do first."

A hand firmly grabbed his arm and Marcus tried to pull away.

"Your shoulder is out of place," he told Marcus. "Do you understand?"

Marcus nodded and he heard the people shuffling out of the man's way.

"Keep him still," the man instructed.

Marcus felt hands grab him from all sides and a man's heel secured itself into his armpit and took his wrist.

The man yanked and Marcus slammed the floor with his good hand as his arm jerked back into place. His teeth clenched as he sat up and he reached for his aching shoulder.

As a boy, he'd suffered the same injury falling off a horse his father bought him. It had been a present for his sixth birthday. His father, General Barsadias, wanted his son to have a stallion of his own when he headed to train at the barracks the following year. To Marcus's pride and joy, none of the other boys his age in Naiden had a horse of their very own. But the horse had a mean spirit. It bucked him off. Those he'd thought were his friends laughed and jeered at him as he slowly got back up, trying to stop the tears, but the shame on his father's face prevented it. Mercilessly, General Barsadias realigned his shoulder and left him in the open field to deal with it on his own. The next morning his father returned to his post in Sidabras, despite his promise to spend the day with him. He didn't see his father for months, and it wasn't until his seventh birthday that they were seen together in public again.

"You'll heal alright now," said the man who was a former shield bearer to his master.

Hands gripped him from all around, assisting him to his feet, moving him to a spot at the back.

Marcus leaned heavily on those next to him. His chest heaved from exhaustion and sweat poured down his face as blood oozed from his wounds. Both his arms tingled as feeling crept back into his blackened fingers.

Favil ripped a small piece from the bottom of her sackcloth dress and began cleaning his scrapes with what she had.

The wagon door opened and Marcus clenched the bench. *They're coming back for me.*

A soldier slid a bucket of water into the cage with a single drinking gourd and the forsaken began passing it around.

Marcus exhaled and Favil lifted the ladle to his lips. He drank greedily, the water gratifying his gnawing stomach.

"Thank you," he muttered to Favil, hoping the others might hear as well.

Favil clutched his hand in hers.

Marcus wiped his eyes, trying to rise above his growing despair. He felt like a caged animal, awaiting the slaughter. His humanity, destined to exist so the creator could mangle and mar him to bits. For years he'd evaded this life. Living as a hermit with his dog Hera. He'd passed the days fishing in the stream and collecting firewood to keep him warm on a chilly night, hoping the world couldn't be darker than the lightless world he saw every day.

But he could only live in ignorance for so long.

One night Hera didn't return home and he went out looking for her, wandering straight into an encampment of soldiers. They stole him from all that was familiar, forcing him into the harshness of reality. Tales of the forsaken used to be ghost stories he and his friends told around a campfire. It was why he ran away, allowing everyone to believe he'd perished along with everything and everyone he knew.

Marcus leaned back against the wall of the cart. Favil hummed a lullaby tune while her fingers traced the lines of his open palm and he drifted into sleep.

VIII

A THREAD IN THE CANVAS

"To your feet!" shouted a soldier, yanking Marcus from his seat as his blanket fell to the floor. He felt a scar reopen and a knife was pressed against his wounded back. Holding his head high, Marcus followed the blade's lead.

The forsaken left behind in the wagon stretched out their hands to touch him, guiding him safely towards the door, hoping his good fortune would pass on to them.

Stepping out of the wagon, the frosty ground shocked the bottoms of Marcus's bare feet. They'd been travelling up a mountain and the air smelled different outside. It tasted like snow and dried his throat. The tarp the men had thrown over the wagon flapped in the breeze and Marcus yearned for his ragged blanket.

Footsteps neared, but he didn't have to hear the

voice to know who they belonged to. It had been a month since his initial crossing and he recognized the creak in the left sole of the boot.

"Leganous,"Marcus said.

Leganous's fist hit him so hard he spun to the ground with a thud. "It's General." He slammed his foot against Marcus's back, knocking the wind out of him. The barely healed scars on his back cried for relief and a cut dripped down his rosy cheek. He'd almost forgotten about the ring each of the generals wore. He'd watched his father fight with it and wiser men took to the shadows.

"Grayson," stated Leganous. "Get the hostage."

Grayson went into the wagon and came out carrying a squirming young girl; at first glance she appeared to be whole. Her jet black hair was long and accustomed to covering her face from prying eyes, but as it stirred, it was clear why she'd been sent to Visadas. The girl's lip was split all the way up to her nose, exposing her dry gums.

The general removed his foot and Marcus was lifted to his feet, his heart breaking at the girl's cries.

"So close to perfection." Leganous grabbed her by the jaw, moving her tangled hair behind her ear. "Two arms, both legs, but the lip—flawed. What's your name, child?"

"Gwen," slurred the little girl.

General Leganous chuckled. "An unfortunate child, indeed. Practically not worth saving." He released her to Grayson's care. "Slit her throat if he tries to run."

Marcus was steered to the front line and chains were put on his ankles as the soldiers lowered their spears.

44

Under his feet Marcus felt cobblestones. Only six people had been taken from the wagons. The barrier wasn't wide, but there was no knowing how deep. Going through a barrier was like peeling an onion. Everyone else was like a knife shaving it a layer at a time, but Marcus somehow slipped between the cracks.

General Leganous began his speech, which Marcus no longer listened to. Overshadowing Leganous's words were the struggles of the young girl in Grayson's clutches. Marcus's hand formed into a ball, the knuckles turning white, striving to control himself, knowing they'd kill her if he didn't. They'd done it the first time. He recoiled at the memory of the man's body hitting the ground.

The call to march pulled Marcus out of his thoughts and without hesitation he ran, trying to outrun the screams in his wake. The waves of the barrier struck his hand like a curse. It flowed over him, encasing him in its energy, drawing him onward until he reached the other side.

And like always, he returned alone.

Back and forth he ran the barrier. Each time more forsaken were dragged from the wagons. As the barrier cleared, some forsaken lived, but they too stopped in their tracks on the other side.

Marcus had come to realize that if the barrier didn't kill you, neither would the priestess. Only the people who tried to run before going through the barrier were killed. If a person ran after making it through, Priestess Cyrene shot them in the leg. It was the army's twisted way of showing respect they hadn't deserted.

Ralakai raised his hand, signalling enough of the

barrier had been cleared for the troops to pass through. His slaves went out into the field, removing the tarnished bodies and placing objects along the safe path. A bit of the barrier still shimmered in the corner of the magician's eye.

Marcus was leaned over gasping as the guards came to either side of him. It didn't take much for him to be winded and the cold air cut through his lungs like a knife. Someone removed his chains, making his feet feel light and foreign. He followed the rest of the forsaken back into the wagon, not wanting to give Leganous a reason to change his mind. He heard Gwen's sigh of relief as the door locked behind him.

"I think you hesitated." The general ripped the girl from Grayson's arms.

"He's throwing her in!" shouted a forsaken and Marcus pounded his fist against the locked door.

"Leganous!" yelled Marcus.

Gwen screamed, begging the general to stop as she kicked and scratched, but he was too powerful.

All the forsaken stood to their feet, but it was too late.

The general threw Gwen into the barrier.

Marcus beat on the door, helpless to change fate, shouting every curse he knew.

"Let's move out!" ordered the general.

The forsaken looked at the ones who'd fallen, especially Gwen who'd turned to stone. The cart jolted forward, but Marcus stood holding the door.

He felt Favil's hand on his shoulder.

"No matter what I do—I accomplish nothing," Marcus lamented, grasping the bars of their cage, trying to hide expressions Favil found so easy to read. She'd become his constant, and he leaned on her more than he cared to admit. Ever since the night they stopped torturing him, the soldiers stayed clear of her, though she refused to speak of it, no matter how many times he asked. She'd tell him there were some truths she was saving for their appointed time.

"You have been amongst the dead and dying for far too long," her voice shook.

"I have nothing left."

"You think being able to walk those barriers is a curse, but it's a gift."

"I can still hear them," he said, defeated. "They fill my every waking moment."

"But you mustn't forget—we all may walk the barriers tomorrow and many of us won't come back. You're our only chance of survival because you're the one who's going to remember us when the new king rises."

"Zoren has reigned for over six hundred years. There will be no new king, Favil."

Unlike the kings before, Zoren had lived an unnaturally long life, and he'd killed many to make it so.

Favil's hand pulled, and Marcus gave in to facing her. "Have a little faith." She took his hand into hers as a gentle smile filled her voice. "My mother and her mother before her were seers. The gift is passed from mother to daughter. We were highly revered and when we walked the streets of the capital, people stepped aside. I was trained in the arts of my mother and my father had found me a suitable match, but all that changed when I never got my monthly. My father sent for a physician and after that every proposal of marriage ceased to exist. They gave me two options as they led me out of my family's villa: become a prostitute in the Temple of Karas, or work in the mines. Every stone I carried was one stone closer to the new reign. Its time is upon us and you're going to be part of it."

"But I can't even see."

Favil paused, her hand turning hot in his as she struggled to find the right words. "A piece of thread can't see its importance in the canvas, but that doesn't make it any less important. Everyone missed my importance because they thought I'd never be a mother, but it is because I never had children that I got to be a mother and voice to so many more than I ever would if I'd lived what was expected of me. You are stronger than you know. There's more to your life past these wagons and you'll recognize it when you're no longer in them."

"These wagons shouldn't even exist," seethed Marcus. "The only truth Leganous ever says is that the elves are our enemy. It's their borders killing us, and they do nothing to stop it."

"We cannot control the actions of others," responded Favil. "Only our own."

"But we have no control," recounted Marcus. "From the day we rise to the day we end, our lives are under the brand of another man. And if you don't see it then you're the one who's blind."

"One day there will be peace."

"Peace," Marcus mocked, forcing her hand to his temple. "Show me peace, Favil. If there is such a possibility then reveal it."

Favil's hand went slack in his grasp. "There's

nothing I can show you that you would believe."

"No. It is because peace is dead and we'll all be dead before she's ever resurrected."

Marcus suddenly felt light-headed and grabbed the cage wall to steady himself. The day's events were taking their toll.

"I'm sorry," he muttered.

Favil took him by the shoulder. "Venting can be very good for the soul." She helped him to his seat. "Rest now, for there are new mercies in the morning."

Marcus felt a blanket against his fingertips. He picked it up and drew it around himself and Favil as she sat next to him.

Gauis, an elderly man on his other side, nestled up against him as well.

The warmth of those around him should have lulled him into an instant sleep, but he couldn't rest. He kept thinking about all the ways things could have turned out different.

IX

SOMETHING SPECIAL

"Up, up, up! Time to eat," hollered the raspy voice of Conway the cook hammering his serving spoon against the cage. Two guards opened the door, and Conway tossed a sack onto the floor ahead of him as two slaves carrying a steaming pot of soup rushed to keep up. The forsaken dashed for the sack, pulling out the wooden bowls it carried within.

The aroma hit Marcus like a knife and his mouth watered. He turned to give Favil a slight nudge, but she was on her feet getting bowls. Instead, Marcus focused his attentions on Gauis, who hadn't budged. Marcus hesitated, knowing the haven of sleep, but the man needed to eat. Shifting his shoulder, he lifted Gauis into a sitting position. Marcus could hear a change in the man's breathing as he awoke.

"Did I oversleep?" The elderly man's eyes cracked open.

"It's time to eat," said Marcus.

Gauis leaned back against the wall, closing his senile eyes. "You take my portion lad. I'm not hungry. I'll be better in the morning and ready to work the fields."

They hadn't gotten a meal like this in days. "I appreciate the offer, but you're going to eat." Marcus sat Gauis back up and found his hands to set them into position to receive a bowl.

Favil came back to her spot and gave Marcus a dish, putting another into Gauis's hand.

Marcus eagerly shifted the empty bowl between his fingers, listening to the stride of the two slaves pouring the watery soup. His stomach growled. They were right next to him. They gave Favil her portion and as they were about to tip the ladle over his bowl the cook shouted.

"That soup is not for him!" ordered Conway.

A feverish heat climbed up Marcus's features as he clenched his empty dish and the slaves moved on, avoiding their row and overlooking Gauis until the cook had had his way.

"I cooked something special up for you," boasted Conway, "and bless my little heart if I haven't been working on it all day."

A knot grew in Marcus's stomach as the chef stood in front of him.

Conway seized his bowl, which Marcus was reluctant to relinquish. The cook placed it on the floor, undoing his belt as he mumbled under his breath. "They think they can replace me. Thirteen years I've been the cook. Citizen scum." He opened his pants and relieved himself until the final trickle filled the dish to the top.

Marcus's back touched the cage wall, and he motioned to stand, but the cook shoved him into his seat as he refastened his belt.

Conway picked up the steaming dish. "A nice warm bowl of soup." The seasoned cook grinned as he pushed it to Marcus's lips. "Drink." He tilted the bowl upwards and urine spilled against Marcus's closed mouth.

Marcus turned his head away, catching his breath, trying not to give the man the revenge he craved. He could hear the guards outside the wagon snickering as the upperclass slave had his fun before he became a forsaken.

The cook huffed and he withdrew as his face reddened. "Well, if you won't drink, I'm sure your friend here would love a taste."

Gauis was too slow to react as Conway shoved the bowl against his open lips. The elderly man gagged and weakly fought back.

Wrath, unlike Marcus had ever felt before, coursed through him, and faster than he realized what he was doing, he knocked the bowl out of the cook's hands and fired to his feet. He grabbed Conway by the neck and threw him into the ceiling. The cook rammed against the roof so hard it bent the iron. Fragments of bone and the deceased Conway plummeted to the floor. The cook's knife fell out of its sheath, and Marcus caught it.

All the forsaken stood to their feet, adding to the chaos. Two guards shoved their way to the back of the wagon, swords drawn.

The cook's knife flipped naturally in Marcus's hand

and without a thought he blocked the soldier's blow, stabbing him through the neck and twisting the handle. The soldier fell backwards as the other guard came at him.

Maneuvering the handle into the palm of both hands, Marcus drove the blade into the guard's chest, piercing both armour and flesh, until it plunged straight into the man's heart.

Both of the soldiers were dead the moment they hit the ground, and Marcus stood victor over three corpses.

And then there was silence.

The knife fell from Marcus's bloody hand, and the forsaken stared, reflecting the same disbelief in their eyes as Marcus felt. He'd never killed anyone before and in a few moments of pure instinct he'd taken three lives. For a split second, it had been like every other sense in his body had awakened, yet the world remained dark around him. He hadn't even been thinking. It was like an ability, not his own, had taken over. Now nothing would be able to stay Commander Grayson's hand from killing him.

And Marcus shook with relief.

His death would be quick once they realized what he'd done. He placed his hand on the bench behind him and sat down, waiting for his recompense. He could hear the soldiers stirring outside, drawn to conflict like rats to rotten food.

Marcus turned to Gauis, who was wiping vomit from his chin. "You okay?" he asked.

Gauis nodded his head, watching Marcus's every move. He raised his hand and waved it in front of Marcus's face, no longer believing he was blind.

Soldiers burst into the wagon, gaping at the three deceased on the floor.

The first soldier was identical to the corpse of the second man Marcus killed. "Cinadon," he whimpered. The man shouted at the top of his lungs and drew his sword.

Blood dripped from Marcus's hands and Gauis shuffled away as Lucias stepped towards Marcus.

"You're a dead man," Lucias proclaimed, but he stopped in his tracks as the cook's knife was thrusted into his side, held in the grasp of another.

"Move and I'll send you to join the others I killed at your feet," Favil cautioned.

Favil, Marcus thought as he moved to stop her, but she elbowed him in the face and he was out.

X

RELIEF

Marcus slowly came to. He felt the bench under him and the back corner of the wagon behind him. He reached up to soothe his aching temple and didn't feel Favil next to him.

"Favil?"

"She's going to be all right," said Gauis.

"Where is she?"

"It's almost over," Gauis tried to assure him.

A whip snapped against skin and Marcus's head jerked towards it. He could hear Favil's muffled cries and he pushed Gauis away. *What did she do?* Somehow Favil was taking his punishment. He had to tell the guards it was him. He tried to stand, but another hand took Gauis's place, restraining him from going to Favil's aid. He shoved them off as the whip struck Favil's back again.

"Fa—"

A hand fastened itself over his mouth and Marcus wrestled whoever it was to the floor. He fought to get the upper hand as the man locked their arms and legs around him.

"Say anything now and her pain will be for nothing," breathed the man. "Seers don't do anything without reason. So come on and stop."

Come on. Marcus remembered his father saying that. The horrors of his past clambered their way into his thoughts. Mizpah, the woman who'd raised him, on her knees telling him everything was going to be okay as his father pressured him to kill her. The shiny new dagger, glowing in the firelight as it shook in his hand. The faces of the people of Naiden surrounding him as they cheered for him to end her life.

Marcus pushed the memory down before it could go any further.

Suddenly, the man released him and Marcus strained towards the door, his legs hardly carrying him as he stumbled against it. White knuckled, he clenched the bars about to confess to the guards standing watch, but the whipping stopped. Marcus turned his head and listened. The fires of the camp cracked and the soldiers on patrol leisurely walked around the camp as the rest began to settle in for the night. He couldn't hear Favil and he didn't know where she was.

What if she didn't survive? thought Marcus.

Marcus's legs shook, but he refused to sit down. Favil was strong. She'd lived her whole life in the mines. If anyone could survive it would be her.

Gauis moved to another seat and the forsaken

whispered to one another behind him.

"How did he do that?" asked a woman, moving to another person she hoped could answer the question this time.

"What is he?"

"Is he an elf?" inquired another.

Marcus might have smiled at their theories if Favil was with him. He knew he wasn't an elf. His mother and father were as human as anyone, yet he could not deny the merit of their questions. He stood at the door waiting until he could hear the rise and fall of every sleeping body in the cart. He breathed along with them, attempting to keep himself calm as the hours passed with no sign of Favil. Marcus was on the brink of slamming the doors when they finally opened and the guards shoved Favil inside.

"Favil," Marcus managed to say. He lifted his hand to her and her ice cold hand took his. All he wanted to do was wrap his arms around her and never let go, but he knew the sting of the whip. A hug would only hurt her more. Marcus didn't know what to say. He wanted to shun her and embrace her all at the same time.

"I might need your arm to get me to the back of the wagon," she managed to say.

Marcus didn't hesitate to give it and together they guided each other to their spot. He held both her hands as she eased herself onto the seat and he sat next to her. The blanket was all tangled behind him and without a word he wrapped it around the two of them. It was all he could do to help her. He knew it wasn't much, but her shivering form drew close to him.

Favil took his hand like she always did and it broke

him further still.

"You've been whipped in my place and yet you offer me comfort."

"It was a stiff whip. You ought to feel the cat-o'-nine-tails. Far more painful."

"Why?"

Favil hesitated. "Because I knew if I didn't they would have killed you tonight."

"You're still here."

Favil winced as she moved to look at him. "I've seen your future and it's far more important than my own."

"Favil—"

Favil cut him off before he could ask what she meant. "I told you if I ever told you your future you'd never believe me. You'll have to figure it out as it comes. I think I need to rest now." She closed her eyes and was asleep moments later.

Marcus couldn't do the same. His mind was in a torrent of thought as the questions about himself and the guilt of what he'd done continued to rise. Unable to wash the blood from his hands, his fingers stuck together. He longed to wash them clean, but there was no way to do so.

XI

THE MESSENGER

General Leganous pulled his cloak closer around his neck as Priestess Cyrene rode up beside him, her eyes glaring at Commander Grayson.

"You wish to say something, Priestess?" he asked.

Cyrene drew backwards. She'd made her mind known. This mountain was on the brink of desolation. He knew no civilization could thrive in the heights where the forests never greened and everything froze. He couldn't help but agree with her.

In the old woman's vision his men hadn't been wearing cloaks. No other army had explored this peak, and maybe there was a good reason. Prior leadership had seen sense.

The company followed Ralakai's white feathered arrows for hours without sight of the scout until Leganous heard a horse on the road.

"Halt!" Leganous raised his hand in the air.

The garrison stopped and Leganous's senses were on high alert. Aided by the power of his ring he listened to a single set of hooves approaching.

"What do you hear?" asked the commander.

"A lone rider." Leganous sat up in his seat.

Priestess Cyrene armed her bow and aimed it at the road.

Out of the haze emerged a traveller wearing the king's armour and a familiar face.

The rider stopped before the army. "General Leganous."

"Captain Haman," uttered a dismayed general. "I'm sure you bring news."

"And supplies. General Quinn of the east has become very intrigued with the happenings in the north," his eyes darted to the wagons, "but this is no place to discuss such matters. Your scout awaits a league up the road with the supply caravan. My tent will be a more proper spot to speak until your slaves can set up your own."

"How did you get ahead of us?" asked Leganous, ushering his horse forward and forcing the young lout to follow.

"You know as well as I how the roads change. I'll bet the road behind you is already different. It's why no one can make a decent map of the territory. We had to use some of your supplies to get us through a barrier, but the pigeon never fails to reunite with her other half," said Haman. "She led us up a different path."

"Any run-ins with the natives?"

"Their presence remains unseen."

"As I thought," remarked Leganous in a tone that ended their conversation. They rode side by side, neither of them speaking. Leganous intended to have a talk with Ralakai when he returned. In the future, Ralakai would come to deliver the news of a supply wagon, not Haman or any other glorified messenger.

Leganous relaxed when he smelled smoke up ahead. Unlike their last little bonfire, there wouldn't be two burning corpses on it. There'd be fresh supplies, and if Haman's slaves had any brains in their heads, they'd be putting on supper.

Haman's small force had set up their tents in short rows and guarded the five supply wagons. Attached to the lead cart were two small bird cages, each carrying a pigeon. The pigeon on the right looked directly past Leganous and into the enchanted eyes of its mate on the lead wagon of his troop. Both of the birds fluttered their wings in excitement, as they saw the one their hearts searched for. The pigeons in the cages next to them paid them no mind, searching in the direction of their own beloved. It was the way the armies found their way through Visadas. As long as the humans held captive the birds, the loving pair would always look in the direction of their mate.

Another spell had been cast to aid them in their hunt for the ancient city, but it lay hidden in Leganous's desk.

Riding between a few of the tents, Leganous stopped his horse.

Ralakai rushed to his side and held the bridle

General Leganous stared down at his scout in disdain. "Report."

"There's another barrier on the other side of that

corner." Ralakai pointed further up the road where it bent.

"They're becoming more frequent," divulged Leganous as he dismounted. He cringed as he stretched his limbs.

"The barrier is narrow and leads into a short tunnel in the mountain. A waterfall feeds the rapids next to the camp and I rode a league in the other direction but found no break in the rock to pass it."

"Sounds promising."

Captain Haman couldn't help overhearing. "If it's so promising, my men and I will follow you to the barrier tomorrow. You may need all the help you can get."

Leganous turned to Grayson as he rode up next to him. "Make camp along the road before the snow falls. We'll cross in the morning."

Grayson set out to ensure his orders were followed. He left his horse with Ralakai, eager to be somewhere warm.

"Priestess." Haman stopped Cyrene before she could ride past. "It would honour my men if we could join you for morning prayer. Long has it been since we paid homage to Karas properly."

Priestess Cyrene nodded her head, nudging her horse to where her own tent was being set up.

Satisfied, Haman gave his attention to Leganous. "General, we can warm ourselves in my tent until yours is ready."

"Lead the way." Leganous wished he could be alone in his own tent eating his meal in peace. But he would force himself to humour the messenger. He was a temporary extension of General Quinn and would be listened to.

Haman opened the tent. "After you."

General Leganous went in as Haman ordered his slave to bring them food and warm mugs of calda. He didn't wait to be offered a fur covered seat by the fire. Taking the iron poker from the fire's edge, Leganous stoked it and the flames rose in response.

The tent's interior was simple. A dirty cot, a few chairs, and a small table in the corner. It was larger than the average soldier's tent, but not by much.

Leganous returned his focus to the fire as the messenger took the chair across from him.

Haman broke the silence. "My men shot a few birds on our way into Visadas. A flat beaked bird with brown and black feathers, for which people in Remisia will pay handsomely."

"If you captured a duck alive, you'd double your money. There's no price the rich won't pay to get their hands on a live bird."

"I've seen a few caged birds at parties."

"But they won't mate outside Visadas. If they escape they fly right back here. The entire land is rank with them. At first their meat was too foreign, but when you've lived in these lands this long, you can forget the taste of steak."

"If I return, I will bring you beef to help you remember," offered Haman.

Leganous folded his hands impatiently. "First you will have to tell me why you're here now."

"I am the response to your letter to the king. General Quinn wishes he could be here in person, but his duties prevent him from doing so."

"Couldn't afford a better horse?"

"I acquired a fresh horse every day and came here as fast as anyone could make it from Masseson."

"If you were my messenger you'd be flogged, wasting time hunting birds. And I never sent a letter to Quinn."

"The king did. Both of them would like you to tell me what happened so I can inform them first hand."

Leganous sat back in his seat. "There's not much to tell."

Haman held onto his every word. "I'm sure the tale bears more weight than you think."

"A blind man walked the barriers unharmed. Grayson tortured him only to discover he had no idea how he did it."

"And is it true he's Marcus the son of General Barsadias, believed to be dead these past eighteen years?"

"His shoulder bears the genuine mark."

Haman sat back in his chair. "Perhaps he's an elf, obscured in magic."

"Ralakai and Grayson found nothing special about him."

"What do we know of his parentage?"

"He's his father's son," recalled the general. "Stubborn as a mule and too young to know about his mother. Barsadias stuck with her even after she lost child after child. Some say Pricilla took matters into her own hands to produce a healthy son. Consulted magics others would deem unholy."

"Fortunate Barsadias's bloodline allowed him to fight as a soldier without an heir to replace him."

"How fathers flocked to him. Offering him their

virgin daughters so they could carry a descendant of the original five generals. Attempts were made on his wife's life, yet he did not stray. She saved his life the day they met and from then on every other woman paled in comparison." Leganous remembered the way the light shone through her eyes. "Although if a priestess asked him, he might not have been able to refuse."

"Nor should any man offered such an honour."

General Leganous doubted this young prick would ever be so lucky. "Priestesses are the highest class of the female sex. My wife was proud when I was chosen to sire a few children of Karas, yet some men will never receive such offers." Leganous struggled to keep a straight face.

Haman's jaw tightened. "We divert from the purpose of our meeting."

"What word have you from General Quinn?" asked General Leganous. "I've not seen him since he became a general. Two years ago now?"

"Three. It wasn't easy for him to gain the respect of his men at first, being so young and receiving such a position, but he's proven himself immensely. King Zoren himself has tested the warriors coming from his barracks in the east and has determined them to be some of the finest he's seen in generations."

"Perhaps I'll be able to see some of them in action when we reach the elves."

"It would honour him." Haman pulled a letter from his satchel, marked with the numeral II and Quinn's crest. "Though General Quinn could not be here in person he has sent this for you. A letter bearing his thoughts, well wishes, and a gift he hopes you will accept." Haman handed Leganous the note. "I'll return when you've finished." He left the tent.

General Leganous broke the seal in half and tossed the envelope into the fire. He read the letter and called for a soldier.

The flap of the tent opened immediately.

"Bring Marcus."

XII

BREATHE

Marcus yearned to stretch out his legs, but a man's back rested against his knees. He shifted his foot and it knocked against another person on the floor. Wedged next to him on the bench, a woman muffled her tears. He waited for Favil to offer her words of comfort, but the seer remained silent on his other side. The newcomers around them whimpered, and she made no move to leave him. Her hand clenched his as though he was about to let go.

And it worried him.

"Two soldiers approaching," announced a man with a missing leg.

Favil tightened her grip.

"Open it up," ordered the soldier.

The keys jangled against one another and Marcus wondered why they'd be coming this late.

"Move!" roared the soldiers.

The man against Marcus's knees staggered to the side and two sets of boots stopped in front of him.

Favil's trembling hand released Marcus's and his body went cold.

They forced him from his seat and to his surprise everyone except Favil protested.

The guards drew him closer, pushing the rising forsaken to the side. An arm broke and a nose busted as the soldiers hustled through the angry mob.

Out of the wagon, Marcus tried to control his rising fear and stop his chattering teeth. They clasped his hands in irons and led him away.

Breathe in. Breathe out. Breathe in. Breathe out, thought Marcus as his heart quickened. *Is Leganous going to kill me?* While Marcus believed death to be far sweeter than what he was living, the reality of it made him wish for more time.

The soldiers led him down a straight line between the tents. He imagined the encampment wouldn't be much different from the way his father's men used to set up outside his home, Naiden. The cowhide tents filled the open fields in their military straight rows. Men sat outside talking around the fires late into the night as he and his best friend Trans snuck around trying to listen.

"Put another log on the fire," demanded a soldier of a slave.

A hammer struck against a tent peg to his left.

"Can you stop that?" yelled a man from a nearby tent. "I'm trying to sleep!"

"The anchors on my tent are loose."

A spoon battered against the edge of a bowl.

"Give me some of that," someone demanded.

"It's not my fault you inhale your food like a swine," a man answered, shrugging him off.

"Best food we've had in months," he said, smacking his lips.

"Seems the old lady did us all a favour," his friend chuckled.

Another soldier butted into the conversation. "Don't say that so loud. Lucias is recovering a few tents down. Besides, I heard the general ordered this cook from Masseson months ago. We owe her nothing."

A fresh wave of guilt welled up in Marcus. He'd played the scenario in his head. If he'd done what Conway wanted, Favil never would have been whipped and no one would have died. But the thought of drinking that man's urine was still revolting. How could he have known it would end the way it did?

The soldier's hand shoved Marcus inside a tent. Instantly all of Marcus's fears fell away and he felt euphoria. Warmth seeped into his skin. He'd forgotten what it was like to feel any heat, and it overpowered him. Roasting meat turned over the flame and without a thought, he took a step towards it, but a hand held him back.

Sipping their watered down wine, General Leganous, Haman, Grayson, and the priestess turned to look at him.

Haman stood to his feet to examine the merchandise. "He's skinnier than I expected."

Marcus followed the sound of his voice.

"Open your mouth," summoned Haman.

Marcus did as he was asked.

Haman's grip locked his jaw open while his finger

entered to inspect the teeth.

Marcus's gag reflex engaged, but there was nothing to throw up.

Haman perused around him with his nose in the air. "He smells worse than a slave's latrine," he scoffed, pulling out his knife. "Yet his hair would be worth a few silver shillings. Men and women would pay handsomely to own a single lock of a descendant."

Leganous put his goblet to the side. "Ask General Quinn for it when he's dead. For now his honour will remain intact."

Commander Grayson took another bite of his duck and cringed. "He'd be better off rowing until he rots. Not going to Ironwood."

I'm going to Ironwood? thought Marcus.

Haman continued his inspection. "To think, by right he could compete."

General Leganous laughed. "He wouldn't survive the first challenge, no matter his lineage."

As the rest joined in mockery, Marcus listened to their chastisement like a fly on the wall. In his current condition he had zero aspirations to enter the Aurelius and fight in the Tournament of Generals, but he remembered wishing he could. As a boy he lay awake at night dreaming of winning and seeing the pride in his father's eyes as he was proclaimed the new general. He used to practice his sword fighting until his hands were raw and tease his friends for wanting to compete. Each of them had to prove themselves worthy to a general, first commander, the high priestess, or the king himself in order to enter, while he'd be the first on their lists.

General Leganous interrupted his thoughts. "Now

that you've seen Marcus is alive and well, you can pay me what General Quinn promised. The letter mentioned sixty shillings."

Haman extracted a pouch from his side and placed it into the general's waiting hand.

General Leganous walked to his desk and tossed the coins to Grayson. "Count it," he commanded and picked up a piece of paper. "Marcus, son of Barsadias of the five hundred and ninety-eighth legion of our King Zoren. It is your right as a citizen to be informed that you are being transferred into Captain Haman's care. Payment of sixty silver shillings has been accepted upon this request. Never again can you ever be returned to the forsaken. You will be taken to Ironwood and General Quinn will take charge of you."

Leganous handed Marcus's papers over to Haman.

"Doran, Gilderoy," said Leganous, addressing the two soldiers holding Marcus. "Put him in Haman's empty wagon."

Haman passed them the keys.

Marcus was led out of the tent and if he thought he was cold before he entered, he was freezing when he exited. The night air took his breath away and his entire body returned to shivering. His only source of warmth were the two arms leading him, but as they walked, footsteps from behind the general's tent approached.

"What are you doing out of bed?" asked Doran, stopping.

Lucias held his side, a few trickles of blood seeping through his bandages. "I heard he was being taken to Ironwood."

Marcus recognized the man's vengeful voice. He was

the first solider to enter the wagons when he'd killed the cook and the two guards. He'd wept for the loss of his brother.

"What do you want?" Gilderoy's voice was agitated.

"You honestly believe my brother was killed by the old maid?"

Doran tried to keep walking.

Lucias wouldn't have it. "You both knew Cinadon since we were children. He was a fighter. He couldn't have been killed by that old woman." Lucias pointed his finger at Marcus. "He's the one who had blood on his hands. I saw it."

Doran interrupted. "He's blind."

"Yet he can pass through the barriers unharmed? It's not natural. General Leganous should have killed him. Probably some inbred with the elves and an enemy of Remisia."

The grips of the soldier's tightened on Marcus's arm.

"We were commanded to put him in Haman's wagon," mentioned Gilderoy, but Marcus could hear reason fading from his speech.

"If the elements kill him, then it's the will of the gods and no fault of ours. Haman said he smelled like a slave's latrine. It's time we gave Marcus here a bath," replied Lucias, who'd been listening to the general's conversation on the other side of the canvas.

"For Cinadon," said Doran.

"And for the good of Remisia," finished Lucias.

Marcus jostled the irons on his wrists and wrestled to be free. They passed through the camp and the half frozen river rushed ahead of them.

Marcus dug his heels into the ground causing

Gilderoy to lose his grip. Turning his body, he slipped out of Doran's as well. On his stomach, he got onto his knees and crawled, but Doran caught him by the ankle and lifted it up like it was a wagon handle.

"This is close enough," Doran said, but he didn't lower Marcus's leg so he felt like a rabbit in a snare.

To another soldier passing by, Lucias yelled, "Bring us a hammer, chain, and an iron peg. Don't want him running away from us, do we?"

"Shouldn't we just throw him in the river?" asked Gilderoy.

"Easier to control him here," replied Lucias.

"Grab buckets of water!" shouted Gilderoy towards the camp.

Lucias crouched over Marcus. "We're going to get you nice and clean."

Marcus wanted to beg them to stop. His heart gripped with fear and he doubted anyone was coming to his rescue. He thought about how he'd fought the cook and the two soldiers. He needed to do it again. Weakly he tried to push himself up and take his foot back.

Lucias kicked him in the stomach and Marcus couldn't breathe. He coughed as another man approached and dropped a large chain next to him. Marcus kicked in a last effort to get Doran to release him.

The hammer struck the iron peg and a shackle was latched around Marcus's ankle.

Marcus's body trembled so violently his back and shoulders ached. Doran released his foot and Marcus shot to his feet, running. The chain unraveled behind him.

Clink.

He reached the end of his leash and he fell face first. He heard his nose snap but he didn't make a sound as he forced himself to stand up.

Soldiers poured out from the camp, hauling empty buckets and pots from the cook's cart. They ran to the river, breaking the ice along the bank to fill their vessels. A circle of men formed around him like it was all a big game.

Marcus picked up the chain and followed it to the iron peg. Using all the strength he could muster, he yanked, but it didn't give way. He was beyond hearing what the men around him were saying. Someone pushed him away, but he wouldn't let himself fall to the ground. Catching his balance, he was about to pull on the manacles again, but it was useless.

The water hit Marcus like a brick wall. He struggled to breathe. He dropped the chain and shuddered away. His skin felt like it was burning, eating at him like heat from a flame. Water struck him from all sides, soaking him to the bone. No matter where he turned they were lying in wait.

They grabbed him and made him bow. Wrenching his face upwards, they slowly poured two buckets of icy water over his mouth.

Marcus's head seared with intense pain. He wanted to scream but knew these men lived on a diet of seeing fear. Marcus held his breath as he continued to fight to be free of their hold.

He had to breathe.

When he did, it was a mistake. Water flowed into his mouth and down the wrong way. About to give up and give in, the buckets emptied, and he inhaled. Coughing and spitting up, he breathed the sharp winds like there wasn't enough oxygen in the air.

They pitched water at him until they tossed the final bucket. Lucias threw him a cloth and a bar of soap. "Clean yourself up."

Large flakes of snow began to fall from the sky. The rest of the men lost interest and returned to the warmth of their fires.

Marcus's hands convulsed so badly he didn't think he'd be able to hold the soap. Surely he would be dead come morn. He was grateful the water hid his tears of defeat. The pain and suffering of this life was about to pass from him, and he would walk into the embrace of the mother he never knew. He imagined her arms around him and warmth spread through his torso. He'd walked this world in darkness longer than he'd roamed in the light and he was tired. What was waiting if he survived this? More torture? He had fought until the end. Marcus's lids drooped and his hands slowed as he moved the bar of soap across his flesh.

His thoughts became laboured and he could have sworn in the haze of his fading mind he heard raised voices. Someone was shouting. Were they shouting at him? Was it time to walk the barrier? Marcus tried to rise, but his legs felt numb. Why would they walk the barrier at night? A boot squeaked next to him.

General Leganous? he wondered.

Something hard hit the ground next to him and the voices made his head ache. Valganen was beginning to call him as the snow stuck in his dreads. He tried to picture it. A land of green by the riverside. Where the fish were plenty and his belly full. The sun would shine down on him and fill him with warmth and the air would smell of fresh leaves and rich soil.

The bar of soap slumped out of his hands as he allowed his eyes to shut in complete surrender to whatever came next.

XIII

SHADOW OF WINGS

The campfires of the guards on duty crackled into the night sky as snow covered the encampment. Those on watch huddled close to their fires, dreaming of a warmer place. Unaccustomed to such conditions, many of them were experiencing snow for the first time.

Something approached in the distance. Riding on the tides of the wind, veering between the trees of the elven forest, the wings of a snow white owl never made a sound.

Further back in the woods, another owl followed, succeeded by another and another until twelve snow-white birds soared towards Leganous's base.

When the soldier's gaze turned in their direction, they swooped behind the trees.

The lead owl's head poked around the edge of the bark and flew into the camp while the others lay in wait.

It soared so close to the ground, its wings nearly scratched the surface. The snow camouflaged its pursuit as the bird made its way to a lone tent. Landing on the roof, its eyes scanned the barracks.

A guard was stationed outside the tent, wrapped in a blanket and tossing another piece of wood on his fading fire.

The owl looked down at the back of his head and a small clear stone around her ankle hummed.

The guard blinked and he rubbed his eyes, until reluctantly his head bowed and he softly snored.

The owl's head turned back and nodded to the others waiting in the trees.

The parliament converged on the tent and the lead owl dove in front of the door, which opened as if a swift wind breathed upon it.

Inside, Marcus lay chained on a bed of buried coals under a blanket. His chest rose, but he barely had a pulse.

The owl pulled the door open with its beak and the other eleven owls flew in, landing on the floor. All of them hopped towards Marcus, gathering around him in a circle.

The lead owl edged closer, until she was upon him. Extending her wings, she spread them over him. The others did the same, weaving together as one. Marcus was completely covered under the shadow of wings and a powerful fiery glow emanated from between the folds.

XIV

A HORN BLOWS

Marcus smelled the familiar as he awoke: urine, sweat, and horse manure. Soldiers walked the camp outside, swords at the hip as tents were torn down and packed on mules, but what was lacking outweighed the familiar. There was a bed of buried coals underneath him, not the wood of a wagon floor. Walls of pure canvas rustled all around him. A blanket fell off him as he sat up and the iron clasp on his ankle rattled. He wiped the sleep from his eyes and hissed when his bandaged finger grazed his nose. He brushed the tip of his finger over it and realized someone had set it back into place.

Perplexed, he finally noticed his clothes were dry and when he brushed his hand through his hair he found something soft sticking between his fingers. Extracting the little object, he stroked it. It was silky like milkweed and had a stem like a leaf. Twirling it between his index and thumb, he thought of the dandelions in the fields of

Naiden, and he had the smallest notion it might possibly be a feather. He remembered Mizpah chasing chickens —one of the only birds to remain in Remisia—away from their nests to get their eggs. She'd come out and her hair would be full of them. He'd stand on a bench and pull them out as she laughed.

How would a feather get in here?

Moving his fingers down the stem he felt for a pod, but the tent door opened and whatever it was flew from his grasp.

"Let's check on our patient." Anzar, the army physician entered. He had a few lengths of white in his hair, and his brow was creased, yet he bore the same uniform as the rest of his brothers in arms. The family crest on his shoulder was a symbol of snakes intertwined in a triangle. "Well, you're sitting up. That's a good sign."

Haman followed in behind. "The general was right when he said he was as stubborn as his father."

"Probably what kept him alive." Anzar sat down next to Marcus.

"Lucias was a fool."

"A dead fool. There was no stopping the general. It was like he was seeing red." The physician removed the bandages around Marcus's fingers and poked them. "Can you feel that?"

Marcus nodded.

"Good. It's quite remarkable. Last night your hands were covered in blisters. Today you can hardly notice. Your hands should feel normal in a couple of days. Helps they're taking you off the mountain. If only some of the soldiers were so lucky."

"Is he fit for travel?" asked Haman.

"Give him a somewhat decent meal and I don't see why not."

"I'll make sure he does. Can't have him dying before Quinn gets his hands on him."

"It was fortunate Commander Grayson heard what the men were doing when he did." The physician rose to his feet.

Haman stuck his head out of the tent. "He's ready to transfer."

A lone soldier came into the tent as the physician went out.

Haman handed him the key. "Anything happens to him and death will be the least of your worries."

A hand grasped Marcus's ankle and unlocked the shackle. He was pulled out of his warm bed. Three more soldiers were waiting outside. They didn't clasp him in irons, but he could feel the soldiers make a formation around him. The men on his sides took his arms and guided him from one cage to another as they put him in Haman's wagon.

The legs of the ragatis hitched to the cart lifted and fell in impatience. Other than that he was completely alone. He took a step further into the emptiness and his foot caught on something. He withdrew, wondering if he really was alone in the cart, and he stood there waiting while nothing happened.

Moving slowly, he touched it again and discovered it was small sack. Marcus turned it in his grasp and found strings. He worked on the knot until it gave way.

Reaching into the pouch, he gasped.

Marcus sat down and drew the satchel closer to him.

He found an apple, bread, cheese, and a few strips of dried meat inside. His hunger awakened and he tore into the bread. The loaf melted on his tongue and he ate quickly, afraid someone would try to take it away from him. But not long after the bread had gone down, his stomach rejected it.

Steering his head away from the other contents of the bag and striving for the iron bars he threw up. He rolled on his side and waited for his abdomen to settle. His stomach wasn't used to food. The key would be to eat slower, no matter how much he wanted to stuff his face. To help practice self control he put everything except a strip of meat back into the sack. He bit into it and chewed it much slower this time. Rolling it around in his mouth, savouring every bite. It was the best food he'd tasted in years.

Joy and sadness suddenly waged war with his thoughts. Without the distraction of others and hunger, the memory of the night before returned. He'd accepted death, longing for the souls waiting on the other side of the veil. He was relieved the unknown was still beyond him, yet his relief was tainted by the bars of his cell.

Sometimes when he closed his eyes he would imagine he was back in the small enclosure where he'd hidden for eighteen years. The nearby stream lulling him to sleep in the evenings and the rabbit he and Hera caught roasting over the fire. She'd saved him from the flames of Naiden and led him to safety when he'd woken up blind. He prayed Elvian kept her safe, knowing if she was still alive, she'd be waiting under the shelter, wagging her tail.

He wished he could speak to Favil about what

happened. She'd known all along he'd one day leave the forsaken, and if he met her once more, he could demand answers. He cursed himself. He'd missed his chance. Now he would never hear her voice again, and that cut him deeper than the questions.

A horn blew and the whip cracked against the backs of the ragatis.

To Marcus's dismay, he noticed his wagon was driving alongside the rest of the army.

The wagons of the forsaken led the way and the snow wasn't deep enough to impede their journey. They travelled for half a league and stopped before the tunnel in the side of the mountain.

The waterfall roared on the right, feeding the valley below with the icy waters from atop. The air shimmered not only from the barrier, but from the mist striking against the rocks in the morning light.

"Bring them out!" commanded the general.

Marcus could hear the cries of the forsaken as the soldiers hauled them out of the wagons and locked their ankles in chains.

Leganous rode his horse into position to speak, but Favil spoke first.

"General Leganous," Favil shouted.

Marcus leapt to his feet and grabbed the bars of his cage.

XV

SPARK

General Leganous watched the old seer step out from the forsaken with her palms raised and her eyes white. Her countenance bore no fear or pain, despite the ominous dark and red stains on the back of her dress. In face of what lay ahead and behind, her expression was peaceful. It was as if she'd known this moment was coming and harboured no grudge against it. She was shivering, but she held her head high as her white eyes peered straight at him. He let her speak, hoping she'd tell him of future victories. Her voice carried to the farthest stretches of the army.

"Soldiers of the false King Zoren. There's not much time left for me, so listen well. Whispers begin to ride upon the winds of Brisa and Casiro's fires of war kindle. The trees of Reeza wreathed in thorns will blossom and the hand that holds its loyalty now will be severed. The dead will rise and sing over the corpses of their enemies, and the birds will feast on the bodies of the citizens. The new king is coming and he will give us vengeance."

General Leganous rode his horse beside Favil. "Your end is now, old woman. Your crimes and these words of heresy have sealed your fate."

Favil fixed her gaze up at him. "And I will watch from on high as you're dragged to the depths for what you did with your life," she responded.

Pulling his foot out of his stirrup, he kicked Favil in the gut. She fell to the ground, but not a sound escaped her lips.

Using the last of her strength, she pulled herself up. "The rising is about to begin and once it does, there'll be nothing you or your false king will be able to do about it." Favil looked past Leganous and at Marcus's pleading face. "In time, you'll see it."

General Leganous kicked Favil harder, and she surrendered herself to the barrier as her body dissolved into water and disappeared.

The forsaken fell to their knees and wept. Marcus cried out the old woman's name and banged on the bars that held him.

Despair rose and the forsaken who waited to walk the barrier turned against Leganous and his men.

The general drew his sword and his men advanced, pushing the revolt into the barrier.

"Bring out some more," ordered Leganous.

The soldiers went to the wagons and instead of the timid forsaken they usually dealt with, the forsaken pushed to get out of the wagon and join the fight. They kicked and hit as hard as they could against the soldiers, rising as Favil had spoken.

Chaos broke out. Soldiers pinned men and women to the ground. Matching their blows with harder ones. The soldiers overtook the forsaken and contained them quickly, pushing the majority back into the wagons. The rest were forced in front of the barrier.

"Lower spears!" shouted Grayson. "Advance!"

The forsaken standing before the barrier stood their ground and waited until the tips of the soldier's spears struck them into the barrier. They screamed as they entered the tunnel and turned to ice, water, plant, and stone.

Ralakai raised his hand and inspected the path into the mountain wall. "It's down," he called back.

General Leganous smirked. The barrier came down quickly and Ralakai's men entered, retrieving those frozen, chiseled, or rooted in their way. His blood pulsed, the warrior within craving the taste of glory. With his sword drawn, he waited as the last of the forsaken were taken away.

XVI

LEAVING

Marcus stepped back from the bars and stood there, not wanting to believe Favil was gone, denying it was possible. His hands felt sticky, as though her blood was upon them. He'd as much drove the knife through her heart as Leganous had driven her into the barrier with his boot. He'd not seen it, but now it stared him in the face. Leganous killed her because of what he'd done. If he'd not killed the cook and the two soldiers, General Leganous would have left Favil alone, but the law forced his hand. It was silly for him to have believed the soldiers would've been satisfied with a few lashes. The spilling of blood had to be paid for with blood.

Shattered, Favil's words echoed in his mind.

There's more to your life past these wagons, and you'll recognize it when you're no longer in them.

And she'd sacrificed herself to bring it to pass.

General Leganous, King Zoren, and the elves were going to pay for every scream. Their deaths would be filled with endless suffering. If he had his sight he'd hunt them down himself. He'd bide his time, but like Favil also said, the rising was coming.

Have a little faith. Favil's words repeated in his mind like a mantra. He was determined to believe for her, but doubt reigned. His father raised him to be a man of strategy and forethought. All he saw were the impossible odds stacked against the rising and to him there was no way out. He was only one man. He was only a forsaken.

XVII

THE OTHER SIDE

The soldiers didn't lower their spears, their eyes intent on the opening in the mountain. Something waited at the other side of the tunnel.

Leganous could see daylight at the other end of the shallow path.

Haman rode up next to him, his sword drawn.

"You best stay here, Captain," advised Leganous. "We may need a messenger to travel at all speed to fetch the rest of the army at Fort Karrlun."

Haman's jaw clenched. "It would be my honour."

Grayson and Priestess Cyrene rode to the general's side and he turned to Grayson. "Leave half the army here."

Commander Grayson lifted his flag to signal the army.

"Present shields," yelled Leganous at the head of his men.

"Three centuries, advance!" ordered Grayson.

Two hundred and eighty men separated from the army and followed their general into the mountain. Shields raised and their spears extended, they pressed forward.

Icicles hung above them, dripping. A puddle of water reflected a partial image of a tree in the opening ahead.

The tunnel opened and General Leganous's eyes were drawn upwards to take in the magnificence of a single tree. He felt like an ant staring up at a boot, it reached so high into the sky. A natural boundary of rock loomed around it. Leganous shielded his eyes as he stared into the branches and saw what hung in the limbs of the massive tree.

Intricately woven treehouses hung from the branches like fruit on a vine and the snow covered roofs were made from gigantic leaves. Within the trunk were circular doors and a winding staircase that connected the small village from the roots to the highest branches. Smokeless chimneys of stone and lightless circled windows made the elf village appear abandoned.

Not a bird made a noise and the sound of the waterfall dimmed on the other side of the stone. The only commotion was the advancement of the army.

General Leganous reined his horse around to face his men. "Destroy it. And kill anything you find."

The soldiers charged the tree and climbed up the staircase, circling up the trunk to the houses above. Smaller staircases forked off the main path to the homes built into the tree itself. Kicking down the doors, they turned over hand-carved furniture and broke dishes made of clay.

Half the soldiers carried double bladed axes on their backs and walked onto the thick limbs of the tree without fear. They were so high up in the tree the general could hardly see them. They approached the vines supporting the elven homes and hacked until they gave way and thundered to the ground.

Priestess Cyrene shot flaming arrows at the structures that fell, while the men who'd entered the homes inside the trunk dropped vials of oil lit aflame.

Smoke started to fill the air as the soldiers completed their work and climbed back down.

Ralakai came to report. "No elves were found and the hearths were cold."

General Leganous basked in the splendour of the moment. Not even the presence of the approaching messenger, who was supposed to stay on the other side with his wagons, could dampen his spirits. "You'll have plenty to tell General Quinn when you see him now."

"I have seen your men in action and they did not disappoint," Haman commended. "We'll leave now while we have the light."

"My men and I will linger here a while. Hoping the moth may be drawn to the flame."

"I wish you all the best."

"And you," said the general. "For luck seems to have found favour with you."

Haman did not understand the implication.

"If Marcus does not reach Masseson alive and in your charge, you will have far bigger problems on your hands than his transfer. I will have reason to speak to General Quinn myself."

"Do you care for him?"

"I'd kill him myself if I thought he was worth my time," confessed Leganous. "But I've seen something that's given me an interest in his future."

"And yet you allow him to leave."

"It is necessary," stated Leganous. "And you may tell General Quinn to prepare his men for war. It soon approaches."

"She showed you something."

"Marcus's crossing will be the spark igniting the flame. Unlike his mother, he survived. Right now he's under the king's protection and it's wise of Zoren to remove him from here. In the tunnels of Ironwood Marcus will be out of sight. Word of him has already reached your ears. Soon it will pass into the furthest reaches of Azuk, unifying the people against us. You will see it before your end. Absolution and the eternal reign of King Zoren will be solidified in stone." The fire of the tree reflected in Leganous eye.

"We will be ready," said Haman, departing.

The village disappeared in black smoke and the tree began to burn from within. Heat from the flame reached into the army, melting the snow around them.

The soldiers joined ranks at the tunnel's entrance, ready for any elf who might approach seeking recompense as Haman turned his wagon around, his mission of acquiring Marcus complete.

XVIII

IRON AND CINDERS

King Zoren rubbed his forehead as the murmurs of his council permeated his skull. Sitting at the head of the table, he pitied the guards stationed around the edges of the decedent room. The marble hall and wooden table had seen many such meetings as this. Sculpted kings of the past and prominent members of old embellished the walls of the room. He wondered if he moved the head of the first king Emil to his seat if the council would notice he'd gone.

Kinkade seemed as bored as he was. He watched the sundial on the window sill and seemed to be willing it to move faster, but not even the gods had that power.

The way the council dragged on about iron shortages could drive a man to declare war. A lone male slave hovered close to the table as the men argued, pouring water into glasses and never letting them become empty.

Counsellor Augustus pounded the table. "The slaves have been digging for months and found very little iron. We need to send a magician to the mines of Ironwood."

Cassius shook his head. "Have you ever witnessed a burning?"

"I know what they are."

"The fire burns so hot it turns white and magicians have died performing it."

"But it'll crumble the stone far faster than any slave." Augustus ran his hand through his hair. "If we don't do this we won't have enough weapons to arm our men or till the fields. It's worth using some of the coffers of magical stones."

"What magician would offer us one of their stones? It's not like we can take it from them," responded Cassius.

"Our warriors can hardly fight with wooden sticks," mocked Augustus.

"That would certainly test the skill of our armies," laughed Livius.

The council members who agreed knocked their fists against the table.

A pale white hand pushed the giant oak door open and a shell of an elf with silver eyes, too big for his narrow sickly face, peered into the hall. He was a tamrasa, a loyal servant to the king. His pointed ears were no more. He'd burned the tips off as a sign of his devotion. No matter the request, Elian and the other tamrasa were bound to the wishes of the king. They'd sold their souls and Elian looked to Zoren like a dog awaiting his master's approval to enter.

Zoren nodded and Elian approached.

"What's he doing here?" demanded Cassius, leery of any elf, no matter their loyalty.

Zoren slighted Cassius with his tone. "I asked him to come." He'd known Elian far longer than all of them combined.

Elian rushed to Zoren's side and whispered in his ear. "He's here," he squeaked.

"Thank you, Elian."

The elf moved to the side to observe.

"Guards," Zoren summoned.

The doors opened and a magician named Othelus entered the council chamber. His richly ornate green tunic glided across the floor and matched the colour of his eyes. The man was getting on in years, but he'd remained strong. He bowed and his long grey hair swayed to the side.

"Your Majesty," he said.

"Othelus," welcomed Zoren, as the magician rose. "I trust your journey with Elian wasn't too much for a man of your wisdom to bear. The matter couldn't wait for you to arrive by horseback."

Othelus's hand quaked. "I can say without doubt I've never experienced anything like it, but the letter you sent was convincing."

"I'm relieved you decided to join us. If you'd prefer to return home by horse, I can arrange it."

"I would like that very much," confessed Othelus.

Zoren sat up in his chair. "What lies beneath the earth is a mystery to most and known by only a few. Your family has served the kingdom well in this area."

Othelus straightened his shoulders back with pride. "It is an art my father taught me and I've passed on to my eldest daughter."

"As any good father should." Zoren forced his face to stay neutral and addressed the members of his council. "Yesterday we discussed the new defences being built around the city and Leon brought up iron. I felt prompted to send a letter to Othelus this morning. I didn't mention it earlier because I hadn't heard his answer. But since he's travelled here, I am hopeful."

Othelus tugged on a chain around his neck, revealing a clear jewel set in an iron pendant. "My family will offer this stone to the cause."

Cassius interjected. "How much magic will it take to reach a new vein?"

Othelus let the pendant fall against his chest. "Having not been there in many years, it's hard to tell."

Cassius eyed the stone and sought another way. He turned to Zoren. "Surely you could do this?"

King Zoren was ready to settle the matter indefinitely. "We are most grateful for this sacrifice, Othelus. When the dwarven mines of Dasarak are reopened to us, your family will be gifted generously."

"You are most kind, Your Majesty. I pray that day will come soon, but I do make one request." Othelus shifted his weight. "As you can see, I'm not as young as I once was and have taken on teaching my daughter's eldest son our ways. I ask that I may be allowed to pass the stones loyalties to my daughter and she go in my place."

"How is your daughter?" Her name was also Othelus. The title passing from parent to eldest child as the head magician of the family.

"It's been three years since she lost her husband, General Titus. She and her two sons returned from

Ironwood to live with me, but she will be glad to have a reason to go back."

King Zoren knew of the prior mistress of Ironwood. She'd attended the Tournament of Generals, crowning General Quinn the victor, but unlike the wives of the past, who'd gone down to congratulate the next general, Othelus never left her box.

"I'm sure General Quinn will welcome her back with an open hand." Zoren turned to the council members. "And Commander Othos will arrange a troop of soldiers to accompany her. Are we all agreed?"

Kinkade was the first to raise his hand and the rest followed. Cassius was the last to raise his hand, but they were all in agreement.

Othelus bowed his head and turned to leave when the doors burst open.

"My lord!" yelled Marwin, his skin and armour caked in cinders and half dry blood. "I beg you for an audience."

King Zoren let the soldier approach and Othelus stayed to observe.

Marwin kneeled at the king's side and grasped the king's hand in his own, placing his forehead against it.

"I received an urgent letter from my wife yesterday morning, demanding I come with as many soldiers as I could find. But when I got there—" The man paused, trying to hold back his sobs. "The bodies of my family were roasting over the courtyard and the fields were on fire. I went to cut them down, but we were overwhelmed and I alone survived."

"How many men did you lose?"

"Sixteen."

"And did you kill them all? Down to the last child?" King Zoren gripped the man's hand tighter.

Marwin looked at the king, confused. "There were too many of them. I couldn't have possibly retaken the villa."

"Kinkade," inquired Zoren to his oldest council member, his face half burned and his arms covered in battle scars. "When your home was overrun, what did you do?"

Kinkade glared at Marwin. "I stood my ground."

Marwin realized what they were implying. "I did not desert my post."

Zoren could feel the soldier trying to pull away, but he'd admitted his guilt. "If you had truly been overrun, as you say, you would not be standing here before us."

"I came here to plead for an army to take back to my home."

"No, you didn't. You ran," accused Zoren. "And while it is in me to not hold the sins of the father against a son, it is not within my will to forgive a man the sins which are entirely his own."

Marwin jerked back, but not fast enough.

King Zoren twisted the soldier around and drew his dagger. He hacked off the man's ear and tossed him to the floor.

Marwin shrieked and scurried away, holding the side of his head.

Zoren rose to his feet. "From today forward, you will row in the galleys." He pointed his bloody knife at the soldier. "Another will finish the work I've begun. They'll sever your other ear, nose, and hair from your body, marking you a traitor and a coward to the masses."

"Show mercy, Your Majesty," begged Marwin.

Zoren looked down at the soldier, disgusted. "You should be grateful your family is dead. None of them will have to live with the shame of their names being joined to yours. They died with honour, you will die without."

Soldiers dragged the man away, and Othelus followed behind them.

Zoren twirled the blood covered knife between his fingers and the room fell silent as he removed himself from the council table. "Tomorrow morning I'll ride out and put down Marwin's revolt myself." He glanced back at the council. "I'll bandage the wound. If the infection spreads, we'll have to amputate a limb to save the body." *The slaves had had their moment of triumph, and very soon the masses would taste the bitterness of the cull.* "Give them one day to relish in victory. If there's anything else you'd like to discuss, we'll address it at our next meeting."

And he departed for the Aurelius.

XIX

A LESSON IN HISTORY

Zoren left the castle and took the bridge to the east side of the city. The stones vibrated beneath his feet as the falls crashed into the rocks far below. On the other side of the rapids, villas of the rich dwarfed in the sovereignty of the Aurelius. The oval structure stood like a mountain next to the river and was the centre of entertainment. Hundreds of thousands flocked to stand within her during the games; their feet resounding in harmony with the accelerated heartbeat of the athletes competing.

Zoren walked through the crowd, unhindered and unapproached. Traders waited at the gates of the arena. A lioness roared as she saw Zoren, her jaw flexing in warning. But he'd seen many lions.

In all his years, dragons were the one creature who'd escaped his sight. He'd sent ships into the farthest stretches of the world to search, but not a single voyage returned fruitful. The elves fought the dragons in the elder days and drove them from the shores of Remisia, forbidding them to ever return.

In the east, the fires of Fearisim still burned with dragon fire. At the end of the war, the dragons burned the corpses of their own from the deepest flames of their bellies, igniting the very rocks they stood upon in flame. The ashes of the fallen rose into the stars above, where their ancestors still reign supreme.

The blade of Zoren's departed wife, Lina, was made from dragon bone. Her mother gave her the sword after her coming of age ceremony and it was Lina's most cherished possession because it was her father's. She'd never met him and it was her way of feeling close to him. As far as Zoren knew, it was the only sword of its kind in existence. Zoren buried her with it, sealing the crypt with blood and moon, making it impossible to open, except by the one she loved most.

Zoren entered the Aurelius and walked around the multitude of painters who were preparing for the next games. He attended most of the events, but the next one was to honour Dirva, the god of earth.

Zoren rolled his eyes as he saw one of the painter's interpretations of Dirva on the arena wall. It was clear the artist was not a painter of history.

They'd made Dirva appear all powerful. His shoulders were broad and a storm of earth quaked in his hand. On his right shoulder sprouted magical stones and adorning his fingers were rings. Embedded in each ring was a different element of the earth. The god's hair was green and his bronze feet were covered in soil. His shoulders pulled back and his head held high, Dirva looked so much more powerful than when Zoren had encountered him.

Zoren thought the games of earth were the dullest of the twelve. Men fighting in mud and tales of Dirva's heroic acts were frequently repeated. There weren't many to tell, which was surprising to Zoren, considering the level of power he felt coursing through his veins.

He stared at the artist's painting, hating it the more he looked at it. Motioning the tips of his fingers, Dirva's face sifted like sand dropping down the hole of an hourglass. The whole image of him was consumed and had disappeared, leaving a vacant silhouette on the stone wall. *Now the image is more accurate to the god's current state.*

Reaching his box, Zoren observed from above, unnoticed by the ones who trained on the sands below. He marvelled at how young the boys were as they struggled through the obstacles. Hanging vertically from poles for long periods of time and balancing on beams, they flipped and jumped. A group of boys raced around the sands, carrying heavy packs filled with rocks in order to survive a long march.

The instructors stood along the course, striking the boys if a limb went out of line, but unseen to the instructors was another group of boys circling around a smaller boy. They'd ganged up on him and were trying to make him yield.

Zoren hastened down the stairs and was upon the boys before they even realized he was among them.

A bigger boy swung his wooden sword at the head of the smaller, but Zoren stopped it by grabbing the blade. The boy stammered back, immediately surrendering the sword to his king.

"Thank you," said Zoren, flipping the sword so he held the hilt. It was lighter than a normal sword, but once the boys learned technique, a weapon of iron would be given to them.

Zoren pointed the sword at the smaller boy. "You show great courage," he said. "Not everyone would stand their ground when faced by so many."

"I only did what any man should," said the small boy. "My father taught me that though I am small, I can have the will to persevere."

"Your father taught you well," said Zoren.

"I am Kelwin, son of Jonas, of the six hundred and sixteenth legion of our King Zoren. It is my duty to protect the realm of Remisia, no matter the cost."

"And who are these boys?"

"A means to an end. With every blow of their swords, I will be made stronger."

Zoren admired the boy's tenacity. "Your strength gives you credit." The rest of the boys shuffled as close as they could behind Kelwin. The instructors stopped the training and listened to every word of their king.

"My father was nothing like yours. He was a butcher, both in trade and heart. I could always smell the drink on his breath as he hit me and cursed my name. I knew nothing of fighting. My comfort was delivering our meat to the market. We were at war with the Azuk at the time, and Remisia was on the brink of collapse. I'd pick up an odd job, sharpening swords and cleaning armour. Earned a few small coins to buy pastries on the way home.

"But when I got home, the door was askew on the hinges. I could hear the muffled cries of my mother on the other side. And when I walked in, four Azuk soldiers were watching while another defiled her on the floor. Anger like I'd never felt consumed me. I pulled one of my father's knives from the wall and I killed two of them before they even knew I was there. I was outnumbered and out-skilled, but I was defending my home and it made me a far better warrior than any conqueror."

"Where was your father?" asked Kelwin.

"Passed out drunk in his chair," said Zoren.

Another boy cried out, "Drunken fool," causing the rest of them to laugh.

"It's why our minds must always be clear. We never know when we'll face our next battle. I took my mother away from there and headed here to find a physician. On the way, my mother came to and asked for a drink of water. I laid her down next to an old oak and went to get her some water with my hands, but as I was doing so I heard the earth stir beside me. A tree of Reeza sprouted up, and when I wrapped my fingers around its small trunk, it uprooted. Lavender leaves sprouted from its branches and this tattoo appeared on my arm. I became king and the trees became loyal to me. They saw the warrior in me, like I see the warrior in you."

Kelwin smiled. "And you turned the tides of war."

"I found the former King Jareth asleep in his bed, his blade still shining like new, and I used it to cut him to pieces. I sent parts of his body to the farthest cities of Remisia and rallied them to win the war."

"How old were you?"

"I was seventeen and had never held a sword in my life," smirked Zoren.

The boys laughed at this. None of them could

remember ever being without one.

"I learned quickly and bought peace with the tip of my blade. The citizens of Remisia came to my side. Something you boys should never forget," said Zoren, addressing the boys who'd ganged up on Kelwin. "There may be a day when you will be surrounded by an enemy and you will have to remember to watch each other's backs. Kelwin here might be small, but he will be fast. He might be fast enough to make a difference between your end and your continuation."

King Zoren handed the wooden sword he'd taken back to the boy.

"Thank you," he said.

Zoren messed up the boy's hair in a playful manner. "Now, back to your lessons. The balance of peace and war is a delicate scale. You must always be ready."

The boys all yelled in unison, "Look to the end."

And they attacked their lessons with new ferocity, inspired by the lessons of their king.

XX

FIRE AND EARTH

King Zoren ordered the fifty soldiers to halt as they reached the edge of Marwin's land. Being back in the saddle a few hours with his army reminded him of the old days fighting the Azuk. Peering down at the scorched villa, he unsheathed his sword and handed it to the First Commander Othos.

Commander Othos hesitantly accepted it. "Would you prefer mine, Your Majesty?"

"I won't need it," smirked the king. "Keep the men here until I return." He kicked his horse into a gallop and his silver armour reflected the sunlight. It was forged by the dwarves. The ornate metal came from the trees of Reeza and kept the ragged appearance of bark. There was no stronger armour in existence. He'd spent centuries trying to replicate it, but no matter how long his blacksmiths held it in the flames, it never softened.

The smouldering gates creaked on their hinges and

Zoren saw the patrols, abandoning their posts, running to whomever was in charge. These were no soldiers. They were farmers and he would slaughter them like pigs.

First he would play their game.

He bent his head as he rode his horse into the villa. The burned bodies of Marwin's wife and children swayed in the courtyard. There was nothing left to distinguish their colour or what they'd been wearing prior to being strung up. Zoren guessed the wife hadn't been wearing any clothes when they'd set her on fire. Her eldest son hung next to her and he saw himself in the child. The two of them could have been him if he'd lost the fight with the Azuk, but he'd been older and had fewer opponents. This family would be honoured. They'd stood their ground, and he would personally pay for their burial.

After years of hard labour, the Azuk had not learned their lesson. He'd tried to teach them, but they forced him to become the most ruthless version of himself.

Zoren dismounted and whacked the rear of his steed as he went up the stairs into the villa. Everything was tossed over and charred. The soldiers who'd come to Marwin's aid lay dead on the marble floor. Zoren saw no one else. He followed the trail of bodies and destruction to the lounge where he found a host of wide-eyed people.

Few of them were armed with any real weapons. Some had picked up the swords of the dead, but most of them carried scythes or pitch forks. When they saw it was him, they tipped all of their weapons in his direction, and stepped aside whenever he got too close.

Zoren caught sight of their leader sitting on a couch and he began to applaud.

He clapped so hard his hands stung and when he saw the look of confusion on their leader's face, he couldn't help but laugh.

"Well done," he said. "Well done!" He shouted, but no one joined in. They stared at him like he'd gone mad, and maybe he had.

Once he stopped clapping, the man on the couch spoke. "King Zoren. I am Nicodemus, direct descendant of ancient Emperor Decimus," he said with a deep voice. "Have you come to kill us?"

"Yes," said Zoren. "I'm afraid as much as I admire your undertaking, I cannot allow it to continue."

"We just want to return home and live in peace."

"You have been living in peace," asserted Zoren. "You're fed, clothed, and given a place to sleep. What more could you want?"

"We want to decide when we sleep, what we eat, and how we live."

"For your actions all you have done is secure when you will die."

"The happenings of the north will not be silenced. If we are the first to rise and the first to fall then so be it." Nicodemus stood up and threw his spear at King Zoren's chest, but Zoren caught it and spun it in his hands.

"A fine choice of weapon." He threw it back at Nicodemus with more force and speed than anyone had time to stop. The leader fell dead on the ground and the room erupted.

Everyone plunged at Zoren, seeking their pound of

flesh. The king relished in their anger. From the right, the left, behind, and in front they attacked, and he met their every blow.

A slave who'd been the entertainer gulped a swig of liquid fire and blew on a torch in the king's direction.

Zoren lifted his hand, and the fire gathered into his palm like a ball on a catapult.

The people stood back.

"What kind of magic is this?" begged the entertainer.

"It's not." Zoren smirked, ramming his hands together, and the flames pulsed out around him, igniting everyone in the vicinity.

The people who weren't on fire ran to the pillars of the room and struck them with sledge hammers. Others fled from the room as the roof became unstable and gave way with Zoren beneath it.

The roof over the lounge collapsed and a wave of dust chased the survivors out the main door. Those who'd gotten out breathed a sigh of relief, believing no one inside could have survived.

That is, until the fragments of the villa shifted and the earth quaked. The rocks rolled to the side and out of the middle of the wreckage the king emerged unscathed, a ball of fire in one hand and earth in the other.

The rebels lost all courage and fled, unsure if the infamous King Zoren was god or man, for no magician had such power. Some begged to be shown mercy, others knew they would never get it. All fell before him.

In the chaos, Zoren spotted a boy shielding himself from the flames. He had black skin, like his own, and similar features, but it wasn't himself he reminded Zoren of. He looked into the eyes and saw the eyes of another he knew. A boy he hated and despised with everything inside of him.

Zoren expanded the flames and took joy in seeing the boy burn.

The slaves tried to flee into the shelter of the corn fields. One by one the earth swallowed them where they stepped, pulling them down to where they could never dig themselves out. They died a slow and painful death as their bodies fought to breathe, finding only dirt to fill their lungs.

Zoren lifted his hands in the air, commanding the fires to gather on the winds above the villa. He manipulated them into the shape of a great dragon. Giant wings of flame pulsed through the air, rising high above the villa until it was the full semblance of the creature of old. It soared over the field around them, and as Zoren swept his hand towards the structures, the dragon moved with it. He caused the earth to rumble as the dragon opened its jaws and plowed into the villa. Flames broke through every window and filled every room, consuming everything in its path. Screams of those who'd taken refuge inside shrieked, but were silenced as the inferno materialized out the other side and dissipated to nothing.

Not a soul survived. Every man, woman, and child, old and young, was dead.

Zoren wiped his brow and noticed some of the vertes on his arms had darkened. One had gone completely black, void of any magic. Using his fingernails he picked it off like a scab and tossed it to the side. He whistled and his horse returned and he rode back to his awestruck men.

"Cut down the family and have them brought back to Sidabras. There they can be buried properly. Leave the slaves where they lay as a sign to others not to try the same. The surrounding farms can take up the fields."

Zoren reached out to Commander Othos. "I'll have my sword back now."

Othos fumbled it back to him, amazed by the acts of his king.

"Thank you," said Zoren.

An aghast soldier mumbled. "That was not the work of a mortal man."

Zoren kicked his horse into a gallop and headed back to Sidabras.

XXI

ALEKSIA

Aleksia stood at the kitchen window with a plate in one hand and a cloth in the other. The cloth moved over the wooden surface as she distractedly gazed upon the dirt road. Evening was beginning as the sun flared between the leaves, but her mind was elsewhere.

She'd had the dream again.

In the dream she was climbing a mountain. Snow plummeted against her as she clung to the ledge, the elements blasting against her pointed ears and neck. A rope was tied around her waist, taut in both directions. Someone was with her, but they were obscured. She couldn't look at them or understand what they were saying, but she knew they were there.

She could see a ledge, her arms strained to reach it, until someone pushed her up. With their help, she pulled herself onto the landing and the feeling of accomplishment swelled throughout her.

Rising to her feet, she was suddenly free of the rope and staring at a buck, unlike any she'd ever seen before.

Its fur was as black as midnight, containing the eyes of a tortured soul. Something stirred within its stare; a silver web, reaching into its very core. The deer timidly limped towards her. The horns on its head the same shade as its body, but broken. Almost the entirety of one horn was missing, the base bleeding.

Aleksia took a step backwards until a sound like thunder came from where she'd yet to look. The buck stood on its hind legs as fire consumed it. Aleksia cried out in horror, drawing her sword, but someone stopped her from behind. The deer fell to its knees in a constant stream of flame. She tried to see where the fire was coming from, but she woke in a pool of sweat.

She hadn't told Jovetta about the dream, and she wondered if she should.

Aleksia put the plate down beside the cooling bucket of washing water and picked up the second one. The vertes of the elvian sparkled on her arms as they caught a ray of sunlight. Usually her sleeves were down, but she'd rolled them up to wash the dishes. To her, they were the most beautiful thing about her. They looked like water droplets all over her arms, back, and chest, but for some unknown reason, she was the only one who could see them. Everything that made her an elf was obscured to anyone who saw her. Even if one of her guardians touched her arm, they felt nothing.

The kitchen in the small cabin was barely big enough to house the two of them, but it met their needs. Two chairs, a table, two plates, two cups, and cutlery.

Next to the grass roofed house was an old barn of stone. In the past it sheltered livestock, but it had been years since even a goat darkened its door.

Aleksia fished in the shadows of a nearby creek, but she'd also carved a bow and arrow, allowing her to hunt bigger prey. Mostly she hunted rabbit or other rodents, but every once in a while larger game were caught in her sights. She'd made it her mission to teach herself to hunt, fight, and survive because she knew one day she might have to. She'd never sparred with another person, but she'd found a few ways to practice.

A chicken scurried beneath the sill, clucking away, pecking the ground for bugs, and she imagined what it would be like to hear the voice of a different bird and to see it fly. She'd heard legends of their songs from previous guardians. Gina teared up at the memory when she spoke of birds. Aleksia had been very young at the time, and she'd asked her to try and mimic their voice. Gina humoured her plea and whistled, and to her younger self it was one of the most beautiful sounds she'd ever heard. She wondered what a real bird would sound like. Just one moment would satisfy her.

Finishing the dishes, Aleksia pursed her lips and whistled a small tune she thought might sound like a bird.

Jovetta sat on a chair outside, listening and drinking in the sound of Aleksia's song.

Aleksia watched her contentment and was filled with envy.

Jovetta sat in the same chair every night, but she didn't appear to mind.

Unable to bear such satisfaction, all of Aleksia's

focus turned to the old dirt road and it taunted her even more. She'd tried to go where it led when she was sixty-seven, but she didn't get very far. Without a map or a guide to take her to the land of her people, she was lost. She could hardly stop at the nearest farmhouse and ask directions.

It wasn't safe. The statement every woman who'd ever come to live with her told her, but how was here any safer? She'd be far safer with her own people in Visadas.

"Aleksia, won't you come sit with me?" asked Jovetta, never opening her eyes.

"Be there in a moment," answered Aleksia, putting away the last dish. She wiped her hands dry on her skirts, walking through the open door as she rolled down her sleeves.

Jovetta's clothing was simple. In the six years she'd lived with Aleksia she continued to wear her brown slave dress, with a sash around the waist. It was well worn and the only thing she owned. The short curls of her hair bristled in the wind.

Aleksia sat next to her without a word.

"I won't press you," commented Jovetta. "I could've prepared another meal and eaten it in the time it took you to do the washing."

Aleksia appreciated Jovetta wasn't one to ask questions. She was the patient type that waited for people to open up. It came from her years of mothering. "What are you thinking about?" inquired Aleksia.

"Chadd," she smiled, closing her eyes. "I can almost picture him coming up the road. I'd imagine he's got little ones of his own by now."

"Did he have a sweetheart?" asked Aleksia.

"There were a few. Vibiana always caught his eye, but he never seemed to have the courage to reveal his intentions."

"Perhaps, you coming here gave him the courage he needed."

Jovetta laughed at Aleksia and nudged her. "Well, I hope so. It's about time he made me a grandmother. I can only wait so long." She giggled, the lines of her face lighting up at the thought of it.

Aleksia smiled along with her, recounting the times she'd heard the story, but she enjoyed hearing it. Stories of life beyond the house on the side of the road were all she had of the outside world.

"My man Aulus, before he was taken from me, would smother that boy. Pick him up in the middle of the night and sit in a chair by the hearth cradling him. I used to tell him, 'if you wake that baby, I'll flog you myself.'" She paused and her face went downcast. "Aulus knew time with his boy was precious. And it wasn't long into our boy's life my husband was sold at auction and I never saw him again."

"Did you find out where he went?"

Jovetta shook her head. "I had Chadd, and I saw his father in him all the time. Sometimes too much of him. He's the one who put my lot in the pile to come up here."

"Do you regret it?"

"There's nothing to regret. I was about to be sent to the barriers," she sighed. "Some days are harder than others," she confessed. "I'd never seen Chadd so happy than when I was chosen. He wanted me to live the last of my days in peace and it has been peaceful."

"I'm glad." Aleksia took her hand.

"No you're not," smirked Jovetta. "You might enjoy my company, I know I enjoy yours, but you're far from content. You've got the same look in your eyes I've seen in many. Eyeing the road like you'll never live unless you get on it."

"I know the risks."

"And I've seen others who knew the risks too. I know you're a lot older than I am, but I like to think I've earned some wisdom to pass on to you."

"You will always be wiser than me."

"For now." Jovetta stroked Aleksia's hand with her thumb. "But this place will not be here forever. Enjoy the peace because one day, you might wish you were back here watching the sun go down."

"I want to go to Visadas and get answers."

"The elves live how many years?" mocked Jovetta.

"I'm not sure. I don't remember ever meeting one."

"From what I've heard of the elves, you've got time. That road isn't going anywhere. It's probably older than you. What makes you think it won't be there when Zoren's gone?"

"He's lived too long."

"His time will come," Jovetta reminded her. "And so will yours."

Aleksia nodded, wanting to change the subject. "Tomorrow I'm going to cut some fresh grass to patch up the roof. It's long enough in the far meadow."

The two of them sat in front of the old house talking until Aleksia sat up, turning her ear to something out of the usual.

"What is it?" asked Jovetta, following Aleksia's gaze to the road.

A horse snorted.

"Go," urged Jovetta.

Aleksia ran to the barn and shut the door behind her, watching the road through a small crack.

Moments went by and nothing happened, but the sound of horse hooves got louder. There was more than one.

Jovetta hadn't moved, but Aleksia could see the tension in her shoulders. She hated the soldiers more than Aleksia, and they'd given her plenty of reasons to.

From behind the tree line three of the king's men rode, along with a horse burdened with supplies.

Let them pass. Don't stop here. Just keep riding, willed Aleksia, but favour was not on her side. The leader raised his hand and they came to a halt. He held himself like a man clinging to power and always eager for more. He wore his well-tended armour proudly, and his arm guards shone in the fading light. The man got off his horse, his two men mimicking his movement, as they walked up to Jovetta, who stood to her feet.

Jovetta spoke first. "Might I help you?"

"Where is your master?" he asked.

"My master sent me here to die, but if I can be of service, I am willing."

"You ought to be with the forsaken."

Jovetta dropped her gaze. "I apologize if my presence here offends you. My master Lysander has his slaves cast lots whenever this house becomes empty to give us hope."

It was always a little bit of a shock when they found me here, thought Aleksia. No one else knew she was here and she had to hide, just as she did now, whenever a slave came to check Jovetta was still alive.

The man accepted her word as truth. "I'm Captain Haman of the five hundred and eighty-seventh legion and my men are hungry."

Jovetta bowed her head. "I don't have much, but what I do have is yours."

Aleksia watched Haman walk into the cabin. "Make us something to eat and feed the livestock."

Aleksia was curious at the way the soldier had said livestock, so she looked once again at the horses still standing on the road. All four horses looked well fed, but then she looked behind, tracing a taut rope, and she muffled a cry of disgust.

There was a man, collapsed from exhaustion, behind one of the horses, his arms hanging limp in the air.

What did they do to him? Aleksia fought the urge to run and help him. The other two soldiers hadn't gone into the house yet.

"Shall I put the horses in the barn before I prepare the meal?" asked Jovetta.

"My men will tend to them," he answered.

Jovetta followed Haman inside, and as the soldiers approached, Aleksia reluctantly left the door and ran into the farthest horse stall. She slid open a hidden door in the wall and climbed onto the wooden ladder in the abandoned silo tower. She scaled up a few steps and fixed her eyes between a breach in the wall as the soldiers opened the barn door.

Last rays of sunlight shone through all the cracks in the building, and Aleksia stayed herself so she wouldn't draw attention.

The first soldier walked ahead into the barn, his

heavy boots thudding with every step. He inspected the integrity of the structure, hitting one of the wooden beams.

Aleksia dared it to fall on him. Then she could put him out of his misery and he wouldn't have even known she was ever there. When the beam didn't break, she almost felt disappointed.

"There's no hay, but it doesn't seem like the building will fall anytime soon. Let them graze outside. We'll chain the forsaken up in here."

Forsaken? Aleksia had seen them walking on the road, wailing in fear, but they'd always come from the south, headed north. How was this man bound for the Elven lands if they were headed in the opposite direction?

Chains announced the soldiers were bringing him into the shelter. The man's feet dragged across the packed floor, his head hanging lifelessly as the soldiers dropped him onto the ground.

They took the chains and clasped them around a nearby beam as the other brought in the saddlebags and gear.

The man neither stirred nor made a sound as the barn door shut and the soldiers went into the house.

Aleksia could see the man's chest rise and fall and everything inside her wanted to help, but she needed to wait until the cover of darkness. Once the men inside the house were asleep, it would be safer. She went down the ladder to prepare.

Centuries ago she'd built a room under the silo. Other men had stopped along the edge of the road and sought refuge in the cabin over the years. Rather than raise suspicion and try to explain her presence one of her old guardians, Sabina, had thought it was best if no one knew she was ever there. During her exile, she'd made it into a home.

An old wool blanket lay upon her hand-carved bed. The mattress was stuffed with leaves from the surrounding forest and her pillow was filled with handfuls of pine needles. There wasn't much furniture. It was difficult to find pieces big enough to make the projects she desired, but she'd managed with a bed and a table and chair where she could work on her carvings. On the far side was a well she'd dug with her own two hands, surrounded with stones she'd found from a fallen building out back. She'd used clay from the river to fasten it together. There was no fireplace because smoke or the smallest crack would reveal her. Aleksia didn't need the light to see like humans. She needed it for other reasons.

On the walls were shelves filled with food, held in baskets of twine, but throughout the room were many objects carved in wood, from animals to dishes.

Above her bed were the perfectly carved faces of each of the women who'd taken care of her. Not that she had any difficulty remembering their faces, but it was a way to keep them close. On the base was their name and a minor detail about them. A picture of a herb they loved or their favourite flower. But on the ledge, right next to Aleksia's bedside, were two carvings without faces and pointed ears. They were the faces she most longed to carve but couldn't. Her first guardian, Gina, might have known, but if she did, the truth of her heritage and how she'd come here had died with her.

Aleksia went to her shelves, taking food and supplies, and placed the items on the bed. She went to the well and filled a water skin. Around and around her little room she walked, mixing herbs into pastes, and trying to divide as many useful items as she could.

When she was satisfied, she grabbed a bag and placed the items inside, but gauging the time, it was still too early to go up.

Rather than twiddle her thumbs and wait in her fear of the dark, she sat at the table, picked up a piece of wood, and began to carve a cup. The man could drink from the waterskin, but she needed something to distract her. Taking her knife to carve always calmed her down.

She only hoped Jovetta was faring well. She kept her ears turned to anything amiss, but there'd been nothing. It was unlikely the men would touch her, but it didn't stop Aleksia from muttering a quick prayer to Elvian.

XXII

IN THE LIGHT
OF THE MOON

Aleksia waited as long as she could, stuffing the new cup into the sack and slinging it over her shoulder. She climbed the ladder, keeping her dagger close. At the top she slid the plank over as quietly as she could, fairly certain the soldiers were asleep, but her paranoia made her stay silent. Rays of the moon shimmered throughout the barn, making it look eerie and forbidden. She proceeded to the man on the floor and couldn't believe her eyes when she knelt by his side. He hadn't moved, and without a shirt to cover his back, wounds both old and new covered his torso. His partly dreaded hair was so filled with dirt she wasn't sure if brown was its natural colour. Dry blood stained the tops of his feet and looking under them there was barely any skin left.

"What have they done to you?" she uttered under her breath.

Aleksia didn't know where to start or what she could do. If she did too much, the guards would notice and that wouldn't be good for either of them.

Where is Jovetta? she thought. She didn't have time to wait and set to work. She set out a blanket and lifted him onto it, placing him on his back and doing her best not to wake him.

I need more water.

Leaving her stuff in a stall, she went back down into her room, grabbing a bucket of water and a cloth. His scars were too filthy to apply any of the herbs she'd brought. Upon returning she dosed the cloth in the water and began delicately washing the grime from his chest. He stirred, but didn't wake.

Aleksia's head shot up when the door of the cabin opened. Light from a torch seeped through the doorway. Hurriedly she picked up her stuff and ran into one of the stalls, pulling out her dagger. All that stood between her and the person approaching was a door that would've blown away in a simple storm. The latch lifted and the door creaked open.

"Aleksia?" whispered Jovetta.

Never had Aleksia felt such relief at hearing her voice. Revealing herself, Aleksia exhaled and put her dagger back in its sheaf. "I thought you were one of the soldiers." Aleksia returned to the man's side.

"Well, I would have shouted, but I didn't think that would help this poor man," Jovetta said, holding strips of cloth and a basket of her own supplies.

Aleksia heard Jovetta's intake of air when she saw him. She struggled to kneel next to him, but once she got comfortable, she dipped her cloth into the bucket and started where Aleksia had left off.

Aleksia came down beside her. "What could a man do to deserve such treatment?"

"Nothing. It's the way citizens are." Her eyes spoke what her words could not.

Aleksia knew there were many stories Jovetta had spared her from. This wasn't the first boy she'd seen in such a state. Watching from the corner of her eye, she saw Jovetta move his hair from his face, stroking it like a mother.

Jovetta's hands shook as she rinsed her cloth again. She'd seen horrors and seeing this man was bringing them back.

"Could you get some fresh water?" Aleksia wanted to spare her.

Jovetta wiped her nose and stood up slowly. "I think there might be another blanket in the house as well. I'll fetch it," she volunteered, her voice trembling.

Aleksia went to the man's feet and began spreading herbs along the bottom of them. If it had been daytime, she could have healed them completely, but the moon still dominated the sky.

Aquila, one of her prior guardians, was adamant she learned to heal using herbs. They'd spent weeks collecting the natural remedies and she'd taught her the uses of each. Aquila always told her there would be days when the sun never came out or the night lasted too long to heal anyone with the rays of the vertes.

The more she looked at the man, the more puzzled she became. He had all of his limbs, a family crest, and long partially dreaded hair, which confused her most. It seemed like he'd tried to maintain them himself. The front was tighter than the back where he couldn't reach. He had to be someone of importance or a great warrior to have dreads. She'd seen a general go by with the same hair once and she'd never seen her guardian, Rosabel, so agitated. That was the day Aleksia decided to dig the room under the barn.

Wiping his face, she smiled. Beneath all the dirt and scratches was a handsome face, or at least she thought so. Aleksia could count on one hand the amount of men she'd seen up close and now she had to wake him up. It was clear from the bones surfacing against his skin he needed to eat. With a little rest and nourishment, he'd be a prime candidate in the king's army.

Aleksia didn't want to make too much noise, but poking him with her finger felt so idiotic. Picking up her water skin, she gently poured it onto his chest and into his hairline before he stirred.

The man's eyes opened and Aleksia understood why he wasn't part of the king's army. A white haze obscured his vision. He was a forsaken because he was blind.

Aleksia was grateful he couldn't see her. He had walked all the way from Visadas, stumbling and depending on his chains to guide him through the darkness. It was no wonder his feet were so ripped and torn.

An image of herself storming into the house and putting her dagger through the soldier's heart with all her strength seized Aleksia's mind. She wished for sunlight. If the rays were to pass through the vertes on her arms, she could restore his sight. How would it be explained to the guards? They would have left a man in the barn who couldn't see and returned to find a man who could. It would alert the king of her presence.

Neither elves nor man could heal using magic. Most died in the attempt, but to her it came as natural as breathing. Yet it came with a price.

The sun was where she got her power, and if she disappeared from Elvian's sight for more than a fortnight, her body turned to stone. Being in the sunlight was an easy price to pay, but King Zoren coveted the vertes and locked her people in sunless dungeons. As the stories went, their screams were heard from leagues away.

The man's body tensed at her touch. He tried to rise and say something, but his voice was desiccated from thirst.

"Don't try to speak. My name is Aleksia and I'm here to help you."

He somewhat relaxed, but not completely.

Aleksia placed her hand against his back. He lurched in pain and she withdrew. "Sorry! Did I hurt you?"

The man shook his head no, rubbing his eyes, as he gradually sat up on his own.

"Would you like some water?" Aleksia asked.

He nodded.

Aleksia poured water into the cup she'd made. There were a few things she still wanted to do with it. There'd only been enough time to carve out the shape and not the designs.

Handing it to him, he drank eagerly.

"Don't drink too fast or it'll come back up again," she advised.

He held out the cup for more and Aleksia refilled it.

He downed it again, but with a little less desperation.

Aleksia kept offering him water. He seemed unsettled. He took one cup and splashed it in his face, moving his hand through the air as though he was searching for something. He was able to sit on his own, so Aleksia sorted through the food. She started with what she'd brought — acorns, berries, and mushrooms — and then thought better of it. Taking Jovetta's basket, she found more suitable options: bread, cheese, and a few slices of the rabbit. Aleksia hated the taste of any kind of meat but her guardians loved it.

"Thank you," he said.

"There's some food here," offered Aleksia, starting with the rabbit. She placed it in his hand and barely touched his skin.

He flinched and dropped it. "Sorry."

"It's alright," she reassured him. "There's plenty." She gave him a fresh piece, keeping the portions small. He made his way through the meat, cheese, and bread, but as she was finishing, the man firmly grabbed her wrist, instantly pulling away as though he'd touched fire. The cup in his other hand burst to pieces.

"There are stones all over your arms," he snarled.

A knot formed in Aleksia's stomach and she slowly rose to her feet, putting some distance between them as an anger unlike she'd ever known consumed his handsome features.

"And your touch —," he winced, "feels just like the barriers."

He knows. Aleksia didn't take her eyes off of him as he stumbled to his feet. His stance fixed on where she'd been before he'd discovered what she was.

"You're an elvian." The man charged, but the chain caught his leg and he tumbled. He was back on his feet as quickly as he'd fallen. "Quit lurking in shadows and fight," he demanded.

Aleksia stayed silent, moving whenever he was in front of her. She was to his left when the hem of her dress brushed the barn wall.

The man's head shot up and he barrelled towards her. Once again his chains caught him and he was on the ground. This time his recovery was slower, leaning on his hands and knees, tears of frustration fell from his eyes.

Aleksia bent down in front of him, knowing she was out of reach. "I am not your enemy," she hissed.

The man raised his head towards her. "Tell that to the thousands of souls awaiting their revenge on the other side." He retreated and sat next to the beam, his body language set against her.

Aleksia went to the barn door and he sat there holding his own hand, as though he cursed it.

"Jovetta's human and she'll look after you."

The man nodded and he was done talking to her.

"I'll spend the night in the woods." Aleksia lifted the latch to exit the barn, but it crashed into her and she collapsed on her back.

Captain Haman drew his sword, aiming it at Aleksia as he smiled at her. "Who would have thought the old woman possessed such a treasure in the barn."

Aleksia strained to hold her position, withdrawing her carving knife. When she'd imagined facing an actual opponent she'd pictured having a larger weapon.

Elvian help me.

Aleksia knocked Haman's sword away, her dagger firmly in hand.

Haman chuckled at her attempts to fight. "Quintain. Porcius," he yelled.

The two soldiers entered the barn, Jovetta between them, a knife to her throat, blood dripping from a fresh cut on her forehead.

Haman tapped Aleksia's dagger with his own. "The longer you hold on to that knife, the deeper Porcius's will go."

"Aleksia!" Jovetta cried.

"Be silent," ordered Haman.

Jovetta's slight intake of air made Aleksia relinquish her knife.

"Quintain, chain her next to Marcus," commanded Haman, taking Aleksia's knife and admiring the craftsmanship.

Quintain's hair grew in at all different lengths and his acne spoke of his youth. He went to the saddlebags and retrieved fresh chains. The smell of him was unsavoury as he secured Aleksia to the same post as Marcus.

"Now show me her shoulder."

Aleksia glanced at the iron clasped around her ankle. Every female citizen had a tattoo on their shoulder, marking the year of their birth. At twenty-one if a woman hadn't married or had a child, they were sent to the mines until her situation changed. It was a law King Zoren invented to ensure his armies were never lacking soldiers. Many slave women tried to hide their daughters from getting branded in order to give them a chance at becoming citizens when they were old enough. It rarely worked, but every so often a girl slipped through the cracks and had to be tested.

Aleksia pulled her arm away, but Quintain, eager to impress, used his knife to cut the fabric of her sleeve and ripped it.

"The tattoo's been singed," exclaimed Quintain.

Aleksia looked at her arm, but all she saw were the vertes. All of them were blind to the truth, everyone except the man sitting as far away from her as he could muster.

Haman had seen enough. "She's coming with us. In Masseson she'll be tested to ensure she really is a citizen and if proven, given the choice of whether she wishes to marry or work."

"No!" shouted Jovetta.

"And you, old woman. Clearly you're not her mother and have been harbouring her. Tell me who her family is and I may spare your life."

Jovetta shivered in fear, but said nothing in her defence.

Haman used Aleksia's dagger and sliced Jovetta's arm.

Jovetta muffled a scream and Aleksia rose to her feet.

"Don't touch her. She came here on my order."

Haman ignored Aleksia, focusing on the one he knew he could break. "Tell me who her family is."

Jovetta elbowed Porcius, and he lost his grip. She fled and Haman hunted her like a cat after a panicked mouse.

He caught her and punched her so hard she plummeted to the floor.

Aleksia forgot her chains and ran as far as she could

towards them. The iron caught her ankle. "Stop!" she pleaded, but through her tears Jovetta gave Aleksia a stern look not to come to her aid.

Quintain pushed Aleksia back, and she stammered to her knees.

Haman asked again, his patience wearing thin. "Who is her family?"

Just say it, implored Aleksia, catching Jovetta's eye.

Blood trickled from Jovetta's lip and arm. Her arms shook under her weight as she pushed herself back up to face her attacker. She looked straight into Haman's eyes and kept her mouth shut.

Haman stabbed Jovetta through the chest with Aleksia's dagger.

"Jovetta!" screamed Aleksia.

Jovetta's eyes were wide as she fell.

"I guess we'll never know." Haman wiped the knife with a cloth from his pocket. "We leave in the morning." He left the barn with his soldiers and posted one of them outside.

Aleksia got as close as she could to Jovetta, straining to fasten her hand around her guardians wrist. The chain dug deep into her ankle, but she got her and drew her near.

"Don't worry, Jovetta. I'm here. I'm going to make it all better," promised Aleksia, barely able to make out the words. She turned to Marcus. "Please help me."

Marcus glanced in her direction, but his back stayed up against the pole, keeping his distance.

Aleksia wanted to punch him in the face. She couldn't hold pressure on the wound and do what she needed to. He sat there, listening to her struggle. Jovetta needed both of them and she'd drag him over by the chain attached to his leg if she had to.

"I need your help," she beseeched Marcus over her shoulder. "Now get over here." Focusing back to Jovetta. "She's human and was here trying to save your life. Don't you think you owe her the same courtesy?"

Aleksia held Jovetta's wound with one hand and sorted through her herbs with the other.

Marcus's chains jangled and he came up beside her on his knees.

Aleksia grabbed his hands, his face cringing at her touch, and she placed them over the wound in Jovetta's chest. "Hold them there firmly until I tell you to lift them," she instructed, grappling to remember everything she'd learned.

Aleksia rolled up her sleeves and tried to capture the moonlight coming in through the small crevices in the wall.

"Stay with me, Jovetta," entreated Aleksia.

She'd healed many people, but moonlight was a pale reflection of daylight. The gems on Aleksia's arms shimmered, only a little, as the moon was covered by a distant cloud in the sky.

Jovetta coughed up blood. She struggled to breathe and her throat gurgled as she tried to say her last words.

"Don't speak. You need your strength." Aleksia grasped her bag of herbs. Her hands shaking, she searched inside and found dried yarrow. Placing it in her crimson hand, she took the waterskin and mixed it together to make a paste.

And then it happened.

Jovetta ceased to breathe and her heart came to a gradual stop.

Marcus lifted his hands as Jovetta's eyes stared blankly at the ceiling.

Aleksia pushed Marcus out of her way, applying the poultice to Jovetta's laceration.

"I'm sorry," he said with reverence. She knew he wasn't speaking to her.

Aleksia's tearful eyes looked into Jovetta's humble face and her chest swelled with unconfined emotion. "No," she cried, her defences crumbling as she took Jovetta into her arms and wept.

XXIII

I SEE YOUR END

In what seemed like hours, Aleksia finally pulled her head from Jovetta's shoulder. She closed Jovetta's eyes and whispered, "I see your end, Jovetta."

Carefully, she lowered her guardian onto the floor and crossed her arms over her chest. She still had some dried yarrow in her bag and placed a bundle in her hands and hair.

"One day we will be reunited in Valganen. If your spirit still lingers near, waiting to cross over into the eternal lands, I pray it is a pleasant journey and that you may find peace in the highest levels. Your children will be proud, and I hope you and Aulus find each other swiftly. You're leaving a giant hole in the world by passing, but you're filling one on the other side. Always remember how much I loved you. You will be avenged, if it takes a thousand years. I will bring peace to your homeland. So rest well and look for my coming."

Aleksia kissed Jovetta on the forehead and took one final moment before she stood up.

Rising, Aleksia searched the room to find whatever she could use to free herself from the shackles. She hated the sound of the dragging chain behind her, but she would not go quietly. She had to escape these men or they could discover what she was and take her in the opposite direction of where she wanted to go.

Marcus had moved as far as his chain would let him to the other side of the room, probably to get away from her. He didn't seem the type to give her room to grieve, but how could he sleep? He might not have seen what Haman and his men did, but he heard it. Didn't it make him want to escape? He'd been to Visadas. If Marcus could somehow get her there, she could offer him his sight in return.

First they had to escape.

Finding nothing to break the chain, Aleksia tried to bend it to her will. She tried so long, her arms hurt. She imagined an elvian who was a thousand years her senior could have ripped the chains in half, but she was too young. Her strength would grow in time, but not fast enough. Right now she needed to be strong enough to bend metal. Another elf probably could have used magic, but she'd only ever been able to heal.

No. Magic and her own strength would not do. She tried once more to find something to break it, and then she saw the beam.

It was made of wood, a material far weaker than iron. She gave the beam a hard nudge. It groaned and dust fell from the roof. Pushing it again, the support shifted and Aleksia smiled at the prospect. She tried it a third time, and the roof caved in a bit. Aleksia's eyes traced the rest of the structure above her and realized if she removed this log it would bring the entire roof down on their heads, probably killing them both in the process.

With a swift tug, she yanked the support beam back into place. She wracked her brain, but there was nothing in the barn strong enough to bend the king's iron.

In a few hours she'd be crossing the threshold down a road she would have given anything to travel the previous day. But now she would give anything to live out eternity in the old house with her guardians.

XXIV

DAMPENING DARK

King Zoren tossed the outdated letter from Captain Haman to the side. There was nothing he didn't already know in the statement about Marcus. General Leganous had likely ripped the silver coins out of Haman's hand, eager to be rid of the spawn of Barsadias, the love of the same woman severing their friendship long ago.

Marcus was en route to Ironwood and nothing more. He needed fresh information. It was the main reason he'd ordered Quinn to take him. The elves never tried to capture Marcus like he thought they might, and Marcus had done nothing new in the month he'd been sitting in elven territory.

Sometimes in battle it was wise to force the enemy to make a move and see what they'd do. It was a risk, but Marcus needed a new environment and obstacles to reveal his true nature. General Quinn would push Marcus in ways that weren't possible in the wagons of death.

The only thing preventing Zoren from taking Marcus himself were the words of his mother and the seer who'd shown Leganous a piece of the future. He feared if he intervened too much on the young man's present course, the future Leganous told him of would not come to pass.

And he needed it to come to pass.

Lina showed him what to do, but she was supposed to be with him. To breach the gates without her at his side was fruitless. He needed an Elvian if the plan was to work. He cursed himself for killing them all, but he'd thought Lina would be the one to open the door. The moment was approaching, and he prayed to Karas that he would find one amongst the elves or all would be lost.

Torturing Barsadias's son was not in his grasp, but watching his every move was.

With a new idea he rose from his desk and left the room.

Zoren was walking the hallways when he saw the black cloak of his mother. She was about to go down the steps to the dungeons when he ran to her, taking her by the arm before she could descend.

"What are you doing here?" questioned Zoren, searching up and down the hall. The slave who was supposed to be watching her was no where in sight.

"I'm going to see my son," snapped Queen Cecilia, taking her arm back from Zoren's grasp.

"I'm your son."

Queen Cecilia slapped Zoren across the face and tried to continue her course down into the dungeons. "I need to sing him a lullaby or he won't be able to sleep."

"I'm right here," Zoren assured her, trying to sound more tender.

Queen Cecilia's eyes filled with tears. "I can hear him crying."

"There was one night you found me crying. Father had beat me to a pulp. I'd stayed in town too long, but you knew what I was up to."

Queen Cecilia searched her memories. "Zoren brought me pastries."

"Yes and on that day, father discovered them. I'd had a good day in the market and brought home one for each of us."

"I dusted them off and—"

"And we left the house. We climbed up a hill, close to home, but far enough away that Father remained in his drunken stupor without finding us."

"We watched the sunrise."

"And you pulled out the pastries. You'd salvaged them from the floor and we ate them side by side."

Queen Cecilia peered into her son's face with a hint of recognition. "Zoren?"

"It's me, Momma," he said, looking straight into her eyes.

Queen Cecilia stroked Zoren's cheek where she'd slapped him. "I'm sorry I slapped you. My mind can play tricks on me."

"You're tired."

"Is it nighttime?" she asked, scouring the stone walls to find a window.

"Yes and you've had a long day." Zoren summoned a guard from the dungeons below.

The guard, Felix, rushed to the sound of his king's

voice. He had a fresh cut on his temple.

"Is there a problem?" Zoren peered down the stairs.

"Prometheus is down there experimenting on the prisoner." Felix dabbed at the blood on his brow. "He put up a bit of a fight."

"Has it been dealt with?"

"Yes, Your Majesty." Felix wiped his hand on his pants.

"Good. Take my mother to her room and replace her maid."

"Of course, Your Majesty," promised Felix, taking the queen by the arm and leading her back to her chamber.

Zoren watched the shell of his mother walk around the corner, her head hunched over as she leaned on the guard's arm. The vertes gave her long years but offered her none of their power. She was seventy-one when she'd stopped aging and the years had not been kind. Telling her the memory of the night they spent on the hill and watched the sunrise was the only way to bring her back to reality. After he told it to her, there was always a moment where she knew he was her son. And it gave him hope that she was still in there, anchored by that memory, when all the others tore her away.

Turning his back to her, he weaved his way through the halls to the door, breaching between the roots of the trees of Reeza. He stepped outside and the falls bellowed to his right as he followed a stairway beneath their raging waters. The hidden pathway was the only way in and out of the lair of the tamrasa.

The dampening dark cave had long ago been discovered by Elian in the early days of the war. He was the first elf to swear his loyalty. Eight others joined over time. Whether by choice or circumstance, they all served Zoren with the same reverent loyalty as Elian, who'd come to him willingly. But when Zoren asked them how to get back to the elven capital, each of them became cursed. The oath, to never reveal the location of Amarisa, could not be broken. As each of them tried, the colour in their skin and hair faded and they transformed into creatures similar to the bats who dwelled in their cave. And as time passed, the memories of their life, before they were loyal to Zoren, faded and they became engulfed in the pledge they'd made.

Zoren walked down the misty staircase to the door and it screeched open.

Rhyland, a tamrasa who was much shorter than the rest, stepped to the side and bowed his head to welcome the king.

Inside the lair, the roof was covered in naturally grown spikes, and it smelled like a breeze had never passed through its door. Fresh bat droppings covered the walls and floors, and the high-pitched peeps of the creatures echoed from above.

A slave lightly stepped along the hall, collecting waste into a pail.

Zoren glanced into her bucket and saw that the tamrasa would eat well. Elian would have to eat well, he was about to go on a long journey.

Rhyland skulked behind, following him to the room where Elian sat at his table, waiting.

The others gathered around the room to figure out why Zoren had come. Amilia and Blandus stuck together like a pair of lungs, never leaving each other's sides. Horus's eyes reflected the yellow flame of the candles set on the table and Vulmar kept her mouth shut, knowing Zoren hated the sound of her voice. Not all were present. Jerome and Antonia were missing.

Likely out searching, thought Zoren.

King Zoren pulled the chair back and sat across from Elian, who was the leader of the tamrasa.

Elian attempted a smile, but smiling didn't come naturally to his features. "You honour us with your presence. Would you like some refreshment?"

"Not this time. I've come with a task for you."

"Name it and it will be done."

"I want you to follow Marcus, son of Barsadias. He's headed to Ironwood, but will stop in Masseson first."

"You want me to discover how he crossed?"

"Yes."

"Then say no more." Elian stood to his feet. "I will depart immediately."

"Under no circumstances are you to kill him. Just observe. He is the one who will lead us to Amarisa. Once he does, you can tear him to pieces."

"It will be as you say."

XXV

PUDDLES AND RAIN

The elf's arm bumped into Marcus's and the screams of the forsaken consumed his mind. He felt like he was back in the barriers. The rain water on his cheek felt like warm blood and his knees went weak. By reflex, his body cringed and his foot splashed into a puddle to get away.

You're not in the barriers, he reasoned to calm himself. *The barriers are far away.*

Two weeks had passed and he still couldn't muster a word to the whimpering elf. The muddy chain and the width of the road prevented him from putting more distance between them. He didn't dare move over any further and risk tripping over a large rock, but every time he got near the elf her touch was like poison.

When she'd first come to him in the barn, he'd been having a nightmare of the barriers. She'd pulled him from the dream, and he'd thought he was still there. The same energy of the barrier hovered around him like a tide he couldn't escape. At first it confused him, hearing the kindness in her voice, and he felt gratitude. Once he'd realized what she was, he'd grabbed her wrist and an anger beyond his control took over.

And then she lost the woman she'd called Jovetta. The sound of Jovetta's short breaths as she tried to escape and the elf pleading he let her live made him shudder.

Marcus was used to hearing people experience the worst, but he wasn't used to talking about it after. It was a moment they never came back from and no one ever spoke of in the wagons.

As a child he'd hated the elves because he was told they were worthy of his hate, yet he remembered going into Octavia's house. She was a painter of history and the one who'd given him his tattoo on the night his life changed forever. Her walls were covered in canvases passed down through the generations; captured stories of the king and his armies fighting against the Azuk and battles with the elves. He'd never seen so many in his life.

He remembered the one that had made him question whether the elves were worthy of his hatred. It was a story of Queen Lina, the most beautiful woman he'd ever seen. Her arms covered in magical stones, but the sadness in her eyes captivated him and as a seven-year-old boy he felt sorry for her. King Zoren held her in his arms, weeping, as the light faded from her eyes.

Marcus let that childhood fantasy go. He couldn't ignore what she was, even if he tried. Queen Lina's face had caused him to doubt his revulsion, but the barriers had changed that. The forsaken died by the thousands while the elves hid in their woods with their legendary power, doing nothing. They did not differ from Leganous and never would.

He stepped into a puddle and it felt euphoric. The water soothed the sores on the bottom of his feet. The horses snorted and trotted at a pace he could maintain. He kept the rope taut, noticing the slightest change in the horse's direction and listening to the horse's hooves, so if they struck a pebble he could maneuver around it.

Marcus didn't mind the plummeting rain as he cupped his hands out in front of him and drank. His thirst quenched, and the sun hidden, he counted his blessings.

Marcus noticed a change in the terrain. Unlike the mountainous hills surrounding Visadas, the ground was flattening. They were descending into the southern lands of Remisia. There was a saying in the south that it was possible to see a fleeing slave from a hundred leagues away.

The chains suddenly went slack and Marcus stopped where he was.

"We stopping for the night?" asked Quintain.

"Any closer and the cornfields will keep us up all night." Haman dismounted. "Porcius, take the prisoners and chain them to that willow tree. Quintain and I will make camp."

XXVI

DRINK

Aleksia leaned against the willow tree. She stretched out her legs and closed her eyes, listening to the stream. There was something about sitting next to the river that soothed her troubled mind. It was like the river was taking her troubles away, restoring her spirits to think of happier times. She wished there was enough slack in the chain to dip her feet into the waters, but her captors hadn't been so kind. Her fingers grazed the blood hardened surface on her tunic and she moved them further down into her lap. The blood stain on her dress had faded and was her constant reminder of what had happened, though she needed no reminding. Somehow that night was sharper in her mind. The slowing of Jovetta's heart and the sound of her final breath. There was no magic powerful enough to change what happened.

Something prickled against Aleksia's neck and she

scratched, but whatever it was moved. She pulled her hand away and it was covered in ants. She leapt from the tree, brushing her shoulders. The critters ran through her hair, tangling themselves into knots, and the bark seemed to move.

The willow was infested.

Marcus had hundreds on him and he lay as far away from her as possible. The ants were burrowing into his hair and climbed all over his skin, searching for food to bring back to their horde. He didn't try to stop them. He opened his mouth, allowing them to enter and snatched them up to eat.

Disgusted, Aleksia pulled her skirts around her legs and sat down, flicking away any who sought to return.

The day was darkening and the cornfields were glowing in the distance. A spell cast over the seeds to stop insects from eating the harvest. If only she had such magic. She'd settle for a flame from Haman's campfire if it meant waging war on the ants.

Haman and his men were roasting fish and the smell of the cooking flesh churned her upset stomach.

Aleksia laid down, trying not to breathe, and Marcus suddenly sat up. She followed his lead and listened.

A horse was approaching. A leather saddle swayed with the movements of its stride, and when he came around the corner, Aleksia saw the soldier come into the farthest reaches of the light.

It was only then that Captain Haman became aware of the rider.

The intruder raised his arms in surrender and stopped his horse at a safe distance. His greasy hair was ravaged by time and there was a wildness in his eyes as he studied those approaching.

Haman got up and kept his distance, his fingers around the hilt of his sword. "Name."

"Hycis, of the five hundredth and seventy-fifth legion of our King Zoren." The fire danced in his eyes.

"And what is it you seek?"

"Rest for the night."

"Your assignment that you'd be on the roads alone at night?" Even though it was clear to all, from the whip and chains on the saddle, what the man was.

"May I?" asked Hycis, pointing to his satchel.

Haman nodded his head, and the man drew papers from his pouch. He urged the horse closer to give Haman his papers.

Haman examined them. "You're tracking five slaves from Gilbert?"

"For two days now," answered Hycis. "Almost caught one of them on the other side of the river, but the bastard got away from me in the field."

Haman took a second glance at Hycis's paperwork, and gave it back.

"Please join us. I'm sure you have many tales to share around the fire."

Hycis swung his leg over his horse, his armour quiet as he planted his feet on the ground. He glanced at Aleksia, and she had to look away because of the desire in his eyes.

In only a few moments the man's horse was settled and he sat next to Haman. They exchanged gossip and food from their saddlebags and Aleksia listened. The newcomer was keen to pass on his knowledge.

"General Printis and his men recently found an

untapped village in the hills of Azuk. The men they brought back across the Olend Sea were untamed and savage. Half of them had no use except to fight in the Aurelius. Too wild to reap a field. The rest they sent to be breeding partners in Masseson. With a stiff whip from birth, they might grow up strong enough to bend iron for the king."

"Perhaps they descended from dwarves," joked Quintain.

"Whatever their lineage, they ended up being no match against the king's army."

Haman stirred the fire with a stick. "It's strange General Printis would make such an aggressive move and take so many at once."

Hycis leaned closer. "Word is, and don't tell anyone you heard this from me, that the people of Azuk have been disappearing. It's been hard to find any new ones to bring in."

"People have been saying that for years," Haman assured him.

"The last ship I saw come into harbour from Azuk barely had a slave on it. More people going to live there than coming."

"Well, they'll have better luck getting citizens to move there than Visadas."

Aleksia's head perked up at the mention of her homeland.

Hycis swallowed a piece of bread, his table manners leaving something to be desired. "You've been through the elven lands?"

"We're returning from there. I had a message from General Quinn to General Leganous."

"And those two?" asked Hycis, glancing over his shoulder at Aleksia again.

Haman's shoulders tensed. "I believe the girl is an evader, but they'll test her in Masseson. The man is none of your concern."

Aleksia wanted Haman to talk more about Marcus, but he didn't.

"Wish I'd get transferred to Visadas. I hear the barriers are a wonder to see."

Haman smiled over his cup. "I can attest to that. Only rivalled by the king's displays in the arena."

To Aleksia's disgust, they talked about what they'd witnessed in the arena until the men slowly called it a night.

Hycis volunteered to take the first watch and as the rest of the men fell asleep, he went to his saddlebag and drew a drink. Swigging the liquid from the wineskin, his demeanour began to lax and he stumbled over to Aleksia. She knew she'd been right to stay awake.

Hycis held out the wineskin. "Might I offer you some?"

Aleksia could smell his breath and recognized his strange behaviour. The man was drunk, and she wouldn't miss out on an opportunity. The scratches all over his forearm caught Aleksia's eye as she took the wine from him. She drank more than her fill and found the flavour pleasant.

Hycis continued. "Made in the northern vineyards of Baachus. They enchant it so it's more potent. I use it to relax the slaves after I catch them. They don't always want to come back."

"And apparently for yourself," responded Aleksia.

"Shhh." Hycis held his index finger to his mouth. "I know I'm not supposed to. But life on the road. All on my own—it makes it easier."

"Have you been to many places?" inquired Aleksia.

"Slaves always try to escape."

"Where do they often run?"

Hycis exhaled and scratched his head. "Everywhere. Think they can make it across the Olend Sea, hide out in the woods, or escape to the elven lands."

"Do they make it?"

"To the elven lands?" Hycis wobbled and held back a chuckle. "Even if they make it as far as the Tondro River, they usually get themselves killed trying to cross it."

"Their strength gives out?"

"They don't know where it's safe to cross. It's not like," Hycis pointed to the river next to them, "that river where the tide meets the shore. No. The Tondro River collides in the centre. Cracking like thunder in a storm, crushing the bones of anyone who gets caught in its trap."

Hycis sat next to Aleksia and she edged herself away from him. "It drives the soldiers stationed at Fort Karrlun mad. The constant drum of the river. Garrison Commander Earlan hasn't had a good sleep in ten years, though a lot of good horses come from their stables. They're not afraid of loud noises. When a barrel of liquid fire explodes, they don't even flinch."

"How would someone get to Visadas?" asked Aleksia.

"First—" Hycis leaned in to kiss Aleksia.

"No." Aleksia, pushed him away.

"You're so beautiful," he muttered, pressing himself closer to her.

Aleksia shoved him harder and stood.

Marcus sat up, and Hycis kicked him to prevent his interference.

Hycis rose to meet her face to face. "Women don't say no to me."

"I just did."

"I'm not known for my patience," he said.

Marcus swung his leg into Hycis's faltering feet, knocking Hycis back onto the ground.

Aleksia stepped on his chest. "I've never heard of you, but the scratches on your arms say much. Is that how you received such an inferior position in the king's army? A dog sent to fetch in heat."

Hycis furiously knocked Aleksia's foot off of him. He jumped to his feet and swung at Aleksia, but she moved so fast his fist snapped against the tree. He cursed and drew his sword. "You'll be dead when I'm finished with you." His broken hand quivered as he pulled a dagger from his belt and tossed it to her.

It was almost within her grasp when Haman intervened, catching it before Aleksia could.

"Enough!" yelled Haman, his own sword drawn. "Who gave you permission to dispel my charge?"

"She attacked me."

Haman grabbed Hycis's broken hand and squeezed, making it crack even more.

Hycis dropped his sword and fell to his knees.

"What reason would she have to attack you?"

"I offered her a drink. I didn't need your permission."

"Yes, you did. And I can guess the plans you had for her once you got her drunk. If you had, it would have been my pleasure to enact the death penalty upon your head."

"She's nothing but slave scum."

Haman set his sword at Hycis's jugular. "That has yet to be proven. You're a shame to your rank and no better than a drunken slave. I will report this when we get to Masseson."

Hycis placed a single finger against the blunt of Haman's sword, veering it away from himself. "No harm done," he taunted, as he stood to his feet. "I'll leave now. The stars are starting to show. The runaways'll be easier to spot."

"Porcius, make sure he leaves. Quintain take the rest of his watch. I don't trust he'll stay away."

Haman put his sword back into place and picked up the wineskin. He smelled it and poured it into the dirt.

The soldiers went back to their fire as Hycis rode off into the dark.

Quintain put a fresh piece of wood on the fire to keep him warm.

Aleksia saw a rock drop from Marcus's palm and he looked like he wanted to say something, but thought better of it.

They left it at that. Marcus rolled over and tried to get some sleep.

A single tear escaped Aleksia's eye that she quickly wiped away. The wine had not affected her. Jovetta's lifeless eyes still lingered in her mind and she longed to feel numb, but it didn't seem possible. So many faces haunted her thoughts, and the rain hadn't washed the blood out of her tunic. Its stench filled her nostrils. No one she'd ever known still walked amongst the living, and it was one of the reasons she ached for the company of her own people. They would never age or get sick or die on her. If she was back in the cabin, she would have been carving a piece of wood into the likeness of Jovetta, a picture of her sitting on her bench as she watched the sunset.

An idea came to mind, and Aleksia made sure Marcus was asleep. His breathing was steady, and she envied his ability to sleep so easily. She found a twig on the ground and carved a line into the dirt.

It was almost daylight when she'd finished, and she couldn't help but smile. Etched into the sand was a perfect likeness of Jovetta sitting in her chair outside the old house, her face painted with the same smile she'd always greeted her with.

Aleksia pursed her lips and quietly whistled like Jovetta used to beg her to do. It was a small service, but it had brought her peace. She was tired of losing people. She didn't know if she had room left in her heart to say goodbye to anyone else she cared about, but today she could keep going. She broke a few branches off of the willow to cover Jovetta's image, putting her to rest. She sat there until it was time to depart and begin a new day in her new life. A day likely to be filled with all new struggles and roads she'd never seen.

XXVII

MASSESON

Marcus had never been to Masseson. He remembered it was the port that brought every man, woman, and child to market to be sold as a slave. The odour, worse than the wagons of death, mixed with the smell of the sea.

When he was a child his Aunt Mariana never looked happier than when she came home from Masseson. The dust of the road flared up under her horse's hooves and a weary line of slaves followed in her wake; an iron brace around their necks and a chain keeping them from straying. She was left to take care of him while his father, the General of the Centre, lived in Sidabras. His father was the champion of the battlefield, and she kept the farm going.

He'd not cared if the slaves were suffering. It was normal then, but now he empathized with them.

A woman wailed in the distance as a child was

ripped from her arms and the whip swung freely to silence her.

Marcus took a step in her direction, but was knocked into the steady line of traffic that moved all around him. He'd almost bumped into the elf, but he'd steadied himself before that could happen.

"Papers!" hammered the guards at the front gate, searching for runaways.

The chains pulled and slackened as Haman's horse came to a halt.

A pair of heavy boots hurried down the stairs toward them.

"The gods be praised," proclaimed Colonel Kendricks, reaching up to shake Haman's hand. "For they have shown you favour on your journey."

"All went according to plan," replied Haman. "Even found a potential evader."

Colonel Kendricks glanced at the elf, taken aback by her appearance. "There are a few families who've reported their daughters running away, but I can't think of any matching her description."

"She'll need to be tested."

Kendricks looked past the elf. "And that's him?"

"See for yourself."

The heavy boots walked over to Marcus and a hand clasped his shoulder. "Well, it's certainly Barsadias's crest. It's hard to tell his age beneath the beard and dirt."

"They'll clean him up at the Vakar."

"General Leganous must have loved him, considering his past with his father." Kendricks released Marcus.

Haman chuckled. "Yes, he did."

"How like the line of Marcus. It's understandable

that not even the barriers would be able to kill Barsadias's family line."

Marcus thought for a second of how his father died and slid his foot back to steady himself.

Haman's horse stomped its hoof. "If only his mother had the same blood."

The mention of his mother was like a punch to the gut. *What did these men know of her?*

"He might not even survive the journey to Ironwood, judging by the state of him."

"Where is General Quinn?" wondered Haman. "I've much to discuss with him."

"He's waiting at the barracks. He'll be happy you've arrived. Tomorrow the Mirtis sails for Ironwood and he hoped to be aboard."

"I thought I could smell a galley ship in the harbour. Smells like a blistering corpse on a battlefield."

"Rain is far kinder than the sun."

Haman turned in his saddle to his soldiers. "Porcius, report to the barracks. Quintain, take them to the market to get cleaned up." Haman reached into his pocket and withdrew a letter. "Give this to Theo and bring back what he gives you. I'll be in the barracks."

Quintain took the letter, and Haman was gone with Kendricks without another word.

Marcus held on tighter to the chain, his mind reeling as people knocked him about. The yells of the auctioneers, gladiators fighting in the small arena, and the prostitutes calling for favours were muffled.

He had no real memory of his mother. She'd died when he was born and his father never spoke of her. He used to imagine his father and mother teaching him to fight. They'd tell him to relax. To keep his feet a shoulder length apart, and to mind his surroundings. In this dream world his father smiled when he got it right and his mother carried him into the house for a dinner of all his favourite foods. He'd found her portrait in a box once and asked Mizpah about it, but she'd been purchased after her passing. Aunt Mariana rolled her eyes and told him she'd died giving birth to him, unable to hide her jealousy as she spoon-feed her youngest daughter. It was like everyone who knew his mother had forgotten her or ceased to exist.

A hand seized his arm and he felt power course through him so strongly he almost shouted. A cart full of produce nearly mowed him over. He jerked his arm from the elf's grasp and held his head.

"Pay attention," she muttered, as they turned a corner toward the pillar of the city and the hub of all slave industry.

The Vakar. It was once owned by a wealthy merchant who sold fine silk and foods, but he lost it when the king amassed a new industry at the beginning of his reign, built on the backs of the people he'd conquered.

Quintain got off his horse and disconnected the chains from his saddle, pulling Marcus and the elf to a table where a man named Theo bartered with a young female citizen about the price of an aging cook. He dismissed her and Quintain pulled on the chains as they approached the desk.

"Welcome back, Quintain. How was the journey up north?"

"Long." Quintain pulled out the letter and handed it

to Theo.

Theo ripped it open and scanned it from start to finish.

"Is she injured?" Theo eyed the blood on the elf's tunic.

"Not her blood."

"Very well, and I suppose he'll be dead within a week of his arrival," said Theo, looking at Marcus.

"Not my concern," moaned Quintain, unable to discuss it.

"A pity," he contended, eyeing Marcus as he handed his notes to his slave.

The slave wrote on two boards and placed one of them around Marcus's neck and the other on the elf's.

Theo filled a pouch with a few silver coins. "Tell Haman what I'm giving him is more than generous. If he has any issues with my payment, he can come to me."

"It's been a pleasure doing business with you." Quintain handed them over.

Marcus felt a tug on the chains around his wrists and followed as the elf was taken elsewhere.

The man leading him wasn't aware he couldn't see. Nothing was familiar or certain and Marcus held out his hands to feel where he was going. He leaned back on the irons around his wrists in an attempt to slow the man down and hit someone.

"Watch where you're going!" an angry man called out after him.

Marcus's face flushed and they went through a door. He didn't notice the step until it was too late. His foot went forward but all it found was air and he lost his balance, colliding into the slave who was leading him.

The slave shoved him firmly and Marcus fell backwards, his hip slamming against the stair. He was only there a moment until he was yanked to his feet and moving again. Gauging the stairs wasn't easy without sight, and his leader seemed to be in a rush. Marcus was expecting another step when they reached the bottom and he almost fell again, but he caught himself this time.

There was a mist on the air, which made it feel thick to breathe. The floor was damp and the room warm. Male voices echoed throughout the space, so it was hard to concentrate on a single one, especially when he didn't recognize any of them.

The man leading came to a halt and took out a set of keys, unlocking Marcus's shackles.

When his bounds were removed, it felt foreign. The chains hadn't been off his wrists since he'd left Fort Karrlun, and he'd become accustomed to them. The black world pressed around him and there was no chain to lead him through it.

The man shoved him into a line of slaves and Marcus collided into the person in front of him.

"Sorry," apologized Marcus to the man he'd hit.

The slave in front of him glanced back and saw Marcus's blindness. "Put your hand on my shoulder."

A whip cracked the air.

Hundreds of men inched onward in a line that seemed never to stop, never to end.

Marcus received a small cloth and a bar of dirty soap. The cloth smelled worse than the market. A pair of hands unexpectedly pulled the drawstring around his waist and his pants fell to the ground. He tried to pick them back up, but his efforts were slapped away. His face went red with embarrassment. He tried to cover himself with the cloth and bar of soap and dreaded the thought they might not give him something else to wear. He prayed there were no women around.

Water splashed up ahead and the air grew warmer.

"Wash yourself off and keep moving!" yelled a soldier.

The baths were originally built for the nobility of long ago, those whose focus was more on the comfort of the individual than the cause of the state. Faded paintings from happier times adorned the walls. A fountain of Vandus, the goddess of water, stood crumbling against the main wall. Her waves of flowing hair were caught up in the torrent of the tide and her toga seeped beneath her breastplate. Her face was broken and cracked from years of neglect and she sat upon a horse with fins instead of legs, the mane entwined with her own hair. Within her hand she bore a spear and a host of creatures swarmed at her feet and all over the marble walls.

The statues of sharks and dolphins had crumbled into pale images of their former glory. Instead of a bath that sparkled and shone, the walls were tinted yellow, like the deep green water the slaves were being pushed into.

The man who was helping Marcus reached up and squeezed his hand as he started to descend. Thankfully, the line was moving slower than the man who'd led him down the stairs earlier. He shifted his toes and felt the ledge before he stepped into the water.

Heat spread from Marcus's foot into his entire body. No longer conscious of his nakedness, he got in as quickly as he could. He lost the man who'd been leading him, but Marcus didn't care. The waters spread across his entire body, seeping into every muscle. He couldn't recall ever feeling this good. He took out his bar of soap and cloth and began to wash himself. The dirt on his body was old and tough. It flaked off his skin as he rubbed at it, the hot water aiding its removal. Patches of clean skin revealed themselves, but it took him a while and he thought about the dirt cloud forming around him.

"Everyone out of the water!" shouted the supervisor.

Marcus was lost. In his washing he'd lost track of where he was in the pool. He tried to sense the direction of the water as everyone was exiting until he heard someone approaching. They took his hand and placed it on his shoulder.

"Thank you," whispered Marcus. The man had given him his space to clean off and returned. They were all led out of the water and given a towel. Drying himself off, Marcus wrapped the towel around his waist to make himself decent. His hair was heavy, but he felt refreshed.

At the next station a shirt and pants were placed into his hands and he put them on. Marcus wasn't the first owner of these stained clothes. The shirt was sleeveless and the pants similar to the ones he'd had. One size fits all, brown and practical. The only difference was that these pants had loops for a string to hold them up. No shoes were given, but Marcus wasn't expecting any. Only household slaves, cooks, and those with an education were given shoes.

Moving into the next room, Marcus could hear the snip and snap of scissors and brooms sweeping the floor. Everyone was being pushed into a line past a man in official robes. Beside him was a giant leather-bound book he hadn't touched once.

Women combed through the line, grabbing men by the hair. Others followed the lice checkers with a brush and a bucket of white paint.

"Shave!" A woman yelled and the slave following her painted a white circle on the man's shoulder. Those who were clean of vermin were sent to the inspector. As the woman reached Marcus she yelled shave, but stopped when she saw his family crest. Instead of making her mark, she shoved him into the line to go to the inspector.

Hands pushed and shoved him to where he needed to be and when he finally stood before the man with the large book, the line came to a stop.

The man licked his lips as his fingers traced Marcus's crest. Marcus could feel the man's breath on his skin, he was studying it so closely. He dragged his finger over the ink, ensuring it wasn't drawn on by a hired artist. To be sure, the man held his hand over Marcus's crest and his green eyes inflamed as he muttered a few words Marcus couldn't hear over the noise of the room.

Marcus's arm warmed and the man withdrew his hand. The shocked man snapped his fingers and the leather book was brought to him by a child slave. Opening the book to an index of all the family crests in Remisia, he searched page after page until he turned back to the very beginning of the book. He settled on a piece of parchment, his fingers moving between the different crests. His rough finger landed on the one that looked exactly like Marcus's and he took a step back. He showed the book to the slave boy.

"Do these look the same to you?" he asked him.

The boy took his time, wanting to be sure and nodded.

With great reluctance, they painted an X on Marcus.

Marcus started to walk, but the man stopped him.

"Wait." The inspector whistled to another slave boy standing by and he raced to his side.

"Make sure this man gets through the rest of his stations without incident. Ensure not a single hair on his head is cut or they'll have to deal with me. I'll send them straight to the Aurelius. They may shave his face and make sure it doesn't grow back."

The boy nodded. "Follow me, sir." He started to leave, but realized Marcus wasn't following. "Sir?"

Marcus always struggled to say the words out loud.

The boy looked up into Marcus's face and took his hand. "You can't see?"

"No," Marcus shook his head.

"That's okay. I've seen many who ain't able to see. I once saw a man who didn't have any eyes in his head. You're lucky, sir. How'd you lose your sight?"

"It's not something I like to talk about," said Marcus.

"Your story's your own. My name's Scorpius." He sounded a little disappointed, but still positive.

"Marcus," he replied, grateful the boy didn't press.

"Most people lose all their hair here, but you got an X. Means you get to keep yours. Your dreads need work."

Marcus couldn't help smiling at the boy's natural curiosity. Favil used to work on his hair in the wagons, using a piece of wood to prick them into place. He could still remember how gentle her hands had been.

The two of them reached a man with an empty chair.

"Marcus, meet my Papa. He's the best hair cutter in here."

"What are you doing here, Scorpius? And how many times do I have to tell you I ain't your father?"

"That's what Mama told me."

"Well, she ain't right in the head," he explained.

"The inspector told me to guide this man through his stations." Scorpius leaned towards the man he'd called Papa. "He's blind," he tried to whisper, but wasn't successful.

"I can see that."

Scorpius helped Marcus take his seat. "Said you weren't to cut his hair. Shave his beard and make sure it never come back again."

"Can you find someone else to bother while I get to work?"

"You the boss, Papa." He smiled.

"I'm not your—" The man's voice faltered, knowing his words would only fall on deaf ears.

Scorpius giggled as he ran to stand against the wall and wait.

"He's a good boy," commended Marcus.

"Thank you, sir," he replied. "First, I'm going to get rid of your beard and then we'll see how much I can fix your hair."

Marcus heard the man moving his instruments and snip his scissors in the air a few times. He grabbed a fist full of his beard and started cutting away.

The man discarded the severed pieces onto the floor, humming to pass the time. His scissors moved over

Marcus's skin in perfect rhythm until he was satisfied enough had been cut away.

He stood up and tilted Marcus's head backwards.

"Stay as still as you can," he urged, as he sharpened his razor.

Marcus had never been shaved. He'd run away on his seventh birthday and he'd been too young to grow facial hair. In the forest he'd never needed to shave and after he'd been captured no one had ever been willing or had a knife to do so. His body tensed as the man placed his hand on his throat and he sensed the nearness of the razor. Last time a knife had been this close he was being threatened with death. The blade stroked his chin and the prickling whiskers released their hold. Marcus felt himself relax and trusted in the man's skill.

Finished, Marcus touched his clean-shaven face. It felt so smooth that he barely recognized himself. Smiling, it was like he was a completely new man. He doubted even Favil would recognize him.

"Just a little longer," said the man.

On the table next to the man's instruments was a clay jar filled with a white liquid. He scooped some onto his fingers and began rubbing it onto Marcus's jaw and neck. Whatever it was, his face felt like it was on fire. He moved to take it off, but his hands were pushed away.

"Don't touch," the man warned.

"What are you doing?" asked Marcus, holding onto the arms of the chair to stop himself from scratching.

"Skustis. Kills the roots in your face and neck. The magicians make it for citizens who don't want their facial hair to grow back and to dishonour the head of a deserting soldier," he replied. "Shouldn't be much longer."

Almost as soon as he spoke it, the pain subsided.

The man put a cloth into a bucket of water and wiped Marcus's face, moving on to Marcus's hair. He cleaned the dreads as best he could in the time he was given.

Scorpius didn't stray very far from his charge and when he saw the man was finished he ran over as fast as he could.

"You look like a new man!" exclaimed Scorpius. "Good job, Papa."

Marcus heard the man sigh at the word Papa.

Scorpius walked around Marcus, admiring the difference. "Put some armour on him and feed him for a few weeks and he'd look like a warrior."

"Don't waste the air with your chatter and keep him moving. I'm going to have a word with your mother tonight."

"I'll let her know you're coming so she can put on something nice."

The man kicked at Scorpius but he moved, leading Marcus to his last station. There he received a metal necklace with a large tag, etched with a symbol of where he was going.

"You're going to the mines?"

"Yes. The barriers didn't kill me."

Scorpius's eyes widened, and he stopped in his tracks. "You lived?"

Marcus nodded his head.

"No one has ever —" Scorpius couldn't finish before asking another question. "What happens there?"

"Something else I don't like to talk about."

"But how did you survive?"

"I don't know," was the only response Marcus had.

"Are you an elf?"

"No," Marcus assured him.

Scorpius was about to ask another question, when a woman's voice interrupted.

"I'll take him from here," she offered, her lips as red as blood. She had a tattoo of a skull. A fanged serpent reared its head out of the eye and a snake's tail hung out of the mouth. On the forehead of the skull was a dead lily to represent her infertility. She gave a man pleasure, but her womb was dead and there would be no life beyond. "The inspector wants you back in the cutting room. Someone vomited and he needs you to clean it up. Plus, he's less likely to get killed between here and the cells if he's walking with me. People might think he's an unarmed citizen."

"But—"

"Go, or it'll be the whip for ya."

Scorpius let go of Marcus and ran back to where they'd come from.

The woman latched her arm with Marcus and he smelled lavender. Others passed watching them, but the woman paid them no mind.

She spoke again. "Come and sit with me a while. I'm Raven and I've got a nice bowl of stew waiting for you." Her red toga swayed against the cobble ground.

The promise of a meal edged Marcus to follow her.

One of her servants had set up a wooden table with two chairs in the alley. She stirred a pot over an open fire and dished its contents into a bowl when she saw them coming.

"Sit," Raven offered. "You must be tired."

Marcus sat where she guided him, but he was

hesitant to lower his guard.

The servant placed the stew in front of Marcus.

"Eat as much as you'd like."

"And what favour will you want in return?" asked Marcus.

"Information," she responded, as she memorized his family crest and pushed the food closer to him.

"I don't know anything." Marcus seized the bowl, and as he moved it, he felt a small object rest against his hand. He held it between his fingers feeling the unblemished handle.

A spoon.

"It's been a while since anyone's treated you as a human," said Raven.

"Maybe I'm not. Scorpius asked me if I was an elf. It could be true." Marcus took a bite of the stew. Following the woman was suddenly worth it. It was invigorating. The thick beans and large hunks of meat filled him with pleasure all the way down to his toes. It was a little salty, but it was the best tasting stew he could ever remember eating.

"Because you walked the barriers like one of their own?" she asked.

"I am not an elf," stated Marcus, annoyed that everyone seemed to think so.

Raven pulled back one of his dreads to look at his ear. "Your ears appear to be human."

Marcus jerked his head from her grasp. "What do you want from me?"

"I've not come to ravish you. You shouldn't believe everything you've heard about prostitutes. Like I told you, I only require information," she assured him, inching closer. "When you crossed the Tondro River, word of your crossing rippled like a stone in still water. Everyone in Masseson, including myself, is wondering about the man who did it. You'd be surprised at how much a man will pay for even the smallest detail."

"No." Marcus felt the edge of his chair and his foot brushed the wall next to him. There was no where else to go. His body tensed.

Raven retreated back to her own seat and Marcus was grateful to have a table between them. "Ahh a man who knows the value of his own story. I could up the bargain," she eyed his emptying bowl. "Give you some more stew."

Marcus took another small bite, trying to make it last as long as possible.

Raven caressed his burnt hand. "How did you get this scar? It looks like the hilt of a sword."

Marcus hid his hand from her view. "I'd prefer to keep it to myself."

"We all have stories we'd rather not share. Not until we have the right person to share them with."

"And you think you're the right person?"

"It wouldn't be the first time," she smiled. "Some speak to their wives or siblings, but not many."

"Do you have family?" Trying to get a read on her.

Raven grinned. "I can't have a husband and I haven't spoken to my siblings in what feels like lifetimes. Do you have siblings?"

"None that I know of."

"How about you tell me your name and I'll tell you something in return? There's no harm in that."

"Marcus."

Raven got up from the table. "That explains your kept honour." She helped Marcus up from his seat and led him towards the building full of cells. "Now I shall give you a piece of advice." She leaned in close to him, her lips almost touching his ear while her eyes focused on the way ahead. "Avoid the cells of Ironwood with holes."

Marcus pulled away. "What's beneath them?"

"Keven," she called to a nearby soldier in a red training uniform, who hadn't kept his eyes off of her since they'd come into view. He jumped at her call. "Would you take this man to the holding cells? He'll need a hand getting there. I'd be very grateful."

"Of course," volunteered Keven, as he took Marcus into his care.

XXVIII

RAVEN

Elian watched the prostitute who'd named herself Raven hold the soldier's eye-line as she stroked his arm.

"I'll be watching you on the training fields," she said, leaving Marcus with the soldier and turning back into the halls of Vakar.

Elian knew where the guard would take his target and felt compelled to follow the woman who'd had no business speaking to his prey. He climbed over and under the beams of the Vakar's inner structure, keeping her in his sights and himself out of the sight of everyone else. She kept an even stride and caught the eye of a few soldiers, but she paid them no mind as she left the Vakar.

She weaved through the crowd of slaves and masters, passing a multitude of stands selling wares. She walked past them all.

Two soldiers sparred in the street, putting on a show

in front of the barracks.

One broke off when he saw the woman.

"Raven!" he called.

"Good afternoon, Ennis." She made him keep up with her. "You shouldn't have broken off your fight. You were about to win," she teased.

Ennis raced until he was at her side and smiled down at her as he stroked the skull on her shoulder. "I was distracted."

"And who's fault is that?" she asked playfully.

"The gods above." His yellow teeth in full bloom.

"Well, maybe you should ask them to help you focus."

"If it was your temple, I would be there every day. Why do you think I spar so close to your chambers?"

"If I were a goddess, I would smite you for speaking such foolishness."

Raven reached the door of her home and paused to face her admirer.

"Will you not give me one kiss?" he pleaded as he put his hand on the door and leaned over her.

Elian watched the prostitute reach her hand up into the soldier's hairline and lean into him. But instead of letting him kiss her, she held his head back by the hair and taunted him. "Maybe if you'd won the fight I would have been more inclined," she said, opening the door and shutting him out behind her.

Ennis knocked on the door, calling her name, begging her to come to the door and let him in.

Elian lost sight of her from the rooftop. She'd entered a building that was riddled with living quarters. Seeking her out, he climbed onto the villa until he was over the prostitute's hovel. Next to her home was an empty alley that he was about to descend into, but the woman was climbing out of a window. Elian crawled back into the shadows as she looked back and forth up the alley. She then made her way south towards the sea.

Her hours of work were about to begin. It was strange that she'd leave as young men with means to purchase her expertise were about to knock on her door. Her stride was less confident, and she peered over her shoulder every second moment.

The tamrasa descended into the alley as she rounded the corner. He focused on her footsteps and glanced into the window she'd just come out of. To his astonishment he saw an identical woman laying sound asleep on the bed.

Elian followed her all the way to the rushing waters of the Olend Sea. He didn't need to get close. He stalked over branch and tree to keep her in his sights.

She walked farther from Masseson's bay and kept to the shoreline. The further she got, the more her pace quickened until she stopped and faced the water's horizon. Kicking off her shoes, she approached the water as it rolled over itself in gleeful welcome. A smile crossed her face, and she whispered to it. The water brushed the bottom of her toga and her dress changed from red to blue, the very sea seeping its way into every fibre. The hair on her head changed from brown to white and her skin darkened.

A fin leapt from the waters in the distance, and as the woman turned her head, Elian saw gills on her neck.

And he recognized her. She was Vandus, goddess of the sea.

I found her. A warmth filled Elian down to his soul. The king would be greatly pleased by this news.

The waves raged towards their goddess and the head of a giant white seahorse emerged. It was very similar to the horses man rode on land, except along its neck were gills, allowing it to breathe underwater. Instead of hooves, it possessed fins to better guide it through the depths.

Vandus stroked the head of her seahorse and climbed onto its back, sinking into the sea.

Elian could not let her out of his sight. He screeched and a bat flew to him. He took the bat between both his hands and emitted a message into the bat's head to pass on to his king and master. He bent over, his back cracking and his eyes turning black as he transformed into the tamrasa—a creature similar to a bat, but with rows of sharp teeth and claws large enough to cut down trees. His tanned wings of skin took off into the horizon and he followed the goddess to wherever she was going.

XXIX

THE FIGHT

Aleksia's face glowed red and was warm to the touch. She'd gotten out of the public wash and was struggling to get the new dress over her head. All she could think about was someone seeing what she truly was and being naked in public. She managed to pull it over herself and stared down at the sunken brown tunic. There were no sleeves. Looking around she sought any other option as a woman passed her a brown sash. Another woman shoved from behind and she tied it around her waist.

The one thing every single one of her guardians told her was, *Don't be discovered,* and she felt like she was about to break her promise.

In the cabin, it'd been easy to keep out of sight. At the first sign of company, she hid in the barn. Here she felt like every eye was watching her, and now she knew it was possible for someone to discover the truth.

Marcus recognized her without even having sight. What would happen if someone with sight could see the vertes? It was still a mystery how Marcus knew by touching her arm. There was something different about him. She'd seen his tattoo, but there was nothing there to determine he had a magic.

Aleksia followed the line of women into an outdoor courtyard, and within it there were women from all walks of life. Older women gripped the hands of the younger, leading them through the process and hushing their tears. All the women in sight had a Z branded on their shoulder; very few female citizens chose to not get married and have babies. Even the priestesses, who were the brides of Karas, had to have a child by twenty-one or suffer the consequences.

Three women worked their way through the line, marking the women with lice. They were followed by a high level slave and his two helpers. His robes were white and from the book in his hand, he was educated.

One woman began searching Aleksia's hair, pulling her long brown hair back and forth, searching down to the scalp for eggs and signs of life. She wasn't gentle, tugging on the finer hair, and Aleksia's eyes watered. When she was finished, an X was painted on her wrist.

She prayed they wouldn't cut off her hair. Rows of women sat in the chairs of the next room as another woman shaved their head clean.

The inspector grabbed Aleksia's arm and she held her breath, praying he wouldn't see through her like Marcus.

"This one needs to be tested." He gestured to a nearby soldier.

Aleksia exhaled and was led away from the line of women being processed to what looked like a round pen used to train horses. It was surrounded by men, both slave and free, shouting and clapping their hands at what was happening on the other side. Some sat on top of the rails, while others watched through the bars. As Aleksia drew closer, she saw why they were cheering and it angered her.

A solider and a helpless young woman fought with long sticks of wood. The woman limped, using every ounce of skill she had, as the soldier toyed with her. He towered over her small bruised form, egging her on, pretending to attack from one angle, then hitting her from another. The woman held her stick over her right side, shielding her wounds from further injury.

Aleksia stepped closer, wanting to jump the fence and put the soldier in his place, but it was too late. The man knocked the woman over the head with his weapon and she rolled on the sand, dropping her sword of wood.

"Slave!" pronounced the mediator of the fight.

The dazed woman crawled on her stomach, trying to escape.

A soldier entered the ring carrying a hot poker with a Z on the tip and offered it to the victor.

They caught the woman and held her down as she screamed and scratched. One of them shoved a dirty rag into her mouth, muffling her cries, but also to stop her from biting off her tongue.

Her eyes widened as the brander approached and the soldiers held her still.

The rag was no match against the woman's cry of agony as they branded her, corrupting the air with the pungent smell of burning flesh. They released her and she rolled on the ground in pain.

Many of the men laughed, but joy was the last thing on Aleksia's mind. She heard the men congratulate the man who'd done this to her, calling him Porthos. She was about to make him pay and the smile would be on her face when she was finished with him.

The gate opened and Aleksia didn't wait to be ushered in. She focused on the man she was about to fight, and Porthos studied her back. He was tall, muscular, and wore nothing except a pair of black army pants. Clearly he was cocky enough to think not a single woman could touch him with the blunt end of a stick.

The sides of the pen filled with eager faces, ready to watch what was about to unfold. Among them was a face she recognized.

Hycis. He caressed his money pouch with his wounded hand, revealing his plan to purchase her if she lost, and she rolled her eyes. She didn't care about him.

Porthos threw her weapon at her while she wasn't paying attention, but Aleksia caught it with little effort. He seemed pleased, and Aleksia wondered if most women dropped it. The wood had many dents in it from those who'd fought. Her mouth went dry.

The mediator, dressed in a costume of red with bells on his ankles, placed himself between them. "The rules of this arena are simple. Stand your ground in combat until the last grain of sand slips through the hourglass and you're a citizen. Run away from the fight or fall on your back and you're a slave, after which you will be branded with the king's mark and sent to market. Do you understand the rules?"

Aleksia nodded.

"Then fight." He stepped aside and turned the hourglass. It was his job to make sure there were no fatalities or serious injuries.

Aleksia tightened her grip on the wood.

"Prove you're a citizen and not a slave," mocked Porthos.

Aleksia's mind was spinning as she waited. She wanted her opponent to make the first move. She wasn't a slave, but she wasn't a citizen either.

Porthos made his weapon glide around him. A method he'd used many times to intimidate his adversary.

Aleksia hadn't even seen a fight before, except the one she'd just witnessed. She doubted even a real female citizen would win against this man. He was built like a wall.

Porthos stopped moving. "Look to the end."

"Look to the end," Aleksia replied, mimicking his stance.

He took a step towards her and drove his stick at her head.

Aleksia blocked his attack, but not his rebound. Porthos shifted his momentum and struck her in the thigh with the other end of his piece of wood. Pulling her leg away, she stepped into what he'd predicted and he pushed her with the centre of his weapon, but as an elf she didn't fall.

The crowd hailed in approval.

Aleksia's face reddened for the second time since she'd entered the Vakar. Her anger was about to get the better of her, like it always did.

Porthos charged again.

She stepped to the side at the last moment and whacked him on the shin.

He grunted and held his cry in. When he turned, Aleksia was there to meet him with an onslaught of maneuvers. His skill denied her the upper hand as they danced around one another in combat.

Aleksia knocked Porthos away, drew her knee up and broke her weapon in half. Armed with a weapon in each hand, she stepped closer to him, where he could get less power from his longer stick.

The hourglass was now half full.

To push her back, he lowered his stick between her legs and lifted up.

Aleksia swung her leg over and hit Porthos in the shoulder with the weapon in her right hand.

Porthos had been training all his life to be a warrior. He spun to face her, breaking his own weapon in two. Aleksia struggled to keep up with him. She'd block a blow and miss another, losing more and more ground to him. The crowd behind her was drawing too near, and she didn't like having her back so close to them.

Porthos kicked her in the gut and she slammed against the wall of the cage. She darted his assault against her head and moved away from the wall. He was about to strike again, but a gong rang and he stopped.

"Citizen!" declared the mediator.

Aleksia threw her weapons into the sand as the crowd raised their voices in satisfaction.

Porthos reached out his hand to congratulate her, but she swept his feet out from under him and walked away.

Soldiers with swords of metal entered the ring and surrounded her.

Aleksia's hands quivered as someone came and painted an X on her shoulder. She spotted Hycis jumping into the ring and she wanted her weapon back. Instead of coming to her he went to the mediator. The mediator's eyes briefly glanced at her and he nodded his head. Hycis handed him the money pouch and left the arena.

What was his plan now?

"This way." The mediator walked ahead of Aleksia as three soldiers came around her. They led her out of the pen and the crowd split, holding their heads down as they brought her towards a building with a black door.

A slave opened it with a smile and waved them through.

On the other side of the door was a small dusky room lit by a single candle on a desk where a man sat, too distracted to peer up from his papers. What the papers contained seemed far more interesting than anything going on around him.

Lurking behind him was Hycis, looking very proud of himself.

Aleksia stood at his desk and the soldiers stepped back.

The man sitting at the table spoke without lifting his head to see her. "I'm Folwin, in charge of the matters of matrimony. I've been searching the documents to find a woman of your description and age, but have found none." He turned the page, his finger dragging the scribbles. "None the less, you have proven yourself in combat and will be offered a choice, which you must make here and now." Folwin made a note about a page in a notebook. "As a female citizen you have two options, marry or work in the mines of Ironwood." He pointed absently behind him with his quiver. "Hycis has volunteered to take you as his bride. The recent death of his wife has left him with a farm and no wife to protect it. You would bear him a child and live your best life."

Folwin finally peered up from his papers and pointed at a door opposite to the one Aleksia came in. "Behind that door are all the arrangements for you to marry immediately."

Aleksia glared at Hycis. "I choose the mines."

Hycis motioned towards her.

Folwin lifted his hand to stay him. "Take a moment. Make sure you are certain that this is what you want."

"No need," said Aleksia.

"Very well then." Folwin opened a drawer in his desk and withdrew a silver necklace. He slid his chair backwards and it shrieked against the floor. He stepped behind Aleksia. "Move your hair, please."

Aleksia gathered her hair and pulled it to the side.

Folwin barely touched Aleksia as he put the necklace on her. It latched around her neck, sealing itself with magic. "You will wear this as your badge of shame. You will receive no family crest or brand, but you may change your mind. Should you desire to leave the mines and marry, alert a foreman at the mines and he'll aid you. It's not uncommon. But if you try to escape on your own, the necklace will be removed and they will brand you a slave with no second chances."

"I understand." She had no intentions of staying in Ironwood. Once she'd escaped and was in the elven lands, she dared them come after her.

"You may take her," said Folwin, returning to his papers.

Aleksia was shackled and taken back outside. Shouts of outrage rose from Hycis and there was a crash as the door closed behind her.

Word of her fight had reached the ears of the entire room, and she could hear their whispers of surprise when she emerged wearing a necklace.

"Probably won't make it down the ladder of the Mirtis," asserted one woman.

Her choice was not a common one, and as Aleksia watched the women, she understood why.

She saw women fighting tears, their eyes darting towards the door ahead, fearing the auction man's verdict. They sat in the cutting chairs, with downcast eyes and hands clasped between their thighs. Most of their heads were shaved down to the skull, stripping them of their beauty and identity. Scars long healed and fresh covered their bodies, and Aleksia couldn't imagine what they'd been through. They shook as though they were cold when they stood, and their feet faltered as they neared the door to beyond.

Aleksia understood how a woman might be tempted to take the easier path. To suffer through an arranged marriage, raise children who belonged to the state, and have power. This place would make any woman want to run. Aleksia looked into the eyes of the hopeless, fearing that one day their eyes would be her own.

Even if she wasn't an elf, Aleksia neither agreed with this society nor could she make herself marry someone she didn't love. In all her years of living with her guardians, her favourite stories were the ones about how they'd fallen in love. It was illegal for slaves to marry, and almost all of them married in secret, vowing to love and cherish one another under a blanket of stars in the dead of night. It was a vow that would never be recognized under the rule of King Zoren, but to them it would be forever acknowledged in the eternal realm. It was the one thing that made them feel free. Hearing all those stories growing up, Aleksia yearned to have the same chance. Someone to call her own. Not because she was supposed to, but because life without them wouldn't be a life at all.

Two soldiers escorted Aleksia out onto the street and past lines of people. The ones yet to go to market bore no necklace, and the ones who had, did. There were fewer people on the street now as the market day was coming to an end.

They didn't travel far down the street, just to another gate on the other side of the Vakar. The room was filled with cells. The soldiers leading Aleksia stopped in front of a cell and written on a board over the door was Mirtis. She was unchained and pushed into the cell. Immediately Aleksia noticed there were mostly men in it. They took one glance at her and moved away, even though there wasn't much room. A sort of path emerged through the crowd to another they seemed to be avoiding. He faced outside the cell and his scarred back was to her, but she knew it was him.

And she felt strangely relieved.

Aleksia walked across the cell and stood next to him.

Marcus glared over his shoulder and pulled away. He'd known it was her without a word. He seemed so different without his beard. She couldn't help but notice he was handsome, and as quickly as she thought it, she pushed the notion away. He was the reason Jovetta was dead, and he hated her. She wasn't going to let a handsome face cover that up.

Aleksia sat down in the cell and wrapped her arms around herself as the light faded. She felt alone in the dark until a man, somewhere in the building, started to sing and others joined.

> *Mount Tikalnus, where is your flame*
> *Another year has gone by the same*
> *Rear your head and burn once again*
> *Our land is waiting for you to mend*
>
> *Your eye's gone dark in the valley*
> *Ellara needs to awaken to rally*
> *The tears of your charge flood the meadow*
> *And your people become like the shadow*
>
> *No rock to stand or sword to fight*
> *We pray you'd come forth and hold back the night*
> *Our hope is a dying flame*
> *Rise up and give us strength to reign*

Aleksia's eyes teared up and she felt their plea. It was prophesied that when the appointed time came for the people of Azuk to rise, Mount Tikalnus, a volcano carved into the shape of a dragon's head by the ancients, would burn once more. The peak lay quiet in the centre of their capital city, Ellara, across the Olend Sea. Since Zoren's victory the people of Azuk had been hunted and brought here. A shell of their former selves. Most of the people around her were born slaves, and if they ever wanted to purchase their freedom, they not only had to repay the money they were purchased with, but they also had to win against their master in single combat. An impossible task, since slaves were killed on site if anyone saw them carrying a weapon of any kind. A slave with no training didn't stand a chance of winning, and few tried.

Soldiers ran between the cells seeking the one who'd started the forbidden song. Aleksia kept playing it over in her mind.

Rise up and give us strength to reign.

XXX

MIRTIS

Marcus sat with his back against the bars as he tried to rub the sleep away from his weary eyes. He couldn't let them close or he'd fall asleep. The people inside the cell shifted on the balls of their feet, waiting for the peace to break. Words were not exchanged, but other cells murmured.

"Did you see the two citizens?"

"Probably spies. Want to stop the rising before it starts."

"You won't catch me anywhere near them, especially the woman."

He knew deep down they wouldn't harm him or the elf, but the law was even more strict if they touched her.

If a slave touched a female citizen in any way she didn't approve, soldiers could execute them on the spot, without evidence or trial. Her word would be enough. If she were killed and no one confessed, every slave in the vicinity would share her fate.

The elf pretended to sleep, but Marcus could hear the rapid pulse of her heart.

Marcus's lids closed and he leaned his head against the bars. He felt a tingling warmth until footsteps walked past and his head shot up.

He rubbed his eyes again. Marcus didn't understand why he wouldn't let himself fall asleep. If they killed him, he'd be saved the aggravation of rowing to Ironwood. It didn't make sense he feared going to sleep, thinking she might be harmed if he did. What was her fate to him? And what could he even do if they attacked? He'd killed the cook and the two guards in the wagon, but he couldn't explain how he'd done that. He should have been killed long ago, yet the gods continued to let him live. Nonetheless, he fought his closing eyes until he heard people stirring as the light of day cracked on the horizon.

A soldier jerked the door open. "Everybody out in single file."

Marcus gripped the side of the cell and stood. He could smell food and a small cart rolled up, stopping in front of their cell.

"Come out, get ironed, and we'll feed you. Anyone who stirs up a ruckus will be beaten and row on an empty stomach," warned a soldier.

The elf went ahead of Marcus and they were the last to leave the cell. Outside the door, a hand stopped him and he felt an iron brace latch around his neck and shackles lock on his ankles. As a reward, a piece of flatbread was placed in Marcus's hands, followed by a plopping spoonful of burnt porridge. Marcus dipped his finger into the goo and tasted it. The raisins were sweet and he folded the bread in half and ate as he followed the line into the quiet street. A breeze brushed against his face, but the clean air thinned as they drew nearer to the harbour.

Marcus knew the smell. He'd recognize it anywhere. It was the smell of human filth and fear. A slave threw up his breakfast and he followed the line to veer around it.

The masts of the Mirtis towered between an opening in the buildings. Its black sails were rolled up, ready to be released whenever the goddess Brisa showed her favour. Designed for war and transport, the black wooden hull was narrow with the oars pulled in. Around each of the oars was a piece of water resistant leather to prevent the sea from getting into the hull. Carved into the front of the ship was a statue of Karas, the god of war and father to the gods of the elements. A mound of elven skulls were his stepping stool and his face cried for war. He was armed with a lone spear, strong enough to impale any enemy ship. Hundreds of shields lined the top of the hull; taken from their fallen foes and nailed there as a warning to all who might think to attack.

Thick pieces of iron branched around the body of the ship with chains stretching into the water that seemed to gurgle around its circumference. The Mirtis wasn't fast, but its ability to be the last ship floating in the aftermath of battle was legendary.

Fishermen avoided going anywhere near her, afraid the crew would need bodies to occupy the seats below.

Marcus stepped off of the street and sand sunk between his toes, covering his feet to his ankles. Ships scraped against the docks and other slaves hurried past them with supplies for the voyage.

The line of slaves were ushered along the beach, until Marcus felt a dock beneath his foot.

"Move it!" shouted one of the slave masters, the sound of his whip piercing the air. "I want to cast off today!"

Up the plank they climbed in single file as the soldiers pressed them onwards like cattle.

Marcus had never been on a boat, so when he put his first foot on the plank and it bobbed beneath his weight, his world felt uncertain. He wanted to grasp something solid to steady himself.

The crewmen were bustling on the deck to get the last of the materials needed on board. The line stopped at a ladder that went below deck.

Marcus's chain slackened and the elf stopped.

A guard licked his lips. "Having second thoughts, dear?" he smirked. "Say the word and you can go back home with me and bear me some children." He took a step closer.

Marcus cringed as the feeling of the barrier entered his mind. He went to pull away but couldn't when he felt her trembling.

"Or have you already found someone?" taunted the guard.

The elf's body tensed and she brushed the man aside. The iron brace was removed and the shackles on her ankles jangled as she slowly stepped down the ladder.

"He's here!" hollered the guard who'd spoken to the elf.

The soldiers must have been informed prior to their

arrival that one rower was going to be blind.

Two men took hold of Marcus and wrapped his body in rope. They tightly tied his ankles together and he had no idea why. *Don't panic*, he urged himself.

"Are you ready?" they called down.

"Send him down!" said another voice from below deck.

They lifted Marcus and he squirmed to get free. *What are they doing?* The soldiers held him over the hole and dropped him.

Marcus wanted to shout and almost lost his breakfast. Several arms caught him and they laughed as he was propped up onto his feet. He was untied and led between the four hundred men and women sitting at the oars.

"Put him here."

Marcus was seated at the end of a bench facing towards the back. He cursed under his breath the moment he sat down.

The elf's magic flowed into his shoulder.

Will I ever be rid of her? he thought. Of all the people they could have put him next to, they had to put him next to her. This place reminded him enough of the wagons of death. He didn't need another constant reminder. But he also knew this place would be different. With the forsaken everyone who entered the wagons knew death was coming, but here someone could spend a lifetime never tasting clean air, motivated by the sound of a drum until they were too weak to go on.

The soldiers drew a chain through a loop on Marcus's ankle irons and latched it to the man behind. If the ship went down, they'd all be going down with it.

The other three men in their row were deserters. The soldiers above kept the peace by splitting citizens from slaves. In the past they'd lost more rowers to fights than they wanted to deal with.

The hatch closed above and the only light around them trickled in through a metal grate further up the ship. Feet hustled above deck, calling out as they still had the tide's favour.

Marcus figured out his surroundings. He shuffled himself to the furthest edge of the bench. His feet barely had enough give to lift off the ground, but he was grateful to have his hands and neck free to move around as he wished. He felt for the oar hanging on a blunt iron hook in front of him. Within the wood he detected the indents of a pair of hands. He wondered how many others had sat in the same seat.

The anchor rumbled against the side of the ship as it rose from the bottom of the harbour, and Marcus felt the boat drift on the waters.

A set of boots passed between the procession of rowers towards the drum at the front.

"Wakey, wakey, gallies! Time to earn your passage aboard the Mirtis," he yelled. "Take up your oars!"

The elf picked up the oar before Marcus could grab it, holding it out to him.

"To our new arrivals, row to the beat of the drum or suffer the whip."

The hairs on the back of Marcus's neck rose. He didn't know what to do. His hands reached for the oar in the wrong place. The elf grabbed his hands and he tried to pull away, but she held firm.

"Let me," she urged.

Marcus didn't want to need her help, but he knew if they were to survive he needed to surrender his hatred. He willed the memories of the barriers and the screams of those it killed to stand aside.

The elf placed his hands onto the oar and pulled it into position.

"I'll help you find the timing with the first few rows," she whispered. "Let me carry the weight until you find the rhythm."

Marcus nodded.

"Hold your hands on the oar and once you get a hang of it, I'll back off."

The drum began to beat.

"Row!" commanded the supervisor.

Marcus felt the oar drag into the water and his body strained to pull against the tension of the sea. He became an extension of the oar, only there to row as his shoulders, hands, and back burned with exertion. Yet there was no stopping. He was now part of the ship, with only one thought. *Row*.

XXXI

TALES OF DESERTION

Aleksia let go of the oar but she still felt like it was tethered between her fingers. Everyone around her leaned back on the paddles behind them and were drenched in sweat. Stretching her shoulders back, she felt relieved being able to move them without the burden of an oar.

Something shifted under the ship. A sound like a large chain rapidly moving thudded against the floor. Aleksia felt a vibration in her feet and the Mirtis accelerated.

How? she thought.

The man beside her spoke. "Marwin, you still alive?"

The soldier who'd had his ear cut off by the king leaned against the oar in front of him and looked at Aleksia. "Unfortunately yes, Kilroy. I will admit, I do feel rather envious that they put the pretty one next to you and not me."

"Thank the gods they didn't take our eyes," laughed Kilroy.

Marwin smiled. "It's so we can see the shock on beautiful women's faces when they see our hideousness."

Aleksia saw the men next to her and knew what they were. They were deserters. Soldiers who abandoned their post and were sentenced to a fate worse than death. Rather than executing them, their nose and ears were severed from their bodies. They bathed their heads in skustis, so they could never return to the life they'd known. If the ship went down and they survived, any man or woman loyal to Remisia would apprehend them and take them back where they belonged. She could tell the one in the middle had only recently lost his features. The wounds were only just healing.

Kilroy smirked. "The beauty of a woman is what got Tavin here." He pointed to the man at the window who hadn't spoken a word. "I doubt he'd make that same mistake twice."

Marwin leaned his arms on the oar in front of him and gazed at Aleksia. "We men do stupid things, like talking about a woman before we've even introduced ourselves."

Kilroy, who sat next to Aleksia, bowed his head. "I must apologize, my lady. I'm Kilroy, deserter of the five hundredth and eighty-first legion of our King Zoren and this is Marwin—"

"Of the five hundredth and eighty-ninth," imputed Marwin. "Seems a day of rowing has nearly killed your companion."

Marcus was leaning against the paddle behind him,

his chest heaving, his eyes closed.

"I'm Aleksia and this is Marcus."

"Marcus?" Shocked at the name, Kilroy reached past Aleksia and turned Marcus towards him so he could see the family crest.

Marcus's eyes cracked open and he lifted a tired hand to stop Kilroy, but he didn't have the strength to fight.

"Do you know him?" questioned Aleksia.

Marwin tried to see past Kilroy. "Is it true?"

"Only the descendants of Marcus can use that name and he has the family crest. Judging by his eyes he should be among the forsaken, not bound for Ironwood."

"Why would they send him here?" Marwin pondered.

"He's barely spoken a word to me," she responded, wishing she could figure him out.

"But what a tale it would be, Kilroy!" exclaimed Marwin.

Aleksia sought to understand. "What happened to him?"

Kilroy calculated what could have occurred. "No one knows for sure. I was told no one survived until today. I rode past Naiden once, that's where his father, Barsadias, General of the Center, kept his villa. There was nothing left. Only a few burnt city walls. When it happened eighteen years ago, there were only a few bodies to bury. Most of them were turned to ash or boiled in the river."

Aleksia couldn't imagine the power needed to boil an entire river. "What could have done that?"

"There have been a few theories. King Zoren's armies were on high alert for months. Everyone thought the elves were coming out of hiding. I'd been just assigned to Azuk at the time. I remember thousands of arrows were being made and everyone was preparing their armour for war."

Is that why he hates me? wondered Aleksia. She glanced over at Marcus, but his head was turned away from her so she couldn't read his thoughts.

"When the elves never arrived, it was a mystery."

Aleksia didn't want to believe her people capable of such a deed. "What else could have done that?"

Marwin interceded. "Zoren."

"You can't know that," responded Kilroy.

"I overheard the soldiers say Zoren ended the revolt at my villa with a flick of his wrist. Burned it to the ground with a flame in the shape of a dragon and made the earth swallow the people whole."

Marcus flinched.

Kilroy shrugged his shoulders. "The only person who can tell us what really happened in Naiden is sitting right next to you, but he doesn't seem like he wants to share."

Marwin cut in. "I'm telling you it was the king himself."

Aleksia wanted more answers, but Kilroy changed the subject.

"Everyone has a theory, but instead of speaking of the unknown it's custom to exchange stories of how we got here. It's not every day we see a woman of your station below deck."

Kilroy and Marwin were both staring at Aleksia and

she could hardly tell them the truth, so she told them the same story she'd told Captain Haman.

"I'm an evader. My father wanted me to accept a marriage proposal, but I couldn't marry him. I took my handmaid, Jovetta, and lived in a cabin until they found me."

"Not uncommon, but very few women don't go through the black door and marry."

"I don't want to marry someone I don't love."

Kilroy leaned in. "I was lucky. My Ciara was the love of my life. It broke both our hearts when she had to disavow me before the court and swear to take another."

"What happened?" asked Aleksia.

"A lie," said Kilroy. "They stationed me in Azuk under General Printis and one day we were taking a few slaves from a village. One of them broke off into the forest. I ran after him and was about to capture him, when Thaddeus, son of Homer, whacked me on the back of the head. He dragged me behind his horse." Kilroy pointed to the burn marks on the backs of his arms. "He accused me of desertion in front of General Printis and with the testimony of a few of his friends, they sent me here."

"Why would he do that to you?"

"The general preferred me over him," explained Kilroy. "If a general fell, I would have been General Printis's first choice to represent him in the Tournament of Generals."

"I'm sorry," apologized Aleksia.

"My children know where I am, but none of them would ever darken the steps of the Mirtis to come and see their dishonoured father."

"How many children did you have with Ciara?"

"Four. Two sons and two daughters."

Water started to be served at the front of the ship.

Kilroy went to say more but was interrupted by Marwin.

"The time for talking is almost over," implored Marwin, who knew once the rations were distributed to the crew they were to remain silent until the following day. The guards allowed them to speak to one another during this time to keep up the spirits of the rowers.

"Apologies, Marwin." Kilroy's eyes filled with the memories of his old life. "It's your turn to speak."

"I'm also here because of no fault of mine." His eyes pleading Aleksia to believe him, the wounds of his betrayal still fresh in his mind. "I was stationed at Sidabras when I got a message from my wife, telling me an uprising had started at my farm. I dropped everything and took a few men with me to help. I get there and the place was on fire. My wife and three youngest children were burning in the courtyard of my villa. Slaves attacked us from all sides. I fought, but there were too many. The farm was overrun. I left to get re-enforcements, but no one else survived and King Zoren believed I deserted. I didn't desert! I left to get more troops."

Aleksia didn't know how to respond. On one hand, she was proud of the slaves who'd risen up to fight, but killing the children—it was something she could never do. She would defend herself and the people around her, but to harm someone innocent was unimaginable.

Marwin continued. "The king himself cut off my ear in front of the entire council, right after he heard my plea. And now I can never go back."

"Would you want to go back?" Kilroy inquired.

"It would be better than living here," said Marwin, a little less confidently.

"We're better off here than where they're going." Kilroy nudged his head in Aleksia and Marcus's direction. "The only people who come out of there are headed for the barriers, so distraught they can't even row."

Marwin spoke. "At least Tavin can row."

"He's never told us how he came here, but I knew who he was the moment I sat on this bench. General Printis used to talk about what happened all the time. He liked to mock General Zale. Three years ago, young Tavin here was sent out on his final test to become eligible for marriage."

Aleksia knew of the test. Young men, who were fifteen, went out one night and hunted a slave.

Kilroy continued. "So they tracked down the slave and found her trying to get across the river. She was smart enough to try to throw off the scent to the dogs. They dragged her out of the water and Tavin recognizes her. He'd been 'sharing relations,'" Kilroy tried to say it delicately, "with her for months when he thought no one was looking. Well, his father found out and volunteered her for the hunt."

"That's horrible." Aleksia shook her head, revolted that a father could do such a thing to his son.

"Tavin's friends decided they were going to have a little fun with her by the lake, and that's when he tried to kill them all. He almost got her away from them, but they didn't make it."

Marwin interjected. "He should have been executed."

"But he wasn't." Kilroy eyed the scars covering Tavin from head to toe. "His father probably made him wish he was dead. Killed the girl in front of him and gave him a beating he would never forget."

Culann, the cook, arrived with the water and handed the drinking gourd to Marcus, whose hands shook as he lifted it to his lips.

Aleksia glimpsed the rawness of Marcus's hands as he passed the gourd back to Culann, and she accepted her water ration.

As the others were given theirs, she took Marcus's hand, but he winced and pulled away.

"I'm not going to hurt you," she reassured him.

Marcus yielded his hands to her, his fingers curled upwards.

Aleksia took them as gently as she could, but with the slightest touch she saw a tear in his eye and an eagerness to withdraw.

"Can you do anything?" Marcus bit his lip.

Aleksia sensed Kilroy watching over her shoulder. "Not as much as I could."

Kilroy turned in his seat. "Culann," he breathed, drawing the young cook's attention. He came back towards them. "Can you pour a bit of water onto his hands? I'd hate to see them get infected. You know what happens to gallies who can't row anymore."

Culann looked around to see if any of the guards were watching and poured a full drinking gourd over Marcus's hands.

Kilroy smiled. "The gods themselves thank you."

Aleksia used the water to wash off as much of the

dirt as possible. And once she was finished, she took her dress and ripped two bandages from the hem.

"I'm going to wrap what I can and hopefully it'll help you row tomorrow."

"Thank you." Marcus removed his hands from her grasp.

Aleksia knew from the emotions on his face he was being genuine. "You're welcome." There was more she wished to say, but she wasn't sure how. "I—" she rolled her eyes at herself. She'd started and now she had to finish. "I don't expect us to be friends, but we seem to be in this together. I was hoping we could help each other out?"

Marcus moved his thumb along the bandage. "Why did you try to help me—back in the barn?"

Aleksia flinched, his question taking her off guard. "I saw you needed me."

"And then you lost everything."

Aleksia hadn't expected him to bring it up. "Yes."

"I'm sorry for that." Barely able to keep his eyes open.

"Neither of us knew what was going to happen that night."

"Doesn't change that I wish it ended differently."

"Something we both share."

Kilroy interjected, "Don't fall asleep yet, lad. Food's coming."

Underneath everyone's seat was a wooden bowl. It slid into a slot in the wood. Kilroy and Marwin showed Marcus and Aleksia where to find it. The soup was handed out and once they'd finished eating, no one felt like talking. After a long day of rowing and a full belly, sleep took over.

XXXII

WORD OF WATER

Zoren watched as the last lion from the animal hunt was put down by the swipe of Jabari's sword. The crowd stood to their feet in joyous expression. The gates opened and the death dancers paraded onto the sands dressed in red with bells around their wrists and ankles.

Carts followed behind them, picking up the smaller animals, as multiple teams of ragatis and horses hooked onto the dead elephants to pull them away.

The hunters galloped around the chariot track and the people chanted the name of their favourite.

"Jabari!"

"Leonitis!"

"Bastian!"

An ambitious death dancer ran to the corpse of a leopard and severed its hide from its skin. Once he finished, he held it over his head with both hands like a banner, flapping in the wind behind him as he ran across the field with it. Eventually he threw it into the crowd and a woman draped it over her shoulders with pride.

Horns blared and the last of the carcasses were removed. The death dancers ran the length of the arena and were dealt rakes to begin their musical number of covering the blood.

The drum beat and the performers moved to the music in symmetry with one another. Scraping in circles, spraying each other with sand, and shifting the dirt until most of the blood was covered up.

Another horn blew and the death dancers ran out of the arena as set pieces were brought in. Giant trees with leaves that mocked the size of the elven woodlands moved into the centre of the sands.

Zoren sat up in his seat, curious about the sets. He couldn't remember a story that involved Dirva and the elves. Typically, a cave was constructed and the actors dressed as dwarves, but as the characters came out he saw they were dressed in elven armour and their ears were exaggerated to a point. Each elf carried a fake weapon made of some flimsy material that flapped in the wind. They had painted their mouths into a permanent frown, and their exaggerated eyebrows made them look angry.

The crowd booed and threw rotten fruit.

Another gate opened and an infantry dressed in black armour marched onto the sand in perfect unison. The lack of a tree on their chests told the crowd they weren't actually soldiers, but they cheered anyway.

A man with a wig made of palomino horse hair rode ahead of them on a white stallion. Zoren smirked when he noticed the man was dressed to look like General Leganous.

The fake general raised his hand and the people went quiet to hear him speak.

"People of Remisia," projected the man. "My name is General Leganous and with every passing day my men and I journey deeper into Visadas."

Commander Othos leaned over to King Zoren. "Leganous better watch out, this man plays him better than he does."

"My thoughts exactly," agreed Zoren, his spirits lifting.

General Leganous continued. "I live for the day when my sword drips in elven blood and the queen's tree falls to the ground before our king. Death will come to them at our hands and we shall end their eternity."

The Aurelius rumbled with applause and Leganous waited until it settled.

"But their end will not come easily, for they are a formidable foe. With strength and agility unmatched by man they plunge us to darkness. But we have some advantage. Not only do we breed faster, but we have the sungazer."

A trap door opened and a lounge of lizards sprung up from the ground, scurrying around the arena and absorbing the heat of the sun.

The mock elves jumped into their fake tree, hiding from the lizards, and the crowd laughed.

One lizard, entranced by a magician in the stands, crept up the side of Leganous's horse and nestled itself into his arms, while the fake general stroked its head.

"Our ultimate gift from the dragon wars," he said,

the crowd hanging on the actor's every word. "The dragons created these beasts to be used as weapons against the elves. One drop of their venom can temporarily take away their advantage. No longer will they be strong or possess any magic. If potent enough, it can make them unconscious.

"Every man, woman, and child here, save our king, needs this venom to defeat an elf. On this day of Dirva I can promise a surprise. Not only for you, but for our king."

Zoren sat back in his seat. This petty game was proving to be surprising. He was relieved to not have to sit through another memoir of the dwarves.

The elves leapt into action and the guard surrounded them in a perfect circle. General Leganous dismounted his horse and whacked it on the rear, sending it galloping around the arena.

"Soldiers of Remisia, attack!"

Nets were fired at the elves from special crossbows. They were much larger than the typical bow and could launch a net far up into the trees.

The people dressed as elves were caught in them and cried out as it burned their skin. An enchantment replicating the effects of the sungazer venom landed on them. They fell out of the trees and fought to untangle themselves but were speared to death.

Soldiers with spikes on their boots launched themselves into the branches.

A soldier and a woman dressed as an elf stood on a branch and fought one another. From below, someone shot a dart at her, hitting her in the neck. She fell to her knees and the guard cut off her head; her body tumbled to the ground.

The crowd cheered, laughing at the falling elves who were being killed left and right. Suddenly, another door in the arena opened and an even larger number of elves charged the scene. The enemy seemed too great to be defeated by a small garrison of troops.

A red-haired elf, meant to be Queen Gretafold, led the elven army. Her garrison cried at the top of their lungs and surged towards Leganous's regrouping troops.

Zoren thought they were outmatched until the actor playing General Leganous tossed a burning clay pot. It landed right in their enemy's midst and broke. A mist filled the air, so thick the actors disappeared from sight.

King Zoren and the entire crowd stood to their feet. The smoke dissipated and the entire elven army was writhing on the ground, too weak to lift a sword.

"Charge!" yelled Leganous, and without much of a fight, they defeated the elves.

King Zoren sat back down. His elbows on his knees and his chin resting in his hands. Not an elf remained alive on the sands and his eyes beamed with delight as Commander Othos sat next to him.

"Has it been tested?" the king asked.

Commander Othos replied, "Prometheus has been sneaking into the palace to use it on the prisoner for weeks."

Zoren tried not to recoil at the mention of the prisoner as his fist tightened on the armrest of his chair.

Othos didn't seem to notice. "Are you pleased?"

"If it works," said Zoren. "The prisoner," the word slicing his tongue like a knife, "is only half elf. Does it affect the men?"

"Not in the least."

"I want it tested on one of my tamrasa."

The fake General Leganous marched his army to stand in front of the king's booth, all of their weapons dripping in blood. "A gift, Your Majesty."

A slave ran up the stairs with a silver platter that carried the head of the woman who'd played Queen Gretafold. He placed it next to King Zoren. Her eyes were glazed over and her face blank. They had made the ears with wire and patches of whitened cow leather. Bringing the head so close broke the illusion, but instead of ridicule, he clapped and the rest of the arena followed his lead, tossing flowers at the feet of the victors as they marched out of the crowd's view.

The crowd moved to get food and celebrate their favourite victories with friends. Death dancers ran out onto the sand to clear the carnage. It would be awhile until the gladiator fights.

Zoren stood to make himself scarce as a mother and her daughters approached. The oldest daughter couldn't have been older than fifteen, and her mother was presenting her towards him like a roast on a platter. He'd learned to hide in his secret chambers between events in order to avoid interactions like this, but today he'd lingered too long. Zoren smiled like he had nowhere better to be and touched the stone beneath his purple robes. The mother's name came to him.

"Cassia, so nice you could come and enjoy the games."

"My king, may I present my daughter, Sephie, and her sister, Amelia."

They were both beautiful, each of them adorned in a

new toga.

"It's very nice to meet you both."

The young girls blushed with virgin eyes, each of them looking at him like he was a prize to be won. He suspected they were fully trained with a sword, but neither of them knew anything of the world. They were children in his eyes. If he ever decided to marry again, he'd choose a woman he saw as his equal and twice the age of these girls, like Nerva when she'd first come to him. He found it difficult to hold their gaze.

He faced their mother. "Are you here all week?"

Cassia gave him a knowing look. "It depends on their prospects. Sephie is here to find a husband. She's found the soldiers at our barracks in Remead not to her liking and hopes to find a man of true ability to match her own."

King Zoren pretended not to take the hint. "I know of some fine young men in our barracks. They'll be getting up extra early tomorrow morning as to not miss the events of the tournament. Maybe she could find someone to her liking there." King Zoren reached behind him and grabbed Commander Othos. "Commander Othos, Cassia is looking to find a husband for her daughter, Sephie. This man has intimate knowledge of all the boys training. Perhaps he can help you."

King Zoren hurried up the steps. Other mothers, daughters, and fathers were gathering and he needed to escape. They called out his name and he pretended not to hear them as a guard blocked their way.

The chamber wasn't far, but he was usually there by now, avoiding the masses. He loved and hated tournaments. He loved the rumble of the crowd and the sight of blood on the sands. He hated them because as king he could never participate. No one in the kingdom was a match, and it made him long for a challenger. Someone who could test his knowledge of the sword and thwart his abilities so he could taste true victory.

A statue of Karas marked the entrance. Turning the sword in the god's hand, the wall gave way and he disappeared inside. He opened the window and sat on the couch, lounging where no one could see him except the painting of his beloved.

Her portrait was the only piece of art he'd allowed on the walls. She seemed to look down at him in a condemning way today, but he ignored it. He marvelled at her stunning face — her full lips, which he used to know intimately, and the tendrils of her hair. He missed the sound of her voice and the way her eyes lit up when she had an idea.

Zoren reached into his purple shirt and pulled out a slim circular disc with a diamond at the centre. Etched in the stone was a phrase in dwarfish. *Brother. Together we live. In heart we live on.* It was called a memoria. He remembered the first time he saw the dwarves wearing them on their foreheads. The dwarven King Sarrgen told him they wore them to light their way underground and that every day, hour, and moment of their lives was stored in the jewel. When they died, others could go into the Hall of Memory to seek the wisdom of those of the past.

Lina had been the first to see the signs of his mind slipping when no one else had. Each day was becoming a drop in an ocean of other days. Earlier memories were sinking to a place he couldn't reach. He couldn't remember the first time he'd seen Lina's face or the first time he'd held her in his arms in the quickening dark. Or a time he wasn't king. A stranger to himself, the memoria had been the only solution to keep him together, to remember every lesson and to reflect on every cause.

Lina stormed Dasarak to steal the memoria. She'd purified it of its previous host and fashioned it to be all that he was. It wasn't long after she'd gotten him the memoria the dwarves sealed themselves shut into their mountain. A seer once had the nerve to tell him the dwarves would rise to the voice of a new king. He cut out her tongue and slit her throat.

Holding it in his hands, the memories long past stirred in the depths of his mind and he swam in their current. Times of joy, sorrow, and fear. He knew he had only a short time to reflect, but as he was sinking into a memory, he heard wings.

King Zoren opened his eyes as a bat flew through the window. He put the memoria back where it belonged and sat up.

The creature hovered in front of him and opened its mouth.

A wave of sound barrelled towards him and in his mind's eye he saw Elian by the shore of the Olend Sea.

"My king, I have done as you asked and found the boy in Masseson, but something far more important has drawn me away."

Zoren felt a flicker of anger that he'd disobeyed his orders.

"A prostitute spoke to him. I found it strange so I followed her to the sea while he was locked in a cell."

The vision changed from Elian, and Zoren watched

a woman in a red dress step into the waters. She transformed into the legendary Vandus, goddess of water. Zoren stood to his feet as the image changed back to Elian.

"I'm following her until Jerome and Antonia can take my place. I will accept any punishment for abandoning the boy." Elian shivered with fear. "I thought this would please you."

Elian disappeared, and Zoren's mind returned to the room.

The bat continued to hover in front of him, waiting for a reply.

"Take this message back to your master," he said to the bat. "Stay with her and send word the moment you know where she's built her palace. I will follow."

The little creature flew out the way it came, and Zoren was left there with a new hope in his eyes. The gods themselves were sensing something was stirring in the land of Remisia. First, he had taken Dirva while he slept, then Casiro, extinguishing the fires of Azuk's mountain of hope, and now he would find their sister and taste her blood on his tongue.

XXXIII

PAULINA

King Zoren excused himself from the rest of the day's events. He rode his horse through the maze of streets to the one place where people were less concerned with the events of the present and looked to the circumstances to come. The House of Seers sat on the eastern cliff of Sidabras. Most of the streets were quiet, as everyone was inside the Aurelius, but some dwelt outside. Slaves bent over fires in the alleys, cooking food to serve the people being entertained.

A man stood outside and threw a large piece of meat to a black bear on a leash. He paced the road to see if the crowds were coming. House servants carried laundry and went about their business as Zoren rode past them.

The House of Seers wasn't as big or as grand as the Temple of Karas. On the gate was a massive eye, mirroring the tattoo on every seer's wrist and it was thrust open as Zoren approached. He dismounted, throwing the reigns to a waiting servant.

In the courtyard was a veranda. It had plenty of desks occupied by little girls being instructed in the art of divination.

He often came here instead of seeking his mother's council. While she was one of the most powerful seers in Remisia, it also took some convincing to get her to show anything of value. Zoren wasn't patient enough to deal with her today. Instead he sought Paulina, the head of the House of Seers.

An elder seer stood at the front of the class with a card in her hand. On the card was a blotched image that didn't look like anything, but the girls were expected to replicate it on their piece of parchment.

Some girls eyes were white as they drew and they didn't even notice the king come into their presence. Others looked over their shoulders but could see they'd be scolded if they said a word and kept to their piece of art.

Decima, who led the class, nodded her head in welcome to the king but did not disturb her pupils from their studies. She'd seen he wasn't there to see the progress of the future generation of seers. "Paulina's waiting for you in her chambers."

Zoren offered a grin of thanks and went into the house.

The air was drenched in herbs and the king felt his throat go dry. Every time he came into this place he'd need a drink to soothe his throat. He started up the winding stair, fighting the urge to cover his mouth.

Embellishing the walls to the higher level were the

paintings of the past and future. Within the house was a gallery of things they'd predicted that came true. Their paintings were far more obscure than the works of the painters of history. Painters of history had to capture the absolute truth of what happened, while seers were open to interpretation of the future.

The canvases on the walls were always changing. Going up the stairs, a few caught his eye. A snowy mountain peak burned in fire. A faceless man with a sword through his heart. A tiny purple flower. A jura and a black dragon fighting in a raging sea. He always enjoyed trying to predict what they meant, but there was too much on his mind to do so today.

The emerald green hallway reflected his black army boots as he walked to the seer's chambers. On either side of the hall were many doors. He could hear a woman mumbling in her sleep, and two women scrimmaged on the other side of another. To learn the basics, seers went to the barracks to train with the other girls when they were young, but as their skills grew, they were brought to the House of Seers to learn to fight on a whole other level. In their skirmishes they were blindfolded and had to predict where their opponents blow would land. It took them years to master, and some even learned to shoot arrows at targets without sight.

They were some of the greatest heroines Remisia had to offer, not only because of their strengths in battle, but also for their ability to predict the tides of war. They advised whether an army should advance and when they should take a step back, sacrificing animals and reading the signs between the entrails of the beast.

Only an idiot would forgo their council, and that

was why Zoren knocked on Paulina's door.

"It's open."

Zoren opened the door and tea was set on the table at the base of the bed in the light of the open window.

"I see you knew I was coming," he remarked.

"Have to keep an eye on you." Paulina's long greying hair swayed behind her as she poured the tea. "Can't have you catch me in a state of undress," she laughed. "I'm a widow who as no more time for suitors or any more babies. I've enough girls to raise without adding any more."

King Zoren sat in the chair and noticed she'd added too much milk to his tea.

"I know," she said. "But I saw you liked it better this way. You're an impatient man and don't want to wait for it to cool. It's also why you've come to me and not your mother."

Zoren took a sip and noticed the addition of honey and mint. "It's good."

"Thank you, but I know you've not visited me for the perfect cup of tea. I'm doing fine and I know how you are, so now we can get right to the matter at hand."

Zoren forgot the tea. "I had her in my sights before, but a seer told me to wait until I had drank the blood of Dirva and Casiro. Elian spotted her by the shores of Masseson a few days ago and now I need to know how I can capture her."

Paulina drank from her tea and ignited the incense to give her mind its clearest eye. She picked up her chair and placed it in front of Zoren. "Are you ready?"

"Yes." He gave her his hand.

"One hand to keep you in reality, the other to take

you into the world beyond." She touched his temple and their eyes turned white.

When she removed her hand, Zoren's eyes danced.

Paulina smiled and told him, "You are more powerful than you know."

Zoren went to leave, but Paulina held onto his hand.

"The time to go after Marcus will be here soon," she reassured him. "Use this as a distraction for now and remember to be patient."

Zoren kissed her on the cheek, and he went back out the door. He had to find Cornelius, his court magician. They needed to start preparations. In the coming weeks, he would face a goddess.

XXXIV

SKIN OF STONE

They rowed until they felt like their backs were going to break and then they rowed some more. The hull groaned in the crashing waves and the wind whistled between the sails above deck.

A storm is coming, thought Marcus.

"Pull them in!" commanded the officer, holding onto a pillar to keep himself steady.

Marcus heaved and staggered to raise the oar onto the hook. It locked into place and the elf's hands were the first to drop. She fell back into her seat and laboured to breathe.

What's wrong with her? He'd detected a change in her. At first he thought he was imagining it, but the touch of her shoulder against his felt less like the barriers and her pull on the oar was weakening.

Kilroy leaned over to Marcus. "Is she alright?"

"I don't know," he stated.

"I've never seen someone go this fast."

"What happens if she can't row?" asked Marcus.

"She'll be thrown overboard and fed to the creature beneath this ship," whispered Kilroy. "A two headed beast, with teeth sharp enough to bite through iron."

"A jura." Marcus had heard of them. An enormous serpent with a head on each end of its body. The Azuk used them during the war. A single jura could take down an entire ship on its own.

"The male sleeps during the day while the female pulls and they use a crane to switch them around at night. Soon it's going to be hungry and the soldiers will come down here and weed out the weakest to quench it."

"But she's a citizen."

"Whose final battle would be against a mighty beast," said Marwin. "An honourable death that any citizen could be proud of."

"How many days till we reach Ironwood?"

"A week. Maybe more if this storm doesn't lift," disclosed Kilroy.

None of them felt much like talking as the thunder brewed in the distance. Water poured down from the open grate and Marcus felt it building up around his feet. The leather seals around the oar holes prevented most of the sea from finding its way into the hull, but if the Mirtis went belly up, they'd all be dead.

"I need you, you, and you," ordered a soldier named Vortigan, unlocking the chains of the strongest further back on the ship. One of the slaves fought back, trying to take the keys from the guard.

He was punched over the head.

"You'll pay for that," said Vortigan. "But not until

after you've spent the night at the pumps. Or do you want us all to drown?"

The tall black man winced and was pushed along with the others.

Seasoned rowers lost their supper. The panicked yanked on unmoving chains. If one of them was pulled to the bottom of the sea, so too would the rest of them.

"Vandus, goddess of the sea, show mercy!" cried a man.

The elf flopped and was about to fall out of her seat but Marcus caught her shoulder. The plea of the people around them overpowered the weight of the barrier on his mind. She was drenched to the skin and shivered. He drew her close.

No one slept until the storm stilled and the torrents of rain changed to a gentle tap above.

Tavin muttered, "I'm sorry," in his sleep as his fist struck the bow of the ship, but it wasn't Tavin who was concerning him.

Marcus couldn't sleep. He sought the elf's brow and it was burning. She moved and her hand touched his.

The tips of her fingers felt like rock.

"It's begun," she breathed, her voice hoarse as she cringed at the smallest motion of her hands.

"What's begun?" asked Marcus as quiet as he could.

"The curse," she whispered. "When Elvian created my kind, she took magical stones from the Vertes Star of Healing, but it came at a price. Our power comes from the sun, therefore our life comes from it as well. If we stray from its rays for more than a fortnight, we return to the form in which we were first made."

"How many days do you have left?" Marcus tried to

piece together how many days they'd been rowing.

"Four." The elf's lip quivered and she fought the oncoming tears. "People heard the screams of my kin leagues away from the city as they died in Zoren's dungeon."

Marcus wrapped his arm around her and she leaned into him.

In the morning, Marcus heard the elf's hands drop against the bench with a thud.

She leaned close enough so only Marcus could hear her. "I can't move my arms."

Marcus bit his lip and took her hands in his. Some of her fingers had completely turned to stone. The infection ran all the way up to her elbow. He needed to figure out a way to get the elf's hands to stay on the oar without her being able to hold it.

Breakfast was brought around to the slaves. Marcus took out his bowl and helped the elf with hers. A plop of sticky porridge was given to all of them, but now that they had the food, the question became how would he feed it to her. It's not like they were given spoons.

"Can you move any of your fingers?" Marcus picked up one of her hands.

The elf nodded, moving the one next to her pinky.

"I'll help you scoop it with that finger and you can eat."

"You should eat first," she said.

Marcus wanted to protest, but Kilroy spoke out of the corner of his mouth. "Guard," and Marcus ate a handful of his own porridge.

"I won't eat until you have," she argued.

Marcus devoured his breakfast as fast as he could.

How is she going to row? After he finished it wasn't easy getting her to shovel it down, but they figured out a system. Whenever a guard approached, Kilroy reached over and tapped Marcus's thigh.

He'd fed her almost all of her porridge.

"Mealtime's over!" the guard called.

A bit of porridge got on Marcus's hand. As he wiped it away on his shirt, an idea came to him.

"Take oars!" yelled the supervisor.

With no time to waste, he stripped off his shirt and took the elf's hands without waiting for permission. As the oar was pushed out, he placed her hands into position. Holding the handle up with his armpit, he tied her hands around the paddle using his shirt.

"Row!" shouted the supervisor.

Marcus's muscles strained against the extra weight. She couldn't use her hands, but she used what strength she had to push along with him so he could find the rhythm of the oar. She maintained it as long as she could, but as the day went on she was helping less and less.

XXXV

THE JURA

An officer walked down the aisle of rowers who moved in rhythm to the beat of the drum. His eyes glanced at the slaves as he wrote on a piece of parchment. The sun was setting in the west and when he gave a nod, the announcer commanded everything to stop.

Marcus released the oar, putting it on the hook, and untied the elf's hands. She collapsed against him. The hairs on Marcus's neck rose as neither Kilroy nor Marwin uttered a word and they helped him lean her against the paddle behind her.

They'd stopped sooner than usual. He'd started the habit of counting the number of strokes to keep track of the passing hours.

A pair of boots paced before the drum.

Men and women who'd been on the ship a long time sat up straighter in their seats and pinched their cheeks.

And then it began.

Soldiers charged down the ladder and the officer pointed to the ones he'd noted. They were unchained and ripped from their seats. Some fought; yet others were too tired to refuse.

Marcus felt a man pass in front of him and heard the rustle of the elf's chains against the floor. Marcus shot up in her defence, shoving the soldier away from her until they restrained him.

Vortigan spoke to the soldier behind him. "Him too."

Marcus's chains were unlocked as the elf was tossed over the guard's shoulder. He was dragged by the scuff of his shirt up the ladder and as he inhaled, he drank in the fresh sea air. The fading sunlight warmed his skin. The black sails flapped in the wind above, but their noise disappeared as he heard the elf roll off of her carrier.

"Let go of me," she demanded, her strength returning.

The crew drew their swords, and a whip flew through the air. She caught it mid snap and ripped it out of the soldier's hand, propelling him onto the deck.

No one moved except a lone man who emerged from his cabin. The scars on his face and arms didn't hinder his beauty. He had the stance of a great warrior, and his soldiers stepped aside to ease his passing. His armour did not differ from the rest, yet he bore a silver ring of ever-entwined branches, set with a vertes from one of the elvians King Zoren had murdered.

General Quinn was the youngest of Zoren's high command. The king had learned early in his reign that a man did not have to be well along in his years to lead men to victory. He walked with precision and calculation, a quality that likely won him the games.

Captain Vortigan broke the silence. "Gallies to be dragged, sir."

General Quinn stared at the elf. "She doesn't look half dead to me."

"Yes, sir."

General Quinn waited for a better explanation.

"In the light she's much improved."

"Perhaps I should put some lanterns down there so you can tell who's dying and who's not."

Vortigan was wise enough to not say another word.

General Quinn held out his hand to the elf. "Please."

She handed over the whip.

"Thank you." He threw it to the soldier who'd lost it and extended his arm to the elf, which she reluctantly took.

"So, this is the infamous son of Barsadias. Even blind his footing matches the stance of a soldier. Unable to die."

Marcus could hear the envy in his voice.

"Shall we test it?" General Quinn asked and his men cheered. "He goes, she stays."

"No!" Aleksia pulled against Quinn's arm, but he prevented her from leaving his side.

Marcus was jostled towards the rear of the ship.

The rest of the gallies were being tied back to back with a partner and thrown overboard into the Olend Sea with a long cord tethering them to the back of the ship.

They paired Marcus with another man who was far taller and broad shouldered. They put a block of wood under his feet to make him tall enough.

A rope entangled their waists and was secured with

an impossible knot around the other man's wrists, leaving Marcus's hands free. A second rope was tied around Marcus's quivering ankles.

He tried to hear the elf, to make sure she was okay, but another gallie cried out as he was tossed into the sea, splashing into the waters below. The block was knocked out from under Marcus's feet.

"Return alive and we'll let you come aboard," stated Quinn.

Marcus and the man tied behind him were shoved off the ship. His hands flailed in the open space. He heard the elf call out his name as he and the man behind him narrowly missed the spikes sticking out of the hull. They hit the sea head first.

His mouth filled with water and he laboured to breach the surface, but which way was up and which way was down? The current drew him away from the Mirtis until the rope went tight around his ankles. He coughed as his head came out of the water.

A screaming woman grabbed him, her nails ripping into his skin. Instinctively, he punched her.

Snap. He broke the woman's nose and she lost her grip.

Another hand seized his head. "Help!" the man cried.

Marcus's head went under with hardly a breath. The weight of all four of them made them sink to where a giant shadow lurked. He tore at the man's forearm and arms wrapped tighter around his neck. Pressure built up in his ears and he could feel his mind slipping.

Bursts of air escaped the man's lungs as he screamed and he was too far gone to release Marcus.

The man behind him kicked his feet, but they were too heavy.

Marcus tried to elbow the man in the stomach, but the water prevented any real power.

The man started convulsing and Marcus grew desperate.

Bending his head as far forward as he could, he found the man's arm with his mouth and bit down as hard as he could. The man's hold loosened and Marcus broke free.

He propelled his arms as hard as he could and felt the man behind him doing the same with his legs.

I need air!

He did not know how far down they were or if they were even heading in the right direction. What air he had left was escaping his lips. His lungs burned and he felt as though they were about to burst when his head finally breached the surface. He turned on his side, allowing the man behind him to breathe.

Both of them coughed, expelling remnants of water from their air passages.

"We have to get up there," said the man at his back, fighting the knot on his wrists. "Now!"

"What's your name?" asked Marcus.

"Trigon."

"Marcus."

"Any ideas of how we're going to get out of this?" pleaded Trigon.

"I'm thinking."

Something clicked, and the water shifted. It surged and an unexplainable wave passed over the gallies trailing behind the boat. They bumped into one another and Trigon came face to face with a dead man.

Trigon kicked him away with his feet.

The ship sped up and those who were still alive became frantic as the water coming from beneath the Mirtis turned black.

The woman next to Marcus screamed, blood dripping from her nose as she fought against the dead woman on her back to reach the bonds at her feet.

A foul odour overwhelmed the air and Marcus's skin felt oily. His body became encased in a foreign substance that tasted like rotten fish and he gagged.

The water shifted as something big passed under them.

Suddenly, blood sprang up amongst the gallies.

Marcus tasted it on his tongue and froze. He was back in Visadas and the man beside him had just exploded as he was running the barrier for the first time.

"I'll go under and try to propel us upwards," said Trigon. He rolled under the water and Marcus snapped back into the present.

He strained to reach the rope at his ankles.

The woman next to them cried out and disappeared. Immediately, her severed feet returned without her and he felt her rope get tangled around the cord at his ankles, giving him an idea.

The creature roared and Marcus's arms were covered in goosebumps. "Is there anyone close to you?" Marcus demanded.

"A dead man."

"Reach him with your legs."

Marcus felt Trigon move and a wave gushed underneath them. He accidentally breathed it in and his insides burned.

The jura claimed another.

"They're too far," yelled Trigon.

"Let me face him."

Trigon went under the water and let Marcus roll over him.

Marcus reached out into the darkness. "Get me towards him."

Trigon kicked his legs and Marcus used his arms until he struck something solid. It was the man's torso. Without hesitation, he used the rope on his ankles as an anchor. Gripping the dead man, he started to lever himself down the man's corpse. Every muscle in his body strained under the weight of the man attached to him. The water plunged against them as they turned horizontal. His fingers were weakening and he struggled to hold on. He could not fail.

The screams were lessening and the jura's eye would soon be on them.

The rope around Marcus's ankles dug deeper into his skin and he shouted against the pain. With a final tug they came up vertical.

Instantly, he yanked up his feet and grabbed the dead woman's severed limbs, clasping onto her rope.

The jura's green, leathery head, snatched the dead man he'd just been holding and he almost dropped the rope in the splash. Its amber eyes spotted Marcus and Trigon, and it dove under the sea. This was its only time to hunt and it wanted to make the best of it.

"Don't leave me!" cried a man who was still alive.

Marcus hesitated.

"Please!"

Trigon snapped Marcus out of the thought. "We can't go back."

Marcus knew he could possibly save Trigon and he hoped his conscious would allow that to be enough.

The man screamed and was gone.

Marcus couldn't let himself stop but his arms quivered and his hands were turning red. He reached and heaved, each move bringing them closer to the hull of the ship.

Trigon fashioned a loop of excess rope around his thigh and worked the cord through his feet, so if Marcus lost his grip they wouldn't have to start from the beginning.

They reached the hull, as the last of the others were eaten.

Marcus fastened his feet against the hull, unsure if he'd be able to carry himself and Trigon to the top. His arms shook as he pulled himself up out of the sea with Trigon on his back.

The water churned underneath them, and Marcus prayed the creature was satisfied. The eel-like creature had only to raise its head and it would have them within its powerful jaws.

They were about to reach the spikes and safety when the soldiers above started throwing stones from their catapults.

A rock hit Marcus in the head and he lost his grip. He swung upside down, hitting the ship, shutting his eyes in pain.

Trigon hollered as both their weights were suddenly on the loop around his leg.

Blood dripped from Marcus's hairline into the water,

summoning the beast.

The jura surged out of the water.

Trigon cried and Marcus shoved himself between the jura and Trigon, opening his eyes.

Light penetrated Marcus's sight, and he looked down with inhuman eyes. The world was spinning and in the shadows he saw something large moving towards him. He knew he was staring straight into the face of the jura.

The jura roared loud enough to make a man's ears bleed; it struck against the bottom of the Mirtis and dove into the waters from which it came.

Marcus felt the ship go even faster. His ears were ringing and he felt so disoriented he thought he was going to be sick. He shut his eyes to calm himself, but when he opened them again, he saw nothing. He hung there, unable to comprehend what happened. He had been at the jura's mercy and yet it fled when it looked into his unblinded eyes.

The crew watched from above, but it was Trigon who brought Marcus back to reality.

"Are you hurt?" The man's voice was shaking.

Marcus could hear his pain and stretched out his hand to take the rope and relieve his suffering. "No."

It took some time to reach the top. Marcus couldn't see and Trigon's only view was the horizon, but once they were between the spikes, it was easier. Trigon stepped onto unsharpened sides and lifted Marcus high enough to grab the next one.

When Marcus finally felt the ledge, he let himself fall onto the deck. His chest heaved and every muscle in his body ached.

He heard the elf's sigh of relief and knew she was alright.

Neither he nor Trigon had time to catch their breath. The soldiers cut them loose and they were brought to their feet.

Marcus felt as though he was going to collapse, but a hand was holding him steady.

Someone approached and General Quinn spoke. "Wonders never cease. Take them below deck. She stays with me."

Aleksia, thought Marcus. He sprung into action, using the last of his strength to jostle himself out of the soldier's grip. He ran towards where he'd heard the general's voice and was knocked out cold.

XXXVI

GENERAL QUINN'S CABIN

Aleksia exhaled what seemed like her first breath since she'd seen Marcus thrown off the back of the ship. Her relief quickly turned to fury as she watched General Quinn's men toss Marcus's unconscious body into the hull. Looking around the deck, she noted the number of soldiers and the weapons each of them carried. General Quinn's sword was close enough to steal, but she wasn't sure what he was capable of. The magical stone on his ring had not escaped her notice either.

"Take her to my cabin," commanded the general. "There are a few things I must tend to."

A soldier took her by the arm and Aleksia considered tossing him to the side and jumping ship. *I could make it*. She stared yearningly at the waters, but she was far from at peace with it.

Marcus was below deck. So instead she allowed the soldier to guide her to the general's cabin and lock her in.

Aleksia hesitated before taking another step into the darkening room. The walls seemed to enclose around her like a cage until something caught her eye.

There in front of her was a large mirror. Her reflection was without blemish. She'd never seen herself in a mirror. They were a luxury only the rich could afford. The only place she ever saw herself with any clarity was between the ripples of a stream. She'd changed much since she'd last seen herself. Her cheeks were shallower and her brown hair a tangled mess. The vertes sparkled within the image of the silver frame.

The interwoven silver branches bordering the reflective surface were unparalleled. Aleksia drew closer. It must have been made by magic. There wasn't a chisel mark from an artist on it.

Aleksia lifted her hand to touch it, sensing an energy emanating from the mirror. Her finger touched the centre and it began to ripple.

Daylight pooled from the mirror and filled the darkness around her. The image within the frame shifted and transformed into a snowy landscape.

It showed her the same summit from her dreams. She saw herself climbing the mountain peak, battling the elements to reach the ledge above her. The rope, tied around her waist, stretched above and below her, but whoever was with her was hidden from the frame.

Someone pushed her onto the ledge and she strained to see who it was. She saw herself rise to her feet and over her shoulder was the strange black furred deer with eyes veined in silver. It was bleeding from the base of its horns, the blood trickling down its brow, just missing its eyes.

Aleksia watched herself take a step backwards and cover her ears as a loud sound erupted from outside her sight. The buck stood on its hind legs as fire consumed it.

More images took the place of her dream. Visions she'd never seen. A young woman with olive skin and dark hair, screaming as she was being dragged to the depths of a body of water. A sea of dead eyes being devoured by rats and decay. A bird with wings of fire, pulsing towards the mirror. She felt the heat on her face until the image changed into an elf sitting in a dark cell, his skin the same colour as his black clothing. The Sapphire King Sarrgen of the dwarves, sound asleep on his throne, covered in cobwebs and surrounded by a room that sparkled blue.

And then she saw Marcus. His face covered in fresh wounds. General Quinn shoved him into a wall and rammed his sword into Marcus's chest. Marcus cried out in pain and slumped to the ground.

Aleksia nearly let go of the mirror until she saw Zoren. The four elements floated in his hands, his arm covered in crystal clear vertes and his eyes looking straight at her. Aleksia released the mirror and turned away, cupping her face in her hands as she wished she could unsee what the mirror had revealed.

The mirror returned to normal as she stammered away from it.

The king, she thought, feeling like he actually saw her.

All those people she neither knew nor recognized. What did they all mean? Were they literal or symbolic?

The visions burned inside her mind as though she were seeing them over and over again. She needed to escape. The room only had one window, and it was a skylight above General Quinn's desk. Aleksia pulled out the chair and climbed onto it. Maps of the coast and ports along the shoreline shuffled against her feet.

He might have a map to Visadas. But there was no time to search between the pages. General Quinn could arrive at any moment. She stood on the table to see if she could break through, but it was to no avail. The window was barred with iron. She could hear two soldiers guarding the door and a host more of them on the deck. She was alone in the room, and she made the best of it. Jumping off, she searched for anything she could use to defend herself. There were no weapons on the walls, only a violent painting of General Quinn kneeling to King Zoren at the centre of the Aurelius. Red rose pedals were falling all around him and the carnage in his wake, like he was some kind of saviour.

Seeing no weapons on the wall, she ran to his bed and searched under the mattress and pillow, finding nothing. The general must have kept every piece of weaponry on his person at all times.

Aleksia searched everywhere she thought might have been a good hiding spot. She returned to the desk and rummaged through its drawers. She settled for sharp objects and wasn't disappointed. There were a few options. A couple of quills tipped with a metal edge, and a letter opener.

Aleksia heard a creek at the door and snatched the

letter opener, placing it against her thigh and holding it tightly under her hand as she stepped into the growing shadows of the room.

Two slaves came in. A man carried two plates on a decadent platter. The woman followed and cleared away the items on the desk, putting them in their proper place. They set up a table for two, lighting the lamps attached to the walls, and as they were leaving, General Quinn stepped over the threshold.

Aleksia's throat went dry. She stood her ground and held her head high, the letter opener cool to the touch in her fingers. She'd never killed anyone, but if it came to it, she wasn't sure how tightly she could hold on to that conviction.

General Quinn approached the table and tore off a piece of the succulent chicken, placing it in his mouth. He licked his fingers as he looked to the corner where Aleksia pressed herself further.

"Please. Take a seat." He motioned to the chair opposite him.

Aleksia considered staying put, but she saw no danger sitting across from him. If anything, it would be a relief to have a table between them. Aleksia sat down, sitting as far back in the chair as she could.

General Quinn poured two glasses of wine and slowly pushed one glass toward her. "Please."

Aleksia took the glass with her empty hand but didn't drink.

"It'll calm your nerves," assured Quinn.

"I'm not nervous," replied Aleksia, refusing to put anything this man had to offer down her throat. The scent of the cooked bird saturated the entire room, making Aleksia want to gag. She loathed the taste of meat and was unsure if it was a quality all elves shared.

General Quinn sipped from his own glass, then picked up his fork and knife. "Tell me your name."

Aleksia looked at her place setting and to her disappointment, saw no knife.

"Aleksia." She turned the letter opener in her hand.

"Aleksia, I'm General Quinn," he said, noticing her disappointment. "I'd offer you a knife, but I don't think that would be very wise of me. I've seen women practice in the Aurelius and from what I've heard, you possess that quality. Have you ever been to the arena?"

"Men senselessly killing one another isn't something I take pleasure in."

"Hardly the word of a citizen."

He couldn't be more right, thought Aleksia.

"I myself have fought in the arena and it made me a better soldier. Hunting was a passion of mine as a boy. I would miss worship at the temple and meals at the barracks more than most. I've led battles and killed many, but when I entered the arena, it was liberation. The crowd watching my every move, thirsting for my blood, and my prey as armed and well trained as I was— I felt peace and more power than I'd ever known." He instinctively held his ring and moved it around his finger.

"Some prey are beyond reach," indicated Aleksia.

General Quinn smirked, taking another bite of his chicken. "Yes, but sometimes if you wait patiently with the right bait, it'll come to you."

"If you have the right bait."

"Every animal eventually falls prey to the knife or the spear. Especially if it's defective." The general cut off a piece of the chicken and held it in front of him. "Chickens are one of the few birds that remained in Remisia after the fall of the elves. They're domesticated and fattened, and even they have an eye for weakness within the flock. When a chicken comes up short to the standard of the rest, the strong will peck it to death. They aren't the smartest of creatures, but even they know the importance of strength. It was a kindness to put the bird out of its misery."

"How would you determine whether someone is strong or weak?"

General Quinn ate the piece of chicken. "The sword."

The sight of Marcus being stabbed by Quinn flashed in her mind and her voice faltered as she spoke. "Not everyone's strength is combat."

"No," he scoffed. "No it isn't. For some it's magic."

Aleksia held her pathetic weapon even tighter. *Did he know what she was? Had he seen her use the mirror?*

General Quinn wiped his face with a napkin. "And that is why I have brought you here."

"I have no magic," said Aleksia, hoping he'd agree.

"No, but in the mines there are many slaves who have been left unchecked. The magical bloodlines of our citizens have been tracked and exhausted. The king requires fresh blood. It's not often we have a woman of your caliber amongst the slaves and if you were to agree to help me seek them out, I can make your life easier in the mines."

General Quinn stood and looked into the mirror. "This mirror can only show me the present. I look into it and I see whatever is around me, but to a seer it can reveal so much more. Answer questions of what's to come."

"Why not ask a slave to be your spy?" inquired Aleksia.

Quinn turned back to her. "You're superior," he smirked, "and they'll already despise you. Slaves fear what the others might do to them if they were discovered."

Aleksia rose to her feet, ready to leave the room. "So do I."

"Are you certain? If you refuse, you will go down into the belly of Ironwood and dig like anyone else."

"I am."

"Guard."

The door opened and a soldier came into the cabin. He stood at attention.

General Quinn approached Aleksia, stroking her arm until he took hold of her hand. "I'll have my letter opener back please."

Aleksia let it drop.

"Thank you." He got even closer to her and moved a few strands of her hair behind her ear. "If you change your mind, let one of the guards know and they'll bring you right to me."

Aleksia could not express her relief when he let her go. She heard him tell the soldier to take her away. Her heart was beating so loud she couldn't hear what he said. She was eager to go back to her oar down below and escape the sight of this man. He made her skin crawl, and she didn't regret refusing his offer. She would dig in the mines with joy if it meant she didn't have to have another civilized conversation with him. All she wanted to do was take his sword and run him through. Maybe she could prevent what she saw in the mirror from ever happening.

The soldier took her back to her spot next to Marcus, and when they were gone, her body shook. She needed to talk to Marcus. She thought he was asleep until he took her hand in his and gave it a slight squeeze.

"Did he hurt you?"

"No," whispered Aleksia.

"Good," he said, his eyes flickering open.

"Are you alright?" she asked.

"I didn't think I would be." Marcus exhaled. "What did he want from you?"

"He wanted me to be a spy."

"A spy?"

"King Zoren is searching for more magicians and General Quinn thought I might point them out to him."

"It's good you told him no. If anyone here found out —I'm not sure what would happen. I'm relieved that's all he wanted." Marcus wrapped his arm around her and for some reason Aleksia couldn't help but feel safe.

"I couldn't believe it when you made it up the side of the ship with that man on your back. I thought you were dead when that rock hit you and you went upside down."

Aleksia felt Marcus's body go tense.

"Marcus?"

Marcus held her tighter and took a deep breath. "Something happened—there was a moment—I saw light and shadows, but it was so bright I had to close my eyes. And when I reopened them, I saw nothing."

"You could see?"

"I don't know. It's never happened to me—I can't explain it."

Aleksia recalled the roar of the jura and how it struck the bottom of the ship.

"I saw something up there too."

"What?"

"General Quinn had a mirror in his cabin and I saw things."

Marcus listened to every word.

"I've had this dream ever since I was a child. I used to tell it to my guardians, but they could never give me any explanation. Eventually I stopped telling them about it. In the dream, I'm climbing a mountain. It's snowing and there are people with me, but I can't see them. Someone pushes me onto the ledge and I see a deer. It's got a black hide and is wounded. I hear a sound like thunder and the deer is encased in fire and I wake up."

"Have you ever seen this mountain?" asked Marcus.

"I don't know." Aleksia tried to recall it, but she couldn't. "It's possible."

"I thought—" Marcus stopped himself from saying elf, in case anyone was listening. "You remembered everything."

"Usually." Aleksia felt the empty space on her wrist where there should have been a vertes. Elves were supposed to recollect the first time they saw their mother's face. "There are things from my childhood I can't remember, like they were taken from me. I remember nothing before I lived in the cabin."

"So it could be a memory," said Marcus.

"Or a warning," rationalized Aleksia. "I saw more."

Aleksia quietly told him about the other images she saw. The drowning girl, the elf in a jail cell, and all the others. But her voice faltered as she got to the vision about Marcus.

"I saw—I saw you in the mirror."

"Me?"

"Yes."

"What happened?"

"You were fighting General Quinn—and you lost."

Marcus sat back in his seat. "You mean I died."

"We can prevent this."

"How?"

Aleksia thought of the vision. How General Quinn knocked Marcus against the wall and ran him through. The pain on Marcus's face as he fell. "In the vision you were blind—" And then the thought came to her. "I'm going to restore your sight."

"No!" Marcus exclaimed a little louder than he should have, before returning to a whisper. "Zoren can't find you because of me."

"He won't. We'll have to choose our moment wisely and escape."

"Escape to what?"

"Freedom. Not just for ourselves, but for everyone else."

"You sound like Favil. She always spoke of the rising."

"Think about it."

Aleksia looked at Kilroy, Marwin, and Tavin sleeping next to her. This could not be their fate or anyone else's. To live under a whip forever and these three hadn't lived their whole lives this way. The rest of the rowers on the ship knew nothing of freedom. They had never been free to decide, not even what they wanted to eat. It was all dictated to them. To give them the freedom to choose what they wanted to do with their lives and fight for it would be worth it in the end. No matter the price.

Aleksia could see Marcus turning the thought in his mind, going through the scenarios and conclusions. She appreciated he was taking her seriously, but from the look on his face, she could tell his answer wasn't going to be what she wanted to hear.

"It can't be done."

"Not on our own."

"There's nowhere to go."

A soldier came down the ladder and ended their conversation.

Marcus shut his eyes and lay his head against the oar behind him, and Aleksia rested against him. She knew what she wanted to do, but she doubted Marcus would ever follow her there. If they did escape, there was only one place they could run. The one place Zoren hadn't been able to find. They would have to run to the elves. Perhaps they could interpret her dream and unweave the mystery of her past.

XXXVII

IRONWOOD

In the early stirrings of the morning when the sun had barely pierced the night sky, Marcus noticed a change in the activities of the crew overhead. A high-toned gong sounded as the mist parted and Ironwood emerged at the top of the plateau.

Soldiers hurried down the stairs, smacking the heads of the rowers who were still asleep.

"Up! Up! Up!" they shouted.

"Prepare to come into harbour!"

Whips cracked against those reluctant to wake.

"Take oars!" commanded Vortigan.

Marcus grabbed the oar and pushed it out to the beat of the drum. He knew he could row today. It was the last day he would ever have to. The drum struck again and Marcus felt Aleksia aligning the oar into position as they dragged it into the sea.

The Mirtis reached the ridge and the drum stopped.

The oars were brought in and the Mirtis was pulled to the dock.

The harbour of Ironwood was a grand place of industry in Remisia. The waters reached so deep next to shore, ships could pull right alongside the rock face.

The deck hands threw the tethering lines to slaves waiting on the dock, and the soldiers started unlocking chains on the rowers. The slaves headed to the mines were easy to distinguish from the ones sentenced to life as a gallie. No woman had ever been permanently placed on a galley ship, and every man headed to the mines wore a shirt and pants, unlike the gallies who were only permitted a loincloth.

The rattle of chains coming undone made Marcus want to lift his legs as high as they could go so they'd be able to unchain him sooner.

When the soldier finally came to Marcus, he looked at him curiously. Seeing his dress and family crest, he put the key into the lock and turned it, releasing Marcus and shoving him to his feet.

Marcus stood and his muscles protested the unfamiliar feeling. Blood rushed to his brain and his mind pulsed. His balance was unsure, and he reached for something to steady him.

Kilroy reached behind Aleksia as the soldier began unchaining her to steady him.

Marcus instantly felt his relief of leaving the Mirtis being tainted by the hundreds of souls they were leaving behind. Kilroy reaching out to him was like the plea of the entire ship, yearning to leave as well. This man had helped him save Aleksia, warning him when the guards were looking, and over the days they'd gotten to know them a little in the few moments they were able to chat. Aleksia had done most of the talking, but Marcus heard the toil in their voices.

Kilroy's grip was lost when the soldier pushed Marcus into the dark abyss. He had no anchor to tell him which way to go. Stretching out his hands, he tried to walk, but collided into people who shoved him away.

A hand took his and he recognized her touch.

Aleksia.

Without a word spoken between them, she stepped ahead, guiding him towards the ladder they hoped to never go down again. The line slowed to a stop the closer they got to the back, but every few moments, Marcus felt Aleksia lead him. He didn't know what he would have done without her and he was surprised her touch was becoming more of a comfort than a reminder of the barriers.

Aleksia climbed the ladder and she took his hand and put it around her ankle so he'd know when to step up.

At the top stood a man inspecting the 'inventory' being taken off the ship, checking each slave's teeth, shoulders, and eyes. Once a slave was cleared, an iron brace was clenched around their neck and a chain through a loop on the side to link them all together.

Aleksia was cleared without incident, but the overweight slave runner, Tarlock, took a single look at Marcus and cringed.

"Blind?" he exclaimed. He gestured his fat fingers to take Marcus back where they found him. "Got no use for a blind man in the mines."

Marcus lunged, but two soldiers nabbed him before he could take a step.

Tarlock kicked Marcus in the gut and he lost his balance, falling backwards over the hole to the gallies.

Marcus spread his limbs out wide and gripped the sides, suspending himself over the hole. His arms strained under his own weight as he tried to lift himself.

A slave pushed him up from behind, cheering him on.

Marcus didn't get enough momentum to stand upright, but he rolled out of the hole. He leapt to his feet and a grip, solid as iron, clasped itself around his neck and suspended him in the air.

"You again," said General Quinn. He saw the guards holding Aleksia back from intervening. "And you."

Marcus struggled to break free as the oxygen to his brain ceased. General Quinn's arm wasn't even shaking under the strain of his weight.

Captain Vortigon stepped in to explain. "He refused to go back down to the gallies."

"He refused?" Quinn stared the man down. "Or your men lacked the skill to subdue a forsaken?"

The captain's cheeks flared red with wounded pride, but he kept silent.

General Quinn didn't let Marcus go as he turned to Tarlock. "He goes."

Tarlock huffed. "I got no use for him."

General Quinn tossed Marcus to a few of Vortigon's men. "None the less." And he descended off the boat.

Marcus grasped his neck and coughed as he took a deep breath.

"I said I've got no use for him," blurted Tarlock, growing bolder.

The general's gaze stopped the slave runner in his tracks.

250

Tarlock looked apprehensively at Quinn's ring.

"Find something," said General Quinn.

Tarlock nodded his head in submission, pushing Marcus towards the rest of the slaves. An iron brace was placed around his neck as Tarlock's chest heaved with anger.

XXXVIII

THE TRENCH
OF THE DEAD

The iron around Aleksia's neck drew her up the zigzag path. The path embedded in the cliff's side wasn't much wider than a deer trail. Marcus was behind her and while the soldiers were occupied with the other slaves, she put his hand on her shoulder, and to her relief he didn't pull away. On the ship she'd felt something change between them. Instead of recoil, he'd helped her row, and when General Quinn was taking her to his cabin, he'd risen to her defence. She hoped they wouldn't go back to the way things were, now that they were off the Mirtis. It eased her to know they could have each other's backs.

Aleksia clung to the rock as the slaves unloading the Mirtis shrank from view. The unprotected trail appeared to be the only way up. *How are they going to get that from there to here?* They were placing the supplies onto a large platform and she traced the lines attached to a pulley system above. It swayed and Aleksia saw the spikes under the platform, a fail-safe in case the enemy ever tried to use it to raise an army to the top.

Marcus's foot stumbled. She grabbed his hand and he steadied.

He was a growing mystery. She'd gone over the incident with jura in her mind a hundred times. The way he'd carried a man on his back up the side of the ship and the roar of the jura as it dove back into the waters. And then he'd said he could see?

Aleksia once had a blind guardian named Myra. She was with her before Zoren started using people to get through the barriers. Myra knocked her head one day and something shifted in her pupils, and for a few moments she had sight. *Perhaps that's what happened?* Aleksia had never healed eyes. She'd been too young when Myra was her guardian.

But there was something different about Marcus. She'd known it the moment they'd met. It was deeper than his blindness. No one else knew what she was and yet he did with a single touch. It didn't make sense and it frustrated her. *Maybe my people would know what he was. Or would he be a puzzle to them as well?*

The narrow path led to a cavity in the cliff's face. Four soldiers guarded the entrance and over the iron gate was chiseled:

Ironwood
House of Life and Power

Those at the gate saw them coming and commanded

the slaves to turn the wheel and open the door.

An enemy had never taken Ironwood. Beyond the cliff, its defences went further still. Around the city was a wall, patrolled by some of Remisia's finest warriors. The mountains to the northwest prevented armies from attacking at any speed and its production of iron made Zoren's armies strong.

Aleksia peered over the ledge, and she almost stopped in her tracks. At the front of the slaves was a creature she'd only glimpsed between the cracks in the old barn. It hauled the wagons of the forsaken north into Visadas.

A lone rider sat upon this ragatis. Being so close to it, she felt its emptiness and its fear. The halter was covered in spikes to make it go in the direction the rider desired. He was a slave as much as she was.

Man had destroyed these noble and kind creatures. Only a few remained outside man's control and it broke her heart. She'd heard stories of the free ragatis. Creatures with fur as white as snow and blue, intelligent eyes. If a boy got lost in the forest, the ragatis were known to guide people back to where they needed to be. That sense was what drove them mad. They felt the suffering of the slaves. Though the ragatis had no eyes, it looked at her like it wanted to charge. It didn't want her pity.

Aleksia understood what they were feeling. To see suffering and not be able to do anything about it was to suffer.

Tarlock attached the chain, linking all the new miners to the back of the ragatis's saddle.

The soldier whipped it, and with a groan of protest

the ragatis moved, yanking the slaves behind it. Some soldiers with dogs took up the rear and the rest were staggered along the line, using their whips of torment on anyone they thought wasn't walking to their standards.

The gate had read, "House of Life," but as Aleksia followed the path into the field, all she saw was death. Rather than a field of crops or a village, there was something far more repugnant.

A graveyard.

Aleksia's eyes widened at the sea of nameless white headstones. In Remisia, it was illegal to be buried within the city walls, and citizens usually placed their dead in the mountains. *What are they doing here?*

A soldier whipped a man further back and Marcus's grip tightened. Her head turned, but as she did she saw something engraved on the reverse side of the headstones.

Azuk. Year three of the reign of our King Zoren. Another stone read, *Elf. Year twenty-six of the reign of our King Zoren.* And the names and nations continued. They were from all over the conquered nations of Remisia's empire. Elves, dwarves, men. It was like they'd buried their fallen enemies where they'd perished.

Flies flew in every direction and stray dogs fought over dug up bones. The few trees standing amongst the graves had long since withered. If a flame was lit anywhere near them, they would've caught fire in an instant.

The road ahead dropped down into a trench that spread across the edge of the valley. Aleksia noticed the slaves hesitating to walk into it and when it came to her turn, dread took root.

One man fell to his knees wailing and another tried to break free, but the chains held him in line. Most walked in stunned silence.

On either side of the dirt path was a trench filled with countless corpses. Smeared in dirt from head to toe, men, women, and children, bloated in the sun, resting on a bed of the burned who'd come before. The charred skeletons on the bottom wore armour, impaled by a forest of iron spikes that stretched around the city. No one had taken a second to put them to rest with dignity and there was no chance of loved ones ever finding them.

A sign screeched on its hinges, reading:

The Fate of Those Who Cross the Iron Wood

Aleksia had no tears or words to carry the weight of this sight. She reached up and interlocked her fingers with Marcus's.

They're skin and bone. The stillness of their bodies in the gentle wind made Aleksia feel hopeless as the red flag cautioning the death site flapped.

A rat scurried over a woman's foot to get to the fresh meat that had been dropped in the trench. She shrieked, kicking it away.

A whip broke the air to silence her.

Other rats watched them from on top, underneath, and in-between the bodies, defending their hoard. Daring the troop of new slaves to come and stop them, all the while licking their lips at their future meal.

This will not be our end, thought Aleksia, as she followed the road out of the trench. *If I have to expose what*

I am and fight every last soldier, I will.

She cursed herself. She'd sat in a cabin for hundreds of years while this nightmare was happening. Had she known, she might have fought harder to escape that life. How had her people not intervened? They knew what was happening here, and yet they did nothing to prevent it. It was only now that Aleksia fully comprehended why Marcus attacked her in the barn. He had heard what she was seeing, and he cursed her people as much as she cursed the king.

Here, surrounded by the people it was too late to save, she made a vow of vengeance, one she would fulfill, even if it cost her everything.

The king and his men will regret I ever witnessed such a sight as this.

XXXIX

HAMMER AND CHISEL

The path suddenly veered steeply down as they entered a deep crater that was bigger than the city of Masseson. Dust rose into the air, creating a haze of fog over the workers who looked like ants moving along the ledges below. The sound of hammers meeting chisels was deafening as the mine came into view. Narrow ledges, penetrated by numerous tunnels, made it look like a staircase descending into the depths of the earth. Giant wheels turned above as two slaves walked in each, pumping the water out so they could collect iron from the deepest avenues of Dirva's domain. Guard towers made of stone were posted around the circumference, armed with bows and arrows to stop any slave from escaping. For many, this was the last time they would see anything of the world beyond this point.

Aleksia watched her step and kept Marcus close as the long trail descended to a flat surface at the base of the mine. She gaped up at its size. There wasn't a tree or patch of green in sight. All she could see was the encumbering mine and the sky.

Children emerged from the holes, bringing out iron in buckets and on slabs. The little ones watched them with open curiosity as they climbed down the manmade paths and threw their iron into a wagon pulled by two ragatis.

Aleksia mirrored the children's interest. She couldn't remember being this close to one and she wanted to hear their voices and know their names. She watched them until they chased each other back up into the tunnels.

Ten downcast slaves awaited the new arrivals. The ragatis halted, and the soldiers started unshackling the new recruits.

All the slaves were organized into three lines.

Tarlock placed himself at the head of the two opposing sides. The veteran miners on one side and the recruits on the other. The veterans watched him, but Aleksia could see them scrutinizing the newcomers from the corners of their eyes.

Tarlock raised his two hands in the air, holding the suspense. He clapped, sending the ten into a flurry of activity. The overseers raced between the lines of slaves, picking and pruning the best of the new shipment.

The youngest and the strongest went first. Many stopped to look at Marcus, but they moved on to better slaves. They approached Aleksia, but none of them wanted her kind of trouble in their tunnel.

An old man covered in dirt took Marcus and

Aleksia. He was a skinny fellow and on his head sat a hat that looked older than he was. His forehead was high, intelligent, and his eyes held a small twinkle of mischief. He stared at his new recruits, his expressions partially masked by a patchy beard.

"I'm Fynbar, but everyone calls me Dig. Welcome to the first step in your eternal misery," he chuckled and walked away, his hand barely gesturing for them to follow.

The group hesitated until a whip set them in motion. They followed the old man across the mine, passing a few old buildings that held supplies, stables, and a few sleeping quarters for the guards, until they came to an old rickety shed, protected by a single guard.

The guard put a key in the lock. The chain holding it closed gave way and banged against the building's wooden side.

Dig opened the door and disappeared. He emerged holding a tool in each hand. He tossed them to the ground and stepped aside. "You'll need one of each," he explained.

The broad-shouldered man Aleksia recognized as the man Marcus bore up the side of the Mirtis, picked the tools up off the ground. A hammer and chisel.

Aleksia took Marcus's arm, leading him to the door to get their instruments, but Marcus was prevented from following. He was held back by their foreman, Dig.

The old man starred into Marcus's eyes. "Well, you're a first. Usually they're taking your lot away, not bringing ya in." He then noticed Aleksia. "An evader and a blind man."

"Yes," said Aleksia.

"I see." Dig left to speak to a guard.

Aleksia and Marcus continued to wait in the line to enter the shed, but Dig returned.

"You," he pointed to Aleksia, "Grab a hammer, and get him a chisel. You'll work together." He turned to Marcus. "You're very lucky she's a citizen, or you'd be on your own."

Dig reached inside the shed and picked up a bunch of clay lanterns, handing them to people who'd come out of the shed with their tools.

The oval lanterns of the slaves were made of clay and stone. At the top was a hole to pour the oil in and a spout holding the wick. It looked similar to a teapot with the handle. They held just enough oil to provide the workers with light to get them through the day. Once the lamps started to go out, it meant the day was coming to an end. It was the darkening sunset of the mines, though it lacked colour.

Dig walked away again, and this time the workers had learned to follow. He led them up the stairs, weaving between the seasoned workers towards the tunnels.

Men and women went by with support beams. Children scurried between them, carrying buckets and planks filled with as much iron as they could handle.

Dig grabbed a hunk of iron from a plank two children were transporting. He eventually turned onto one of the higher ledges and they passed tunnel after tunnel.

Aleksia could hear the men and women toiling away in the darkness, and she felt her heart drop as Dig stopped in front of the one they'd be traveling down.

"Hand this around." Dig tossed the piece of iron to

the nearest slave. "Take a good look at that rock. It's what you're here for." He was about to leave, but paused. "If you see a stone with magic, don't touch it. You're not a dwarf and it's worth more than your miserable life if you take its loyalty." And he headed into the tunnel.

Aleksia lit her lantern on the guard's torch and took one last glance at daylight.

It's only for a little while, she reassured herself as she walked into the hole.

At first she didn't have to bend her head, but as the tunnel twisted and turned it slowly closed in. Eventually, lanterns became the only source of light, though Aleksia could still see fairly well with her elven eyes.

She distracted herself from thinking about how far she was from the sun by pondering what Dig said about the magical stones. She didn't know much about dwarves, except that they were all male and were the best miners of magic because they couldn't use it. She'd never held a magic stone and if she was the first to touch it, it would be loyal to her and no one else. Magical stones were handed down through family lines and a magician could give it away, but she'd heard it wasn't easy.

A new light appeared ahead as the tunnel narrowed and the roof slanted. They came around a small bend and found six guards and fifty workers.

A few of the workers glanced at them, until they caught the sights of a guard and went back to work.

Dig yelled over the hammering. "See how everyone else is doing it and do the same. Find a spot and get to work."

Aleksia's hand balled into a fist as she exhaled slowly, trying to maintain her calm. The smooth handle of the hammer moved against her fingertips. She wished to have her carving knife. She wanted to create something beautiful and clear her mind.

"Aleksia?" asked Marcus.

She heard his concern, but pushed it away and concentrated on a man chiseling. Every time the hammer collided, he shifted his chisel to get a cleaner hit. Chunks of rock fell and they would kick them behind. The children came along side and picked up the broken shards. She got the idea and moved to an open spot near a small vein. Leading Marcus to it, she took his chisel and hand, placing it over the iron.

"Whenever I hit, shift it around till it connects with the wall again. And try to keep it in the same place."

Marcus nodded. "Save your strength."

Aleksia heard his tone of warning. If she hit too hard, they might suspect she was more than what she claimed to be.

The man from the Mirtis came up beside them and Aleksia watched how far his chisel went in on human strength.

Clunk. His chisel struck.

It didn't go in very deep. She would be expected to have to hit more times than him to get results.

The woman on Aleksia's other side coughed. It was deep. Purple veins trailed up the woman's feet and into her ankles. Worms were eating her from the inside.

Aleksia had to take another breath. If she couldn't carve at least she got to hit something.

Marcus held the chisel in position, and she struck it

so hard it buried itself a few inches into the wall.

Marcus's hands gave way and he cursed as he rubbed them together to relieve the pain. "I said save your strength!" He gritted between his teeth.

The tall black man next to them stared and lifted his eyebrow.

Aleksia yanked the chisel out of the wall and shoved it back into Marcus's hands. "I must've hit a soft spot." She guided it back onto the wall and hit it again, this time with a force Marcus could sustain.

"That's better," he said.

But Aleksia wished she could have hit the chisel harder.

XL

A FULL PORTION

Marcus's fingers felt foreign when they finally stopped. The vibration of the metal handle continued to pulse through his limbs. It was like a string was tied around his hand, stopping his fingers from stretching out. The fresh blisters popped and when he pressed the tips of his index finger and his thumb together, he couldn't feel them. His arm protested as he lifted it up onto Aleksia's shoulder.

People surrounded them as they followed the guards out. Everyone was so close, Marcus felt the nose of the person behind him in his hair.

As they neared the exit of the mine, Marcus heard a rumble. The closer to the exit he got, the louder the noise became and at first he couldn't make out what it was. Water rushed over the surface of stone. *It's raining outside*. It was a strange sensation. They'd been so engulfed in rock and work, they'd been oblivious to the moods of nature.

Stepping out of the mine, the rain pounded against Marcus's tired muscles. The air was clean and the dust gone. Slaves lost their footing on the slippery stone and slid into the mud.

Marcus tread carefully as they declined the mountain side onto the floor. Slaves waited at the bottom with wheelbarrows to throw their hammers and chisels into.

Aleksia took his and put it into the correct one.

The soldiers bullied them to where the slaves spent their nights. The entrance to the tunnel wasn't much larger than the openings to the mine shafts. Beside the passage, a few soldiers sat under a tent, roasting food and trying to keep the rain off as they guarded the cells.

Along the well-trodden hallway were a series of cells; all of them had iron bars from floor to ceiling. Each cell could hold a hundred slaves or more, depending on how the soldiers felt that day.

"Move it!" yelled the guards, anxious to get to their supper.

Pregnant slaves stood at each cell with pots of lentil soup and flat bread.

Marcus's stomach grumbled.

"Put your hands out," Aleksia instructed.

Marcus slowly took his hand off Aleksia's shoulder and put both hands out in front of him.

A slave woman, who looked ready to deliver her baby, saw Marcus coming. He held out his hands and she gave him a bowl with only half a portion.

Marcus took a step to leave, but a firm grip stopped him.

"Wait," said Trigon, the man Marcus saved from the jura. He addressed the slave. "He's earned a full scoop, woman."

She scowled at Trigon, who towered over both of them in size, and gave Marcus the rest of his portion.

"Don't let that happen again," Trigon warned. "You tell the others."

Trigon kept a tight grip on Marcus's shoulder as he received his bowl with his other hand. He guided Marcus into the cell and around the hole at the centre of the room.

Trigon let go of Marcus's shoulder and took his free hand, placing it against the rough wall. "Here's the wall. Lean up against it and let your back rest."

Marcus heeded the man's advice. He sat down, his back tingling as the tension shifted away and he let himself relax. This was a straw-stuffed mattress compared to the conditions on the Mirtis. He wondered if he would be able to get back up in the morning, but at least he had the night to recover. It was funny. On the galley he'd dreamed of standing, yet now he couldn't wish for anything more than to stay right where he was.

Trigon planted himself right next to him and took a bite of his soup.

"Thanks," said Marcus.

"You saved my life, and that's a debt I have to repay. I don't know what I would have done if either of us stayed on that ship. Certainly would've made my job harder."

"You would've done the same if your hands were free. Probably would have got us up faster."

"You didn't see the jura."

Marcus took another bite of his soup. *But I did.*

"There was a woman with me," inquired Marcus wondering where Aleksia had gotten off to.

"She's over looking at the hole in the floor."

"There's a hole in the floor?" said Marcus, remembering Raven's warning to avoid the cells with holes.

"It's covered by a wooden slab and someone's sitting on it."

"Why would there be a hole in the floor?" Marcus muttered thinking out loud. *What's down there?*

Trigon looked around the cell and saw that everyone was keeping their distance and Aleksia was the closest person to it. "I don't know." He studied the shivering man sitting over the hole. "But I'd keep away from it. I'm surprised she's not over here with you. You two seem to be inseparable. From getting paired up on the ship to working together in the mine. Now, you I have a debt to protect, but her, I'd happily protect for free."

Marcus was humoured by his new friend. "She can protect herself."

"I'm sure she can. The way she knocked that chisel into the wall — I wouldn't want to get her upset." Trigon took another bite of his soup and gagged. "This soup's worse than the stuff they fed us on the ship," he said as he took another bite, "Makes you forget the decent food your Mama used to make, like jumba or leek soup."

"Lymana soup?"

Trigon nearly dropped his bowl. "A citizen eating lymana?" he laughed. "I've never heard of such a thing. My previous master could have used some. Would have put some hair on his head."

"What did you do before you came here?" asked Marcus.

"I was a shield bearer to a citizen who could barely hold a sword. And he claimed I had no talent."

"Why did he sell you?"

"He was a coward. Filled his boots with his own urine every time I handed him a weapon. Been a lot of uprisings and he thought I'd challenge him to win back my freedom. Would've probably won it too if I'd had the money."

"You still might get the chance."

"I won't miss it again."

Marcus thought about Aleksia and his plan to escape and how she promised to restore his eyesight when the timing was right.

"And how did you come here?" wondered Trigon. "A blind citizen being sent to the mines must have a story."

"A long one."

"Which has nothing to do with the forsaken who crossed the barriers?" Trigon took another bite of his soup as he gave Marcus a knowing look.

Marcus took another sip of his soup and felt Aleksia sit down next to him. She was shaking. The energy of her touch pulsed through him and it relieved him to have her near. He couldn't help it. When she'd taken ill and General Quinn took her to his cabin, he wanted to protect her. In the ever-present darkness she was becoming the only thing familiar and he knew her well enough to know something beyond the work of the day made her tremble.

Trigon noticed everyone returning their bowls to the cage door. "Are you done with those?"

"Ye-Yes," said Marcus, holding out his bowl. It still had a few morsels in it, and Trigon devoured them on the way to the door.

A tear escaped the corner of Aleksia's eye. She wiped it away, but another followed. Leaning against Marcus, he wrapped his arm around her as she cried into his shoulder and he waited until she was ready to speak. It's what Favil had always done with him.

"For years all I wanted to do was escape and see what the rest of the world had to offer — after today —"

"You wish you never left."

"Part of me does," Aleksia admitted. "The graveyard. These people. I was living a lie. I knew the world was bad, but now I realize I didn't have the smallest inkling of what was going on. Every time I close my eyes —"

Marcus held her tighter. "I don't know who I pity more. The people who've met their end or the people who know it's only a matter of time."

Aleksia looked down at her hands. "Today I envied you."

"Why?"

"Because even though we walked the same path, you'll never have the faces of the dead to haunt you."

"Ghosts already haunt my memories and you never forget people burning alive in the streets and bodies boiling in the river."

"How did you survive?" asked Aleksia.

Marcus took his arm away from her and sat up. The memories of that night fought to breach the surface of his mind. The remnant of his father's infantry making their last stand. He'd run to his father's corpse and picked up his sword.

Marcus touched the brand on his palm. "I can't explain it," was all he was willing to say.

Trigon saved him from having to answer more of her questions. The two of them spoke until Marcus's eyes could no longer stay open and they all fell asleep.

XLI

LUCINDA

Marcus was sound asleep against the wall but he woke suddenly.

Something moved in the dark. A creature far bigger than a rat.

Scratch. Scratch. Scratch.

Marcus could hear a struggling breath. He shifted his head, trying to determine where the sound was coming from.

Scratch. Scratch. Scratch.

He thought of Raven's warning about the holes in the cells.

"Help," beaconed the muffled voice of a tired old woman from under the floor.

Marcus tenderly lifted Aleksia's head off his lap and started to stand.

"I wouldn't do that if I were you," whispered Dig.

"What is it?"

"Lucinda."

Small bony fingers crept between the tiny crevices where the hole ended and the board began. She clawed at the sides, shifting the dirt, trying to gain leverage.

BANG.

Lucinda struck the bottom of the board, waking the man sleeping over the hole. He threw his hands over his mouth to prevent himself from screaming. He lay down in the fetal position, whimpering as Lucinda struck harder and harder against the one preventing her from rising. The man's breath came in spurts, waiting for Lucinda to come.

Marcus moved to help.

"Stay where you are," advised Dig.

Marcus ignored him and strained to walk towards the noise, but he didn't want to hit anyone. He was about to turn and get Aleksia when Lucinda ceased.

He stood there a moment, waiting and listening. He jumped when she pounded on the base of another closed hole further down the hall. There was truly nothing he could do to help them, so he sat back down.

"What is she?" he asked.

Dig sat up. "No one knows. She's been down there as long as anyone can remember. Most believe she's a servant of Dirva, here to collect a pound of flesh for the iron we take from his earth. Every few weeks she comes up and drags a man, woman, or child down into the hole."

"What does she do with them?"

"I try not to think about it," shuddered Dig. "Those who've seen her say she's got three scars over her right eye. Some of the miners even worship her, hoping that if they pay her homage, she won't take them. But I figure there are three ways out of here. Dying, Lucinda, or being taken by the guards to something far worse."

"Where's that?" asked Marcus.

"The elven lands."

"Becoming a forsaken."

Dig clasped his hands together. "Something I've heard you're all too familiar with."

Marcus shook his head. "They die in horrible pain."

Dig pushed the conversation further. "Yeah, but I've been dying here for decades. The barriers sound like a quick way to go."

"Do you wish you were taken?"

"I'm too valuable here," said Dig proudly. "I'm a witcher of iron. I can smell a vein through five feet of rock. I've even been told I'll live long enough to see the next king rise."

"Who told you that?" asked Marcus.

"A seer."

Marcus smiled. "Favil?"

Dig's eyes widened. "You know her?"

"She lived a lot longer than most in the wagons. General Leganous kept her around after she showed him a prophecy."

The old man smirked. "Favil used to walk around the cells at night, showing people things she probably shouldn't have. A lot of people cried the day she left."

Marcus wished she'd shown him more. "I heard her voice on the field the day I was taken away. She died declaring the new king."

"It's a shame to hear she passed."

Marcus nodded and Favil's last words ran through

his mind. *The rising is about to begin and once it does, there'll be nothing you or your false king will be able to do about it.*

Dig wiped his eyes. "She knew things before they happened and she was never wrong. Every day miners come with stories of slaves turning on their masters. It's only a matter of time and if Favil said it, you can count on it."

"Favil always knew what to say."

"You should have seen her in her younger days. She was a beauty."

Marcus smiled. "Both inside and out."

"Yes. Yes, she was," said Dig, as he went back on his side to sleep. "Yes she was."

But Marcus was awake now. He heard Lucinda striking the boards of other cells, but never heard any screams. She'd been thwarted tonight.

Marcus stretched out onto his back and heard Aleksia breathing next to him.

Aleksia. The girl. The elvian. The one who'd nearly broken his hand with the first thrash of her hammer. The guilt of their initial meeting gnawed at him. She was trying to help him and because of him, she'd lost her freedom and her guardian in one night. If he could have been her eyes to shield her from what she witnessed, he would have. The horrors of his past partnered his every step. What were a few more? She was innocent, and he wanted her to hold on to that forever. He wondered what she looked like. He'd heard others say she was beautiful. He struggled to remember what beauty was. Mizpah had been beautiful. Sometimes in his dreams he heard the sound of her voice singing him to sleep and he sought to remember it now.

The cold stone felt good against his back as he lay waiting for sleep to return, but as he did, he was unaware that another spied on him through the darkness.

On the other side of the room, a woman observed Marcus's every move with her one good eye. Scars of her own making veiled the right side of her face. Smaller scars covered her arms, legs, and back, and as Marcus fell asleep, she watched him.

XLII

THE CULL

King Zoren walked down the hall of his palace after training with Cornelius and a few of the tamrasa all afternoon. The fresh shirt on his back was seeped in sweat and his long black hair felt damp against his neck.

Time to train had run out. In the morning, he'd depart and head to the shores of Remead, where Elian found the goddess of water's underground palace. Now it was time to draw her out and face her. Paulina showed him how he would do it and he would not fail.

Zoren was passing an open window and a company of soldiers riding across the western bridge caught his eye. At the head rode Zale, General of the Centre, returning from the wars in the northern mountains of Kyrox. An untamed and unchecked people, but their borders lined the upper parts of Visadas and Zoren was determined to fence the elves in from all sides.

He changed direction to walk out and meet them. Zale and his men were dismounting and greeting the others as he arrived.

General Zale, of the five hundred and eighty-seventh legion, and son of the High Priestess, Nerva, spotted his approach. He stretched out his arm to Zoren and he seized it, giving it a single shake. He didn't wish to encourage the rumours that they were father and son, even though it was possible. He wasn't blind to their similar appearance, but Nerva had had many partners in those days. According to the laws of the temple she could never say for certain if he was Zale's father, though it was clear by the way the general looked at him, he believed it.

"How go the wars in Kyrox?"

"The people of Kyrox are cowards who shoot from behind trees. We had a few of them on the run the day I left. Tried to follow them to one of their villages, but the barbarians ran up into the trees and were gone like ghosts. In the months I've been there, I've yet to see any signs of habitation."

"They sound like elves."

"If I'd not seen the corpses myself, I would think they were elves."

Some of the soldiers passed by and Zoren patted their shoulders in welcome. He shared in the joy of their return. Unfortunately, he wouldn't have time to visit them in the barracks. Tonight, he and Zale had much to discuss.

"You must be hungry," said Zoren.

"Starved."

"You'll have to tell me all about your conquests as

we dine," asserted Zoren. "I'll meet you in the courtroom as soon as we've both cleaned up."

Zoren went to his chambers. The double door balcony was opened, and the curtains caught in the gentle breeze. A tub of hot water simmered at the end of his bed and he slipped out of his dirty clothes and sank himself into the lavender leaf water. It wasn't as warm as he'd hoped, but he fixed that by igniting his hand in flame. He placed his hand against the side of the bath and the metal underneath him became searing hot. Since he'd drank the blood of Casiro, he could sustain boiling water. It drove the servants mad, but it soothed his tired muscles.

Cornelius had been relentless in their training and he was about ready to drive a knife through his green eyes. One more session with the old man and he might have. The water steamed against his limbs, dripping back into the rolling water. He wondered what it would feel like to control it. To bend it to his will and make it defy its own nature. It wouldn't be long. The power of controlling it was just beyond his fingertips.

He soaked longer than he should have and got up to dry himself off. On the silver bedspread was a purple tunic. He'd never really liked the colour, but since becoming king it grew on him. Silver and purple were the colours of the king's trees and he wore them proudly. He pulled the tunic over his head and thought of the leaves his trees used to have.

The elves claimed he'd poisoned the realm of Remisia with his lust for power and that was why the leaves had disappeared. He did not agree. The reason the leaves were gone was because he'd made the people strong enough to survive without their shelter. The fat of the land had been trimmed and now it thrived.

King Zoren looked at his arm. A few more of the vertes had turned black. He pulled them off and opened a secret compartment in the leg of his bed. He retrieved a small purple pouch and poured its contents onto the mattress. A pathetic number of the vertes remained and he'd told no one except General Quinn. He was desperate to find another elvian and take over Amarisa soon, or perish. He'd only two more elements to capture and rumour was Brisa, goddess of wind, held her kingdom in the heavens over Kyrox. Soldiers spoke of hearing her sing on the winds of evening, lulling the world to sleep with a gentle breeze.

He needed to be at full strength if he was to leave the shelter of his trees. He put a few of the remaining vertes on his arm and power surged through his veins.

Dressed, he headed towards the courtroom where General Zale and the rest of the council were waiting. He sat at the head of the table and Zale took his place next to him as the rest of the party did the same.

A gong was struck and the room filled with the smells of venison. Zoren hadn't noticed how hungry he'd been until he smelled it.

A young woman Zoren knew to be the cook's daughter, Miriam, brought in a plate of biscuits to go with the meal. He watched as General Zale's eyes never left her.

King Zoren wanted to grin, but he didn't want to give himself away. He knew the attraction his poor general had for the young woman, but he'd never give in to it. Zale's oldest son, Tavin, rowed on a galley ship because he loved a slave, and he refused to do the same. The poor general would head home and take his frustrations out on his own wife. It amused the king tremendously to watch him catching a glance of her.

The conversation started light and amusing. They caught up on the happenings of Kyrox as General Zale told stories of the victories and defeats in the north. He'd left his armies in the care of his Commander Dulius, whom he trusted to carry on the good work.

"Went by my sister's place on the way here. Had a few upset slaves nailed to her gates," Zale laughed.

Zoren leaned back in his chair and ensured all the slaves had left the room. "Word of Marcus's crossing, despite our efforts, is beginning to spread amongst the slave population. A population that outnumbers our soldiers twenty to one. I think the time has come for us to propose a cull."

A slave walked in the door and dropped his water pitcher. It shattered across the floor but no one said a word.

Zoren continued. "Our men can only contain so much and their number has grown too great."

Kinkade spoke, "How many?" His eyes eager.

"A quarter."

"I agree with Zoren," stated General Zale.

The council members exchanged glances. Augustus's face reddened and Leon took another sip of his water while Kinkade smirked at the prospect of a good hunt. Of course General Zale agreed. He'd yet to defy a single order. He wasn't like General Barsadias, who'd questioned his every idea. In a way, Zoren missed that. He wondered if his son Marcus would've been the same.

Apparently, he was fairing far better than expected. He'd faced a jura and lived to tell. The gods had shown favour to the son of his former general, but the unrest amongst the slaves wouldn't be tolerated.

Zoren had them exactly where he wanted. He'd been patient. If he'd suggested it in a previous meeting, they would have dismissed it without a second thought.

Cassius broke the silence. "Your Highness, this is a decision that should not be made lightly."

Council member Brennen concurred. "Word should be sent to other cities to hear if they agree."

Augustus hesitantly spoke as well. "There is much labour to lose if we do this. A cull will stir up much dissension among the slaves."

"It is a necessary risk," rebuffed Kinkade, loosing interest in his meal.

"It's been decided," declared King Zoren, ending the dispute before they'd have to call another election. "General Printis's letter of approval arrived this afternoon. The cull will begin on the eve of the next full moon."

"But the farms and the mines —"

"Will have more than enough bodies to keep them going," said Zoren. "Right now the number of slaves is too great and what good is a sword against an avalanche?"

Augustus smacked the table. "Shouldn't you wait to announce it? When the slaves hear our plan, they'll riot even more."

"The strongest of our citizens will hold them off, but our soldiers have become content. If there are soldiers, like Marwin, who abandon their posts at the first sight of an oncoming storm, then our men deserve to be usurped by those beneath them. There is no room for weakness in our ranks and as long as I draw breath I will not witness the destruction of our people again. The sword of Remisia will be sharp and ready to strike. We are close to finding Amarisa. I've never felt it stronger than I do now. General Leganous saw a vision of our soldiers fighting beneath Gretafold's tree. If we go to war against our strongest enemy, we must go into it with the best of our warriors."

The slave cleaning the pieces of clay off the floor moaned and caught Zoren's attentions. "Send your messengers."

The slave's head hung low and his body was shaking.

King Zoren spoke to him. "I can see this has upset you."

The council searched amongst themselves to see who Zoren was speaking to.

The slave raised his head, his red eyes full of disdain. "Yes."

"Why?"

"You talk about people like they are cattle for the slaughter."

"I've seen the insides of both and from what I've seen they are similar."

"And then you claim you do not hold the sins of the father against the son, when all you have done is that. What are my sins that you would persecute me?"

Zoren tossed a knife onto the floor and kicked it towards the slave.

He picked it up and rose to his feet.

"Do you wish to kill me?" provoked Zoren.

"Yes," he admitted, but he made no move to do so.

King Zoren watched the man's eyes, fascinated by the war within. He was balancing the scales of whether he could or whether he should. He most definitely did not have the skill, but if he succeeded, Zoren revelled in the very idea.

"You would curse yourself?" Zoren taunted, as the slave's knuckles whitened. "You would live a hundred years, I'll give you that, but every day would be a torment as your body slowly decays while you're still alive. The agony would only increase, until one day you'd pass into Valganen and burn. Only two have ever attempted it. The one even came back for seconds. Yet here I am."

The slave placed the knife on the floor in front of him. "I cannot."

"And I cannot allow you to live. Rhyland."

The tamrasa jumped down from his perch where he'd been hiding.

"Please ensure word of the cull does not reach the slaves before the masters."

A high-pitched screech blared from the back of Rhyland's throat.

The slave tried to run, but he was caught between the gnashing teeth of a hideous creature. The slaves bones crunched within its jaw as Cassius turned away and Kinkade perked up in his seat to get a better vantage point.

No one could dispute the king's declaration, though Zoren could tell by the way some of them held their heads, they did not agree. No one openly challenged him. Not even the queen of the elves had the power to defeat him. All of them were children, and he was their father, trying to lead them through life as they passed and he carried on.

"I've an early morning. I will be leaving by horseback first thing."

"You're not going to ride on the wings of one of your abominations?" cringed Cassius as the bones of the slave's back cracked in half.

"My mother shrieks at the sight of them. If she's to be there to wish me farewell, I'll take a horse out of the city and ride on Horus's wings till I reach Remead."

"Of course, Your Highness."

"Sleep well, Your Majesty," said Livius, who'd not spoken a word throughout the entire meal.

King Zoren headed back to his chamber, and as much as he wanted to sleep, his mind would not stop going over Cornelius's lessons. Vandus was strong. If he was found wanting in front of his men, word would spread of his failure and that would not be a good thing right before the cull was announced. But if he was triumphant, there would be no one to question him. What it would feel like to control water consumed his thoughts. He fantasized what it would feel like to wield it in war until his mind drifted and he fell asleep.

His slumber didn't last long; it was dark when his eyes opened. He heard the rooster calling.

Why didn't the elves take the chickens as well? he thought sourly, dismissing the notion to hunt the animal down and butcher it.

He readied himself, setting his armour over his chest and placing every weapon he carried in its spot. A knife was all he required to slice open the goddess, but it comforted the men to see a sword on his hip. Made them believe he was still human.

King Zoren was ready far earlier than expected. He thought of going to the garden but he couldn't face her today. Lina would want him focused on the plan and he was determined to make her proud.

He went and had breakfast at the barracks. Not many of the boys were up yet, but when they saw him at a table with a bowl of porridge, they came over to sit with him. He recognized a few of them from the arena and offered a few pieces of advice. All of them scrambled to get close to Zoren's table, admiring his armour. He sat with them until the gong rang.

"Are you coming with us to prayers?" asked one of them.

"Not today." Zoren stood up off the bench. "I'm heading on a hunt."

The boy nodded his head. "May it be a fruitful journey."

King Zoren thanked him and left. Half of his council were standing on the steps of his villa, along with General Zale. The other half of the council were at the temple.

"Where were you this morning?" questioned Cassius, whom Zoren wasn't at all surprised had weaselled his way to the farewell.

"I had breakfast at the barracks this morning," said Zoren. "They served porridge."

Queen Cecilia came down the steps with her newest maid. His mother looked solemn, like she was on the verge of a breakdown, upset her son was leaving.

Priestess Nerva was the last to arrive. "I apologize if I've held you up. You forget how many people travel to the temple when you're always there to lead it."

"You honour us by being here," responded Zoren.

The high priestess pulled out the piece of burnt offering from a bundle wrapped in white cloth. He opened his mouth and she fed it to him. She took his hands in hers and closed her eyes.

May Dirva's iron keep you safe
And give you a solid ground to stand on.

May Casiro's fire light your journey
And keep you warm on the coldest night.

May Vandus's water keep you from thirst
And the blood of righteousness flowing in your veins.

May Brisa's winds fill your lungs with the purest of air
And show your journey favour.

Go with Karas's skill in battle and Elvian's will to live.
And may you be blessed.

"Look to the end," said everyone present.

Nerva pulled out a small vat of oil and stroked the lids of his eyes. "Look to the end and see the victory of war, not the shadow of a single battle." She kissed him on the lips and stepped away to stand at her son, General Zale's, side.

Zoren went to his mother and stood a few steps below her like the young boy he once was. She reached

287

out and held his face, her eyes pleading him to stay.

"Lina's too close to her time for you to leave now," she whispered.

And Zoren knew where her mind was that day. Rather than fight with her he lied. "I'll be back this afternoon."

Queen Cecilia relaxed. "I see the child will be born in the evening. You will not miss it," she smiled.

King Zoren stepped up and kissed his mother's cheek. "I'll see you soon." He saw the love in her eyes and it was enough. Zoren was given a water canteen and two soldiers rode up in armour to join him until he reached the field where Horus was waiting. He strode down the steps and mounted his horse, not looking back at his fragile mother waiting on the steps for his return.

XLIII

SHIVERS

Marcus felt like he'd been at Ironwood for years, even though it had only been a few days. The routine was unchanging. They'd wake up, eat, dig, eat, and go to sleep. Like a bee in a beehive, his only mission was to create honey and serve the monarch until the day he died. In a way, he wasn't far off. Honey bees never seemed to stop working until the sun went down and they followed without question.

The miner's day started with the sun and ended with the moon. Marcus had memorized the steps between the cells and the tunnel. He'd counted, but he'd yet to make it there and back on his own. With so many people around, it was easier to let Aleksia or Trigon lead him through the obstacles.

Every morning Trigon woke them up and pushed them towards the cell doors. During the first few mornings of their stay, Trigon realized that the people latest to breakfast wouldn't get a slice of flatbread to hold their porridge in. Without the bread, eating the porridge was a messy affair, and they ended up losing most of it on the ground.

Trigon vowed after the first time it would never happen to them again, and so far they'd been successful.

The woman who'd denied Marcus his full portion the first night never tried to give Marcus a half ration again. He sensed Trigon staring down at her every morning and evening, making sure she wouldn't. And to Marcus's disbelief, he noticed his figure was growing a bit. His ribs weren't as deep and the shallows of his cheeks were filling in. Holding the chisel while Aleksia hammered against it was the easier task. At the end of the day he had to massage the tendons, but the calluses on his hands hardened.

The food was better than anything he'd had in the wagons. It didn't taste good, but if he was to survive, he ate it no matter how sour the raisins.

His survival had become Trigon and Aleksia's mission. He hadn't fully accepted Trigon's life debt, and he did not feel worthy of the level of loyalty the man had shown him. While he was grateful, he wished he could offer something in return. Every once in a while Aleksia went off to help someone else and he could tell it gave her a peace of mind to know Trigon would pick up the slack.

Trigon filled the hours with song, much to the delight of those around him, and today they joined in. Keeping in rhythm to the movements of their tools, it made the day go by faster. The man had the vocals of a true baritone, reaching the lower notes with ease as he switched from songs of love, to songs of harvests and yesteryear. The guards made no efforts to stop them, so long as they kept working.

I once knew a lass
All covered in grass
With the heart of a dragon or two

I saw her one day
On a much higher plain
Shouting out at the Mountains of Rune

Cursing the stars and the skies
Asking all questions why
She's there

No one could hear her
And no one would see her
She cried for the one who'd prove true

Her river of hair
Running loose as the bear
She searched in the valley bellow

Day after day
In her heart grew dismay
For the one that she searched for was gone

Cursing the stars and skies
Asking all reasons why
He'd gone

Never believing
It all was deceiving
She cried for the one who'd prove true

The miners broke into another verse, but the hairs on Marcus's arm stood up and he nearly dropped the chisel as Aleksia was about to hit it.

Aleksia grabbed the chisel and held it straight. "Keep it like this."

"Sorry," Marcus said, ignoring his instincts and refocusing, but he couldn't shake the feeling that something was amiss. It crawled on the edges of his mind and he didn't even realize the labourers changed to a different tune. He listened for the conversations beyond, the ones that spoke only in whispers, but with the singing and hammering and chiseling it was impossible.

The day was barely half over and he felt like his arms were going to fall off. The aches and pains increased by the minute, but as the day passed, the numbness of repetitive work set in.

Lamps flickered and a few of them went out. They were on the brink of evening when the soldier who'd been standing next to the scar-faced woman approached. But it wasn't Marcus he sought.

A soldier with three scars covering half his profile placed his hand on Trigon's shoulder, turning him around to face him.

"You're with me," said the soldier, shoving Trigon towards the exit. "There's a fresh load of timber and I want it moved before dark."

Trigon made eye contact with Aleksia, silently

asking her to look out for Marcus until he got back. It was only when Aleksia nodded, Trigon gestured the soldier to lead the way. As Trigon was leaving, he reached down and helped a little girl carry her bucket.

The rest of the digging shift was done in silence. The lead vocal had left, leaving the work to drag on until someone collapsed.

XLIV

THE SACRIFICE

Aleksia stayed her hammer. A woman cried out and crumbled to the floor.

Marcus started to say something.

"Shhh," Aleksia hushed him, taking a step back and peering from behind the man on her other side. She could barely see the woman, but she saw the soldier.

"Get up," he ordered.

The woman panted, her eyes barely open and her mouth dry. "Water," she moaned.

"You'll get water when your shift is over!" The guard drew his whip.

She tried to get up, scratching the side of the walls with her fingers, but her head drooped against the stone.

Aleksia shoved her hammer into Marcus's grasp and dashed towards her.

Dig stepped in Aleksia's path. "You might not want to do this."

Aleksia thought she saw something in Dig's eye, something he wasn't telling her. The soldier slapped the woman across the face and Aleksia forced her way past.

Placing herself between the slave and the man's fist, she shoved the guard away.

Aleksia leaned down and turned the woman onto her back. She was warm, but it was hard to tell whether she had a fever. Sweat perspired from her temple; it could have been from a day of hard labour.

"She needs water," demanded Aleksia as she looked into the man's stone cold face.

"Look at the lantern," he retorted.

Aleksia reluctantly did as she was told.

"Does it still burn?" he asked.

"Yes," said Aleksia.

"No one gets more water till the end of the day."

"She can't work without it."

"And you're going to need a new face if you don't get back to work."

Aleksia stood, planting her feet for combat. "Water first."

The soldier made no move to draw his sword. "Why help her?" he jeered. "She's no one."

"I hope someone would do the same for me."

"But would she?" he taunted. "Possibly you see a friend where you should see an enemy."

Aleksia didn't understand his meaning. He looked at her as though he had a secret. A secret she wasn't privileged to, and the heartbeat of the woman she was trying to help sped up.

Aleksia looked into the face of the woman and saw a smirk. Aleksia withdrew as the slave stood to her feet unhindered and picked up her hammer and chisel as though nothing was wrong with her.

"Marcus," she breathed, as she realized he was no longer there.

Aleksia cursed herself. The soldier tried to stop her, but she kicked him to the side and headed out of the tunnel. She followed the drag marks in the dirt until they disappeared.

She pushed herself to run faster, passing a little girl frantically picking up her fallen bucket. Whoever had taken Marcus must have knocked her over.

Why didn't I restore his eyesight? He was vulnerable, and she didn't want to guess why the soldiers had taken him. She was going to save him and then they could follow through on their plan. General Quinn wanted Marcus dead, and now he'd hatched a plan to make it so. Even on the ship, Marcus had been a target. He was nowhere close to death, yet he'd been thrown to the jura. It's why she and Trigon had an unspoken agreement to keep an eye on him. There were plenty of ways for a man to "accidentally" die in the mines and the general must have found one or they wouldn't have removed Trigon and distracted Aleksia.

She spotted Marcus as they were about to reach the opening of the tunnel. The setting sun was blinding but Aleksia could see a guard carrying Marcus on his shoulder. What puzzled her was the slave woman walking beside them.

The woman spotted Aleksia and wielded a wooden dagger. "He must be sacrificed," she hissed.

Aleksia had no idea what the woman was talking about. "Give him to me and we'll go our separate ways."

The woman charged and Aleksia tossed her aside, sending her flying to the ground.

The soldier drew his sword and let Marcus drop.

Marcus groaned, and a wave of relief flooded over Aleksia. They hadn't killed him.

The man swiped his sword through the air and Aleksia jumped backwards.

At the same time, the woman got up on her hands and knees and crawled to Marcus.

Aleksia went to intervene and the man stepped into her path. She noticed the same markings on both their faces: three slashes across the right eye. A few people in the mine had them, but she hadn't thought they symbolized anything. She'd assumed they'd all gotten the scars under the end of a whip.

The soldier sliced his sword through the air.

Aleksia stepped back, but this time she rushed him before he had time to draw it forward again. She grabbed her enemy, knocking him into a wooden pillar with the full capacity of her strength.

The earth around them rumbled. A wave of dust and rock plummeted from above. Aleksia saw the woman hauling Marcus into the sunlight, as powers beyond Aleksia's control separated them.

The tunnel cracked above her and Aleksia plunged deeper into the tunnel until darkness overtook her and she became ensnared in the rubble.

XLV

AFTERMATH

Whatever foul drug Marcus's captors soaked the dirty rag in was wearing off. His eyes flickered open as something crashed behind him and the air filled with dust. The ground vibrated under his feet.

"Cave in!" someone yelled from below.

Marcus stirred as the top of his head tingled with the sensation that something was not right, and he realized he was being dragged. He tried to pull himself free and the person stopped. His hands dropped and he was on his back. A hand shoved a rag over his mouth and nose as whoever it was sat on him, trying to pin his arms with their legs.

Marcus rolled over, noticing his attacker was female when she cried in outrage. He staggered to his feet, shaking his head of the cobwebs. Every cell in his body was on high alert, listening in the darkness. He feared to move. Not sure know how close he was to the side of the ledge or where his attacker had gone.

The woman jumped onto his back. She drew her arms around his neck and pulled, cutting off his air passage.

In his ear, she hissed, "Lucinda must be appeased. The weak must be sacrificed for the sake of the many or her spirit will bring down the entire mountain on our heads. Your friend tried to prevent it and she has paid the price."

Marcus stumbled and nearly lost his balance as his foot found the edge to the mine floor below. Now that he had a bit of his bearings, he turned his back to the wall and rammed her into it.

But she held on.

Tearing at her grip on his neck, he tried to loosen her hold. He coughed and his head tingled. He called on the rage he'd felt in the wagon. The power he'd used to kill three men. He wanted to feel adrenaline surge through his veins. He'd faced the jura and seen, but one of his legs gave out and he fell to a knee. Her grip tightened and his body thrashed. He gasped for breath; he couldn't let his world go black.

Miners ran past them and no one stopped. They'd seen the cult of Lucinda do this and were happy it wasn't them being targeted. The woman's intentions were not to kill him here. She would let Lucinda have that privilege. She and many others in the mine believed Lucinda controlled the flow of iron, but there was a price. In exchange for the iron, Lucinda took life, but people sat on the holes preventing her from collecting. The cult were her servants, and they set out to capture the weak and offer them to her as a sacrifice. Marcus had been the perfect choice. His only weakness was his sight. They didn't want to upset the spirit with a weak offering.

Marcus heard a woman cry out in anguish at the sight of the cave in. He let his body go limp as a last effort to lure his attacker into a false sense of security. She held on and Marcus wondered if she would ever let go.

She finally did and he didn't waste a second. Her arms loosened and Marcus wheeled onto his back and kicked her in the stomach. She flew over his head and screamed as she tumbled over the edge. Her neck snapped on impact and her body turned in an impossible position on the mine floor.

Marcus rose to his hands and knees, his lungs grappling to breathe. Blood rushed back into his head and he waited for the sensation to pass.

Soldiers rushed to the front of the fiasco, attempting to regain order. The voices muffled in Marcus's ears and the instant seemed to last an eternity.

"Marcus," said Trigon, like a light in the darkness, placing his hand on his shoulder and anchoring him back into reality.

"Which cave collapsed?" Marcus asked, his voice hoarse.

Trigon hesitated and Marcus's heart sank.

"Get me to the front."

Trigon levered his friend to his feet. "How did you get out? And what happened to your neck?"

"I'll tell you later."

Trigon pushed their way through the crowd until they were at the front of the line. Miners were trying to clear the rubble, but the soldiers pulled and pushed them away.

"This is the will of Dirva. The shaft has been closed and will not be opened," a soldier named Ravlin yelled.

Marcus didn't care what it took. Aleksia was in there — the elvian who was afraid of the dark and whose curse moved against her. Climbing up onto the rubble, Marcus started shifting away the debris.

Ravlin yelled at the crowd, "Get back to your stations! I'm warning you." The soldier positioned his sword at Marcus.

"He's pointing a sword at you," described Trigon, prepared to defend Marcus.

Marcus straightened his back and he felt fire stir within him. "I'd raise a white flag, but — I'm sure it's very difficult to keep anything white here. I'll raise my hands if that makes you feel safer."

"I'll run you through if you don't get down and seek reassignment," decreed Ravlin.

"The day is almost finished. All we want to do is get our people out and possibly rescue a few of your own." *If the miners on the other side hadn't turned on them.* The thought made Marcus fear for Aleksia all the more.

"You cannot defy the will of the gods," yelled Ravlin.

Another soldier named Aninai pipped in. "How about you fight him for it?"

"What are the terms?" asked Ravlin, intrigued by the thought.

Aninai was quick to respond. "You fight with swords. No proxies. And if he can disarm you, we'll give him the night to dig."

"And if I win?" inquired Ravlin.

"I'll be dead and you'll have the honour of killing a descendant," said Marcus, egging him on. "But if you don't think you can beat a blind man, I'll understand."

Ravlin smirked. "Make the circle."

Marcus stepped down from the rocks onto the ledge as Trigon hesitantly guided him into position.

Everyone moved to surround Marcus and Ravlin, but there wasn't a lot of room to do so. The path was narrow and no one wanted to fall over the side.

Trigon tried to stop Marcus. "You can't fight him — you're — "

Marcus wouldn't stop now. Aleksia would've done the same if their positions were exchanged. "It's our only shot."

"Then let me fight him."

"No," affirmed Marcus. "And if you step in, you'll be killing everyone in that tunnel. You cannot come to my aid."

Trigon nodded, but Marcus didn't see it. "Is there anything I can do?"

Ravlin taunted. "Come now Marcus, son of Barsadias. It's time someone finally killed you."

"You know my name, but I don't know yours," Marcus ridiculed.

"Ravlin," he responded. "Would you like a comb and a vat of oil to prepare yourself for burial?"

"Would you?"

"It won't be necessary," he chuckled.

Aninai tossed a sword at Marcus's feet.

The sword scraped the ground so loudly Marcus nearly had to cover his ears. Suddenly, everything around him was heightened as he focused on the man standing between him and rescuing the ones trapped in the mine. He could hear the heartbeats of everyone standing around him, and the one that was beating the fastest lingered in the chest of his opponent. "So you say." Marcus touched the hilt of the sword with his toe knowing exactly where it was, like when he'd fought the three men in the wagons of death.

Aninai shouted. "Enough of this chatter! Let's see some fighting!"

The soldiers cheered while the slaves mourned the ones that would never emerge. They watched helplessly as Marcus was the only thing standing between them and their loved ones, and they doubted he could win.

Marcus closed his eyes. He could hear Ravlin's heavy breathing and the shifting of the man's armour as he raised his sword. He heard him take the first step to charge.

Marcus jolted the sword up with his toe into his scarred hand and disarmed Ravlin with a single move. He knocked his opponent to the side and he let his sword drop. He walked through the line of silent spectators and started to dig.

A few hands clapped and slaves shyly moved to follow Marcus.

Ravlin's pride was wounded enough. He pushed everyone attempting to dig away. The people protested, and he shut them up, pointing at Marcus. "The deal was that he could dig all night. Not you. So clear out."

Other soldiers came to stand next to him, drawing their swords, and as much as the crowd wanted to assist, it wasn't worth their lives. They cleared away and were herded to the cells, but Trigon remained.

"I'm staying," said Trigon, towering Ravlin in size.

Ravlin opened his mouth, but Aninai spoke up first.

"Let him have one person." He sheathed his sword. "What difference will it really make?"

Ravlin washed his hands of the mess and stormed away as Trigon stepped up to help Marcus move a large rock. The sun slipped behind the mountain. There wasn't a moment to lose.

XLVI

AN ARRIVAL

Othelus reigned her horse to the side. An ornate litter, carried by eight slaves, barrelled around the corner. The stone on her neck warmed and she nearly set the litter's yellow curtains aflame. She'd forgotten how chaotic Ironwood could be and weeks in the saddle had made her temper short.

She revelled in the familiar smells and sounds of home. Her entourage entered the main market and she breathed in. The smell of exotic spices turned her head. Freshly dyed linens of every colour dried in the wind.

A slave woman walked by with a basket of meat pies and Othelus's stomach churned in hunger.

Music with a heavy beat resounded from every tavern on the street. Two drunk slaves dressed in gladiator costume danced, heralding the soldiers to come watch them fight later.

Othelus would have loved to have stayed in the market, but as she and the king's best soldiers passed through the gate of her former home, she welcomed the sight of the villa. The first thing she noticed was the statue of her husband, General Titus, had been removed from the courtyard. It used to stand in the middle of the circle. Someone replaced it with a statue of Karas.

Looks more like Zoren, she thought.

Waiting on the steps of the villa was a welcoming party. She instantly recognized General Quinn. She'd watched him take her husband's title in the arena over three years ago. Against tradition, she hadn't gone down in person to congratulate him. It was better that way. If she'd gone down there, she might have killed him herself. She'd been sick to her stomach watching him covet what was Titus's.

Othelus closed her eyes at the thought of her husband's untimely death. She prayed the jura devoured him when his ship went down. It pained her to think such a powerful man drowned in the raging sea. Her only comfort was that he'd died fighting Vandus herself.

Standing next to the general was his very pregnant wife, Daphne, in a coral blue dress. Her head was shaved, unlike most married women in Remisia who only cut their hair above the shoulders.

Over the last three years, Othelus had been her own woman. She'd let her copper hair grow and gained many attentions from the men in Remisia. Several had asked for her hand in marriage but Othelus could not accept. She would not allow herself to go backwards and marry a foot soldier. She'd tasted the authority that came from a powerful man at her side. No man less than a general or the king himself would satisfy her lust. She considered taking the tests to become a priestess. On a whim she could bear the children to the mightiest men of Remisia in the name of Karas. Possibly lure the king into her chambers, but everyone in Remisia knew he favoured the High Priestess Nerva. She'd bore him several children, though she could never admit they were his.

General Zale was rumoured to be one of those children.

She and Titus laughed about it in the dead of night. How it must've tortured Zale to know the lineage but not be able to declare it.

As a child, she was unable to become a priestess. Being the eldest child in her family, the succession of head magician fell to her. Her father taught her personally how to fight and wield whatever magic he could spare. The two of them were teaching her own son and the family line was intact. She had performed her duty and gave her son a bloodline that was worthy of the house of Othelus. She'd ensured it and used any and all means necessary to make it so.

General Quinn took a few steps down the stairs towards Othelus as she reigned her horse to the base of the stairway. He held the beast as she dismounted, her emerald silk tunic trailing behind her. Her father's jewel rested between her breasts, and weaved into her hairstyle was a net of magical stones. They'd been passed down through the generations.

Both of her legs trembled as she stepped on the cobble court, but no one could tell how tired she was by the way she stood.

"Ironwood welcomes back its former mistress," announced General Quinn.

Othelus feigned a smile. "It's a pleasure to be back, General Quinn."

General Quinn offered her his arm and Othelus took it as he led her up to his waiting wife. The slit in front of her dress was fashioned to halt at the thigh, and her leather sandals crisscrossed to below the knee.

Daphne gazed down on Othelus, her face an open challenge. "Welcome, Othelus."

"Daphne." Othelus kissed the woman who replaced her on both cheeks. "I had no idea you were expecting."

"Due any day."

General Quinn moved to stand at his wife's side.

"What are you having?"

"The seer says we're having another boy, but I pray we'll have a girl. We've had two boys and I long to have a daughter amongst my pupils."

"I've heard you're to be congratulated. Three of the girls you trained have become priestesses."

Pride filled Daphne's eyes. "Two have remained here and serve at the Temple of Karas, but the other has gone to Sidabras."

"And your sons?"

"Our oldest Macklin will soon be off to the barracks and the other wishes he was."

"My two boys were the opposite. Because of our bloodline, my oldest was jealous when my youngest Philis went to train."

"I remember that now about magicians. The eldest stays home and trains with the mother or father who's the magician."

General Quinn interrupted. "Dear, Othelus looks tired and you shouldn't be on your feet," he advised with more concern for the child than his wife.

"We'll talk more later," she said.

General Quinn instructed one of his slaves to assist his wife into the villa. The rest of them were sent to get the soldiers settled at the barracks and unload Othelus's personal items.

General Quinn and Othelus moved ahead of the slaves, talking as they walked through the atrium. It was a large and open room with pillars stretching to the ceiling. A pool of lilies was its crowning feature. A hole in the roof kept it filled and it fed into a cistern underground. Potted plants and couches wrapped the circumference of the room. The villa was older than Zoren's reign and featured marble carvings in the walls of people drinking wine and feasting on the spoils of harvest.

"I saw some soldiers coming into the city covered in dust. The slaves aren't revolting here as well?"

"There was a minor cave-in as the shift was ending today."

"How many men did you lose?"

"At least six," accounted the general. "The cave-in occurred at the mouth of the tunnel and it is shut to us now."

"My father used to take me into the mines when I was a little girl. It smelled horrible and the slaves were terrifying, but I would watch the burnings. He'd show me how as he did it. I remember one time a slave was stoking the flames and got too close. To see him thrashing — It stuck with me."

"Materials and the slaves will be waiting for you when you arrive at the mines tomorrow."

"And I'll need the slave they call Dig."

General Quinn stopped walking. "He was in the cave-in."

Othelus kept following the slaves to her chamber. "Then your men best find him. I require my divining rod."

"We don't dig out collapsed tunnels," said General Quinn. "Dirva has spoken."

Othelus left General Quinn in the hallway. If Dig was dead they'd have to use magic to find iron. She didn't know how old the slave was, but even her grandfather used him. Her father once joked that King Zoren himself had blessed Dig with a vertes so he'd live longer, but Othelus doubted there was any truth to it. If she'd been a suspicious woman, she would have thought he was an elf in disguise or found favour with Dirva the god of earth. Dig was one of the most valuable slaves in all of Remisia, but she doubted even he knew that.

She felt covered in dust. Once she was in her chambers, she ordered a bath to be drawn and a fresh tunic to be prepared. As the former mistress of the house, she would look her best at the dinner table. The stone her father gave her weighed around her neck and she held it. Its warmth sank into her skin and she pitied its waste on something so futile as a burning.

XLVII

LAST ONE STANDING

Aleksia opened her eyes and saw nothing. Her ears were ringing and she coughed. The air was thick with unsettled dust and her breath came in spurts. She cursed as her fear gripped her whirling mind and seemed beyond rationality.

What have I done? She'd caused this. She'd risked the lives of everyone in the tunnel for the sake of one man and now she was going to die. If the darkness didn't turn her to stone first, the crumbling rocks around her would. She clasped her chest, trying to slow down her heartbeat.

Everything is going to be okay, she told herself. *You've got time. Sit up and move.* As a last resort, Aleksia slapped herself across the face.

Sitting up slowly, she lifted the neckline of her dress over her mouth.

Two struggling figures blurred in and out of focus,

illuminated in the light of a dying lantern. One was on top of the other. Aleksia's head throbbed and she lifted her hand to soothe it. She had to get to Marcus. He needed her help, but as her eyes adjusted, it seemed she had to help herself first.

A throng of rocks covered the soldier who'd taken Marcus and a slave woman named Veeta was bashing his head in with a rock. The skull cracked and she turned on Aleksia; the stone dripping in her hand.

Aleksia frantically pushed the stones off of her, but her leg was caught between a stone and a piece of wood.

Veeta aimed her weapon at Aleksia's head and she stopped it.

Aleksia yanked the woman towards her so they were face to face and jerked her leg free.

Veeta tried to free herself, hitting Aleksia, but the hold was unbreakable.

Screams drew Aleksia's attention. Without letting go of the woman, she stood to her feet. "We have to help them."

Veeta spit in her face.

Aleksia released her and despite her fear hurried deeper into the darkness. She ran beyond the point where Veeta could see and only an elf could.

Rocks littered the ground ahead but she jumped over them with ease. The ceiling shifted and the supports groaned. Aleksia almost missed a little girl huddled against the wall. Her bucket was turned upside down over her head as she made herself as tiny as possible. The girl pushed herself into the wall.

Aleksia stopped and bent down to her level. "It's okay, little one." She perceived right away she was speaking in a voice that was more upbeat and cheerful than usual. This was the first time she'd ever spoken to a child, an instinct from deep within revealing itself. She couldn't tell how old the girl was, but she was impossibly small. "I'm Aleksia."

"Rose," she said.

"Okay Rose." Aleksia tilted the bucket up.

Rose's features were smudged in dirt and she bore a fresh gash on her forehead.

Aleksia melted at the girl's frightened eyes. "Do you want to come with me to find the others?"

Rose stretched out her arms and Aleksia welcomed her embrace, lifting her up and carrying her to the rest of the survivors.

The light ahead was hazy, but it grew the closer they got to the dig site. Amongst the screams of the wounded, there were sounds of struggle.

Dig stumbled around the corner. "All these years and finally Dirva's had it with me," he yelled at the walls. "Couldn't have done this years ago, you jackass!" He saw Aleksia and Rose and held up his hand to stop them coming any further. "You don't want to be here," he told Aleksia.

"The tunnel's blocked."

Dig cursed under his breath.

"Someone took Marcus."

"It doesn't matter now. You best give her to me."

Rose clung tighter to Aleksia.

"Why?" demanded Aleksia, shifting the child in her arms.

"Because I'm not going to fight them when they come for your head," he proclaimed. "I'm too old and I'm not ashamed to admit it. They've killed half the soldiers in there."

Aleksia thought of the woman killing a soldier at the entrance. Chaos and mayhem had descended.

"Perhaps we can hide until they dig us out."

Dig chuckled. "No one's coming. They figure if Dirva shuts a shaft it's his will." Dig took Rose from Aleksia. "Seems the soldiers are going to be the first to go, followed by you and then us. I just hope we all stop breathing before we have to eat. If you know what I mean."

No one is coming, Aleksia panicked. She wanted to pound the walls with her bare hands and unleash all control of her emotions, but what good would it do? Letting fear win never accomplished anything. If they were to rise into the sun, they all needed to band together and dig.

Aleksia didn't want the little girl to witness the atrocities of the other miners. "Find a way to dig us out."

Dig nodded and turned back up the tunnel while Aleksia went to confront the very people who'd try to kill her. She noted a hammer and chisel on the ground, possibly the ones Marcus dropped, but she didn't pick them up. If she went in there armed she'd never be able to prove she was on their side.

Aleksia stepped into the light with her hands held up in surrender. The soldiers had been overwhelmed. The tools broke bones far easier than stone. One soldier remained and he was at their mercy. The dead lay among the wounded who cried out in pain as they held broken limbs and severed skin. Every man and woman pointed a weapon at her.

"I want to talk," said Aleksia.

A man with no front teeth, no hair, and purple-veined feet stepped to the front, his hands and chest covered in another man's blood. "Grab her," he coughed.

They seized her and pushed her to her knees. She allowed them to do it as a sign of goodwill. Knowing they might turn on her.

"A citizen will say anything when they're on their knees begging to live."

"I didn't beg to live, I asked to speak."

The man raised his hands in the air. "Then speak, oh mighty one, so we mere mortals might hear and not obey."

"I come in peace," Aleksia vowed.

All the miners laughed, their leader the loudest among them. "Citizens don't want peace!" he exclaimed. "War is rooted in you like a tree. Even if you hack away what's above, the roots remain."

"A tree can be made into many things," divulged Aleksia, thinking about all the things she'd carved.

"We're not talking about trees," he rebuffed. "We're talking about you who'll say anything to get us to follow your rule. But we will not die bowing to it."

"Why die? We can dig ourselves out of here," said Aleksia. "Have you given up? Given in to death before it's even come for you?"

"I've tasted revenge," he laughed.

"And yet you've stopped here. The rest of the miners aren't free. Is your fate as sealed as the end of this tunnel or are you willing to shift the cracks in the wall and fight to live?"

The man placed his chisel against Aleksia's chest and held his hammer over the end. "Before I came here, I worked in a tavern. Every day they got me drunk and tossed me into a ring to attack another slave who was just as drunk as me. We'd battle for the entertainment of the crowd who mocked us till we nearly beat each other to death. We'd dry up and they'd bring in another pair of men. I'm not stupid enough to think I could beat you—" he gestured to the one soldier left, "or him in a fair fight, but I think we'll find it entertaining to watch you try to kill each other. Whoever survives, we'll tie up in a corner and allow nature to take its course."

The miners cheered in approval as the man withdrew his chisel from Aleksia's chest.

"What if I don't want to?"

"Then we kill you both right now. I would rather die down here than serve the king a day longer. I'd like one final piece of entertainment to look back on as I burn in the lowest levels of the pyramid. I want to see citizens killing citizens," he yelled into the air, jerking his fists.

Aleksia saw no way out of this and swallowed hard as she glanced at the last solider standing. An area cleared and she was allowed to her feet.

The slaves pushed her opponent into the dirt.

Lucka grunted and cursed at the miners as he lifted himself back up.

Aleksia recognized him as the soldier who'd refused to let the woman have any water. It seemed the miners kept him alive to give him the special treatment. She suspected he was in on Marcus's abduction.

Lucka stumbled on a bad leg, his face shimmering in his own blood. His voice was coarse as he spoke. "What are the terms?"

"No weapons," said the slave in charge. "If you wanna win, you're going to have to use your fists."

Lucka spit on the ground. "You see," he spoke to Aleksia, "show them compassion and they'll turn on you the first chance they get."

"They're just doing to you what you've done to them all along," claimed Aleksia.

"Now I understand why you never married," stated Lucka.

A slave shoved Lucka from behind. "Stop talking and fight."

"Fight! Fight! Fight!"

Lucka stepped closer to Aleksia and she steered clear, never showing her back to him. A hand pushed her from behind and the circle suddenly seemed smaller. Her heart was beating like a drum, pulsing into the side of her temple. Lucka had probably done far worse to others, but to kill someone with her bare hands was something Aleksia never thought she would do. She'd feel his life leave his body as she killed him. Others lived to beat a man to death, but she'd rather not kill at all.

Oh help.

Aleksia thought of her fight in Masseson. She'd barely made it, but this time her opponent was wounded. There was a chance she could hold her own and fighting would buy her time. She hoped he wasn't aware of her nervousness.

He noticed and landed the first punch.

Aleksia fell into the crowd and they pushed her back in. His punch was weak, but she'd wanted to know how hard he hit. It was going to be difficult to make the fight appear real. Her goal wasn't to lose or win but to endure.

XLVIII

DIGGING

Marcus searched for the next rock he could pick up from the top of the pile. Midnight had long come and gone and he no longer felt any pain in his arms or back. His mind disconnected and left him with only one goal: to keep moving. Not a whip flew or a guard cared. Whether they worked or slept, it didn't matter. But once morning came, Marcus doubted they'd be able to dig. They'd be coerced to go elsewhere and sleep would not be tolerated.

Trigon came up next to him. "We need a bar to wedge this boulder out of the way or we'll never get through."

"Could we use one of the broken timbers?"

"I'll see if I can find one." Trigon, whose eyes had adjusted enough to see, moved around. He searched through the rubble, finding a few pieces, but almost all of them were broken in two. It took him a while to find one that would work, though it was hardly long enough to make do. Trigon stuck it in under the rock and the two of them levied it up. Using all their strength and weight, the stone rolled out of their way.

Marcus knew this would have been impossible if he didn't have Trigon to help him. All of their work might have been futile, but the man had stuck with him through it all.

"Thank you," uttered Marcus. The words felt so empty on his lips, but he couldn't think of any other words to express his gratitude.

"I'm not letting you out of my sight," Trigon grinned. "The moment I left you alone, a cult nearly killed you. And if it was my wife, I'd be doing the same thing you are."

Marcus started moving another stone. "I didn't know you were married."

"She's like you," said Trigon, picking up a heavy rock and heaving it to the side. "For years we worked to hide it. The children helped. They'd work next to her in the fields and I don't even know if she's still there. The guards might have found her by now."

Marcus heard the eagerness in Trigon's voice. He had a question, but was too afraid to ask it. "What's her name?"

"Linet." Trigon used the piece of wood to lever another big stone out of the way. "Did you ever — hear of someone with that name?"

There had been so many in the wagons and it was hard to know anyone. The only person he'd let himself be close to was Favil and she was dead. She would have been able to tell him.

319

"No," said Marcus.

"Well then, there's still a chance," smirked Trigon. "Help me with this."

Marcus realized why Trigon had been so understanding with him as he felt Trigon place his hands onto the wood and they pulled. "How did you two meet?"

"We were born on the same farm. I knew her all my life." The stone gave way. "At first I ignored her. She was far too skinny and her hair a tangled mess. And she didn't care for me either," he chuckled, moving some of the smaller pebbles. "She always hated whenever I brought in more than she did from the fields. We liked to make it a game. Made it feel a little less like we were slaves. We usually avoided working together because I was afraid she'd try to steal all the harvest. But there was this one day—I ended up working near her and I heard her singing. I'd never heard a voice as sweet as hers. I teared up. Her voice was like my heart. Singing about our homeland and its beauty, though neither of us have ever seen it, we both had the same dream to return to Azuk."

"How old were you guys?"

Trigon smiled. "I was eleven."

Marcus hoisted a stone and passed it to Trigon. "Eleven?"

Trigon threw the piece of rubble over the ledge. "I knew I was going to marry her. I was taken away to be a shield bearer for my master's son, Percy, but every time we came home I would see her. We got married in the apple orchard one night by an elderly man who still practiced the old ways. I'd captured a lizard on my journeys. He severed it in two, symbolizing that if the two of us were ever separated, the pain of it would be like the lizard, cloven in two."

"And you had children?"

"Four of them. Three boys and a girl. Our youngest never leaves her mother and helps her in the fields. Percy's father likes to keep families, says it makes the workers happier and happier workers rebelled less. There was one slave Master Lysander sold. My brother. Bastian had a gift with horses. He could get them to mount up on their hind legs or bow when the master came. Lysander's wife let him ride in their pen. A friend from Sidabras came to visit one afternoon and the next morning my brother left with them. Went to work in the Aurelius as far as I heard and became a chariot racer."

"Those in the arena with talent can be well treated," said Marcus, drawing the loose sand away.

"I suppose." Trigon tossed a broken piece of wood. "But I'll never see him again."

Marcus heard the guard shift in his seat. "You never know. My nurse, Mizpah, had many children and as a child I wondered where their father was because I'd never met him. It wasn't until I was six that I realized there would never be a father to claim them. They weren't born out of a place of love. But she loved them until her dying breath. She held them close as a wall of fire charged towards them. Mizpah was as scared as her children, but she faced fire for them."

"Nothing is certain, except that there is nothing we won't do for our children or the people we love."

Marcus brushed off what Trigon was hinting at and picked up another rock. He couldn't let himself think about Aleksia in that way. She was an elf and he was a blind man who would never be worthy of her.

Trigon kept talking. It helped pass the time. He knew Marcus wouldn't sing with him if he started a tune.

A small tunnel developed through the debris, but they were still a long way away from reaching the other side.

XLIX

A WAY OUT

Lucka rushed at Aleksia as she moved left, grabbing his arm and using his own momentum to flip him on his back. He lurched himself up and swung, striking her in the gut. Aleksia let it connect, elbowing him in the head and breaking off a fraction of his front tooth.

He spit it out and attacked again.

Aleksia held him off with little effort. Kicking him in the stomach as he wheezed, but no matter how many times she knocked him to the ground, he got up again. The crowd was getting restless. The fight had gone on too long and soon someone would break into the circle and take matters into their own hands.

This is a waste of time. They should be digging themselves out, but no one seemed to care. Everyone present had lost sense and only saw the present moment, licking their lips for death.

Lucka grasped Aleksia's head in his palms and swiftly jerked it to the right. The muscles in Aleksia's neck strained, and she saw something in the corner of her eye.

The crowd veered as though something was moving amongst them.

Aleksia butted heads with Lucka, breaking his hold. He fell and she braced herself for whatever else was coming.

Little Rose burst through the crowd, running towards her.

But Lucka was closer and before anyone could stop him, Rose was in his grasp, with his hands around her throat.

"Back up or I snap her neck," Lucka shouted.

Coward, thought Aleksia; she didn't dare take another step.

The leader of the miners shifted his fingers along his hammer, contemplating the loss of Rose against the principles of his people and others were doing the same.

Rose's eyes pleaded to live. Aleksia couldn't let her die. Her life was only beginning. Anything she said or did could sway the mob in either direction.

Lucka took a quick look over his shoulder. "Everyone behind me clear the way for me to get out of the tunnel."

The people reluctantly shuffled away from the exit.

"One step and she's dead."

Aleksia knew he meant it. If he killed her, he'd lose his leverage, and he would take as many slaves as he could with him.

The miners cleared the way behind him until there

was no one there.

Lucka grinned and tried to take command. "Now everyone, pick up your hammers and chisels and follow me. You're going to—"

CLINK.

Lucka grunted and struggled to breathe. A dark line of blood trickled from his lip. Rose dropped from his hands and she ran to Aleksia.

Lucka kneeled and tried to pull the chisel out, gurgling in his own blood. He fell onto his face, breaking his nose, the bone snapping straight into his brain.

Dig stood in the gap with the matching hammer to the chisel imbedded in Lucka. "Have you all had your fun?" He stepped over the body, taking in all the carnage. "I, for one, want to get out of here. Once these bodies start to rot, it's only going to get worse."

"First, we kill her," said the man with the missing teeth.

"She'll help us," maintained the foreman.

"She's one of them!"

"I don't care," said Dig. "She's one more pair of hands to chisel our way out of here."

"And if she tells them what we did?"

"I won't," swore Aleksia.

"See." Dig took Aleksia at her word.

The leader spoke again. "Maybe I don't want to. Maybe I'd rather die here than work another day in this mine."

Dig ripped the chisel out of Lucka's back. "If you want to die, Clarance, I'm sure someone here can help you with that. I haven't lived this long to die in a cave-in. Now pick up your tools. I'll jimmy something up here to collapse this section of the cave so no one will know what you did to the soldiers. That way if we do get out of here it won't be a short trip."

All the slaves headed out of the cave, but Dig stopped Clarance. "I'm going to need your help here."

"But you—" started Clarance.

Dig smirked. "I need someone here who doesn't care if they live or die. In case the cave collapses before I'm ready. I've shown Veeta where to work. Together we should be out in a week."

"A week?"

Dig forced his hammer into Clarance's hands and walked into the small area of the tunnel, stepping over the fallen as he examined the walls.

Aleksia leaned down to help one of the wounded, but a man stepped in front of her, preventing her from going anywhere near them. She and Rose found some tools. She couldn't find her own, but there was a chisel in a woman's hand who'd died in the cave-in. Removing it from her hands she closed the woman's eyes and prayed she'd found peace.

Rose found a hammer. "I couldn't find a bucket."

"We'll get yours along the way." Aleksia picked her up.

None of the others walked anywhere near her. They avoided her like a leper.

A week, thought Aleksia, only slightly relieved. She'd be weak and wheezing in seven days, but she wouldn't turn to stone. *If only I could use the power of the vertes for more than healing.* She'd heard tales of magicians performing wonders with stones of magic and she needed to be more than she was right now.

Everyone else wouldn't last long without water, and when the lantern oil ran out, she doubted even her eyes would be able to see. The soldiers kept a small pitcher of oil for emergencies, but it wouldn't be enough. This wasn't a dwarf mine where the walls illuminated themselves with glow worms. In this place the only light was fire and it devoured.

They'd extinguished the majority of the lanterns. Leaving one with Dig and taking one with them to illuminate the path out.

Aleksia held on tight to Rose. She stepped over fallen rocks and followed everyone else's lead. Aleksia could see where they were going, but she stayed behind to not draw attention. The two of them found Rose's bucket and brought it with them.

Arriving at the collapse, the woman Dig called Veeta stood there with a hammer and chisel in her hands, blocking Aleksia's way.

Aleksia put Rose down but the little girl held on to her leg. "Dig said you could show us where to start."

"He did, which means I'm in charge. Or are you going to whip me into submission?"

"I'm here to help," offered Aleksia. "Are you going to waste time talking to me, or are we going to get out of here?"

Veeta addressed the rest of the group. "I figured we'd work in shifts. Half of us work now, the other half in a couple of hours. I want people digging at all times. Who wants to volunteer to take the first shift?"

Aleksia came forward, knowing they'd chastise her if she didn't.

Veeta looked down her nose at her. "You'll always

be working, that is, if you want to keep on living."

"Like you said, you're in charge."

Veeta motioned to a section of the wall with the biggest rocks.

But if anyone was going to have the strength to move them, it was going to be her.

Veeta went about shouting orders at the rest of them. A few of the men lit one of the extra lanterns to find broken pieces of wood for supports. An assembly line formed and people started removing the rocks from the top.

Aleksia thanked the gods when she saw little Rose curled up against the wall asleep. She'd stayed close, and Aleksia was grateful to have at least one more ally in the tunnel.

The work had barely begun when a crash came from the other end of the tunnel. The cave groaned and rocks tumbled from the roof. Aleksia ran to Rose and threw herself over the child as all the lanterns went out and the earth fell around them.

L

EMERGENCE

Marcus scrambled to find a loose stone that wouldn't bring the small tunnel down on him. He moved his hands to feel the stones around him, but the wreckage seemed to have wedged together like a wall.

The peak of dawn was minutes from piercing the sky, and neither Marcus nor Trigon felt they'd gotten closer to rescuing anyone. They didn't even know if there was a single person left to save. Rocks could've filled the passage from beginning to end.

Marcus's bloody hands stained the stones as he found another loose one. He passed it back to Trigon. He'd ignored the man's attempts to make him stop, becoming more and more frantic as time was running out.

He heard footsteps coming up the path.

"Soldiers," muttered Trigon.

Marcus shoved himself further into the hole. *What if we're almost there?*

"Remove them," said a woman's voice.

Trigon lifted his hands and stood to his feet, knowing it was futile to resist.

Marcus, on the other hand, did not go quietly. The soldiers grabbed him by the ankle and he kicked up a fight. He tried to latch onto a stone to anchor himself, but his hands were so worn he couldn't hold on. They lifted him up and took him to the base of the rubble to stand before Othelus.

"We finally meet, son of Barsadias, whom I've heard so much about," she asserted. "I'm Othelus. My Father's youngest brother, Piper, served under your father. He was with him when Naiden fell. Can you tell me what happened to him?"

"No." Marcus remembered the guards sitting around the campfire, his best friend Trans sitting next to him as the soldiers tried to decide who to ask to dance under the stars.

"Can't or won't?" she asked.

Marcus didn't reply.

"I could make you tell me." Her hand caressed the stone around her neck.

Marcus knew what she was, her family name revealing her lineage as much as his own. "Nothing I say can change what happened to him, witch, so why speak of it?"

"Perhaps you need to speak of it," she observed, getting closer to him.

"I've put it to rest."

Othelus searched his eyes. "No, you haven't."

General Quinn rode up below them on his horse and dismounted. "Othelus!"

"General Quinn." Othelus withdrew from Marcus. "It's early. I thought you'd still be in bed with your wife."

"What are you doing?" he snapped, making his way up to them on the mining path.

"Getting my divining rod."

General Quinn drew the witch close, speaking in hushed tones, but Marcus could still hear them talking. "The magic of that stone was not intended for rescuing slaves."

"Like I explained last night, it's going to take a lot less magic to move a few stones and find one man than search the entire mountain."

"If he hasn't died."

"His odds are far greater than you ever had in the arena." Othelus gazed at the scars along Quinn's handsome face. "It's a bit of a risk, but isn't that how you became a general? Twelve men go in and only one comes out. At the end of the tournament, there is always a victor, no matter the cost. I believe my father would do the same thing, but it's up to you."

Marcus held his breath.

"You have until the sun comes over the ridge."

The rays of light illuminated the clouds over their heads as Othelus walked around the general and climbed up onto the rubble. She extended both of her hands towards the hole Marcus and Trigon dug. She closed her eyes and tilted her head.

Rivers of sand trickled from between the cracks, loosening the larger stone. The sand moved around the edges of the tunnel to fortify it; creating a smooth edge.

Stones fell as though a large finger was flicking them out of the way. The gravity of the earth took them the rest of the way out of the tunnel and over the ledge, nearly hitting Quinn's horse. The hole dove deeper into the wreckage.

CRACK.

Othelus opened her eyes and let her hands fall. A tiny vein of white appeared in the crystal.

All eyes fixed on the hole.

Marcus listened. Waiting to hear the faintest sign that someone was coming through. He heard General Quinn's horse's hooves scruff against the ground, but mostly he heard his own heartbeat vibrating into his throat. The fear of not knowing if Aleksia was alive tore him up inside. Right now there was still hope, but if she didn't come out—it was too much to think about. Everyone he ever cared about was gone. From the day of his birth when his mother was taken from him, he thought he'd hardened against loss, but somehow he continued to let people into his life and every loss cut him deeper. He wasn't sure he had the strength to hold on if he lost another.

Something manifested in the dark, and Marcus heard the pants of a lost soul emerging from the depths.

Marcus fought to curb his hope. One survived. It didn't mean Aleksia was among them, and if she survived, she might not be the same. She was strong, but she was also alone in a tunnel full of men and women who hated the very sight of her. There was no knowing what might have happened.

A man emerged, covered from head to toe in a thick layer of dust. He shielded his eyes from the light.

"Not another step," said Othelus.

Another person was waiting to come out but was blocked by the man who'd come out first.

Marcus didn't know why Othelus had stopped them from coming out. While everyone was focused on her, Marcus crouched down and picked up a stone.

"Is your foreman among you?" Othelus demanded.

"Dig?" the man asked.

"Is he still alive?"

"He's somewhere back there."

"Alive?"

"Yes, my lady."

"Tell your friend to back up. Not another slave comes out of that hole until I see Dig. If someone else comes out, I will reseal it. You will all spend weeks dying of hunger and your deaths will be long and painful."

"Get back!"

"What are you talking about?" asked the voice behind him.

"She wants Dig out first."

"But we're already at the opening."

"Get back or she's gonna kill us all."

There were murmurs of outrage from within the hole, but they obeyed.

When Dig finally emerged, he jumped at the sight of Othelus. "The scorpion," he muttered under his breath.

"Dig," said Othelus, her smile brimming. "Get yourself cleaned up. We've work to do." Othelus stepped aside. The soldiers General Quinn assigned to her followed in her wake.

Dig protested as they took him away. "I like to be as close to dirt as possible. If you wash me, I don't think I'll be able to divine anything."

Othelus called back to General Quinn. "Do what you will. I have what I came for."

"Let the rest of them out," snarled General Quinn, taking charge.

The people inside the tunnel started to come out of the hole, young and old, but there weren't very many of them. Only twenty-two out of fifty survived and none of them soldiers. Only one person with neither a brand or family crest came out of the dingy hole.

Marcus heard a voice in the dark say his name and he dropped the stone in disbelief. Aleksia embraced him and he welcomed the feeling of her magic in his arms. He let it course through every fibre of his being. She was alive and, better yet, she was with him again. Pulling away, Marcus cupped her face in his hands. "Are you hurt?"

"A few scrapes and bruises," she assured him as she noticed his hands.

Marcus beamed with relief, lost in the moment of her return, until a whip cried across the quarry.

"Where are the soldiers?" asked General Quinn, speaking to Aleksia.

Aleksia stepped out of Marcus's embrace and faced the general. "They died in the cave in."

"Yet the rest of you survived."

"They were talking in the far corner when it happened. There was nothing anyone could've done. One soldier died at the mouth of the tunnel, but it looks like a rock rolled on his head. His tattoo might be the only way of identifying who he was."

"Were you harmed?" asked General Quinn, noticing her cuts and bruises.

"No, but there are a few wounded in the tunnel who need help."

"Good." General Quinn spoke to two of his soldiers. "Kill the dying and have Tarlock and his gravediggers bring out the rest. The iron in this tunnel cannot be left to waste."

The two soldiers went into the tunnel and General Quinn departed.

Marcus's face heated as he heard the screams of the injured being killed.

"You'll get a ration of water and then you'll be off to work," declared a soldier.

A faction of guards herded them back down to the mine floor.

Marcus took a step to follow Aleksia, but the ground felt like it was tilting underneath his feet and he crashed into her back.

Trigon rushed to his side and Aleksia turned to catch him.

"He hasn't stopped since the collapse." Trigon put Marcus's arm over his shoulder.

"Doesn't look like you got much rest either," said Aleksia.

Marcus fought to keep his eyes open.

"I had a few minutes here and there," stammered Trigon. "What about you?"

"I don't know how I'm still awake," she lied.

"Well, at least they're going to give us some water. Even they know a person can't dig without something in their stomach."

"Exactly."

It was early enough now that the rest of the slaves

335

were coming out to work. Marcus, Aleksia, and Trigon were being taken to another hole to dig until the dead were removed and the tunnel reenforced.

They gave each of them water, and Marcus felt a bit of his strength return. He no longer needed to lean on Aleksia and Trigon to stand. The ones handing out the water had been generous and gave them more than the regular portion of water to sustain them.

They passed another line of slaves and Marcus felt someone put something in his hands. It was warm and gooey to the touch, soothing to his bloody hands. Another person put something in his hands until his hands were filled with food. Word had spread to the rest of the miners and they wanted to help. Marcus wished he had a way to repay their kindness.

LI

TO ENSNARE A GODDESS

King Zoren watched the waves crash against the shoreline, the crystal blue water beckoning its sailors to join in, as he sat on the rocks. The western shore hadn't been a side of the empire he'd frequented, but it had its merits. The west was known for new beginnings, and though it was a poor sector of the realm, it was a far friendlier place than the east which burned in dragon fire. Colonel Lann and the barracks of Cavar had been most welcoming to their party. They'd had nothing but the best food the night they arrived.

The small fishing vessels bobbed in the harbour and he eyed the one they'd be taking. It wasn't much, but it would serve his purpose. It had a chance of going unnoticed.

His armour was hidden under a grey fisherman's

cloak and a sash tied around his waist. A necessary evil to look like slaves, but the armour comforted him underneath his disguise. He would have felt naked going into battle without it. It was part of the trees he could take with him. A bandage was wrapped around his wrist and forearm, hiding the mark of the king.

Colonel Lann volunteered his own slaves to fish on the way to Vandus's underwater palace. Zoren waited impatiently as the final preparations were made to depart.

A soldier was about to pass him by, but Zoren took hold of him. "Get those slaves to go faster or it'll be nightfall before we sail."

"Of course, Your Majesty." The man waved more soldiers to help. They pushed and shoved and even commandeered slaves from the surrounding ships to get the craft ready to take off.

Once the boat was prepared, a handful of soldiers boarded and his tamrasa emerged into the light of day.

Elian waited on the dock and Zoren joined him. The tamrasa did not blend in as he stepped onto the ship. His grey hair and smooth skin gave him away in an instant. And that was if they didn't spot the burns on the tips of his ears. Elves had a way to disguise themselves to look human, but neither of them wanted to waste magic.

Horus stayed behind to guard the cell he'd built to hold the goddess. Not that he believed anyone in Remead would seek to destroy it, but he wasn't taking any chances. It was essential he got Vandus out of her element in order to rip into her veins.

King Zoren stepped aboard and felt the wood shift beneath his foot, the single white sail swaying in the wind overhead. He couldn't remember the last time he'd been on a boat. He'd have to consult the memoria in order to recall, but he'd left it safe in Sidabras. He wouldn't dream of bringing it and risk it falling into the goddess's hands. It was one of the last things Lina had given him and it carried his every memory of her.

The sun reflected off the water into his eyes and he squinted. They should have waited for a cloudier day, but the plan was in motion.

The vessel pushed out onto the waters and King Zoren felt an exhilaration he had not experienced in centuries. He was far from home, but unlike his council he didn't fear being away from the shelter of his trees. Every battle he'd faced since he'd taken Casiro's fire had been a sure fight. There was no risk, but this was a war of true power. Only the gods had the might to kill him now. The goddess was a predator older than time and he was a shark rising to challenge.

Zoren scoured the waters, but the horizon was empty. The fishermen cast their nets, catching nothing, and he hoped they didn't. Somehow, the goddess was connected to everything in the sea, including its creatures. The last thing they needed was a dolphin swimming up next to their ship and telling the goddess of their approach.

They didn't stray from the shore. If the goddess realized their intentions before they were ready they would have to flee. It was why he'd risked bringing Elian. If anything went wrong, he was to fly him to safety.

Zoren dared not speak to any of the men as the hours passed. He stood at the railing watching the shores of Remead pass by. Some shepherds watched their flocks on the shores and waved. He hesitated to return the action because they were no one of importance, but he figured a slave would wave. He thought he heard one of them shout, but their words were lost on the wind. White sheep grazed the green fields and Zoren's mouth watered. He preferred beef, but a lamb would do. If only he had a sheep to butcher. It would calm his mind and help him focus. He toiled with the idea of how he would cut it. There was a lot of fat around the heart. He often passed the time stripping it of the excess and feeding it to his dogs.

Zoren was on the verge of losing his sanity when Elian pointed out into the water. He saw a pinnacle of one of the goddess's towers. If she'd made her home a little less conspicuous, they might never have found her, but her vanity would be her undoing.

Our dream is coming true Lina, he thought.

"We're in position," said Elian.

King Zoren sat in the middle of the deck. Crossing his legs and closing his eyes, he urged himself to relax. Breathing in, he stretched his mind towards the water and below.

Specks of sand drifted on the base of the sea, and Zoren filled himself with every grain and every stone of the goddess's home. A crab climbed the edge of the structure and starfish clung to the walls. He adjusted his focus into the castle and felt the touch of the goddess's feet on the floor. She walked down the hall of her palace, seemingly unaware of his presence, and he followed.

Coral and urchins grew all around him but she was his constant. He waited until she walked into the small chamber Paulina had shown him. It only had one window and inside there were many trinkets from ship wrecks. The goddess carried a clay jar and searched for a place to put it.

Zoren commanded the earth to build over exits, shutting her off from the rest of her castle.

Instantly he felt the water resist and he concentrated on building the exterior to trap her.

Hostile waters built up against the walls and Vandus churned them to slam Zoren's cage.

Suddenly, she pointed all of her efforts into the roof, and the seal ruptured. A wave carried her out of his clutches and Zoren began his next line of attack.

The boat shifted underneath him and his men cried out. Barrels fell over and seasoned sailors lost their sea legs as the waves sought to destroy them.

Zoren commanded every wall and pinnacle in Vandus's castle to give way. The water became saturated with dirt and grime. He pressed it onto the goddess's flesh as she strained towards her white seahorse swimming to rescue her. The goddess summoned a rushing current to carry her, but the weight of the earth pulled her down. The layers of her crumbling home thickened on her arms and legs until she couldn't move.

Vandus yelled and Zoren filled her mouth with earth to silence her. She continued to struggle as she disappeared into a pile of hardening materials and landed on the bottom of the sea.

Zoren drew the hardest materials he could find, ranging from sea shells to diamonds. He trapped her in a solid sphere where nothing could escape.

Stirring the sands underneath her prison, he built

the ground up a layer at a time, raising it, until it breached the surface. He could feel her pushing from within, but she was weak and Zoren drained every drop of water out of what he'd built around her.

The ship hands cheered and Zoren opened his eyes to see his prize.

LII

GOBLET OF BLOOD

King Zoren sealed the hole shut behind him, closing himself and the goddess off from the nightly campfires of his men, who waited outside. The circular chamber he'd built to hold her was split in two by a glass wall he'd fashion using sand and fire. He only hoped it was thick enough to hold her.

The goddess of water stood entrapped in her prison on the other side and he wondered what was going to happen the instant he released her.

She could be more powerful than expected.

In her family, she was the third oldest. Brisa, the goddess of wind, was the oldest and floated on the vacant air before the earth was even formed. Dirva was her older brother, and while he was strong, he was also lazy. He moved with the tilt of the sun and shifted whenever the wind blew. Vandus followed after him, but she was always on the move. Casiro was the youngest and the most ill tempered. He was Karas's son and the spawn Elvian, the goddess of life, regretted ever having. His desire to destroy only paled in comparison to his father's. The earth remained as long as Elvian lived at the centre of creation, preventing them from destroying everything she loved.

Of course, Karas and Casiro still caused chaos, but it was nothing compared to what they had the potential to do. In some deep-seated way, they loved Elvian and waited for her to resurface.

Dirva was asleep when Zoren met him and Casiro had tried to kill him with fire when he'd entered Mount Tikalnus. This was the first time he'd been prepared to speak to one of them.

Queen Gretafold, rumoured to have been one of the oldest elves to walk the earth, was the oldest being he'd ever spoken to, but this was someone who'd been present at creation. She'd seen the changes of the world and he hoped, if she was willing, she'd speak to him about it.

Zoren willed the stone around the goddess to fracture. He peeled it away, moving the discarded fragments to fortify the prison even more against the goddess's might.

Vandus shattered the pieces holding her. Her deep blue eyes peered through the glass at him and her coral blue toga flowed gently over her mahogany skin. The white hair on her head drifted around her face like she was still under water. She studied him, searching for something she could not see.

Zoren faltered to speak, so she spoke first.

Vandus breathed in through her nostrils. "Your cage

is thick, tyrant king, but I imagine if this glass was broken I would smell something other than the vertes on your skin."

"Magic has grown scarce in these lands. I've adapted to protect my people."

"You lie like a child," she scolded.

"I remember what it was like to be a child in Remisia before I took the throne. There was chaos and now there's peace."

"But at what cost?"

"I don't remember you intervening."

"My existence is to encourage the waters to move along their natural paths. Not manipulate it to my own ends."

"Your palace under the sea did not appear natural."

"I merely swayed it to be something more."

"That is what I seek to do as well."

"You have upset the balance of what must be. Taken power you do not understand and like an infant, you're a child choking on solid food," She stepped closer to the glass.

"I seek answers."

"As well as power."

"You are almost as old as time itself. Have you no wisdom to pass?"

"You're a fool who should have died when your time was up. Men are born. They grow old. They die. And the cycle continues. Wisdom is to know when to let go and be at peace."

"Is there peace on the other side?" Zoren hoped his beloved had found it.

"Only for the worthy," she responded. "And your

sins are stacking up against you."

"War makes sinners of us all," said Zoren. "But I would rather burn than let any army slaughter my people."

"Your defence of your people is admirable, but lives suffer under your command."

"The ones I've conquered would have raised their armies against Remisia one day. Just like the Azuk. Remead, Patrelis, Antioc, Dalos, they all would have followed and Remisia would have been destroyed."

"Why do you see enemies where there are friendships to be had?" asked Vandus.

"I trusted the elves more than once and it nearly killed me. Whenever trust is extended, you offer a dagger and they'll use it at their first opportunity."

"Then you will never fully control the wind and waves. To be swept up in their currents is to trust that they will carry you."

"Thank you for being so insightful," mocked Zoren. "The elders of my village used to debate what it would take to make a god bleed. 'Do they even bleed?' When I found your brother Dirva, I held my dagger over the inside of his leg, and that question plagued me. For if they didn't bleed, and he awoke, my plan would erupt to nothing. But I discovered something. You're nothing but flesh and bone like the rest of us."

"You think my brothers are dead?" Vandus took another step, approaching the glass. "Has the earth cracked or the fires of the hearth gone cold? My brothers await me in Valganen, held back by my father who will ride his chariot over the wreckage of war and laugh at the little boy who tried to become him." Vandus laughed and Zoren lifted his hand, pushing the glass towards her.

"Now, I'll take what I need from you."

Zoren felt the force of her will against his, but without access to her source of power, she could not withstand him. He manipulated the glass around her features, encasing her like ice around the face of a dead man.

Vandus lifted her legs against the back wall and pushed, but her legs gave way and she crouched into a sitting position.

Zoren waited until the thickening glass fully embraced her to stop its advance. He repositioned the glass around her left arm and lifted it in front of him. In another section of the glass he fashioned a goblet and it rose up to his hand.

He nicked Vandus's wrist with a shard of glass from the inside and funnelled it down, filling an air pocket with Vandus's blood. He sealed any access Vandus would have to it and opened a passage for the blood to fall into his waiting goblet.

Until the last drop struck the red surface, he could see Vandus's eyes shifting as she tried to make a final effort to stop him. He lifted his glass to her and drank.

The blood was cool against his lips and tasted salty, filling his nostrils with the smell of the sea. It invigorated him like he was walking into refreshing waters. And he felt an urge. Something was calling him home. In his ears, he heard the lull of the sea, steady and calm. His mouth went dry and his pulse quickened.

"Stop," breathed Vandus through the glass.

Zoren transformed the glass encasing the goddess

into a thousand knives and propelled them into her. He broke through the wall of the prison, causing the horses of his men to rear. The soldiers raised their weapons and torches, thinking it might be Vandus escaping, but they lowered them the moment they saw their king.

"Your Majesty, is the goddess dead?" asked Colonel Lann.

Elian watched the king intently, waiting for what he'd seen happen next.

Zoren felt drawn to the waters beyond his reach and ran. It wasn't far, but a cliff separated him from what he desired. He dove off the edge and into the night.

The water embraced him and he felt nothing but delight as it tickled his skin and washed over every part of him. He dove until his ears popped and he planted his feet on the bottom of the Olend Sea and tested his newfound strength.

Twirling his hands, the waters channeled to his command; swirling around him with such strength he could hardly contain it. He pushed it away from him and the waters roared as the starry heavens opened overhead. Zoren stood on dry ground, his hair shifting like a tornado above him as he walked back to the shore and released the sea.

Nothing had prepared him to hold such power.

LIII

DIVINING ROD

Othelus trailed behind Dig as they entered a shaft her great grandfather had long ago abandoned. Spiderwebs cascaded their path, melting in the heat of the two torches wielded by slaves who were unlucky enough to go first. A pair of soldiers edged them on, and another two took up the rear.

The witch moved around the fallen rocks but nothing was large enough to prevent them from going further.

Two fruitless days of searching and disappointment. The old man had sensed a few small pockets of iron, but nothing to warrant using the power of the crystal.

He muttered under his breath, likely cursing her, but she hadn't gotten what she wanted.

Dig held out his wishbone shaped rod, anticipating its vibration in his hand. Some unknown individual made it before Othelus was even born. He swayed it at the walls, holding it up, down, and all around, rummaging to find what they were looking for.

They were running out of shafts to check. She'd used the crystal to pull him from the earth and she would use the same magic to put him back if he didn't find iron. Leave him to rot with his curses. It had never taken him this long to find a vein, and it meant Ironwood's days were likely numbered. King Zoren would have to find his iron elsewhere if they came up empty-handed.

"Ah," exclaimed Dig, as he stopped in his tracks.

"What is it?" asked one of the guards.

Othelus recognized the excited face of her divining rod.

Dig turned to the right and stepped down a hidden path Othelus had almost walked right by. It was a short little venture to a dead end. It appeared the men who'd dug the original tunnel had tried to follow a dried up vein. The old man raced to the end and Othelus could see his hands shaking.

Dig's eyes lit up and Othelus touched the rod. It was vibrating like never before. Somewhere on the other side of the wall was the mother lode of iron.

Othelus spoke to the soldiers and slaves. "We'll burn here."

They pulled slaves from other caverns, forming a line from one end of the tunnel to the other. They passed wood and stacked it against the wall Dig's rod had pointed to. An empty tub was brought in by eight slaves.

Once the vat was in place, buckets from every part of the mine were handed down the line, filled with a mixture of water and vinegar. The soldiers worked to ensure not a single drop was wasted and punished any who failed to uphold the weight.

Othelus watched as the four slaves began setting the flame.

Kindling was set and the flint was struck.

The fire blazed.

Four slaves fanned the flame as it grew hotter and hotter.

A bead of sweat dripped down the centre of Othelus's back and her toga dampened on her skin.

The vat was filled and the lineup of slaves was ushered out until only Dig, four soldiers, and the four slaves stoking the flames remained, getting it as hot as they could without magic.

Othelus had the guard pull the slaves back, and she immersed herself into the magic of the stone around her neck. Using the power of the stone, the flames turned blue. She expanded the blaze from floor to ceiling. The air thinned as the fire burned and Othelus wiped her brow to still the dizziness.

Two of the slaves fell to their knees, clutching their throats, but it wasn't time to release the flames yet.

Othelus watched the wall, holding for the exact moment. If she extinguished it too soon, the cracks would not go deep enough, but if she held on too long, none of them would be alive to care.

Just a little longer, she thought. *Almost there.*

The guards shielded themselves from the heat; Othelus saw the worry in their eyes. They were young and had seen nothing like it.

The flame turned white and she released it, reaching

her magic into the tub. She drew the cool water up like a tidal wave and rammed it against the flames. The liquid turned to steam. She drew it from the air and hurled it back against the wall. She repeated the process until the wall crumbled.

The guards called to retreat and Othelus heeded their counsel, certain her work was finished. None of the slaves needed encouragement and Othelus caught Dig by the front of his shirt as he tried to see how far the burning went. She pushed him ahead of her and he cursed her like he always did. Had he not been so valuable she might have cut into his flesh, but she still needed him.

Coming out of the cave, the breeze felt good. She placed her hands on her hips, every inch of her soaked in dust and sweat, but they'd made progress. She retired to her litter to drink and freshen up. Soon the guards would send the slaves in to clear away the rubble and they'd do another burning.

Othelus looked down at the necklace and noticed the veins of white growing throughout it. *Such a waste*, she thought.

LIV

ROUND UP

Aleksia followed the crowd out of the mine, but the line was congested and they came to a stop. *This has never happened.* She stood on the tips of her toes to see.

"What's happening?" Aleksia mouthed to Trigon.

Trigon turned to the person next to him.

Rose ran to Aleksia and she picked her up. "Do you know why we're waiting?"

Rose nodded her head. "They're taking the people away."

"What people?"

Rose shrugged her shoulders. "They check your teeth, eyes, hair, and some people go in a wagon. For-for —" Rose didn't know how to say the word.

"Forsaken?"

Marcus winced.

Rose nodded her head and leaned into Aleksia's

shoulder until she saw a boy running to the front she wanted to follow.

Eventually, the soldier stepped aside, allowing them to come out, but the pace was slow.

Aleksia took a step out of the mine and onto the path. She'd never seen this many slaves outside at once.

Soldiers, both male and female, with bows and arrows stood at the top of the crater and guard towers. There were way more soldiers than usual, and some of them were even in red uniforms to show they were in the final stages of training.

Aleksia avoided their gazes. Most of them would be looking for a wife and she did not want their attentions. She used her hammer to cover her necklace, hoping it would be enough.

All of them were headed down to the mine floor, but past the wheelbarrows where they always dropped off their hammers and chisels was a large wagon, and Tarlock and his men were checking people's teeth, hands, feet, and hair colour.

Aleksia, Marcus and Trigon were about to drop their hammers and chisels into the wheelbarrows when the line came to a stop.

Tarlock grasped an old woman's face and parted her lips. Most of her teeth were gone and the ones that remained were black. He held a torch in front of her face and looked into her eyes, the light of the flame revealing thick cataracts. Her hair was braided and within each braid there was a different person's hair: black, brown, blonde, and some copper. At night she'd skulked around her cell cutting off chunks of people's hair in an effort to make herself appear younger.

Tarlock wasn't fooled and took her out of the line to go into the wagon.

The woman, named Iris, let her legs go limp and fell into the dirt. "No," she whimpered.

"To your feet."

Aleksia held Marcus back. He grappled to push past her and she grabbed the other end of his chisel to take it from him, but he didn't let it go.

"There are some battles we can win and some we have to lose," Aleksia whispered, trying not to draw attention to them. "This isn't one we can win."

"No," Iris yelled, pressing herself into a ball. She'd lived her entire life in the mine. To leave was a fate worse than death. She feared what waited outside the mine. She'd never been on a boat or even seen a flower in bloom. A sickness rested upon her mind at the thought of leaving all she knew. "Please," the word barely escaping her chapped lips. "I swear I can keep working," she pleaded. "Don't send me to the barriers."

Tarlock had no more patience and lifted her off the ground.

Iris wailed at the top of her lungs and she tried to break free.

"We can't do nothing," Marcus hissed.

Aleksia's muscles strained to hold him back as he advanced two steps. She dug in her heels. "Right now, there's nothing we can do."

A soldier punched Iris in the face to silence her. Gasps of sorrow emanated from the depths of the old woman's chest and the streaks of her tears parted the dirt on her face. They threw her into the wagon and closed the door.

The bottom of Marcus's lip quivered, the cries of the old woman opening wounds fresh and old.

Aleksia could never forget the state he was in when she'd first seen him. He was so weak. He'd suffered months of starvation. She didn't know how he was still alive when she'd found him in the barn. Only he knew exactly what lay in store, and it was killing him.

Marcus surrendered his chisel and Trigon took him.

Aleksia was about to put the chisel into the wheelbarrow, but she noticed it was indented, like someone had gripped it too hard. She'd been looking at it all day and knew it hadn't been bent earlier. She traced the markings and placed her fingers into the edges.

Marcus had known what she was from the first day they'd met. Haman chained her next to him and she'd used every ounce of her strength to bend the latches of iron, but it was to no avail.

Who and what is he? she wondered. He'd survived the barriers, faced a jura, fought Ravlin even though he was blind, and no ordinary man could've bent the metal like this.

Aleksia tossed the chisel into the wagon and ran to catch up with Marcus and Trigon. She needed to have a talk with Marcus, but would he even know the answers to her questions? How much did she really know about him?

LV

THE PLAN

Marcus held his supper but he couldn't bring himself to eat the double portion the serving woman had given him. His stomach churned as memories of the barriers roused his every thought and he could concentrate on nothing else. Aleksia and Trigon were talking with Dig about something but he didn't hear a word.

The woman's scream coursed through him like a bolt of lightening and the food dropped from his hands.

"We need to do something," voiced Marcus.

"Like what?" questioned Trigon.

Aleksia took his arm. "What do you need?"

"Gather as many people as you can." He turned to Trigon. "Watch for guards."

Marcus sat and waited against the wall. Some turned their backs on Aleksia, but a few came, and that's all Marcus wanted from them. He needed them to hear.

The other cells were oblivious to their silence, and Marcus hoped their chatter would be enough to mask the conversation he was about to initiate.

Aleksia sat down next to him. "They're listening."

Marcus hesitated a moment, not sure how to begin, other than to say it. "I think it's time we escaped."

"Shhh!" someone hushed as they all turned to ensure the soldiers weren't at the door.

Dig was the first to say anything. "It's impossible," he chuckled. "Do you know how many shmucks I've seen die trying to break their way outta here? I've lost count."

Others nodded their heads in agreement.

"So you'd rather wait till your body gives out or a guard beats you to death. Or maybe you'll live long enough to be thrown into the barriers, if you survive the journey. Your freedom will not be given to you. You have to seize it."

The miners glanced at one another, stirred by what Marcus was saying, except Veeta. Her eyes were cold.

Veeta spoke. "Living here is better than dying out there, which is what's going to happen if a guard catches wind we even talked about this."

"We're all dying here," argued Marcus. "It just takes longer."

"And who's going to lead us to freedom?" Veeta scorned. "You? You'd trip over the first rut in the dirt."

The other miners muffled their laughter.

Marcus tried to ignore the sting of the woman's words, but he knew they were true.

Aleksia leaned in. "I'll guide him."

"To where? Even if we escape, there's nowhere to go."

Marcus restrained the impulse to raise his voice. "Anywhere would be better than here." He'd lived eighteen years on his own, but he'd only been one person. If they all escaped, there'd be no hiding from Zoren's armies.

Dig mumbled. "No point in talking about destinations if we don't have a way out. To dig, — " he exhaled with his whole face as his mind calculated and he scratched his head, "would take years. I definitely wouldn't see it."

"Tunnels." Marcus realized he'd spoken aloud.

"You mean Lucinda's tunnels?" jeered Veeta.

"They must let out somewhere." The thought took shape in Marcus's mind as he spoke. "How else do you think she's alive?"

"By eating us!" grumbled a woman.

That made little sense to Marcus. "But she only takes a person every few weeks, hardly enough to survive. Meat doesn't last that long. She has to have another food source and water."

Venom poured from Veeta's lips. "She'd kill us all." She nudged the woman next to her. "Tell him the story you told me."

Marcus wanted to throttle Veeta as she destroyed the confidence of the group.

The woman shied away from speaking and her mouth went dry. She hated being the centre of attention.

"Go on, Martha," Veeta pushed. "Tell us all what you heard."

Martha closed her eyes. She took a deep breath and shifted in her seat as she twiddled a stone in her fingers. "I've been here all my life and when I was little, an old man told me a story. One night he saw fifty soldiers go down into

Lucinda's lair and not one of them came back up. Their corpses smelled up the cells for months. The citizens weren't going to waste any more of their men getting them back."

"You'd be leading us to our deaths," claimed Veeta.

"Lucinda is not invincible," said Marcus, but he knew he'd lost them.

"Are you volunteering to go first?" taunted Veeta.

"Would that make you feel better?"

Veeta didn't respond.

"Would it?" Marcus asked again.

"If you killed Lucinda, I imagine a few people would follow you down that hole," mentioned Dig.

"Who'll go with me?"

Aleksia grasped his hand. "I'm with you."

Marcus's heart warmed to know she'd follow him and he gave her hand a slight squeeze.

"As am I," said Trigon.

But no one else volunteered.

"If anyone changes their mind, we're going down tomorrow night," declared Marcus.

Everyone dispersed, whispering uncertainty amongst themselves. Escape had never happened before, so why would it happen now?

Marcus, Aleksia, and Trigon sat in a circle.

Trigon patted Marcus on the back. "So what's the plan?"

Marcus wondered that himself. "If we are going to kill Lucinda, we'll need weapons. The hammers and chisels are dropped into the wheelbarrows every night and the soldiers hold their swords too close."

"What if the story Martha told was true?" Aleksia asked.

Trigon smiled. "There'd be fifty sets of armour and swords down there."

Marcus added. "More than enough for the three of us to wield." He doubted anyone else was coming. "Dig."

Dig lifted his head and shook it. "I ain't coming."

"Do you remember the story Martha spoke of?" asked Marcus.

"I'm old, but I'm not that old, you jackass," he bickered. Dig shuffled to the other side of the room, sleeping closer to the hole than he'd ever dared, but he needed to get away from them.

"He won't tell us anything," said Marcus. "Tomorrow night we go down, but if we don't find any weapons, we come straight back up. We can't face her without them."

If there weren't any weapons down there, they'd have to find them elsewhere. Hide the hammers and chisels in their clothing somehow. They couldn't face Lucinda with rocks.

The three of them spoke quietly as everyone else fell asleep, but then a guard whistled in the hall.

"Down," Trigon bid.

The three of them pretended to sleep as one young man stood up in their cell. He whistled back as he walked to the cell door.

The soldier named Aninai stopped to whistle again and the man at the cell door returned it, wrapping his fingers around the bars.

Aninai saw him and came to the cell. He reached through the bars and stroked the man on the face tenderly, kissing him. He smiled when the slave returned the gesture and opened the door. Hand in hand, they left to find a place more private.

"I guess people find escape where they can get it," said Aleksia.

Marcus knew it happened all the time in the barracks. He hoped the slave didn't exchange favours for favours. In the morning, the entire guard could be alerted of their plan of escape.

LVI

YOU DON'T HAVE TO

No one else wanted any part in entering Lucinda's tunnel. Aleksia listened to the others talking about it in hushed tones when they believed no one else could hear. But Aleksia heard them. She heard their fear and their doubts and their mockery.

They'd been foolish to believe any of them would want to come, especially since Lucinda was not only feared, but worshiped.

"Did you hear?"

"Yes."

"They're going to get us all killed."

"Lucinda could bring the entire mountain on our heads."

"Everyone in that cell is as good as dead."

If they knew what she was, would that change their minds? Aleksia wondered. It might've encouraged them to know they had an elf on their side, but none of them could be trusted. They did not want to fight to be free, but there was every chance they'd bargain for it. Even if it meant giving the king exactly what he wanted.

If they were successful, it might sway them enough to escape, and yet Veeta's question rang in her ears. *Where would they go?* She'd always wanted to go to the land of her people, but would they even accept her? Would she even find them? Or would she spend centuries wandering through the giant forests of Visadas, searching for a people who didn't want to be found. The elves had never come to find her. No one ever did.

They could steal a ship and sail to lands beyond Zoren's reach. Kingdoms of elves existed in the deep south and other cultures who'd never been affected by Zoren's touch were out there. But there were thousands of workers. They could pack as many as they could on a galley, but some would be left behind. And how would they feed everyone? They could get stuck on a windless vessel and starve to death. People wanted certainty, but they could know nothing for sure.

Night arrived and no one came to offer their help. There were fewer people in the cell than usual. They'd chosen to cram themselves elsewhere, but curiosity had gotten the better of some. If they were successful and killed Lucinda, they wanted to say they were there when it happened.

They waited in hushed murmurs. Everyone avoided their gaze, unsure what to say to people they had a feeling wouldn't be coming back.

One person in particular surprised Aleksia.

"Dig?"

Dig avoided eye contact. "There wasn't room in any of the other cells," he muttered apprehensively. "But since I'm here, I might as well wish you good luck."

It warmed Aleksia to hear him say so. "Thanks."

Dig rested himself against a wall, rubbing his hands together nervously.

Trigon paced the room, every so often peering between the bars into the hallway, listening for signs the guards had been told of their plan.

The only person who didn't seem to be nervous was Marcus. He sat against the wall with his eyes closed and his chin tilted upward.

Aleksia thought he might be asleep, but then he patted the ground next to him. She felt her face flush.

"Anyone else coming?" he asked.

"No," she shook her head as she sat next to him.

A hint of frustration crossed his features, but then they relaxed. He raised his head. "You know you don't have to come if you don't want to."

"You know my answer," she said.

"I just wanted you to know I wouldn't look at you any different if you stayed behind."

"Look at me?"

"Think of you. I wouldn't think any different of you," he joked.

"And since Trigon and I are going, you have to come with us," smiled Aleksia. "We all know what happened last time we left you on your own."

"I seem to remember Trigon and I digging you out."

"Because you got kidnapped."

"Well, I doubt the cult of Lucinda will try to feed me to her now since I'm going willingly."

"It might be a good thing." Aleksia thought out loud. "Might mean a double blessing if the victim willingly sacrifices themselves."

Marcus's body shook as he tried to contain his laughter.

Aleksia laughed alongside him. It was probably the nerves talking, but this was the first time she'd heard Marcus laugh. The others probably thought they were insane.

Trigon butted in. "What's so funny?"

"We were trying to figure out if the mine will be doubly blessed since we're jumping in willingly," said Marcus.

Trigon pretended to ponder it. "Well, if we kill her, we might curse the whole mountain. Surprised none of the cult has tried to kill us already; but then again, they could be singing our praises."

Marcus piped in. "Cause we're saving them the trouble of finding their next victim?"

"Exactly. Might even build us a shrine if we don't come back."

"And if we do?" inquired Aleksia.

"We'll have to escape quickly," Trigon smirked.

Marcus stretched out his hand and Trigon took it, lifting him to his feet. "Then let's go."

Two men had volunteered to open and shut the hole, but that was all they were willing to do. They all wanted freedom, but none of them would do anything about it.

Marcus was suddenly serious and said to Trigon, "You know you can stay if you want? I know you have a family."

"You didn't leave me to the jura and neither will I

leave you to Lucinda," Trigon replied.

Aleksia, Marcus, and Trigon stopped at the covered passage.

Dig was the closest he'd ever been to the hole, standing next to Aleksia.

Aleksia gave Dig a pat on the back and her hand came back covered in dust. She wiped it off on her dress.

Trigon swallowed. "Are we ready?"

Marcus nodded.

The two men lifted the board, but as they did, a hand pushed it up from below and they flew across the room.

Lucinda grabbed Dig's ankle. He fell to the ground as the evil spirit heaved on him.

Aleksia dove to catch his hand, but she missed it.

"Help! Please help me!" Dig yelled. He disappeared and his screams echoed into Lucinda's lair.

LVII

A LONG-AWAITED CONVERSATION

Aleksia jumped in after Dig and something broke under her left foot. She looked down and jumped. She'd cracked the skull of a child, and it wasn't alone. The ground was riddled with bones.

Marcus and Trigon came down behind her as the board above was dragged over the hole. The tunnel darkened and there was no sign of Dig.

"I can't see anything." Trigon peered up. "Should we go back?"

"I'll lead." Aleksia took Marcus's hand and placed it on her shoulder. She could still see, but Trigon would have no idea how.

They passed under the other cells with holes in them. There were a few cracks of light in one of the boards above and Aleksia could see the movements of the person laying over the hole. They were restless, worried Lucinda would come for them if they failed.

The tunnel lowered as they moved away from where the miners were kept.

Aleksia lifted her hand and touched the damp ceiling. "Watch your head," she uttered back.

All three of them had to bend to make it through the narrow passage until it opened up and they could stand again. Aleksia thought it looked a bit brighter, but not much. The path split and she couldn't fathom how far the tunnels were taking them.

"What is it?" asked Marcus.

"A fork — I'm not sure — " *Which way should we go?*

A cackle came from the tunnel on their left and Marcus's grip fastened.

Lucinda breathed in deeply through her nostrils. "I can smell you." The voice drew closer. "You can't hide from me, child of the light."

The voice passed right by and Aleksia turned on the balls of her feet. She picked up the bone of someone's leg to defend herself, but nothing else crept in the shadows. She broke it in two and gave half of it to Trigon. Having a weapon in her hand felt good, but they were going to need more to defeat Lucinda.

She turned down the hall where she'd heard the laughter. The tunnel opened up to their right and Aleksia saw a little girl. Blood trickled down her brow and onto her sackcloth dress. Her head was smashed in exactly the same place as the skull she'd stepped on earlier.

"Aleksia," the girl whispered, walking towards them. The little girl's eyes flashed with hatred as she sang.

Come find me, for here I'll be,
Standing in the darkness.
A valley of bones, here it grows
The light snuffed out by darkness.

Aleksia stepped backwards, bumping into Marcus. The more times the girl sang it, the more her voice morphed into the voice of Lucinda.

Another child ran past Trigon and he shuffled to the side as a boy's laughter reverberated through the passage.

Aleksia's pulse sped up as the little girl was almost upon her, and she stood there frozen in fear. She felt Marcus's hand reach down into her's.

"Aleksia?" he muttered.

The girl disappeared, and the singing stopped, but Aleksia couldn't steady her breathing.

"I can't trust my eyes," she confessed.

"Close them and let me lead." Marcus drew her behind him and held on to her hand. He dragged his other hand against the wall until they came to a larger cavern.

Trigon peered from the back. "I can see a little bit in here."

Marcus didn't have a wall to guide him anymore. "I'll need a walking stick. Trigon, help me find something we can use. Aleksia stay here and keep your eyes closed."

Trigon searched. Aleksia heard his hands graze something that crinkled. He retracted his hand but nothing happened so he reached for it again. It sounded like dry autumn leaves on a dead tree branch. "Wait. I think I found something." He followed the vine to something bigger.

Aleksia listened to the shuffling in the dark until Trigon cried out.

"Linet!" he sobbed, dropping the broken bone Aleksia had given him.

Aleksia's eyes shot open and she saw Trigon holding a corpse held up by vines, whispering apologies and prayers. She moved towards him.

"Aleksia, stop!" Marcus snatched her.

Aleksia froze.

"There's a barrier," explained Marcus.

A barrier? thought Aleksia. *But that was elf magic.*

Marcus went ahead of her with his hand outstretched, leading her around the outskirts of the elven spell of protection until he found Trigon. He knelt beside his friend.

"Trigon," he softly said.

"She's gone," Trigon wept.

"Look at her," Marcus persuaded.

Trigon was blinded by tears, unable to help himself.

"Look at her," he said again.

Trigon looked into the face, and scurried away in disgust. He saw the screaming skull of an enemy soldier encased in roots.

Aleksia didn't know who Trigon saw, but she gathered whoever Linet was must have been special. It was clear Marcus had some idea of who Trigon was seeing. Someone he feared had gone to the barriers.

There were over a hundred soldiers and all of them died in different ways. Whether by vine or stone, the ground was covered in bones and dried blood, far more soldiers than Martha described.

Lucinda's chorus began again, but this time the words were different.

Come find me, for here I'll be
Waiting in the darkness
Trees on bones with hearts of stone
The final scream in darkness.

"Do you see any weapons?" asked Marcus.

Aleksia saw a few on the ground, but she wasn't sure it was safe. "I see them, but I don't know if we can get to them."

"I'll go ahead of you and you can lead me," said Marcus.

Aleksia stood behind him as he shielded her. She'd never been to the barriers and was afraid to touch them. She wasn't sure if all elves had the gift, as Marcus did. She'd heard people with magic could see them, but she couldn't discern any sign of a barrier. Between the corpses, the barrier had faltered, making the swords easy to get to. They had to break a few hands of stone to free the weapons, but each of them were armed.

Marcus took a few steps and stopped.

"Marcus?"

"Stay here a moment." He lifted her hand off his shoulder and tread lightly along an invisible line on the cavern floor. "There's no way around it."

"Can we get through?" Trigon glanced hopefully at Marcus.

Marcus exhaled. "I've never taken anyone with me."

Aleksia had a feeling Lucinda was on the other side of the barrier, and now she wanted to face her more than ever. "I'll go."

"No." Marcus put himself in her way.

"I don't think it'll harm me."

"But we don't know."

Trigon interrupted. "What makes you think it won't harm you? Are you not seeing what the barrier did to the soldiers?"

"I'm not like them," she said.

"I could go on alone," volunteered Marcus.

Trigon tapped the weapon Marcus was holding. "Tell me what that sword in your hand looks like and we'll let you go alone."

"You could go first and we'll put Trigon between us," said Aleksia.

"Maybe we could try to find another way." Marcus retreated from the barrier.

Instantly, a stream of rocks fell into the path they'd come from.

"She's sealing us in!" yelled Trigon.

Aleksia instinctively took a step to stop it, but the way back to the cells was gone. They could only go forward and into the barrier.

Marcus's expression told Aleksia everything as he stared at the ground. *He blames himself.*

"We'll make it," Aleksia assured him.

"No one's ever made it," he deflected.

"Dig needs our help."

Marcus sighed. "Then get behind me."

Aleksia ushered Trigon between them and placed her hand on Trigon's shoulder, prepared to watch his feet so she could match his gait and stay as close as possible.

Marcus lifted his hand. "Ready?"

"Yes," responded Aleksia, and they advanced.

The barrier hit Aleksia like the warmth of a fire on a cold night. It sunk into her skin and filled her with a sense of belonging. The air smelled of springtime and every instinct ignited within her. She suddenly felt connected to something beyond herself. It made her long for something she'd only dreamed of. It wrapped itself around her like a friend welcoming her home after a long journey. She basked within it, longing for it to never end, until it was gone and all she was left with was the loneliness. She was tempted to let go of Trigon and return to it, but Marcus kept going and she had to follow.

Marcus's steps remained sure, as though he knew the way. She worried about Trigon. He did not know what either of them were. The man had an inkling there was something different about Marcus, but he never brought it up. If they survived this, she thought it might be time to tell Trigon what she was. She could try to explain Marcus, but even she didn't know what he was.

"There's a light up ahead," said Trigon.

Aleksia was no longer certain if it really was a light or if it was another hallucination from Lucinda. Or perhaps everything they'd seen since they'd stepped into the tunnel was real.

They came around a corner and stepped into an illuminated cavern.

Aleksia marvelled at the walls, feeling like she'd stepped into a galaxy of turquoise green stars.

It's beautiful, she thought, and as Aleksia tried to look in every direction at once, she noticed that the stars were moving.

Glow worms.

The cavern was big enough to fit a few of the prison cells. *How did Lucinda do this on her own?*

And then she saw her.

Lucinda stood upon a large rock with Dig at her feet. The right side of her face was disfigured by three deep scars that ran from her throat to her forehead, blinding her in the right eye. Aleksia guessed it was from a cat'o nine tail whip. Her black dress was frayed and torn, but what caused Aleksia's heart to ache were the pointed ears poking out from her nest of black hair.

Lucinda stared intently at them. Her one good eye, darker than the midnight sky, shifted between them. There was something untamed about her and it was clear she was a power to be reckoned with.

Aleksia lowered her sword. She saw no sign of malice or evil intent and she wanted to be the first to initiate a truce, but more than anything, she wanted to meet someone of her own kind.

"She's an elf," said Trigon.

Aleksia heard Marcus's pulse skip a beat and he clenched the hilt of his sword.

Lucinda's expression warmed. She spoke and her voice was not what Aleksia was expecting. It was graceful. Almost like music. "Marcus, Trigon, and Aleksia." Lucinda's eye dwelt on Aleksia. "I apologize for the theatrics I used to guide you here. I cast a spell over the tunnels long ago." On her wrist was a metal clasp, embellished with a fading stone. "I could not waste magic taking it down before its hour. Long have we awaited and prayed for this moment; when the time of the elvian would return."

"What elvian?" questioned Trigon.

Aleksia's throat went dry as she took a tentative look at Trigon and Dig.

Lucinda stepped down from her rock and approached Aleksia with tears. "You don't know how much joy it brings me to see one of your kind again. Elves are known to be patient, but lifetimes have passed." Lucinda cocked her head to the side and stared at Aleksia's arm. "Though you remain hidden."

"Can you see the vertes?"

Lucinda shook her head no. "Someone very powerful tethered you in a veil."

A *veil*? thought Aleksia. She'd known something was preventing everyone from seeing her, but she'd never given it a name.

"Have you ever used magic?"

Aleksia took another quick glance at Trigon and saw the confusion in his eyes. She'd have to explain it all to him later. "I've healed people."

"But beyond that?"

"I've never held a stone of magic."

"The vertes don't only give elvians the ability to heal. They are more powerful than this stone on my wrist."

"All my life I was raised in a cabin and elderly slave women came to keep me company."

"May I?" Lucinda motioned to touch Aleksia's arm.

"Of course."

Lucinda clutched Aleksia's wrist and closed her eyes. "Not only have they blocked anyone from seeing you, but they've blocked you from accessing the deeper magics. Elven parents inhibit their children's access to magic till they're old enough to understand how to use it.

A few visions might have passed it, but very little. Whoever tethered it to the vertes was another elvian." Lucinda released her. "And they took your earliest memories. Only the stone that was taken can restore them."

Lucinda pointed to a vacant spot on Aleksia's wrist where a vertes should have been.

"Can you remove the veil?" Aleksia wanted to ask Lucinda a thousand questions. *How could someone have taken my memories? Who were my parents? Where can I find them?*

"Yes, but removing the veil would also reveal you. You're safer going unnoticed. Only when we reach Amarisa should it be removed."

"We?" interrupted Marcus.

A herd of people stepped out of the tunnels. Trigon and Aleksia looked all around them as the room filled with the individuals Lucinda had taken.

"You saved them?" stated Aleksia.

"The time has come for us all to be saved."

They were surprised, but no one's eyes were wider than Dig's as he looked at all the people he'd thought were long buried.

Aleksia couldn't believe it. All the men and women sitting over the holes were preventing their own rescue. The legend of Lucinda, the spirit of the earth, held them all so tightly that a cult worshiped her. They'd almost killed Marcus, but she'd not harmed a single one. "How have you survived all these years?"

"Dwarves can live their whole lives underground if they have to." Lucinda looked at the walls carved with the names of the dead. "It's not been easy. I took as many as I could, but I could only take so many without drawing attention. I've been trying to get Dig for years, but as you saw, there's nothing the witch wouldn't do to retrieve him."

Dig gave her a slight, yet terrified, smile.

"And now you have led the witch to our doorstep." Lucinda glared at Dig.

"Me?"

Torches lit all around them.

"Look at the wall, foreman, and tell me what you see."

The crowd parted and Dig ran to the wall. His eyes danced and he ripped off his hat and twirled. He yipped and he yahoo'd at the sight. He was standing inside the mother lode of iron he'd sensed. The walls were branched from top to bottom. There was enough iron to support the armies and plows for the next century.

"I found it. I've been—" but he stopped as the tension in the room grew.

"Yes, you've found your mother lode, but now you've jeopardized the escape of us all. The time has come for the rising to begin."

Marcus's head lifted.

"Not all have seen the promise of freedom. My initial plan was to escape through the city, but we hit an underground river to Ironwood and decided the only way to give the miners their best chance of escape was in the other direction. This war is not going to be won on the strength of elves alone. If we are to win we will need humanity to help us."

Marcus let out a breath of frustration and Aleksia's face flushed as she braced herself.

"Help you?" snapped Marcus as he stepped forward, avoiding a large stone in his path.

Lucinda's eye flickered between Marcus and the stone.

"Do you know what your people are doing?" articulated Marcus.

"Of course I do. I helped design the barriers."

Aleksia saw rage fester on Marcus's face.

"You designed them?" Marcus huffed and lifted his sword.

"I built them to protect my people. Zoren killed Queen Gretafold and I barely escaped with my mind and my life after he tried to turn me into one of his tamrasa." She tugged her hair away from her mutilated face. "I escaped here and have been saving people ever since."

"And what makes you any better than him? It's not the king who suffers, but the forsaken! The least fortunate! And you're telling me it's your doing?"

Lucinda's expression never changed from calm and controlled. "The barriers look at the heart. Whoever was destroyed by them was no fault of mine."

"They had no choice."

"Neither did we," she stated. "But it's clear to me that since you are here and they are not, you never really made the ultimate sacrifice. Or are you hiding more than you appear?"

"There was nothing I could do."

"Are you sure?" she inquired, as though she knew something he didn't. Aleksia wondered what it was but sensed it wasn't the right time to ask.

Lucinda walked up to Marcus and tilted his sword

down. "We'll find healing in time, young Marcus, but until you've sacrificed all that you are for the sake of another, you will never truly see what can be done. Forty years ago the king revealed his weakness. He uses the forsaken because he is desperate for vertes and if he runs out the war is won. But if he finds Amarisa or gets his hands on Aleksia, all is lost. So right now I cannot exaggerate the need to escape."

"How do you intend we escape?" interrupted Aleksia.

"Now we are getting to the matter at hand. My workers and I have been digging to a spot one league away from here. From there, people can travel north to Amarisa where the elves are waiting."

"But I thought you couldn't lead us there?" said Aleksia. "Isn't that why the tamrasa transform into beasts?" She'd lived in the cabin all her life, but the women who'd come to live with her hadn't. They all had stories to tell about Zoren and his creatures.

"We cannot intentionally bring anyone to our capital who seeks to destroy our people or who's not been invited by the phoenix. Zoren intends to burn our kingdom to the ground, which is why they are cursed."

Trigon, eager to leave and find his family, piped in. "Is the tunnel ready?"

"We've reached the other side, but we need a day to clear away rubble if our escape is to be swift. The magician is too close to the tunnel. Tomorrow night, there's to be a storm. The thunder will dull our movements and the rain will wash away our scent. Anyone who wants to leave will have to come now."

"But not everyone will," mentioned Aleksia. Marcus

had completely detached himself from the conversation.

"That is their choice," responded Lucinda. "But I fear for the survival of all who remain behind. I will have time to answer all of your questions on the way to Amarisa, but now you must return to the surface. Tell them it will not be easy, but never are the paths worth taking without trouble. The path is narrow, but it will lead to freedom. If they wish to stay behind, tell the people to simply go to one of the cells I've not marked. It is their choice. A powerful thing, if not handled with care. And finally, take this."

A man gave Aleksia something small and wrapped in cloth. The fabric had a slight blue glow and as she unraveled it, a luminescent mushroom fell into her hand.

"Take this as proof that the words I speak are true, but get rid of it after you've shown everyone in your cell. Word of it will spread and the people will come."

"Thank you."

"Do you know the way back?" asked Lucinda.

Marcus interrupted. "We'll find it."

Aleksia could hear that he was eager to get as much distance between him and Lucinda as he could.

Lucinda nodded respectfully. "It will be unhindered." And as the crowd parted and they were leaving, her eyes never left the back of Marcus's shoulders.

LVIII

PROMISE

Aleksia, Marcus, Trigon, and Dig hurried back in silence.

Aleksia didn't know what to say to Marcus. She hadn't seen that kind of fury in him since the night they'd met. His hand shook against her shoulder. All paths seemed to lead back to Visadas, and to him, going there was the equivalent of her going to Sidabras. The thought of it made her want to flee, and she'd never even been there. But he'd never met the elves. He'd run their paths and suffered. In every war, there are two sides, and so far the elven side of the tale had been silent. She needed Lucinda to take her to Amarisa and maybe find out the mystery of her past.

They reached the hole they'd come down and discarded their swords. The weapons would be there if they needed them later.

Aleksia climbed up to the board covering the

entrance. She tapped it. No response. She hit harder. People muttered fearfully and scuffled above. The board sagged, like more weight was being put onto it.

They think Lucinda is coming for revenge, thought Aleksia. She couldn't help grinning. Their unfounded fear came across as comical once the truth had been revealed. Maybe they should have brought Lucinda with them as a testament, but bringing her would have drawn the attention of the guards if their fellow cellmates screamed.

Aleksia hit it again.

"Who's there?" asked one brave soul.

"It's us," whispered Aleksia.

"Who's us?"

"Get off this board right now," demanded Aleksia. *One of us should have stayed behind to make sure they'd let us back up.*

Aleksia listened as they seemed to discuss whether or not they should let them up. But Aleksia was growing impatient. Rather than break the board and send them all flying about the room, Aleksia thought of a better idea.

"Dig. Come up here. They'll recognize your voice better than mine."

Dig cursed under his breath as Marcus and Trigon gave him a boost.

"Careful, you jackass," he yelled because Marcus almost dropped him.

Dig hauled himself up, wheezing as he reached the top.

Aleksia moved to help him, but he stopped her.

"Can't have both of us fall," he said. "Now you tap it again," he told Aleksia.

Someone was crying, praying they wouldn't be taken and killed by the wrath of Lucinda.

"Stop your muttering and lift up this board," ordered Dig.

At the sound of the foreman's voice, the people moved.

"Should've let me come up in the first place," he growled, as the board was removed and people reached down to help them.

"Quickly!" they urged, fearing Lucinda.

Everyone was bewildered they'd come back alive, but they couldn't draw the attention of the guards. Once Marcus and Trigon were up, they all huddled together and expectant faces turned to Marcus.

Aleksia handed him the rolled-up mushroom and he took it with a trembling hand. His interaction with Lucinda had left him more rattled than the rest of them, but she watched as he put his feelings aside, placing the item on the floor and unwrapping it. The miners snatched it and passed it around.

"Lucinda gave us that to show you," Marcus began.

A man's eyes went wide. "You spoke to her?"

"Yes. Along with the other people she's taken over the years."

"They're still alive?"

"And they've been digging a tunnel. It surfaces a league from here."

"But where would we go?"

"Lucinda's an elf and she's offering safe passage to the elven lands. If you don't want to go there, you could steal a ship and sail to Azuk or find refuge in the mountains. It's up to you what you want to do with your freedom."

"We'd be living on the run," said a woman.

"You can stay if you want to, but if you want to live free, you're going to have to come with us tomorrow night. If you don't want to come, be in a cell without a hole. Spread the word."

Marcus left Aleksia's side and felt his way to a wall where no one would bother him. He might've ignored her, but she followed and settled down next to him all the same. They sat side by side in the growing silence as the slumber of those around them deepened and there was no one else to hear them. Aleksia almost thought he'd fallen asleep.

"Aleksia?" he breathed.

"I'm still awake," she replied.

"I need you to do something for me."

"What?" Aleksia sat up.

Marcus exhaled. "Tomorrow—if we're to escape this place—"

"It would be easier if you could see."

Marcus nodded. "I hate to ask it." He picked up a rock and moved it between his fingers. "If anyone were to discover—" his words faltered and he discarded the stone.

"I know the risk, but I made a promise."

"I released you from that promise long ago," he stated. "But I can't help feeling useless. I would rather stay here than slow everyone down."

"Do you remember what it was like to see?"

"Sometimes," he said. "I don't even know what you look like."

Aleksia blushed. "Ask."

A grin claimed the side of Marcus's mouth. "That's all."

"I can't promise an accurate description," she teased, but she wanted him to know. She wanted to see his eyes light up at the sight of her.

"Well if you lie, I'll know," he chuckled.

Aleksia took his hand and guided it to cup her face. He stroked her cheek gently with his thumb.

Marcus leaned in and placed his forehead against hers. "I want to know what you look like."

Aleksia's heart felt like it was going to come out of her chest. "Just one more day."

He grinned and opened his arm for her to lean up against him. With his arm cast over her shoulder, she felt safe. Even though she could protect herself and do it on her own, she knew with Marcus at her side, she would never have to.

LIX

SEEDS OF DOUBT

By noon the following day, every worker in the mine heard about what transpired in Lucinda's tunnel. For most it was an anthem to rise to the call, but others wavered at the mere thought and would not be darkening a cell with a hole that night. The miners hadn't been trained to fight. Most of them started on farms until their owners sold them to Ironwood.

Marcus didn't blame them, but he did pity them.

It was like the parable of the man who lived on the edge of a cliff all his life. He drank when it rained and ate the scraps the birds brought him. He lived high up in the sky and watched the world from above. The deer roamed through the trees; the river rushed along the shore. Children swam in the waters as they laughed and played. Every day he wondered what it would be like to live alongside them.

One day, a large eagle landed beside him and offered to fly him away from his prison, to take him to green pastures where he'd live a full and happy life, but the man refused. Fear gripped him so severely that he did not trust the bird. He might have fallen. The mountain was steady and sure, but to fly away would endanger everything. And he remained there until the end of his days.

Marcus had known freedom. It was easier to take the risk because he knew what was on the other side.

He was grateful Aleksia agreed to heal his eyes, but he feared what it could do. King Zoren would kill her to get the vertes on her chest and arms. Marcus had seen how weak she got when she'd been out of the sun on the Mirtis. He didn't want to imagine the sound of her screams if it had gone any further.

Aleksia worked, but her blows were less consistent. *Was she worried Trigon and Dig wouldn't keep her secret?* They'd both sworn to. At that moment, Trigon had gone to convince others to join them further down the tunnel. Marcus imagined Trigon attempting to speak in hushed tones with his overpowering voice.

Aleksia handed him the hammer. "Do what you can till I get back."

Marcus placed the chisel back against the wall and missed. He heard Dig speaking until he was interrupted and he figured that's where Aleksia had gone. He wasn't doing a very good job on his own when someone came up beside him.

"That burn mark on your hand," observed Veeta. "Where did you get it?"

"It doesn't matter," he replied, not caring. On the

flower, she was the thorn that drew blood. She'd almost killed Aleksia.

"I've never seen a burn like it," she said.

"Is there something else you want to discuss?"

"I want to know how you expect to lead us out of here when you can't even lead yourself."

"I'm not the one who's going to be leading," he promised, as he missed the chisel.

"You seem to act like you are," she contended.

"I only found a way out."

Veeta leaned in closer to Marcus. "Well, I'll tell you, son of Barsadias, that if you're in that tunnel tonight, there are many who won't be joining. You're cursed. With you, all we'll feel is the very iron we chisel, ripping through our chests."

Veeta left, moving from person to person, spreading her doubt and fear, convincing people to stay behind.

He sought to ignore what she'd said, but her voice spoke of the doubts he'd refused to say out loud. If Aleksia couldn't cure him, he'd have to convince her to go without him. It wasn't what he wanted, but it would be best.

Aleksia returned and she abruptly seized the tools from him. She rammed them against the rocks. The wooden handle on the hammer broke and the chisel was bent beyond use. She took both of them, keeping Marcus at her side, and approached the guard who was talking to Dig.

"What do you want?" asked the soldier.

Aleksia presented the fractured instruments.

"Go to the shed and get another one. Another slave can help him dig till you get back."

Dig laughed. "He'd only slow them down." Dig

reached over and picked up a bucket full of rock waste. "Have him carry this to the wagon."

The soldier waved her away.

Aleksia grabbed Marcus's hand and led him. He stumbled a few times to keep her pace, but he kept up with her through the twists and turns. They emerged onto the ledge and headed to the toolshed, but she turned and Marcus felt the sun leave his shoulders.

The abandoned tunnel echoed under their feet. Aleksia muttered the way to herself until the shaft opened up and they were standing in a large cave. The roof was tall and a beam of light poured down from above. There was a hole, big enough to see the sky and, on a dark night, the stars. A pool of water glimmered in the rays of light, reflecting them as they danced on the walls with a haunting glow.

"Where are we?" wondered Marcus as Aleksia let go of his hand and walked to where the beam of light almost struck her shoulders.

"The place where I'm going to heal you," she revealed. Aleksia walked back to him and took the bucket from his hand. She put it to the side, along with the broken chisel and hammer. "Dig helped me find it."

Marcus perceived her smile of pride as he searched for a hard surface to steady himself. For over eighteen years he'd lived in the dark, recognizing people by their voices. He'd dreamed of being able to see, but never believed he ever would.

"Are you ready?"

Marcus didn't trust his voice he was so nervous. "Yes."

"Remove your shirt."

He did as instructed and tossed it to the side. She held his arm and placed him on the opposite side of the cavern, where the light reflected off the water most. She turned him to face the beam of light she was about to step into. "Keep your eyes open."

Marcus lifted his head and his stomach turned in knots. His heart pounding faster than he thought his chest could sustain. There didn't seem to be enough air to fill his lungs.

"It's time."Aleksia stepped backwards into the light.

Instantly, every inch of the cavern filled with light. The moisture on the sides of the wall amplified it, pouring over Marcus like a wave.

Warmth like he'd never known surrounded him. Every scar on his body began to heal. The markings from the shackles on his wrists and ankles, the scars from Grayson's torture, even the wounds from his childhood disappeared like he'd never had them. His skin became smooth and he felt refreshed.

Aleksia released the sunlight but Marcus never saw it. He touched the old scar on his hand and realized it, too, hadn't healed. The marks from his seventh birthday were still part of him, just like the memories he wished to forget.

"Marcus," said Aleksia, her words faltering.

"No." Marcus stopped her right there, his voice soft, but hurting. "I guess there are some injuries that can't be cured. It was silly to hope."

Marcus prevented a tear escaping the corner of his eye and he crouched down and sat, unable to trust his legs.

"It's okay Aleksia," he paused. "It's okay." Trying to

convince himself. He'd lived this long without his sight and now he could give up hoping.

"Maybe I could try again."

"No."

Aleksia sat down beside him and then she asked him the question he never answered. "Perhaps, if I knew how you lost your eyesight."

Out of habit, he closed his eyes and struggled to think of something else, but his life was filled with so much sorrow it was easy to let the good times fade. Ever since that night, he'd kept the tale to himself. Not even Favil knew how he'd lost his sight. Perhaps she'd never asked because she'd seen who he was meant to tell.

"It was the night of my seventh birthday—"

LX

A FAREWELL PARTY

Thousands of fireflies danced in the trees and crickets sang their melody on the eve of young Marcus's seventh birthday. A farewell party was in full swing outside the walls of Naiden and all had come to celebrate, even those from surrounding villages had gathered to send off this particular boy. They wanted to see the general's only son take his first step on the journey all their sons shared.

Surrounded by fields of glowing corn and in the clearing beside this party was a group of people cheering and watching two small figures circling one another. Both boys bore sharpened blades and neither of them wanted to make the first move. The crowd anxiously awaited the beginning of a good fight.

Marcus's heart beat so fast he could've sworn Trans heard it as it drowned out all the noise around him. He knew the look of determination on his friend's face and he couldn't help but smile. Even though he was smaller, he'd bested him many times, and he was confident he could do it again. Marcus's father had taught him well.

Trans returned the smile and Marcus revelled all the more. His opponent was big and tough and Marcus looked like a twig next to him, but Marcus would always be faster.

He started calculating the pace he wanted to set. Many people watched and he debated if he wanted to make it long or send Trans running to his mother's toga sooner rather than later. The thought made Marcus chuckle.

This fight hadn't been his idea but he'd welcomed it. He wanted everyone to know they were sending off a warrior they could all be proud of. They all expected him to be as good as his father and deserving of his bloodline, but the young warrior knew he was lucky to not be facing his father. Only earlier that day, his father had him on his backside in less than three moves.

"Hah!" yelled Trans as he charged.

Marcus swung his sword and blocked his advance, their swords gleaming in the evening sun.

And the fight began.

Deflecting Trans's blows with ease, Marcus felt like they were in a conversation. Each of them saying something with their swords, the other responding in kind. He flipped and let Trans push him to the edge to make the fight more entertaining. He listened to the crowd and knew he was doing a good job of it.

"I can't look," said a woman.

"He's done for," chuckled a man.

"Careful," mentioned someone who was a little more

concerned. "Wouldn't want anyone to get hurt."

Marcus thought the same thing, but if anyone was going to get hurt, it wasn't going to be him. He blocked another one of Trans's pathetic blows and brought the fight to an end. He lifted his sword in order to bait Trans into the position he wanted and his friend raised their weapon in perfect response.

Marcus reached down swiftly and pulled out a dagger, placing it against his friend's throat.

The crowd cheered.

Trans's eyes widened and dropped his sword in surrender. "Where did you get that?"

"Father," replied Marcus, as he pulled the dagger away. "He gave it to me this morning as a gift to take to Sidabras. We spent the afternoon sparing with it."

Trans's face was red with humiliation. "That's not fair. I didn't have a dagger."

"Tell that to the elves on the battlefield," smirked Marcus.

An elderly man who was watching butted into their conversation. "Come on boys, follow the rules of engagement."

Marcus sheathed his sword and his dagger and grasped Trans's forearm. "Look to the end."

"Look to the end," said Trans.

The crowd called for the next fight as Marcus and Trans left the apex. People patted Marcus on the shoulder and offered congratulations, but their focus was on who was about to enter the ring. Two other boys entered, and they were even younger than Marcus and Trans.

"Can I see it?" asked Trans, eyeing Marcus's fancy new weapon.

Marcus reluctantly handed it over.

The black leather sheath was embroidered with silver thread. The hilt was made from two pieces of fine black metal which intertwined to a silver piece bearing his crest. Trans pulled it out of its sheath and noticed the simple, yet perfectly crafted, blade.

Marcus wondered where his father could have gotten such a blade, but at the same time, he didn't care. It was his, and everyone knew it.

"This must have cost your father a fortune," remarked Trans, unable to keep his jaw shut.

Marcus smiled with pride. "I am the only son of a descendant and my father is the General of the Centre." He came from a long line of generals and he wouldn't be the one to halt the family tradition. It was only a matter of growing up and waiting for another general to die so he could take their place. He'd fight in the tournament and the title would be his.

Trans returned the dagger "Do you think once you get to Sidabras you'll meet the king?"

"I already have."

"You never told me that! When?"

"Last year. Mizpah and I went to visit my father for the king's six hundred and fourth celebration of his reign."

"What did he say to you?"

"That he looked forward to the warrior I'd become."

Trans kicked the dirt. "You're so lucky! And you get to start your journey tomorrow."

"It can't come too soon." Marcus ran up to one of the many tables of food that were adorned with rare delicacies.

Tomorrow. Marcus had lost sleep for weeks thinking about it. He and his father would depart at first light to embark on the same journey all his ancestors had gone on since King Zoren's reign began. He barely remembered what Sidabras looked like, but he remembered his awe as they rode over the waterfall on the bridge to Zoren's villa as the trees swayed in welcome.

Marcus stepped to the side of the party. The other laughing children who'd gotten glowing corn stuck in their teeth, and the melodies of the dance floor faded as he peered down the road. It was a two-day journey to Sidabras, and on the day he arrived he would swear his allegiance to King Zoren. He would live in the barracks until the day he became a general, died, or retired, and even then it was optional to leave. There, he'd become the warrior his father could be proud of.

A gentle hand on his shoulder interrupted his thoughts. Marcus peered up and saw his nurse, Mizpah, in a fresh house slave tunic.

"You fought very well tonight." She bent down in front of him.

Marcus paused, the thoughts from before she arrived still churning in his mind. "Do you think I'll make a good general one day?"

Mizpah placed her hand on the small of his cheeks. "Yes," she said as she tried to keep the tears from her eyes. "Just do everything your father tells you and you'll be alright."

Marcus nodded and grinned. He knew Mizpah loved him and that she would tell him the truth. His father loved him in his own way.

"Now, what do you have here?" Mizpah pointed at Marcus's plate full of treats.

Marcus shoved another sweet into his mouth. "After today, I'll have to eat the food at the barracks. I hear it's terrible, so I figured I better eat all the good food I can now."

"Well, make sure some of that good food includes some meat and vegetables." Mizpah kissed him on the cheek, breaking the law of slave to citizen interaction. "I'm going to miss you."

Marcus smiled. "But I can't stay here."

"No," she professed. "I guess you can't."

Marcus wiped the tear. "The king needs me. I'll come back and visit."

"I know you will," said Mizpah. "With plenty of stories to tell."

"Marcus!" yelled Trans, his plate even fuller than Marcus's with sweets.

Marcus glared at his friend.

"It's okay. Go on. I'll see you later."

Marcus spun on his toes and ran after Trans, grabbing an ear of corn and a piece of beef off the tables.

Mizpah rose to her feet, watching him as another tear fell from her eye.

Trans eyed the soldiers sitting around the fire. "Should we go?"

Marcus nodded, guessing the soldiers would be trying to choose a partner to dance with.

Trans started approaching a fire he'd been watching, but Marcus pulled him by the back of his shirt to another one where the majority of the soldiers were gathered. They were greeted with many congratulations and well dones. Most of them had watched their fight.

As Marcus predicted, the men were trying to figure out which young lady to ask to dance. Some of the men weren't officially soldiers yet and wore red shirts, marking them as such. Most of them had yet to marry and were searching for a woman to give them an heir. A man couldn't go into battle until he had an heir to replace him, so they were eager to find a proper wife, but not just any girl would do.

The one soldier, Piper, dressed in a red training uniform, glanced from woman to woman, observing whether or not they met his list of requirements.

Jasper sat next to Piper and whispered in his ear, "Do you think if you recited poetry into that maiden's ear she'd want to dance with you?" Jasper pointed at a long-haired maiden who was trying to avoid staring at the entourage of soldiers.

Piper smirked. "Who cares if she prefers poetry. There are far more important things to consider when choosing a wife. If she can't bear me an heir or put down a revolt, she can brush her long hair all she likes."

Another man piped in. "What woman wouldn't want to dance with you reciting poetry in her ear the entire time?"

Jasper was unable to control his laughter. "She might even throw in a punch for free."

Piper was not amused. "I'm sure your wife loves the dreaded language. My wife, she'll actually be able to run a household while I'm away." He chugged the rest of his drink and split off from the group, headed towards a different young lady who'd caught his eye.

Marcus watched as Piper walked up to the woman

and she curtsied. He extended his hand and she took it. Marcus joined in with the rest of the soldiers as they whistled and hooted.

Piper looked as though he wanted to kill them all, but that would only prevent him from dancing with the potential wife he desperately needed.

Marcus laughed along with the rest of them as he watched the men and women dance under the lanterns. There were few men among them. Those that were in attendance were either retired or too young to be off training. But all of them knew how to dance. Line dancing was taught to both men and women throughout their education. It taught the people of Remisia to fight in sync and kept the women healthy for childbearing.

Marcus couldn't help but gape enviously at the uniforms. The black breast plate encased every muscle on the torso and the silver tree of the king stretched across it. Every soldier carried a curved sword on their hip and the knee-high boots had a shin guard built into the front. There was no protection on the back of the calf. Any man who turned his back on the enemy deserved to have the back of his legs slashed. Marcus coveted the armour and couldn't wait to get some of his own.

He saw his Aunt Mariana walk by. She gave him a quick glance and he saw her hatred. Tonight she could barely look at him. She'd laid with many partners to have a son, but every nine months she held disappointment in her arms. She took care of him while his father was away but she'd never shown him any tenderness. His mother died when he was born and he'd lived with his aunt ever since. The line of Marcus was about to end and because his father refused to remarry, the rest of the family line fell to her.

Most of his family had either died on the battlefields or in the arena. All of the other five lines of general descendants had disappeared for the same reasons. Marcus and his father were the only two remaining male descendants. She wanted one of her own.

A hand knocked him on the shoulder.

"Marcus."

Marcus looked up. "Father." He straightened up in his seat.

General Barsadias glared at Trans.

Terrified, Trans picked up his food, spilling half of it as he ran. The general took his place.

Marcus could feel the tension exuding from his father like the heat from the campfire. He didn't speak to his men, nor did he smile. He stared into the flame with his jaw clenched and the soles of his feet firmly planted.

Marcus stared at the ground, squeezing his hands together.

"I saw you fight," his voice shattering any hope Marcus had of a job well done. "Look at me." Barsadias took hold of his son's face and forced him to look him dead in the eye.

Marcus didn't shy away.

"Don't you ever let me see you fight like that again. I taught you better."

Marcus nodded and tore his face from his father's grasp as he fought the tears of frustration he felt building in his eyes. He'd won and still his father wasn't proud of him.

"Don't," the general said. "If you can't fight, I might

as well run my sword through you right now, cause you won't live through the training. As my heir, I'll kill you myself before you ever embarrass me on a battlefield."

Fireworks exploded in the distance and Marcus used the distraction to wipe his eyes. He tried to ignore his father by watching some soldiers tie a slave to a fence post and pour wine down their throat. They were going to get the man so drunk he wouldn't be able to walk straight. It was funny to watch a man walk around like a fool. Some of them even became violent.

The fireworks rose over the city, but Marcus noted his father wasn't watching them. Naiden's gates were opening and Octavia, a woman with grey hair and an apron, stepped out.

"It's time," said Marcus's father.

Marcus stood up and followed his father. As they passed, men and women put their hands on his shoulder congratulating him. A sort of tunnel assembled as Marcus drew closer and closer to the woman waiting at the gate. An old retired soldier waved down at him from the watch tower. He sat next to the old warning bell that had never been rung. Younger boys looked at him in awe and young girls with respect. He did his best to make himself look dignified.

They reached the gate and the general passed him into the woman's charge. "I'll see you soon, son."

Marcus looked back at his father, nodded, and followed her into the city.

The crowd outside cheered as they disappeared from view.

LXI

INK AND SKIN

Marcus walked in the woman's shadow as she turned to the first house within the gate. It was made of stone and was nothing extravagant to look at from the outside. It could have been mistaken for a slave's home.

Unlike most citizens her dress had sleeves and he couldn't see what her family crest looked like. He'd seen her walking the streets of Naiden a few times, but she mostly kept to herself.

Octavia swung open the door and left it ajar for Marcus. The house smelled of ink and still air. He shut the door behind him as he listened to Octavia wheeze into a room further down the hall. *Do her slaves ever clean?*

Marcus hadn't been in this cabin since his first birthday and tonight his tattoo would be completed. He assumed the place hadn't changed much, from the layers of dust on the shelves, but what struck him about the house was the endless array of paintings on the walls. He'd never seen so many of them in his life. His family home had a few, but none were as detailed.

There were paintings of men and elves fighting in the wars, battles with the Azuk, and images from a time he'd never learned about.

Marcus looked at as many paintings as he could as he strode down the hall to the same door Octavia had gone through. Stepping into the room there were even more paintings. Canvases piled along the floors and overwhelmed the shelves.

In the centre of the room was a reclining chair. Octavia had set it so he'd be sitting upright, but on the side of it were levers and handles so she could adjust it if she needed someone to lie down as she worked. She didn't only ink people with family crests, but often people would come to her to get symbols of victory or love or whatever they desired.

"Please sit on the table and take off your shirt," said Octavia.

Marcus did as he was told and his body began to involuntarily tremble as he became aware of the sharp sticks, brushes, and a vat of black ink on the table.

Octavia sat down in her chair next to him. She pointed at the number on his shoulder. "I gave you that on your first birthday." She rolled up her sleeves and her arms were covered in tattoos.

Marcus swallowed back his fear. "Did you do these?"

Octavia smiled. "Some of them. My mother gave me this one of her and my father. And this one of my favourite horse growing up. You probably can't tell through all the wrinkles, but she was a black and white paint with blue eyes. Followed me everywhere I went. My daughter's added to them and I taught her, so you have nothing to fear. She'd usually be here, but her husband came with your father."

"I've never seen so many tattoos on one person."

Most were made with black ink, but within hers was a tint of navy blue and a tattoo that was the most intricate family crest that he'd ever seen. The circular tattoo was a picture of a sun and moon. Standing in front of it was a perfectly balanced scale, and the arm of the scale looked like a paintbrush. Suspended on the scale were two eyes, one dark and the other light.

"It's my story," Octavia rolled down her sleeves. "My mother and her mother and so on painted these canvases. I come from a line of painters of history. Along with my regular training, my mother taught me how to paint. She made me memorize the story behind every canvas in this house till I knew the smallest details. I decided at a young age to cover my arms in a story I'd lived and not a story I was told."

"So these all happened?"

"Yes," she responded, stirring a clay jar of ink.

"How do you know they looked like that?" asked Marcus, pointing to the first painting he saw.

The woman smiled. "You see these eyes?"

Her eyes were two different colours.

"The blue eye sees truth and the brown is brown because they're telling me—" She was about to say a word, but she held back. "Lies. And if they're lying or not telling me the whole story, a grey area appears on the canvas."

Marcus saw there were a few grey areas. A lot of them on the paintings from the elven battles. He looked at them with growing curiosity, knowing it would take a lifetime to learn them all.

"Now this is going to take a bit of time." She leaned in, delighted to tell one of her tales. "Every person who sits in my chair gets to hear a story about a painting while I work, but first I must discover what story you're meant to hear."

Octavia placed both her hands on Marcus's head and closed her eyes.

Marcus didn't know whether he was supposed to close his eyes as well, but since she didn't say anything, he left them open and watched her eyes move beneath the surface of her lids. She opened her eyes and sat back in her seat, staring at Marcus as though she was seeing him for the first time.

Octavia stood to her feet and rummaged through many canvases, searching through the depths of her collection. She pulled out an old and withered painting. She surveyed it but didn't show it to Marcus yet.

"My ancestor, Merlana, painted this." Octavia hesitated to even show it to him, and when she did, Marcus's eyes were instantly drawn to it.

An elvian woman in a white flowing night dress lay dying in King Zoren's arms. Tears of grief streamed down both their faces, and Marcus stared at the elf's beauty. Her arms were covered in what looked like water droplets, but her torso was bathed in blood. Zoren's sword pierced straight through her and onto the floor behind her. A strange-looking sword was discarded on the floor, beyond the elvian's reach.

Marcus recognized King Zoren's black hair and skin as he held the sword in her chest. His other hand cupped her head close to him, tears of his own agony flowing freely from his eyes. Anger stirred in Marcus towards the king who'd caused pain to something so beautiful.

The rest of the room was occupied with soldiers and all of them carried spears, pointed at the elf. Marcus almost missed it. The soldier closest to Zoren's side was holding a white blanket.

Octavia broke the silence. "The story of Queen Lina, the elvian." She picked up a piece of string and used it to draw the lines of the tattoo on Marcus's shoulder. She didn't speak until it was fully drawn. Once she was satisfied with the design, she took up two sticks. One with a small needle on the end to puncture the ink into the skin by tapping.

Marcus winced, but kept still.

"A long time ago, not very far from here, a man strode into Sidabras carrying his wounded mother and a silver tree of Reeza. The streets crowded with celebration. A new king had come to save them. We were on the brink of becoming slaves to the Azuk, and he was the answer to everyone's prayers. He carried the mantel of war and led his people to victory. And as the dust settled, King Zoren ensured our nation would never falter again. Boys at the age of seven trained and lived by the sword and for women it was much the same. Every citizen was given a sword to bear and an enemy to vanquish. The people of Azuk were brought here to serve, and our people devoted themselves to protecting the realm."

"But having the support of his own people was not

enough. King Zoren's men conquered the surrounding realms. First Remead, then Antioc, followed by Patrelis. An invitation from the elves was extended, and he went to share in their power."

Octavia shifted in her chair. "Queen Gretafold had Zoren and his men escorted to Amarisa blindfolded and welcomed him with a smile, but it lacked trust. As Zoren stood in the queen's throne room, her daughter Princess Lina entered and he instantly fell for her and she for him. Queen Gretafold saw a darkness inside his soul and refused their union, but the two consummated their love and bound themselves together. It was a union that not even the queen could break."

"Lina became queen of Remisia and was her husband's most loyal subject. Even as the war between men and elves rose, she did not leave his side."

"What happened?" asked Marcus.

"Iron fought against iron, and despite the efforts of the elven warriors, they were overwhelmed. The king's men had become numerous and strong with the aid of the sungazer venom. No matter what Zoren did to Lina's people, torturing, mutilating, and killing them, she never flinched. She led Zoren's armies to attack the dwarves and captured her own people, turning them to stone and binding their magic to her husband. But then one day Lina turned on Zoren. With her sword drawn and her eyes filled with vengeance, she stormed the king's court. They fought, but he had become more powerful than she and stabbed her in front of his men. Regret flooded Zoren's soul, and he wept like no man ever before. She died in his arms. He carried her body out of the palace. Despite the war, he disappeared, placing her in a crypt somewhere within Sidabras's walls."

"Why would she attack him?"

"No one knows. It's believed that before Lina attempted to take her husband's life, she gave birth to a son."

Marcus realized the small bundle in the soldiers's grasp must have been their child. "Where is he?"

Octavia shrugged. "Rumours spoke of a baby crying and left for dead in the cells of the castle. But suddenly one day they stopped. Some believe he still lives down there. How else is our king able to step onto the battlefield without an heir to replace him? King Zoren is as bound to the laws of Remisia as his people. Only descendants of the original five can enter battle without a child."

"So the boy could still be alive down there?"

"If he is, I pity him. It would've been kinder if he'd died. Probably gone mad."

Marcus couldn't imagine never leaving a single room all his life. Zoren's son would never know what the stars looked like.

Octavia was almost finished. "There's only ever been one other person who came close enough to killing our king. One night, after her daughter's death, Queen Gretafold mysteriously got past the trees of Reeza, but the king defeated her too. And neither elf nor bird has been seen in these lands since."

The door opened and Marcus's father came in.

"All done." Her eyes went white and Marcus's tattoo felt warm. "Now the tattoo will grow as you grow."

General Barsadias came around and inspected the fresh tattoo.

Marcus saw Octavia move the painting of Zoren and Lina out of sight while his father was distracted.

His father seemed pleased and pulled out his money pouch, offering Octavia five silver coins. "You tell him a story?"

"Of course." She motioned her head to a painting on the wall of King Zoren on a white horse, charging the fields with the head of an elf on the end of a spear. "I saw to tell him the story about the king winning the Battle of Fearino where General Mortegan defeated the elves by sneaking themselves into the elven camp by the river."

Marcus listened to her lie, but didn't dare to correct her. He knew the punishment for lying to a general, but he questioned why she lied. *If the story was true, then why shy away from it?* It did not speak of the king in the lightest of lights, but it spoke of his humanity. Perhaps Zoren didn't want to appear human or let his people know he'd killed his wife. Marcus had certainly never heard of how she'd died.

General Barsadias inspected the painting. "That's the same one you told me."

"Well, he's a lot like you," said Octavia.

Marcus pulled his shirt back on and looked proudly at his family crest. It was exactly like his father's and now he was one step closer to becoming like him. His father motioned him to follow outside.

"Thanks," Marcus mumbled, unable to look Octavia in the eye. He knew to keep his mouth shut.

Everyone in the crowd cheered as he and his father joined the party again.

Marcus felt a bit dazed by it all, but he put on his best smile as the people called out his name.

General Barsadias grabbed his wrist. "And now comes the final event of the evening."

Marcus tried to make eye contact with his father, but the general wouldn't look at him. He didn't know what his father meant. He'd gotten his tattoo. *What else is supposed to happen?*

The partiers split into an aisle towards where his father was taking him. Marcus tried to take a step back as he saw what was ahead, but his father tightened his grip around his wrist.

Before them, bleeding on her knees and tied up, was Mizpah.

The colour drained out of Marcus's face and he wanted to dig his heels into the ground and flee.

"Get out your dagger," his father said.

"Father?" Marcus questioned, dragging his gaze from Mizpah's weeping face. The people he'd known all his life smiled down at him with encouragement.

"Come on." General Barsadias pushed his son closer to Mizpah and dug his nails into his shoulder.

Marcus slowly reached down and drew his dagger, holding it shakily in front of him.

A cut bled from Mizpah's forehead, trickling into her left eye and dripping onto her always clean tunic.

The last thing on Marcus's mind was harming her. If his father would release him, he'd do the opposite. He would've fetched a cloth and soaked it in water to clean her wounds, like she had done for him every time he'd gone to her growing up. The dagger felt heavy in his hand and all he could do was stare at her, not believing this was truly happening. It felt like a nightmare, and no matter how many times he blinked, he didn't wake up.

Mizpah's eyes never left him. Her breath came in spurts as she tried to stay calm for his sake.

Sweat dripped on Marcus's forehead and he fought the urge to cut Mizpah's bonds and tell her to run. She was only an arm's reach away and if he thought either of them would get away with it, he would. There were too many of them and they'd never get very far. Mizpah wasn't old. She had a child close to his age, but she was no match against the citizens surrounding her.

Marcus's father knelt down beside him. "Now remember what I told you, the best place to kill is the neck or up through the gut and into the heart." General Barsadias traced his fingers on the skin of the woman who raised him, showing him the best places to kill her, like she was an animal they were about to butcher. "Given this is your first official kill, you'd probably be best to go for the neck."

Marcus turned to face his father, not believing the words he was saying. This woman had been his mother. His Aunt Mariana had paid him no mind or shown him a fraction of the care this woman had. When his father was away, she'd been the one to take care of him. She'd been the one to tell him she wasn't his real mother. The one who'd nursed every bruise he'd sustained when he fought his father.

General Barsadias pushed him even closer to Mizpah. "Come on, son," commanded his father, his pride getting the better of him.

As much as Marcus fought the tears, one broke as he looked into Mizpah's loving face. He felt the anguish of her loss drenching his soul.

Mizpah broke the silence and whispered. "It's okay.

412

Remember what I told you. Listen to what your father tells you."

General Barsadias grabbed his son's hand and urged it upwards.

Marcus closed his eyes as he felt his hand moving closer and closer to Mizpah's throat, when suddenly, a noise, unlike any he'd ever heard, pierced the night sky.

LXII

NAIDEN

The current of wind sent chairs flying. Trees broke in half, and everyone in the crowd fell to the ground, screeching in terror. Every fire in the city went out and only the fallen corn glowed in the darkness.

The world went silent. The crickets were gone. The music was stopped. And General Barsadias slowly rose to his feet.

Marcus's dagger lay forgotten as he looked at the sky and the moon darkened as insects fled to find sanctuary.

Dogs howled and broke free from their chains, yelping as they took off with their tails between their legs. One dog's chains were too thick and it yipped to get away.

Children ran to their mothers and everyone searched the skies, unsure of what was happening or what was coming.

Marcus reached out and grabbed his father's hand and, for the first time in his life, he gave his hand a slight squeeze. "Father—"

Another wind resounded over them like a thousand arrows, knocking those who'd risen back onto the ground. Marcus lost hold of his father's hand and houses crumbled.

Marcus watched his father rise and draw his sword. "Men!"

All of the soldiers followed their general's lead.

"On me!" he yelled.

A roar shook Marcus to his very core. It broke the silence, and a pillar of fire struck Naiden.

"Dragon!" shouted a man in horror.

Marcus stood paralyzed until he heard his father shout his name.

"Go," cried the general.

Marcus snapped out of it, but he wouldn't leave Mizpah. As his father and his men charged the flames, Marcus picked up his fallen dagger and cut Mizpah's bonds. He gave her a quick embrace but they didn't have time to speak. The dragon was turning back in the sky and would soon be upon them.

"Run to the river. I'll meet you there." Mizpah kissed him on the cheek and ran to get her own children.

Marcus headed northeast towards the river. Heat burned against his side, and he didn't dare enter the city.

The dragon passed again, knocking him down and stoking the flames. He got up and a wall of fire blocked his path around the city, compelling him to go through Naiden.

Men and women screamed as the dragon breathed,

setting another part of his home ablaze. Women ran with a sword in one hand and a child in the other, while the men raced to the remaining rooftops to fight off the creature.

Marcus waited outside the walls for the dragon to pass. Between each sweep of the dragon, there were a few moments to get through. As he waited, his mind calculated how long he thought it might take. He and Trans had raced it many times, but this was a matter of life and death. He was knocked to the ground. Fire erupted at the end of the city, and Marcus shot up and ran.

Nearly every building in Naiden had either fallen or was gorged in flame. The timber groaned and gave way, fragments just missed him as he swerved down another road. The air was thick with smoke, choking the life out of those still alive.

Marcus coughed and leaned over to catch a breath. He'd never make it unless he did something.

A woman ran past him, covering her mouth with an apron. With only his shirt to protect him from the heat, he didn't want to remove it, but he wouldn't survive if he didn't take it off. He saw a line of laundry in the street and picked off the first article of clothing he could get, holding it against his mouth. Keeping low to the ground, he worked his way to the other side of Naiden.

Marcus exited the north-eastern gate when he saw Mizpah with her three children. He changed his course, heading towards her, but the air shifted above them.

"Mizpah!" Her eyes met his but it was too late. A wall of fire made him stop and she and her children were gone. He couldn't believe his eyes. One moment she was there and the next she wasn't. He wanted to go to her, mourn, scream, and fall into despair, but as he moved to go to her, a fire laden beam blocked his way.

Screams cried out only to be silenced. The air surged over the river and the dragon exhaled a white flame into the water. Those who'd sought its sanctuary boiled alive.

Marcus couldn't stay a moment longer and raced back the way he came. The river was no longer safe.

On the outskirts of the city and beyond the burning remnants of Marcus's birthday party stood Marcus's father and the last of his regiment. There weren't many left to fight, and it gave Marcus hope to see the general leading the charge.

Marcus felt the wind pulse like a slow heartbeat, filling his ears and his entire body like a drum.

The dragon, as black as midnight, landed on the burning embers of Naiden. It cocked its head and let out an earth shattering roar.

The general ordered his men to fire arrows at the beast, but they were useless. They burned to nothing before they could even reach the creature's hide. The army looked like children.

Marcus caught Barsadias's gaze, and he saw him say, "Look to the end," as he and his men were consumed in the fiery breath of the dragon.

Marcus screamed and ran to his father. He knelt next to his father's ashes as the dragon drew closer. Tears poured from his eyes.

"I—I see—I see your end," he faltered.

I am alone. My parents, aunt, Trans, and Mizpah have all gone to Valganen. There's no one left.

The creature stood on its hind legs and cried out in challenge.

417

Marcus covered his ears, his little heartbeat pounding. *I don't think I can do this.* And like a response from the grave, his father's sword caught the fire light. That dragon had murdered everyone he cared about. He picked up the sword. He ignored the searing pain of his flesh burning against the hilt and looked into the piercing amber eyes of the black dragon. *My father was brave, so am I.*

He rose up from the ashes, holding onto the faces of those he held dear. Anger festered in his soul. He raised his sword to vanquish the creature who'd taken everything from him and he charged.

The dragon stepped on another building and it gave way. It stared Marcus straight in the eyes, never losing contact.

Marcus held its gaze, storming the outer field with every ounce of his strength.

The beast cocked its head back and blew air from the very depths of its lungs.

And the last thing seven-year-old Marcus ever saw, as his world turned black, were the eyes of the creature he hated most.

LXIII

DON'T LOOK BACK

"I woke up, but I couldn't see."

Aleksia watched the final moments of the memory of that night pass through his eyes and all the good times seemed to fade.

"I knew what they'd do if they found me, so I ran. Trans and I had a cave in the woods where we used to camp and I found my way to it. There were a few things there to get me started."

"How did you survive out there on your own?"

"My dog, Hera, was the one who found me. The dragon was gone, and she helped guide me through the years. I knew how to fish and my father taught me how to make snares. The hardest part was keeping a fire going. At first, I didn't want to even try to make a fire. Within the crackles, I could hear the screams of the ones who didn't survive, but I couldn't eat my food raw."

"Perhaps you could help me with my fear of the dark."

"I'm sure an elf in Amarisa will be able to help you far better than I."

"Would you come with me?" she asked, her eyes pleading.

"I can't," he breathed.

"Why?"

"Because I'm staying here."

Aleksia couldn't believe what was coming out of his mouth.

"I'll hold as many of the guards back as I can, collapse Lucinda's tunnel if I must. I can give you a head start."

"But you're the one who started all this."

"For everyone else," he explained.

"And why not you?"

"I'll slow everyone down."

"I'll help you," said Aleksia. "If you'll let me."

Marcus stood to his feet. "I'll stand between everyone else's freedom and the sword. Lucinda was right. All those people walking the barriers and I never —"

Aleksia rose to challenge him. "You can't blame yourself."

"There are a lot of things I blame myself for." Marcus reached out and touched her shoulder, moving his hand up to find her cheek. "If this is to be our last conversation, I need you to know how much I regret what happened the night we met. You touched me and all I could hear and feel were the barriers. I spent every day hating you for what your people did to me, but now I can't imagine—" His voice faltered.

Aleksia covered his hand with her own. "I was naïve

when we first met. It's only since I've been at your side that I've seen the truth. I understand why. But neither of us will ever know if Haman and his men would have found me anyway."

"This time I'm going to make sure you get out. Lucinda can lead you back to your people and Zoren will never find you."

Aleksia could see his mind was made up and it broke her heart to see him do it. He was giving up. *If only his eyes had healed. Why hadn't they healed?* Was dragon fire beyond her skills? Tears of frustration fell from her eyes. "Please. Let me help you get out of this place."

Marcus pulled away from her hand. "Don't shame me, Aleksia." His face downcast. "Leave me behind and don't look back."

Aleksia wiped the tears away, anger and frustration building a new resolve within her as she picked up the bucket and broken tools. "Then find your own way out of here." And she left.

LXIV

FROM THE
SHADOWS

Veeta held her breath as she pushed herself into a crevice in the wall until Aleksia passed. And then she grinned.

She poked out her head to see Marcus staggering in the light of the cave. All the whipping scars on his back and the scratches on his torso were gone. She watched his shaking hands pick up his shirt and put it back on. His left hand stretched out to find the wall and he walked towards her.

Veeta was apprehensive he'd discover her and warn Aleksia of her fate. But Aleksia would not be escaping with the rest of them tonight. At her feet she saw a rock and bent down, careful not to graze the walls and alert Marcus to her presence. Grasping it tightly, she lifted it without a sound.

Marcus halted in front of Veeta's crevice. He'd lost

contact with the wall and stood there, wiping the moisture from his eyes.

You will weep far greater tears when you learn of Aleksia's fate, citizen, thought Veeta, revelling in the pain she would cause both of them. She'd followed them, thinking she'd catch them formatting a plan to betray them all with their lies, but she was leaving with a far better prize than she'd hoped. There was only one species in all the realms who could heal, and it was the one creature King Zoren desperately wanted.

Marcus looked up as though he'd heard something and Veeta tightened her grip around the stone. She was on the verge of attacking, but he kept walking and she relaxed.

General Quinn will be pleased with this news, she thought. Of all the magicians she'd turned in, surely this would be her greatest reward. She was ambitious. If given the chance, she could learn to do something other than crush rocks.

Veeta exhaled and emerged from her hiding place. She constrained herself not to run and draw attention to herself as she sought to find Ravlin, the guard who was as desperate to prove himself as she was. Ever since he'd lost the sword fight to Marcus, he'd suffered the scrutiny of his peers. He usually patrolled the eastern wall, passing through the hustle and bustle of young children and men carrying support beams. She weaved through them and felt a surge of adrenaline when she finally spotted him.

Ravlin saw her and swept his gaze over the mine. He was going to walk right past her but Veeta took his forearm. "I've found one."

"Who?" he asked.

"Not here," she whispered, knowing what he'd do.

"Start struggling." He wrapped his arm around her waist.

Veeta pretended to struggle in his arms and he lifted her off the ground. She let out a small cry and he smacked her.

"Be silent."

No one helped. Everyone diverted their eyes to the side as though nothing was happening, and even though it wasn't real, it still hurt that there was no one who would come to her rescue.

Ravlin dragged her into the horse stable and released her.

"I need to speak to General Quinn," said Veeta.

"What's the information?" he asked, pressing her against the wall in case another slave came in to tend the horses.

Veeta kissed him and while he got lost in it, she wedged her way out of his embrace. "I'll only tell General Quinn." She wouldn't let him take the credit. She saw a few horses in the stable, and one of them was outside, fully tacked to go. "We should ride there now."

"Tell me what you know."

"Trust me," pleaded Veeta. "Has my information ever not been good?"

Ravlin picked up a batch of chains to attach behind the horse, but Veeta wouldn't have it and strode to the horse outside.

"There's no time for me to run behind the horse to Ironwood or to wait till nightfall. The general will want to know now." Veeta threw her foot to catch the stirrup, but the beast moved and she missed. She cursed under her breath and chased after it. She grabbed the mane and Ravlin came up behind her, hurling her into the saddle. Her body tensed as the horse moved underneath her.

Ravlin untied the steed and took its reins. "You only ride until the far edge of the graveyard." He got on behind her, wrapping her in his arms to take the reins, and kicked.

Veeta had imagined hammering a soldier off a horse and riding away plenty of times, but the real thing had no comparison. The breeze moved against her skin as they climbed up the path and out of the hole in the earth they called a mine. The horse started to canter and she felt like she was flying. Her body moved to its rhythm. With her information she hoped she'd never have to go back.

Ravlin made her run once they reached the end of the graveyard, but both of them walked through the city gates. The smell of the fresh bread and unabashed laughter hit her first. Civilian children ran down the street and their nurses chased after them.

She'd never seen so many people roaming the streets of Ironwood, usually the guards dallied until nightfall to bring her here, but the market was crowded.

Handmaids carried umbrellas over their mistresses as they rifled through togas or swords. Slaves bartered like dogs trying to get a pat on the head from their master. They carried silver but none of it was theirs. Not a single slave owned the wares they were selling or purchasing. It was all for the sake of their owner. Some of the slaves were smiling as they did it. It disgusted

Veeta. *They call this happiness.*

Both citizen and slave looked at her with revulsion and covered their noses as she passed, laughing at her expense. She wouldn't let these fools get to her. She didn't need their approval or their pity. They'd been born with a silver spoon in their mouths and she licked a wooden bowl for every scrap. Reverse their roles and they wouldn't last a day enduring what she'd come to call normal. Soon it would be all over.

They came to General Quinn's villa. An ornate litter sat in the courtyard and the gardens smelled like the highest level of Valganen. They climbed up the stairs. Ravlin pulled a silk string and bells rang.

A housemaid came to the door. She glared at Veeta and scrunched up her nose. "Can I help you?"

"We need to see General Quinn," replied Ravlin.

"I'm sorry. The general is busy at the moment and won't be disturbed."

Ravlin pushed her aside. "We can't delay."

Veeta knew she'd picked the right soldier to deliver her message. His desire to move up in the ranks was almost as strong as her own.

The doors to General Quinn's study opened and Veeta saw the general sitting at his desk with his family. A tiny infant rested in his arms as he teased it with a small wooden sword, whispering tales of war in its small ear.

The general never looked up from the child, and the mother did the same, watching in adoration. Her stomach still appeared like there was a baby inside, but it only spoke to the recent birth. Dark rings framed Daphne's eyes, but her perfectly polished sword remained at her hip. Even after giving birth, she would be a tough opponent. She was a legendary swordswoman and taught other girls to be the same.

To Veeta, they looked like the perfect family, but she knew it was a deception.

Ravlin broke the silence. "Congratulations on your newest son, Augustin, General Quinn and Mistress Daphne."

General Quinn's eyes flickered up, and Veeta saw his annoyance at their interruption. He stroked the side of his child and spoke. "Did I not say I wasn't to be disturbed?"

"Yes General, but—" started Ravlin.

"But what?" General Quinn passed the child to his wife.

"This slave has information, which requires your immediate attention."

"What information?"

Ravlin remained silent and his jaw clenched.

General Quinn stood to his feet, approaching the soldier until they were face to face. "What information?" he asked again.

Still Ravlin admitted nothing and Veeta didn't want to draw attention to herself.

General Quinn grabbed Ravlin and threw him across the room. The soldier smashed into a bookcase and the books fell on top of him as he hit the floor. The child stirred in Daphne's arms.

Veeta hadn't even seen the general move and she took a step back.

Ravlin's breath was rapid, trying to control his temper. "I don't know," said the soldier as he pushed himself up to stand back to attention.

"You don't know?"

"I don't know, sir."

General Quinn went and sat on his desk with his hands held together in front of him. "So you bring me a slave with 'immediate' information and you don't know what it pertains?"

"No, General," confessed Ravlin through his teeth.

"Get out."

Ravlin moved to take Veeta with him.

"Not her," instructed General Quinn.

Veeta felt all the blood drain out of her face and her knees weakened as Quinn went to his wife and whispered something in her ear. He kissed the child's brow and they departed out another door.

Ravlin washed his hands of Veeta and left. The door thudded shut and Veeta didn't take her eyes off the general as he sat back down at his desk. He picked up the wooden sword he'd been taunting his son with earlier and started sharpening it with his dagger. Veeta prayed he wasn't sharpening it to kill her. She should have kept her mouth shut and stayed in the mine. Now she would die and all the others would escape.

"Speak," said the general, as the wood shavings hit the table.

Veeta wasn't sure if she had a voice to find, but she tried to keep it level as she addressed the general. "I want out of the mines. I want a better life after I tell you what I saw."

General Quinn tested the blade's sharpness with a touch of his finger. "How about I let you live?"

Veeta's resolve caved. "I saw an elf in the mines."

General Quinn smirked. "An elf? What did this elf do?"

"I followed her and Marcus into an old abandoned tunnel. There was a hole in the roof and after he removed his shirt, she stepped into the light and the whole cavern filled with light. She tried to heal him of his blindness."

General Quinn stopped carving. "Was she successful?"

"He's still blind, but almost every other scar on him is gone."

"Who?" General Quinn rose from his desk and drew closer to Veeta.

Veeta's voice staggered. "I want out of the mines."

"Done, so long as what you've told me is true. If not," he paused, "I'll skin you with my son's wooden sword until it dulls, and still I'll keep cutting."

"It's Aleksia."

"The female citizen?"

"Yes," Veeta scowled.

General Quinn studied her features. "And you hate her?"

"That's not why I accuse her."

"It better not be," he warned. "She is protected by blood. You are not."

"I swear on my life."

"And so it will depend," he said. "Guard."

The doors to the hall opened immediately.

"Take this girl to the dungeon and bring me Othelus. I have a job for her."

LXV

DARKENING IN THE SOUTH

Aleksia kept looking over at Marcus. He'd picked up his own tools at the shed and was trying to work alone. He kept missing the chisel and he wasn't even hitting the right spot. Aleksia wanted to toss her own tools to the side and help him.

Trigon had come back to dig with them and he stood in front of Marcus so the guards couldn't see his poor progress, but neither of them would be there in the morning.

Will Trigon stay? He'd made a vow to Marcus to watch and protect him; she wondered how strong his countenance was.

Trigon kept giving her looks. He knew something happened, but this wasn't the place to discuss it. She had to speak to him about dragging Marcus with them. He'd be eager to help. Together, they'd talk some sense into him and they'd all be rid of this place.

Marcus's disbelief and disappointment was etched into her mind like one of her carvings. It was all her fault. She'd made a promise she couldn't keep.

What purpose did the dragon have for killing so many people and blinding Marcus? Dragons always had a reason. A few of her guardians built shrines to the beasts, but she knew little about the species. She never took part in their prayers and she admired their devotion. They believed fire would one day rise again from Mount Tikalnus's mouth like a volcano in rupture. A force of nature that could not be contained and it would ignite war.

A soldier entered the cavern and started pulling miners.

"I wasn't aware of any transfers," declared the one in charge.

"A storm is coming. We need to move the timber inside," he replied as he took another person.

The man grabbed Aleksia. "You too."

She saw Marcus and Trigon motion to help but she held up her hand.

"The rest of you, keep working," said the guard.

Aleksia followed, surrendering her hammer and chisel outside the tunnel. She was directed to a fresh shipment of timbers on the mine floor.

Rose passed by, carrying an empty bucket.

Aleksia gave her a slight wave.

The girl's eyes lit up, returning the gesture as they passed one another. She disappeared out of sight into a tunnel.

The sky was grey, and darkening in the south.

"Pick up that lumber and come with me," a soldier

ordered Aleksia.

She lifted it over her shoulder, watching to see how many the others were taking. They lifted one at a time, so she did the same. The soldier led her to a cave on the far western side of the quarry where she'd never been before.

"Bring as many as you can and put them in there." The guard pointed to one of the tunnels and left her to finish the work.

The guards in the towers overlooking the circumference of the mine kept her in their sights, armed with arrows to ensure she didn't step out of line. Aleksia didn't need to escape yet so she put the piece of lumber in the tunnel and went to grab another. There was no need to stir up any trouble.

LXVI

CAPTURE

Othelus's emerald eyes glowed with delight under the darkening sky. Her prey was alone, separated from the herd like a doe in a vacant canyon, and she was the wolf, licking her lips for the kill.

Three soldiers awaited her command to move in, but their hopes of taking down an elf were dashed. General Quinn wanted the elvian brought in unharmed and there was only one way to do that.

One soldier carried a wicker basket and Othelus reached into it. She felt the sungazer crawl into her hand and she lifted it out. The brown lizard wrapped its body around her arm and nudged its dragon like head into her palm affectionately. She stroked it as she drew on a little magic from her stone and sunk into its mind, taking command of its instincts and desires.

Othelus's pupils transformed into slits like the lizard

she commanded, and she filled the sungazer with her will. The lizard stuck out its tongue and she tasted the air on her own. Smells of rock, sweat, and the afternoon breeze overwhelmed her senses. The cooks on the other side of the mine turned their pots of rolling soup and she fought the creature's instinct to go to it. Turning it to sweeter meat.

An instinct receding back to its creation took hold of the lizard. Its eyes fixed on Aleksia and it leapt onto the ground, dashing across the rocks. Claws extended and breath even, it was unhindered.

Othelus urged the creature to camouflage itself and suddenly green became far more vibrant and everything else dulled in comparison.

But what surprised Othelus most was when the lizard fixed its gaze on Aleksia.

Up and down between the crevasses of its walk, Othelus caught glimpses, but there was no doubt in her mind the woman was an elvian. Through the veil of the lizard's eye, she saw the pointed ears and the dazzling vertes all along her arms and neck. The rest of the world around her seemed to dull in comparison to her beauty. To think she'd been under General Quinn's eye the entire time and he'd never noticed.

The sungazer got a little ahead of the elvian, but when Aleksia passed, it pounced, sinking its fangs into her skin and releasing enough venom to bring her to the ground.

LXVII

TO FREEDOM

Marcus didn't think he'd have the heart to say goodbye to Aleksia as he walked back to the cells next to Trigon. They'd been through so much together and he didn't think he could muster the right words. What he was doing was logical and it would keep her safe. The longing to speak to her, and the fear that he would, were opposing one another in his mind. He had to do this, but if she asked him one more time to go with her, he wasn't sure he'd have the strength to refuse. He cringed at how he'd reacted when her magic failed to heal him. Never once did he blame her and he wanted to make sure she knew that before she left.

Maybe she'd come back with an army. This certainly would be one of the first places he'd attack to weaken the king's hold on the land. He'd cut off the king's iron and free the people to go spread the word that Zoren's days were numbered.

A silence hung over the crowd. People were trying to decide whether to take a chance at freedom or accept their fate. Marcus hoped when they saw him enter a cell without a hole it didn't discourage them from seizing their freedom.

He hadn't even mentioned his plan to stay to Trigon. Trigon had a family to get back to, people who lifted their heads as they worked and searched for his coming on the horizon. His wife Linet and their children needed him far more than he did, though he would miss him. It had been a long time since he'd had a friend.

A hand grabbed Marcus from behind, stopping him in his tracks, but it wasn't Aleksia.

"Marcus," said Ravlin.

Marcus recognized the voice as the man he'd beaten after the tunnel collapsed.

Trigon stopped to help.

"You, keep walking," he commanded Trigon, as he constrained Marcus to walk with him.

What did he want? A rematch? They walked faster than the others, and Marcus lost count of the steps. He wasn't sure where they were headed, but he guessed the young soldier wanted revenge. Marcus tried to wedge his arm free from him.

Ravlin slapped him. "Stop."

"What do you want?" Marcus demanded.

Ravlin turned.

The walls echoed and Marcus knew where they were. They were in the cell tunnels and he dragged him to the closest one. The slaves serving the evening meal watched as Ravlin roughly shoved Marcus into a cell and slammed the door.

"King Zoren will be here by nightfall," said Ravlin.

All of the colour drained out of Marcus's face. "Why tell me?"

"I think you know," taunted the soldier as he leaned in as close as he dared. "There's not a mark on you."

Marcus grasped the bars and his knuckles whitened.

"I only hope the king keeps her here, so when she screams you'll hear her as she turns to stone and Zoren rips the vertes from her mangled corpse."

Marcus reached through the bars to hit Ravlin, but he'd stepped back.

Ravlin smirked and walked away.

Marcus punched the bars until his knuckles bled. The cell was full of strangers and Marcus grasped the first person he could get his hands on.

"Lead me to the hole in the floor."

The man shook his head no.

Marcus softened his voice. "Please."

"There isn't one," said the man stepping away.

Pressure built in Marcus's temple as his mind yearned to figure out a way to get to Aleksia. They'd taken her to move timbers, and he'd let them. Maybe Ravlin was lying, but he couldn't be, otherwise how would he have known Aleksia was an elvian? He went back to the door and pulled. It rattled but never opened. He felt his way to the cool metal hinges and dug at them with his nails but they didn't budge.

"Marcus!" Trigon whispered from the cell across the hall.

Marcus grasped the bars with both hands. "Is Aleksia in your cell?"

"No."

Marcus punched the bars again but it didn't make him feel any better.

"What are you doing in there?" asked Trigon.

"Ravlin threw me in here but I have to find Aleksia. I think Quinn has her."

"I'll find out."

Marcus heard the board in Trigon's cell shuffle to the side. He could hear it only because every sense in his body was alert. He wanted to vomit but he'd been denied supper. It seemed like hours had passed when he heard Trigon speak again.

"Lucinda's going to all the cells but still no luck."

"Tell her to check again," entreated Marcus, cursing himself. It was his fault. If she hadn't attempted to heal his eyes, she'd probably be cursing him from the cell across the hall, but she would've been safe. Now, who knew what General Quinn was doing to her.

"There's no sign of her," said Trigon.

Marcus sat down with his back against the cell door. He ran his hand through his hair and didn't know what to do. The escape happened at midnight; he didn't have long. He had to get out now. He could try to dig, but it would be to no avail. Even with tools, it would take days and would draw too much attention. People in the cell would probably think he'd gone mad. He didn't care. He had to get to Aleksia before the king did.

He pushed on the door again with his back but met the same result.

"What can I do?" offered Trigon.

Marcus could hear the desperation in Trigon's voice. "Go. Be with your family and don't look back."

"But—"

"You've been there for me ever since the day we met, but your family needs you far more than I do."

"I'll stay."

"Don't," begged Marcus. "Please."

Trigon sat against the bars in the cell across the hall and huffed. "If it wasn't for them—"

"I know. You've saved my life in more ways than you know," vindicated Marcus. "Go and hear your wife sing in the fields and kiss your children."

"I'll tell them about you."

"You better," Marcus smirked.

"Crazy citizen who ate Lymana soup and faced the jura."

"Don't leave out a single detail."

"I won't."

"Good."

And there was nothing else to say. Neither of them were any good at goodbyes and Marcus had to figure out how he was going to get out of the cell. The people around him laid down and mimicked sleep, but Marcus felt like not a single slave would sleep in the cells that night. All were sitting in wait for the ones who'd chosen to slip into the darkness of freedom.

In the hours that passed and as the cells grew dark, Marcus hadn't moved until he heard a sound coming from down the hall of the prison. A sound that formed a pit in his stomach.

Aninai was whistling.

Marcus leaned his head back against the bars, knowing what he'd have to do. And it filled him with dread. Sweat perspired on his brow as he exhaled, trying to build up his courage to do it before another soul could answer his call. He pursed up his lips and whistled.

Aninai stopped and Marcus stood, though his body willed him to stay. He stuck his hand outside the bars and whistled again. Aninai's footsteps drew nearer, looking to see who'd sang his song. The soldier's eyes lit up when he saw Marcus.

"Hello Marcus." Aninai reached between the bars and placed his hand on Marcus's face. He pulled for a kiss and the thought of the man coming anywhere close to him made his skin crawl.

"Not here." Marcus nudged his head back at the others in the cell.

"They're asleep." His face hovered in front of Marcus's.

Marcus looked down, his cheeks burning.

Aninai relaxed and moved further away, mistaking Marcus's discomfort for being bashful.

"Never mind. We've got plenty of time." Aninai took his hand off of Marcus's face and opened the door. Marcus stepped out the door and he felt Aninai lightly run the tips of his fingers down his arm. "But will you hold my hand?"

Marcus reluctantly nodded. He knew this was part of his routine. "I'm going to need it to get to where we're going." His voice barely staying steady.

Aninai put his keys back on his belt, and Marcus made a mental note of their location. He'd require them in order to get back into the cells.

Their hands interlocked and Marcus counted the steps to Aninai's secret spot.

Marcus hoped it wasn't too far away, but he wanted

it to be far enough that when he turned on Aninai, they wouldn't be heard.

Aninai took a flaming torch from the cave wall as they left the cells behind. They walked past the tool shed and climbed to the highest level. He turned into one of the tunnels and Marcus had a feeling he knew where they were headed. It was the same passage Aleksia had taken him to. It made sense. There was a pool of water, a skylight to the moon, and all the privacy anyone could ever want.

Aninai let go of Marcus's hand and put his arm around Marcus's waist.

Marcus was grateful Aninai wasn't big on talking. If he'd wanted to talk he might've seen right through his charade.

The cavern opened up. Aninai placed the torch in a metal loop Aleksia and Marcus hadn't noticed.

Marcus tuned his ears to every movement Aninai made as his thoughts clambered to think of what to do. He'd gotten this far, but he sensed Aninai draw closer to get what he'd brought him there for. He had to come up with a plan quickly.

Aninai unlocked his belt and the keys and weapons jangled to the ground.

Marcus surrendered to his senses and as the man drew close, he took action. He swung and missed.

Aninai punched Marcus in the face and dove for his weapons, but Marcus moved into his path. A fist hit his jaw and he kicked Aninai with all his might.

The soldier slammed into the wall next to the torch. He grabbed it and brandished it against Marcus who stumbled out of its way.

The flame raged past him and he fastened his grip on Aninai. The man turned Marcus into the wall, shoving the flame into Marcus's face.

The torch blazed against Marcus's skin and his hands quivered as Aninai pushed it towards his cheek.

Marcus thrusted his knee into Aninai's groin and the fire fell to the ground. He kicked it and it rolled into the water, giving him an upper hand. A faint light shone from skylight, but the soldier didn't have time to let his eyes adjust.

Aninai seized Marcus's arm and threw him into the water.

Marcus hit the water, and his head smacked against the edge of the reservoir. He instinctively tried to soothe it and his feet searched to find the bottom but it was beyond him.

Aninai splashed in next to him.

Marcus ventured to the other side but he wasn't fast enough. Ensnared by his opponent, he was plunged under water without a breath. Aninai's grip was solid around his neck. The weight of the water slowed Marcus's punches so much they barely hit his adversary. His arms flailed and his legs kicked, but the soldier would not relent.

This was a fight Marcus couldn't afford to lose. He craned his head down and bit hard into Aninai's forearm. His mouth filled with blood and he clenched his jaw down deeper.

Aninai withdrew and Marcus rose from the water, spitting a piece of flesh from his teeth.

He used his opponent's pain to his advantage and charged. This time, his fist connected with its target and

Aninai sunk down into the water.

Marcus retreated. Finding the edge of the pool, he went to lift himself out of the water, but his hand found a rock.

The water shifted behind him and Aninai approached like a jura in deep waters.

Marcus tightened his grip around the rock and wielded it, striking Aninai across the head. The man went limp in the water, facing downward. Whether he was dead was unclear, but Marcus had to be sure. If he left Aninai alive, he could alert the entire guard and any chance of rescuing Aleksia would be lost.

Before he could let his conscious find a way to let the soldier live, he found Aninai's head and held it under. The body trembled and Marcus's hands with it. He'd never killed a man by holding his head under water. It felt cowardly. In combat, the sword was a vacant extension of himself and his adversary died with pride, but this felt wrong. It was wrong, but as Aninai's body seized and thrashed, Marcus didn't let go. He didn't have time to think about the black and white of what he was doing. There was only grey and to let the man die was the lesser evil of the two.

In moments, Aninai was dead.

Marcus pulled the body to the rim of the pool and got up out of the water. He lay there. The cut on his brow bled along the profile of his face and he got up and washed away the blood, tensing whenever his hand touched the cut.

He yanked Aninai out of the water and traded clothes. The guards wouldn't look twice at him if he was dressed as one of them. He found the belt with Aninai's

443

weapons and keys and strapped it around his waist. Marcus was considerably smaller than Aninai and he had to make another hole in the belt so it would stay put. The sword felt foreign at his hip, but he knew he'd need it once he arrived at General Quinn's villa. He'd use Lucinda's tunnels to get there without being seen. He gripped the wall and set out.

Marcus was on high alert as he stepped outside the tunnel. He hoped none of the guards were near the mines when all the slaves were locked up in the cells.

Thunder and lightening rolled in the distance. A few raindrops fell against his skin. It wouldn't be long now and the storm would cover the sound of the slave's escape. Marcus's dreads weighed heavily on his neck and he prayed for an increase in rain or the guards might see water trickling down the back of his armour when it shouldn't.

He worked his way back slowly, counting the steps from one end to the other and trusting his memory was taking him the right way. He listened to the nearby chatter of the guards as he neared the opening of the cells and hoped they kept on talking.

None of them paid attention to Marcus as he slipped past. They were more focused on a pot of stew. He stayed close to the walls until he heard a familiar voice.

"Marcus!" burst Trigon, his voice turned to concern when he saw Marcus's red stained skin and fresh wound. "What happened to you?"

"Have you found Aleksia?" Still hoping Ravlin had lied.

"No. And Lucinda's checked everywhere," said Trigon. "Lucinda and I were about to go get Aleksia

444

without you."

Marcus handed Trigon the keys. He found the one to open the cell. Marcus went in and shut the door behind him. The rest of the slaves looked at him and shied away. They didn't like the sight of a guard's uniform and they guessed how he'd gotten it.

"Make sure she didn't end up in one of the cells without a hole," Marcus said. "Lucinda wouldn't be able to check those. I'm going down."

Someone helped Marcus to the centre of the floor and another opened the hatch.

Marcus jumped in and crouched as his feet hit the bottom. Urgency made him want to yell Lucinda's name at the top of his lungs, but he made himself whisper. He heard a clatter up ahead and he stood under the gap of another cell.

"Lucinda," he called.

A set of footsteps approached, and as they neared, Marcus recognized the woodland scent.

"I need to get to General Quinn's villa," he said, not wasting time on ceremony.

Lucinda smacked him upside the head. "How could you have been so stupid?"

"I—"

"There are no words to cover up the actions of a fool."

Lucinda walked down the path and Marcus followed her mumbling voice. "Couldn't have waited to heal yourself till after we were outside of Ironwood. I don't know why I even try to help. Humans sabotage everything I do for them."

"Tell me how to get into the city."

445

"You don't need to know how to get there."

"Why?"

"Because I'm going with you."

Marcus didn't want her help. "You should stay behind and help the miners get to Visadas."

"That's poor strategy. As a descendant I expected more. A general does not leave his best warrior at home when he goes to war. My people know the way to Visadas and the elves will guide them the rest of the way. I don't think you realize the weight of the general taking Aleksia."

"I know what she is," responded Marcus.

"Yes, but you don't know why Zoren wants her. He'll move mountains to get to her."

"Which is why I have to get to her first."

"I agree." Lucinda lifted her wrist bearing her magical pendant. "Now it's likely when we find Aleksia she won't be able to fight or possibly even move. You'll have to carry her while I get us out. If Zoren arrives before we can leave, I'll send her away using this and she'll be safe."

"You should send her away the moment we find her," insisted Marcus.

"Then none of us are getting out of there alive. Unless you've got magic to use against the witch?"

"Let's go."

"You and your friend Trigon go ahead. You'll require this." She held up a torch and lit it with magic, illuminating Trigon as he approached. "Both of you follow this path and I will join you once I've grabbed weapons." She ran in the opposite direction.

Marcus turned to Trigon. "You're sure? If you come,

we could be caught or killed."

Rather than answer, Trigon placed Marcus's hand on his shoulder and started down the path Lucinda had pointed to.

The path was ever winding. Trigon called out whenever the tunnel lowered or was about to descend or if there was a rock to step over. He stopped when they came to a fork in the road.

"Why have we —"

Something fluttered behind them, pulsing on the still wind not far from where they stood. Then it was footsteps and Lucinda came barreling around the corner. She threw a sword to Trigon.

"I've enchanted it to help you in battle since we don't have the time or the magic for further instruction. Don't lose it." Lucinda ran down the path to the right and they raced to keep up with her.

Rats scurried at their feet and the air smelled of rotting meat and fire as they passed under the trench of the dead.

None of them spoke, saving their energy, not knowing what they'd encounter at the other end. They ran past caverns full of glowing mushrooms and food that thrived in darkness, and down the tunnels that were more vast than any the miners had ever dug.

Trigon's torch illumined an end to their path and he came to a halt. "A dead end?"

Marcus's heart faltered. They didn't have time to have taken the wrong path.

Lucinda scolded Trigon like a grandmother teaching a lesson to a toddler. "You must learn, Trigon, to not be deceived by appearances." Closing her eyes, she lifted one of her hands. The air cracked and the path opened up.

Water rushed ahead of them.

"I hope both of you can swim," she said, going through. "The underground river passes right under the city wall and feeds the well in the market square. We must be wary of the guards on the walls, but we've gone up many times and not been seen. From here, we must be careful with our speech. Our voices could carry on the waters and echo into the courtyard above. We'd hate to be discovered before we rescue Aleksia. Leave the torch on the shoreline here, it will lighten our path until we get to the bend in the river."

Lucinda walked into the water and Trigon tossed the torch as they swam upstream.

LXVIII

THE COURTYARD

Marcus kicked his legs in vain to help them go faster. It didn't help, but he felt like he was doing something other than merely holding on. The underground river gushed over his ears as he strove to stay close. He held tightly to Lucinda's side and her power surged through his arms. He wanted to forget her past sins; he couldn't deny she'd helped. If it wasn't for her, the journey to Ironwood would have been impossible.

He hoped they weren't too late. He prayed Brisa, the goddess of wind, would slow the king's arrival and give them the time they needed to get Aleksia out. And then he prayed to Vandus, the goddess of water. He implored her to move her waters in their favour.

A rope tied to a bucket swayed in the current ahead and Lucinda slowed her pace as they came under it.

"Hold on to the rope." Lucinda grabbed Marcus's

hands and placed them around the frayed cord. "You come up after me. I'll give a signal."

The rope hardly jostled as she climbed, her body light and her movements smooth. She'd wedged herself into the awning over the well, poking her head down to see if anyone was coming.

Marcus felt a tug on the cord and he put one hand in front of the other. The rope swayed and sometimes he over or under extended his hand to grab the line. He panted, using his legs to leverage himself upwards. *How did I do this with Trigon on my back?* It seemed like years had passed since they'd been there.

"Wait," he heard Lucinda whisper, and he stopped.

Footsteps crossed the market and voices chatted amidst the thunder.

Marcus's arms shook as the pain moved deep into his shoulders. Aninai's armour weighed against him. All he wanted was to take a deep breath but he worried they might hear him. His hands slipped and he tangled his foot in the rope to stop himself from going down. He hit the side of the well and muffled a cry.

"They say he's coming tonight," uttered a patrolling soldier.

"Any sane man wouldn't travel on a night like this."

"Whoever said the king was sane?"

"Seems the whole city believes he's on his way. Never seen so many candles in the windows this late at night."

The voices sounded right next to the well.

"You want a drink?" The soldier stretched out his hand to draw the pail.

Lucinda's hand moved to the hilt of her sword.

Marcus didn't think he could hold on much longer.

"Nah," responded the guard. "We'll stop by the tavern and get a cup of calda. It'll warm us up."

"Give us a moment out of this weather too."

The voices trailed off.

"Come," prompted Lucinda.

Marcus dragged himself back up until a hand seized the cuff of his armour and tossed him into the square. Rain plummeted his skin and lightening forked the sky.

Lucinda tugged on the rope to signal Trigon and she came out of her hiding place. She grabbed Marcus and led him to an empty market booth, shoving him out of sight.

"Stay here." Lucinda went back for Trigon.

Marcus sat in the dark. He was wiping the water out of his face when something crashed next to him. His head jarred towards it and he withdrew his sword. Had he been spotted?

There was no alarm and he didn't hear any boots on the cobble.

SMASH. A clay jar fell on the ground.

Marcus turned his sword in its direction. *It's getting closer.*

A stray cat purred up against his leg and Marcus jumped. He exhaled and smiled to himself. He lowered his weapon.

"You scared me half to death," he breathed and pet its short wet fur. The cat rubbed its head against his hand, moving its body against him.

It ran away as Trigon and Lucinda joined him. He felt the absence of his little friend.

They pulled him up to his feet and Marcus huddled

between them, sticking close to the sides of buildings.

Lucinda led the way down the empty alleyways.

Few but the guards left the comfort of home in a downpour. They made their rounds on the city streets and strode upon the walls, watching over Ironwood. Rumours of the king's arrival and the storm distracted the guards from looking down into the city streets, blinding them to three individuals stooping along the wall of General Quinn's villa.

"We're here," muttered Lucinda. "Get up against the wall."

The rock wall was covered in vines and Marcus pushed his back into their embrace as the shadow of a guard crossed the house on the other side from them.

"No turning back now," she said.

Marcus swallowed hard as Lucinda ascended the wall. She twisted the vines into an unbreakable cord, using magic so they could heave themselves upwards. She climbed to the top and they heard a small thump. A body rolled down the vines, each vine gripping the body and slowing its descent. The dead soldier slumped onto the ground and the vines drew him against the wall to hide him.

"You go first," whispered Trigon, keeping an eye out.

Another body tipped over the side and rolled to the bottom to join the other, adding to the sound of the rain.

Marcus began his ascent.

Lucinda crouched as low as she could, her eyes darting and water dripped off the end of her nose.

She didn't help Marcus over the side this time, letting him fall on his stomach.

Lucinda hauled him up. "Go stand in that corner and

pretend to be on watch."

Marcus moved. With Aninai's uniform, he could blend in and replace the soldier Lucinda killed.

He dragged the sheath of his sword along the wall to know where he was. He felt a corner and held his shoulders back, pretending to scan the horizon. He wasn't sure how to stand. He tried to remember what the soldiers looked like on the walls of Naiden as he rode in on his horse. Did they hold the hilt? Were they allowed to pace to keep themselves warm? Marcus remembered hearing the training at the barracks was brutal in teaching recruits to survive the elements. *Whatever the weather, a soldier should be able to carry out his duties.* It killed him to stand still.

Aleksia, he thought. He needed to speak to her. Assure her it wasn't for a world without her he'd chosen to stay, but because she needed to go on. He prayed nothing had happened to her, hoped that she was valuable enough to them because she meant everything to him.

"Nice night," a soldier mocked as he appeared on his other side, away from Lucinda's watchful eye.

Marcus shielded his face, but it was too late.

"You're not—" he started.

Lucinda's blade pierced his armour but it wasn't good enough. The soldier cried out, alerting the rest of the army to their presence.

Lucinda grabbed Marcus, shoving a shield into his hands and thrusting him over the wall into the courtyard.

Nothing but air flowed beneath Marcus and he shouted. He slammed into a pile of hay and rolled onto the ground. Trigon and Lucinda landed behind him.

Soldiers marched into the square and Marcus stood to his feet, drawing his sword and raising his shield.

Lucinda shoved him and Trigon behind her as she backed them into a corner to defend themselves.

"I'll wound them, and Trigon, you kill them. Marcus can shield you from the arrows." Lucinda raised her bloody sword to meet the first soldier that came at her.

In two moves, the soldier was down and she propelled him to Marcus and Trigon. A few she killed on her own; the bodies were piling up. A horn blew and the courtyard filled with soldiers. The entrance to General Quinn's villa was in sight but they'd have to get past an army of eager soldiers to reach it.

LXIX

REVELATIONS

Aleksia's head ached. Opening her eyes, the world spun so much she had to shut them again. Whatever lay beneath her was softer than anything she'd ever slept on. She sat up slowly and chanced opening her eyes again. She was perplexed and saw herself staring back at her. Aleksia rubbed her eyes, knowing what she saw couldn't have been possible. It followed her actions. Had she heard of this before? Her brain was all jumbled up as she leaned in closer to it. Her other self mirrored her actions. Afraid to keep looking at it, Aleksia sat up in an elaborate room and slowly recalled how she'd gotten here.

There'd been timbers.

She was assigned to move them. She was on her way back from delivering a beam and something happened. Her neck was throbbing. She touched it. Pain seeped through her and she felt like she was falling over. She'd never been sick. Over the years there had been a few cuts and bruises, but nothing like this. The closest she could come to describing it was when she'd started turning to stone on the Mirtis, but unlike then, the effects were not instant. Something still dwelt inside her, jostling her mind and keeping her weak. It coursed through her. It felt like sand was moving through her bloodstream.

"King Zoren's been looking everywhere for you." General Quinn stepped closer to the bed Aleksia was lying on.

Aleksia jumped at his voice. She hadn't realized she wasn't alone. "Doesn't he have enough vertes?" Her voice was groggy and unlike herself.

"Possibly, but that's not what he wants from you quite yet."

"What does he want with me?"

"Perhaps you can ask him when he arrives," smirked General Quinn. "I sent word to him after one of my men confirmed the tale Veeta told me about you. The king should be here within the hour."

Aleksia weakly pushed herself off the bed and toppled to the floor. Everything was spinning and there was a vile taste in her mouth. She had to put her head on the marble floor. It cooled her brow, and once her body settled, she used her elbows to drag herself across the floor.

General Quinn did not try to stop her leaving. He strolled next to her and she could tell he was enjoying himself.

There has to be a door somewhere in the room. She lifted her head and saw the open door. A tightness built across her forehead and her stomach churned as everything spun ahead of her. She had to stop.

"I do admire your zeal," said General Quinn. "How long have you evaded him?"

Longer than I can remember, thought Aleksia as the world settled and she strove towards the door once again.

"What were you doing in a cabin in the middle of nowhere?"

"I don't expect you to understand," she responded. "I'm sure you've heard the stories of what your king does to my kind."

"Not directly," exhaled General Quinn. "The king doesn't really like to talk about it."

"I'm sure he doesn't like to talk about a lot of things," said Aleksia. He killed his own wife.

Aleksia strained through the door into the next room. Lightening flickered and thunder cracked in the sky above. The room was far more open. Pillars lined the walls and there was a hole in the roof. A curtain of rainwater poured into a pool of lilies and it made the air smell sweet. The others would be escaping soon.

Aleksia's eyes strained to focus. For some reason, the room felt familiar. She'd seen pieces of it before, but her mind was too fogged to remember where.

"I—" Aleksia glanced over her shoulder. General Quinn came through the doorway, and she knew where she'd seen this room.

Marcus. The tunnels underneath the cells not only led away from Ironwood, but to it. He would come for her and Quinn would kill him like she'd seen on the Mirtis. The general's sword would pierce his chest and he would throw Marcus against the wall as he breathed his last. Aleksia prayed to the goddess Elvian that he wouldn't come, but she knew Marcus was on his way.

"Ah, Othelus," said General Quinn, as she entered the atrium.

"There's a disturbance in the courtyard," Othelus smirked.

"What's happening?"

"An elf, a slave, and Marcus are killing your men."

"Seal the door," commanded the general.

Aleksia tried to lift herself to her feet, using a nearby chair.

General Quinn's eyes flickered to Aleksia. "Othelus."

Tiny feet clawed against the floor and this time there was more than one sungazer.

Aleksia found her footing, yet her balance was all over the place. She needed to stop Marcus.

A lizard scurried at her feet and she struggled to kick it away without losing her balance, but as she did, another crawled up her leg and its teeth buried themselves into her flesh. Aleksia screamed and her leg gave way. Another lizard bit into her back. They were all over her and as she tried to fight them off, but her body fought against her.

LXX

TRUE SACRIFICE

Another arrow struck Marcus's shield as Trigon dispatched another one of Lucinda's adversaries. An archer was shooting from the roof of the general's villa. Marcus assumed it was a woman, possibly Quinn's wife, for a bow and arrow was typically a woman's weapon.

Lucinda sliced an arrow in half and her blade cut through the soldiers like they were air. Ironwood stood far from Visadas and this was their first encounter with an elf.

The air snapped louder than thunder and something crumbled.

"We need to move." Lucinda sliced a soldier's throat. "Shutting the gate will only slow them down. They'll be coming over the walls as soon as they can find some rope or a ladder." And as if she'd spoken it into being, the heads of soldiers starting erupting over the side of the villa's wall. "Follow me!" The elf carved a path along the wall towards the entrance.

With their backs exposed, Marcus stammered to keep up with his companions. He tripped over the fallen bodies and barely blocked the arrows with his shield. He lingered between Lucinda and Trigon, feeling more a burden than a help. Once inside, they'd find Aleksia, and he'd be the pair of hands to carry her. That's when he'd be useful, that is, if he made it.

He'd nearly died many times and he'd reluctantly accepted death, though his life had felt unfulfilled. This time his death would serve a purpose. He prayed Aleksia would forgive him for knowingly walking into it. She'd seen General Quinn kill him and she would've wanted him to have escaped and live a life outside the clutches of King Zoren. But he would not leave. Not unless she was running next to him.

Lucinda pushed Marcus back and an arrow struck the wall where his head had been.

They drew close to the stairs leading up to the entrance and a garrison charged down the steps. Lucinda's sword found the weak spot between boot and shin guard. She sliced through the muscle holding the ankle and foot together, finishing the job as they fell, carving a path of carnage to the doorway.

Quinn's army saw a slave pretending to be a soldier and tried to remind Trigon of his place. His movements were not as graceful as Lucinda's but he held his ground, protecting Marcus and fulfilling his life debt again and again.

Lucinda yanked Marcus onto the top stair and pushed him behind a pillar. "Trigon, cover me." She faced the locked doors of Quinn's villa her magic struck the doors like a battering ram. The hinges burst and the doors caved in.

"Get inside," she exclaimed as she took the first step into Quinn's villa.

Trigon shoved Marcus through the doors.

The archway collapsed and Trigon held onto Marcus until they were safe. Dust stuck to their wet skin and Marcus coughed.

The soldiers in the courtyard could not follow, but on the other side of the door, they faced new enemies.

Othelus raised her hand and Lucinda hurled against the wall as the witch charged.

Trigon lifted his sword and Marcus held out his shield.

Marcus threw his shoulder into his safeguard and braced himself for the oncoming storm until it was struck. His feet slid back and he pushed with all his might. A hand tried to rip the shield from his grasp but he used it to smack the jaw of whoever was attacking him. General Quinn waited between the ceiling high pillars at the rear of his army, waiting with Aleksia on the floor at his feet.

Marcus turned himself out of a soldier's grasp, seizing their dagger and slicing their arm. He plunged the weapon into the warrior's neck.

Marcus was pushed to the ground and away from Trigon. He rolled back up onto his feet and a fist punched him in the face. Arms wrapped themselves around his torso. They weren't trying to kill him; they were trying to take him alive. Marcus struggled and kicked the soldier who came at him. He couldn't break the hold of the soldier who held him no matter how much he thrashed. They suddenly let him go and he toppled to the floor.

Something grazed his hand and he recognized her touch. He reached out to find her again. Aleksia's magic felt faint as he drew her in his arms, stroking her hair back from her motionless face. It was like when she was turning to stone on the Mirtis. He felt for her neck to ensure there was a pulse. Between the faint beats he sensed her blood on his fingertips. She was alive, but the touch of her blood made his own boil. For General Quinn and his witch there would be no mercy, no little voice of conscience to stop him.

Soldiers stood on either side of Marcus and a pair of heavy boots stepped in his way.

"Did she tell you what she was from the beginning?" asked General Quinn.

"What did you do to her?" demanded Marcus, praying Aleksia would open her eyes.

"There's only one way to deal with her kind," said General Quinn. "Honesty, I'm surprised you didn't kill her yourself. You've witnessed firsthand what her people do to ours."

Marcus remembered their first encounter. He thought he was dreaming of the barriers, and when he realized he was awake, he tried to kill her in the barn. He thought that by killing her, he would avenge every soul he'd heard lost within the barriers, but that was in the past. Now he was the one standing between her and his people. Trying to protect her when she couldn't defend herself like she'd done for him.

"I'm taking her with me," declared Marcus.

"You won't be taking her anywhere," responded Quinn. "The king will be here to fetch her any moment now."

"Then I'll have to kill you quickly."

"Kill me?" smirked General Quinn. "Only one of us will be dying this evening, Marcus. You have committed treason against your king and for that, the line of Marcus will end."

Marcus reluctantly set Aleksia down. He didn't want to leave her side, but as he rose to his feet, he drew out his sword and prayed he was facing the right direction. Aleksia would leave with him or he wouldn't be leaving this room at all. He didn't care that Aleksia had seen his death. If he died for her chance at life, then he died. Zoren would not have her.

Quinn's sword sliced Marcus's arm and he fought to keep hold of his weapon. He stumbled back, knocking into a pillar. He regressed as Quinn's sword thrashed against the column, spraying marble all over the floor.

Marcus receded, holding his sword ahead of him as the marble crunched, marking Quinn's footsteps toward him. He sliced his sword through the air but it hit nothing.

Quinn came from behind and threw Marcus across the room into a potted plant. It crashed against his back. A piece of the clay urn imbedded into the back of his shoulder. He grimaced as his hand trembled to pulled it out. The general was toying with him. Marcus got on his hands and knees to rise again.

General Quinn kicked him in the stomach and Marcus felt one of his ribs crack.

Every instinct told Marcus to run but he could not.

His body fought his every move as he used his sword like a cane to help him back to his feet. He needed to get Aleksia out. If King Zoren arrived and took her somewhere he'd never be with her again.

"I'm taking her with me." Marcus blocked General Quinn's blow.

General Quinn's sword spun around and Marcus felt his weapon fall from his hand. He was completely exposed and Aleksia's vision came to pass as his adversary's blade pierced him straight through the heart.

Marcus's hands stammered towards the hilt of Quinn's sword as his body cried out and his mouth filled with his own blood.

General Quinn shoved Marcus into the nearest wall. "I see your end, Marcus, son of Barsadias," he said as he twisted the blade.

Marcus inhaled. His arms felt numb and his legs gave out. The world around him muffled as General Quinn withdrew his sword and he fell on his side. A trail of his own blood streaking across the wall behind him as he died.

LXXI

OUT OF THE DARKNESS

The earth beneath Marcus's side felt soft and mossy. Pine needles, fresh soil, and a morning breeze captivated his senses. His chest ached as he shifted and sat up with a tree trunk at his back. Twitters of birds sang and wings beat to the sharp ache in his chest. He recognized the atmosphere, but had no idea how he'd gotten here. Had they escaped? Had Aleksia healed and carried him back to Visadas? Opening his eyes, he saw nothing.

"Aleksia?" he muttered, trying to stand to his feet, but his body resisted.

Almost as an answer to his call, he heard a large set of wings float over him. Nothing like the dragon of his childhood, but it cast a shadow over his body as it landed.

A vibrant bird adorned in red and blue wings with

eyes as blue as sapphires and claws as long as fingers stood in front of him. A phoenix.

Marcus, echoed a woman's gentle voice in Marcus's head.

"Who's there?" he pleaded.

A friend.

The voice sounded young and ancient all at once, but it was reassuring and compelled Marcus to trust it.

The phoenix flew closer to him and Marcus pushed himself back into the tree which was as wide as a house.

"What are you doing?"

You've lived in darkness for far too long. It's time to come into the light.

"Who are you?"

Please, the voice said. *There isn't time. Lie on your back and you will find understanding. There are two things I must give you before you can return*.

Marcus lay on his back, anxious, but eager.

Open your eyes.

Marcus did as he was told.

The phoenix jumped next to Marcus and hovered its head over his eyes. A single tear fell on his pupil and he felt warmth surge through his eye. The misty white fog parted, like a heavy wind splitting smoke. Beneath the cloud, there was clarity. Deep sky-blue eyes reacted to daylight for the first time in over eighteen years.

Marcus squinted as he slowly sat up, overwhelmed at what he was seeing. The leaves danced on the morning breeze as the sun flickered between them. A honey bee covered in black and yellow fuzz flew past him towards the meadow of flowers. It possessed more colours than he remembered existed. Moss grew on the bark of the maple tree and a squirrel scurried up an oak. Ample tears poured down his face and he was afraid to close his eyes. He'd forgotten. He'd forgotten the vibrance of green and the shades of an early morning sky. Then he gazed at the phoenix.

She stepped back and burst into a flame of red and blue. And standing there was no longer a bird but an elf. A crown of eternal woodland flowers rested in her copper hair. Her skin reminded Marcus of the stones one found on the bottom of a riverbed, smoothed to perfection. She moved with inhuman poise and untamed beauty. Small lines of time crevassed beneath the vastness of her eyes and made her look older. Yet even with all her years, there was kindness within them. But they were so full of time, Marcus could barely look at them. Her blue dress was frayed along the bottom and glided with her as she moved.

"I am Gretafold, queen of the elves, and I've waited a long time to speak to you."

"Am I dead?"

"No. You are neither here nor there."

Marcus stood, gripping his chest as the pain of General Quinn's blade still ailed him.

"I know I don't deserve your trust Marcus, but I need you to believe everything the elves have done has had a purpose."

"And what is that? To slaughter thousands of innocent people?"

"There are greater forces at work here. Greater than any of us realize, but everything will be revealed. You must be patient."

"Tell me now."

"I can only show you what you are meant to see."

"And what is that?"

The queen lifted her hand to touch Marcus but he moved away.

"Please," she beseeched.

Marcus didn't take a step towards her, but he didn't recede when she drew nearer. She took his hand and placed her other on his temple. Their eyes turned white as their minds were transported elsewhere.

Marcus found himself alone in the middle of a great hall. Light shone between the columns, leading to a chair at the apex of the room.

A throne made of purest silver.

On either side of the symbol of power were two large urns. The one on the right was as black as midnight. Carved into the ashen marble was a dragon gnashing its teeth at an unseen enemy and standing on the limb of a silver tree of Reeza. The other was as white as snow, with handles like the wings of a dove. Etched into its face was another dragon. Its wings extended over a host of people; the wings casting a shadow of protection.

A flame, the same colour as each urn, vibrated restlessly from within though there was no wind upon the air.

The silence was broken as the sounds of a battle drifted on the air and the drums of war beat in rhythm with Marcus's heart.

A black dragon rose from the black urn and a white from the other. Each was followed by a host of its own. A colony of bats screeched behind the darkened creature and a dole of doves cooed behind the other.

The two opposing sides crashed in the middle and a

light flashed so brightly Marcus closed his eyes.

A silver dragon emerged at the centre and the multitude transfigured into a silver tree of Reeza. A new throne was forged and the lavender coloured leaves blossomed to the ceiling and shaded the room.

Peace overwhelmed Marcus's soul. The limbs of the tree seemed to sway in contentment and the room became warm, soaking his every sense. He could have sworn he could hear someone singing a merry tune, but it slowly vanished as Queen Gretafold's hand solidified in his and he was back in the forest of Visadas.

"What was that?" asked Marcus.

"A prophecy. Born the moment General Quinn's sword pierced your heart. Many will try to interpret it, but we must not get set on what we think it is saying or its true meaning could pass us by." Queen Gretafold stepped away, pondering what they'd both seen. "The time for war has come."

"Will you fight?" demanded Marcus, bending over as the pain in his chest grew and his eyes burned.

"First you must come to us."

"What's happening?" The pain becoming too much to bear.

"You have finally awakened," she smiled. "Use this gift well Marcus, for it was not given lightly. Forged in a dragon's breath and brought to life by an act of true sacrifice, it is your responsibility to bring Aleksia to Amarisa. There is much to say, but some things cannot be spoken until you're within our borders."

Marcus fell to his side as everything inside him felt like it was scorched in flame. Queen Gretafold disappeared in a pillar of fire.

LXXII

THE ATRIUM

Marcus wanted to die. Every muscle in his body convulsed, and his veins glowed as red as molten lava. His sword was abandoned next to him but he couldn't pick it up as he struggled to maintain his sanity. He thrashed on the floor, striking it to dull the pain as his body doubled in size.

Everything was so bright and the noises throughout the villa muddled through him in endless waves. Lucinda's and Othelus's swords crashed against one another. General Quinn commanded his soldiers to form ranks and search the rest of the city. Trigon's foes had grown too great and his chance of survival was turning against him. The sword had given him the ability to fight but not the endurance. It was all too much. The courtyard outside the villa was filling with soldiers and he could hear the rodents scurrying in the walls.

And then he heard a sound that brought everything inside him in tune.

"Marcus," whimpered Aleksia.

He honed in on Aleksia and made her his focus. The sound of her beating heart, her breathing, and the comprehension that she needed his help flowed through him.

The pain ceased and Marcus lifted himself off the floor, his senses feeling every speck of dust rising off the ground around him. He opened his eyes.

He blinked and the piercing amber eyes of the dragon that had always been there appeared.

A soldier jumped at him but Marcus caught him mid-air and threw him down so hard the floor cracked along with the man's neck.

A sungazer ran across the floor at Marcus and he stamped it with his heel, killing it instantly.

A woman lay on the floor, her arms covered in small lizard bites and gems that looked like water droplets. He knew it was Aleksia, though he couldn't see her face.

Lucinda kicked Othelus out of her way and looked expectantly at Marcus, a smile crossing her lips and she dove back into her fight with the witch.

The general loomed over Aleksia, the tip of his sword dripping with Marcus's blood.

Quinn faced him, his face illuminated in wonder. "So — this is what she saw in you."

Marcus kicked up his abandoned sword and caught it with his hand, charging the general.

A soldier tried to come between them and Marcus gave into his instincts, wrenching the man's blade from his hand, breaking the soldier's every finger and stabbing him in the face.

General Quinn held a sword in each hand and drew on the power of his ring. "Who would've guessed?"

Marcus raised his sword high to bring it down on Quinn's head, but the general blocked it with one sword while striking the other at Marcus's torso.

Marcus avoided it and struck again, sparks flying from their blades. Steel met steel and Quinn sliced Marcus's side. For a moment there was pain, then the wound instantly healed.

An infantry of soldiers moved around Aleksia and one of them hoisted her into their arms. Marcus moved to go to her but Quinn blocked his path.

The general chuckled as he lunged at Marcus once more.

Marcus lifted his sword to meet the attack but it shattered to pieces. He dashed to pull another from the hand of a dead soldier. The general had two swords and now he had none. He raced to stay ahead. A soldier came up against him and Marcus broke the man's neck. He caught the man's sword before it could fall.

General Quinn twisted the ring on his finger, checking its clarity as it glowed in the darkened room.

Strength alone would not bring Marcus victory. He had to recall the lessons he'd learned as a child.

Relax, he heard his father's voice say as he took a deep breath, blocking Quinn's assault.

Feet shoulder length apart. He remembered his father kicking his boots into the correct position.

Mind your surroundings.

Marcus expanded his perception beyond what was taking place between himself and the general.

Lucinda and the magician were matched blade for blade. The pendant around Othelus's neck glowed as she drew enough magic to face Lucinda. A host of her lizards were dead. The rest of the soldiers had stepped to the side and one of them held a sword to Trigon's throat to encourage him not to move. They'd make an example of him to the other miners and they would not be kind. Marcus moved around the pillars and hurled his sword at Trigon's attacker, freeing him to keep on fighting.

Marcus dove for the sword of the soldier he'd killed and was back on his feet.

Turn the environment to your advantage, said General Barsadias.

Marcus deflected Quinn's crosscut and each of their blades searched to fortify their position. Marcus ducked as his adversary swung to take off his head. He darted down and sliced Quinn's side.

The general launched a whole new assault.

Marcus evaded, diving over a couch to the other side of the room where he found a lamp hanging on the wall.

He kicked Quinn in the gut with such force the general soared halfway across the room.

Marcus broke the lamp with his sword and the oil poured over his blade. His rival was back on his feet and attacked.

Their blades struck and Marcus dragged his weapon against Quinn's. The oil ignited.

Quinn's eyes widened and he took a step back, but Marcus wasn't going to let up. He needed to get the general's ring. Using the flaming sword, he sieged his opposition with a fresh onslaught, using everything he had. He had his opponent on the defence as their blades crossed back and neither was willing to give up without a fight.

Marcus knocked one of Quinn's swords out of his hand and pushed the general against one of the pillars. He thrusted his adversary's sword hand against the marble. The ring gleamed in the firelight and he amputated it from the rest of Quinn's body.

The general shrieked, holding his hemorrhaging limb, and Marcus punched him in the face, knocking him out cold.

Marcus turned his focus on the soldiers rushing to their general's defence, cutting through them like butter. Aleksia was just beyond him when an energy threw him across the room. He crashed hard against a pillar and hit the ground. He raised his hands beneath him to rise, but in a burst of lightening he saw a silhouetted pair of wings upon the floor. The water falling into the atrium shifted and the flame on Marcus's blade went out.

A man landed in the pool and parted the plummeting water like a curtain with the move of his hand. He emerged perfectly dry and his eyes focused on Aleksia.

The king surged towards her.

"Lucinda!" yelled Marcus as he rushed to stand between Aleksia and Zoren. "Get them out of here!"

Lucinda pushed off her opponent and Othelus crashed into the wall. She reached deep into the stone and the room was cascaded in a blinding light.

Marcus shielded his eyes and Zoren roared in outrage.

When the light faded, Aleksia and Trigon were gone.

The stone in Lucinda's hand was black, void of any more magic. She discarded it on the floor and wielded her sword ahead of her. She charged at Zoren, but she'd barely taken a step and the walls and floor around her shifted, capturing her. Everything but her face disappeared into its embrace.

Marcus was the final line of defence and attacked.

King Zoren raised his hand and a ball of fire surged towards Marcus.

There wasn't any time to avoid it, but when it struck him, Marcus felt nothing but warmth.

The king's angry face made a quick study of him, taking in Marcus's eyes and build. He drew his elaborate sword.

Marcus had heard of it. It was made from the bark of Reeza and was unbreakable. His own sword would be like a single strand of yarn, but rather than back down, he stepped up, ready to fight the legendary king he'd once admired.

He was no match against the king.

His sword shattered in an instant and Zoren moved faster than Marcus thought possible.

Zoren returned his attack, and for the second time that night, Marcus was stabbed through the heart. He lay on his side, choking on his own blood as the king released his weapon. His vision blurred until he saw no more.

LXXIII

LOYALTY

Marcus tried to lift his hand to his aching head but it wouldn't move. He opened his human eyes and saw Zoren. He jolted to fight but his body didn't budge. Chains wrapped around him from his shoulders to his knees.

"Marcus, son of Barsadias," said Zoren. "It's been a long time since your father brought you to Sidabras. I told you I looked forward to the warrior you'd become, but I'd never imagined what was beneath the surface. What spell or incantation did you mutter in the dark to gain such power?"

Marcus concentrated on his left arm and pushed against the marble column to gain leverage over the chains. A few bent but repaired themselves. He searched for the magician but couldn't see her.

"Regretfully, this power has been wasted on you, but you may still have your uses." Zoren pulled out a tiny glass vial from his tunic that faintly glowed in the darkened room. "Do you know what this is?"

Marcus didn't recognize it. He leaned his head back against the pillar and met Zoren's gaze. "I don't care what you do to me. Aleksia is out of your reach."

Zoren continued as though Marcus hadn't spoken. "In the early days of my reign, a man named Eonan was a blacksmith. He worked with the trees of Reeza and was trying to turn its bark into armour like mine. He failed. While he worked, a silver sap dripped from the trees and he placed it in a vial. He summoned a few unwilling volunteers and made a discovery that's served me well over the years." Zoren looked to someone behind Marcus. "Hold him still please."

Two pairs of gloved hands came from behind and constrained Marcus's head.

"Whether it will work on you is yet to be determined. When given to humans, the effects are instant, but elves need a little persuading. You appear to be neither." King Zoren opened the bottle. "It's time for you to show loyalty to your king." He wrenched Marcus's mouth open and poured.

Marcus gagged. Zoren plugged his nose, and the drink seemed to have a mind of its own, ripping into him from the inside. Rapidly, the sap branched into his heart, and as it touched his mind, he howled at the top of his lungs. The hands holding him let go as he convulsed. Within his eyes grew veins of silver, consuming everything he'd been, was, and had yet to be.

Zoren handed the bottle to one of his soldiers.

A lone tear strayed from Marcus's eye as the last of his soul was taken from him. He blinked, and it was like looking into the eyes of a stranger.

The chains fell to the ground and Marcus found his footing. He moved slowly at first, suddenly realizing the newness of his body. His steps were different and his shoulders broader, but his first action was to bow at the feet of his master, the benevolent King Zoren.

"To your feet, son," said Zoren.

Marcus rose a little shorter than Zoren, but the two of them towered over the rest of the people in the room.

"Do you know where the elf sent Aleksia?" asked Zoren.

Marcus shook his head. "No."

"A pity." Zoren turned to a company of soldiers. "Take the elf to the dungeons. I'll be down to question her momentarily."

The wall released Lucinda and she was dragged away.

"I'll take whatever punishment you deem necessary," volunteered Marcus.

"It is unfortunate, but I will let it go this time if you promise me something." Zoren picked up a sword and placed it in Marcus's hand. "Bring the elvian back to me unharmed and kill anyone who gets in your way. Othelus will assist you."

The copper haired witch came to stand at his side.

"It'll be as you wish."

Marcus left immediately to see it was done. He blinked and the dragon's eyes replaced his own. He was ready to hunt, and he would throw Aleksia at his king's feet no matter how much she pleaded him to stop. There would be no mercy, only the king's desire to have her and his will to make it so.

ACKNOWLEDGEMENTS

I'll be the first to admit that there were days I wanted to do nothing more than light this manuscript on fire and never think of it again, but here we are today with a completed novel that had more good days than bad.

Writing these books has been one of the highlights of my life. I went to film school in 2017 and was told by my instructor that my film ideas needed to be books first. Almost six years later and I've written the entire trilogy. So, if you enjoyed reading this book, take heart, it won't be long until you're holding book two in your hands.

They say writing is a lonely art, and for the most part it is, but I did not finish this novel on my own.

The first people I would like to thank are my friends and family. They never looked at me like I was crazy when I said I wanted to write a fantasy novel. Mom and Dad, you are the best parents a girl could ask for and I love you both so much. To my movie quoting sisters, Lynn, Laura, and Leah, I always look forward to getting together with you and will sing with you any day of the week. You've always been encouraging and you don't know how much that has helped me get to where I am today.

To all my truck drivers and fellow staff at Drain Brothers who listened to me vent about a difficult chapter or celebrated with me when I felt I got a chapter right, thank you. Being a scale house operator with no internet is the best job a writer could ask for.

To my first editor Rebekah Smith. You made me dig. The structure of my novel was there but you were the one who helped me find the hidden jewels of my characters and get rid of all my ramblings. This novel used to be ten thousand words longer and I didn't lose a single plot point. Through your council, I gained a clearer and more effective novel. Thank you for being my first fan!

To my second editor, publisher, and cover designer Alanna Rusnak of Chicken House Press, I cannot thank you enough for agreeing to publish this book. I don't think I could've done it without all your hard work.

To my illustrators. Rick deHaan and Kristine Wannamaker, thank you for taking my rough sketches and bringing them to life. Special thanks to Rick for the amazing world map. I did what I could and you made it even better.

Finally, to the person holding this book. You've read *Out of the Darkness* from beginning to end. I cannot begin to express how thankful I am that you gave me a chance to tell you a story. Picking up the writings of a stranger is always a gamble, one that I am very familiar with. I hope you've come to love my characters as much as I do and that I've left you with enough desire to see where they go next.

Hope to see you all in book two of The Forsaken Trilogy: *Into the Light*!

Elisabeth Rodgers

Elisabeth Rodgers's love of fantasy, combined with her vast imagination, inspired her to write her debut novel *Out of the Darkness*. She currently lives with her family in Ontario, Canada.